DEAD MEN DON'T CHEW GUM

A MARTIN AND OWEN MYSTERY

NINA CORDOBA

ACKNOWLEDGMENTS

This book would not have been written if not for my awesome, geeky husband and kids. And I especially want to give a shout-out to my two favorite beautiful, but geeky, Latina's: Sierra Acy, thanks for making me watch Harry Potter, showing me what "cons" were, and teaching me that it's always "Doctor Who" not "Dr. Who." Melissa Vargas-Chanyarlak, thanks for lending Rika your old job as an E.coli tester and making me laugh for a couple of hours straight last time I saw you. I wish I could have fit some of your hilarious true stories in here, but maybe you'll want to use those yourself, someday.

Also, thank you to a dark and creepy road in South Texas (you know who you are) where I first got inspired to write a mystery series, and to my beta readers who reassured me I was capable of writing a mystery by showing their excitement and support after they read it.

As always, thanks to RWA members who lend help and support whenever it's needed and my editor Jennifer Bray-Weber who always keeps her sense of humor.

And to Abel: I luh you, Papi! And you have my permission to make out with Shakira if you ever get the chance.

This one's for Sisi.

CHAPTER ONE

Rika Martín

"What's wrong with these people?" I muttered as I drove past the last building in a town that ended thirty seconds after it began.

So much for Bolo, Texas. Maybe I should have expected this when the sign touted a population in the hundreds instead of millions like I was used to. But, jeez, ten-fifteen on a Wednesday night and everything was closed?

The McDonald's. The Sonic. Even the Mary Queen, which was clearly an old Dairy Queen that had lost its franchise. The "Mary" part was painted in black letters on a white tarp and thrown over the front half of the sign.

But, while it was plausible that people didn't eat late around here, what about gas? The two convenience store-gas stations on either end of town were locked up tight as if no one could ever possibly need gas in the middle of the night.

My Honda Fit got good mileage, so gas wasn't my big priority at the moment. But I was starving. I was thirsty. And I had to pee like nobody's business.

As I pulled up to a red light, I ripped open a pack of gum—

the last thing I had in my possession resembling food—and stuffed a stick of it into my mouth. I tapped my fingers on the steering wheel impatiently.

No cars across from me.

No cars to the right or the left.

Not a soul in sight.

After living in L.A. and New York, this place looked like some post-apocalyptic movie set.

Then I noticed the antique three-story houses sitting on two of the four corners and realized this was the intersection where I needed to make my big decision. I could take the route the GPS, Google Maps, and MapQuest told me to use, or I could take the shortcut my friend Marly recommended, which would presumably get me to civilization faster. Otherwise, why would they call it a shortcut?

Shortcut it is.

When the light glowed green, I took a deep breath and turned left. A half-mile later, I turned right at the yellow flashing light...

Onto the darkest, most desolate two-lane road I'd ever seen. Or maybe it just felt that way because the moon, which had shone on me consistently the past couple of hours, suddenly disappeared behind a blanket of clouds.

All I could see was the pavement in front of my car and the vague outlines of stubby trees and scrub brush on the sides of the road. My hand jerked up to rub the nervous tingle off the back of my neck.

Maybe I should turn around and take the other route.

Either way, I had to admit it was a terrible idea to try to hide out for a couple of weeks before heading home to L.A. to face the I-told-you-so's from my grandmother and aunts.

What a shitty f-ing day this had been.

Actually, I'd been driving for three days, stopping to nap at state rest areas when I got tired. But the time blurred together in my mind like one very long, lousy day.

It started when I went to my job as an E.coli tester in the lab of a meat-packing company in New York and worked for four hours before my boss arrived to inform me I was laid off.

Effective immediately.

As he shoved a wad of cash into my fist, he was wild-eyed, ranting about the FBI and a money laundering operation. I figured better to be jobless than imprisoned and got the hell out.

When I returned to the apartment I shared with my boyfriend Brandtt—okay, technically *his* apartment—I found a blonde with legs up to her neck, standing in the lobby, directing movers. Elias the doorman explained to me that Brandtt had found someone new, and I'd need to find another place to live.

Also effective immediately.

Nice.

The "good" news was that my belongings were already boxed up, and Elias had been keeping them safe for me. I nearly tipped him for his trouble, then decided if this situation were ever written up in an etiquette book, the dumper would be responsible for the tip, not the dumpee.

Shell-shocked, I sat on one of my boxes in the lobby for a half hour as I tried to call my boyfriend of two years. When Brandtt —"with two T's," as he always pointed out—didn't answer my calls or texts, I had to accept that I'd actually managed to lose my job, my man, and my home in one morning.

As I held onto the steering wheel with my right hand, I pressed my left palm to my stomach. It felt like someone had dropped a wet rag in there. I'd experienced the same sensation over and over, each time my mind replayed the lobby scene, all the way from New York to Texas.

And that was a lot of freaking times, let me tell you.

Okay, Brandtt and I were over, but couldn't he have handled the breakup another way? A way that didn't involve the doorman peering at me, dewy-eyed with sympathy, looking like he wanted to take me home and let Mrs. Doorman feed me *pasteles* or

3

tamales or whatever New York Puerto Ricans ate. Elias was so broken-hearted on my behalf, I felt like *I* should be comforting *him*.

Even worse, I could no longer ignore the nagging feeling that had plagued me for months. The thought that Brandtt, my handsome, charming boyfriend worshipped by millions—okay, thousands—of women...was a *tool*.

I guess on some level I'd known for a while, but I considered myself an intelligent person, and what smart person wants to believe she abandoned her own life to follow a tool all the way across the country?

Jeez. I rolled my eyes at myself for about the thousandth time since I left New York.

I met Brandtt when I was still in L.A. One night, I attended a stage adaptation of *The Matrix*—a terrible idea for a play, by the way—in celebration of finally reaching my goal weight. He walked out onto the stage in his black trench coat and tall, chunky boots and I was a goner. I was sitting in the front row of the tiny theater, and he sent a stagehand out to invite me back.

And, I mean, who can resist Neo?

I hate to admit it, but the sting of humiliation was much worse than the ache of losing Brandtt. Okay, there was no ache at all.

It had become clear a while ago that he and I didn't belong together. I just hadn't figured out what to do about it, yet. But being dumped unceremoniously from his life like yesterday's iPhone still burned. Left me feeling like I'd felt throughout my teen years. Like I wasn't worth so much as a conversation.

I had nowhere to go in New York, since my three girlfriends had already flown to South Padre Island to stay at Marly's aunt and uncle's condo for a few weeks. I'd passed on the trip because I didn't think it was right to go off with a bunch of very single women while I was living with a boyfriend.

But with him no longer in the picture, recuperation time on a far-off beach sounded a lot better than heading back to L.A. with my tail tucked between my legs. I made a snap decision and headed south while I formulated my new life plan and procrastinated about facing the woman who raised me.

In my defense, I did tell Brandtt I couldn't go to New York with him, initially. I'm not an idiot, and following a boyfriend across the country seemed like an idiot move. But he begged me to come.

"How can you make me go alone?" he'd whined.

I'm a sucker for a good guilting. I blame my grandmother.

Of course, explaining Brandtt's new job on *The Real Millionaire Bachelors of New York* to her had been the hardest part. "If he's not a millionaire, why would they give him a job on the show?" she kept asking. She also still believes pro wrestling is for real.

I spotted a bend in the road up ahead and crossed my fingers that I'd find a truck-stop diner or at least a 24-hour Walmart on the other side. I sucked in two big lungfuls of hope, slowed, and started around the curve.

Damn it. No Wal—

My headlights reflected off glass and metal on the right shoulder. In the moment it took my brain to register that a vehicle was parked, facing the wrong way on the right side of the road, a motor roared and the cab of the red pickup truck lunged in front of my car.

I jerked the steering wheel to the right to avoid colliding with the bed of the truck. My foot mashed on the brake while the truck's tires sprayed my windshield with gravel they'd collected from the shoulder. The tiny rocks crunched under my tires as my Honda left the road and slid to a stop.

I twisted around just in time to see the truck's tail lights pop on before it disappeared around the curve. I'd avoided smashing into it by mere inches.

Pressing my hand to my chest, I deep-breathed, reeling over my near miss with a drunk driver. He had to be drunk, right?

Who else darts out from the wrong side of the road with no lights on?

As my pulse slowed, my bladder began nagging at me again. I was amazed I hadn't wet myself when the truck jumped out at me.

I turned to peer into the dark through the passenger window. What kinds of wildlife did they have in Texas?

Rattlesnakes? Coyotes? Bobcats?

But I couldn't drive another mile in this condition. Glancing around, I found my cell phone, which had slid from the passenger seat to the floorboard when I slammed on the brakes.

I leaned over and plucked it from the mat. I tried to turn its built-in flashlight on, even though it hadn't worked since a month after I bought the phone, the one negative I'd mentioned when I reviewed it on Amazon. I didn't return the phone because I loved everything else about it and that one feature hadn't seemed important in the bright lights of Manhattan.

My lightsaber key chain—Yoda version—would have come in handy. Unfortunately, I'd felt obliged to switch it out for the expensive Michael Kors key chain Brandtt had given me. He hated my lightsaber key chain, along with all my other geeky possessions.

So, the light from my cell screen was my only option.

I tried to learn lessons from my mistakes. *Never give up the geek.* That would be the lesson I took from tonight.

As I got out of the car, a warm breeze ruffled my thin summer skirt. At least I wouldn't have to wrestle with skinny jeans to make this happen.

Holding my phone out in front of me, I tried to look ahead, but the puny light only allowed me to see a few inches around me. I imagined snakes slithering on the ground and rose up on the balls of my feet, trying not to disturb them. My knee-high leather boots would have come in handy, but since I didn't pack the boxes in my trunk, I had no idea where to find them.

The Sketchers I was wearing would have to do. I'd put them on before leaving the lobby of Brandtt's building—the only *screw you* I could think of, since he'd always hated to see me in anything that wasn't designer and certainly wouldn't approve of a skirt-tennis shoe combination. Pretty lame as *screw yous* go, especially considering only his doorman was watching.

The night was surprisingly noisy, full of the buzzing and chirping of insects. Chewing my gum faster, I tiptoed away from the road. Soft, barely discernable footfalls padded nearby.

Like a bobcat stalking its prey?

I imagined what it might feel like to become a bobcat's bedtime snack. Would he at least make sure I was dead before gnawing off my limbs?

I halted, held my breath and strained my ears to determine the direction I needed to run away from. But when I stopped walking, the sound stopped, too.

Duh. I was the bobcat.

I started moving again, hoping to get far enough from the road that a passing car's headlights wouldn't expose my naked ass to the driver, but not so far as to make me look like easy pickings to whatever carnivores might be prowling around. When I scratched my leg on something spindly, I imagined accidentally squatting on a cactus. *Eek*, that would make for some miserable driving.

Something slithered by my foot, for real this time. I squealed and fled, lifting my knees high in an exaggerated jog until I ran right into a stubby version of a palm tree.

Ouch!

Stupid smart phone. How smart could it be if it didn't even keep its owner from running into major foliage? I felt around the trunk, moving to the backside of the tree, and did what I'd been needing to do for the last three hours.

Whew!

As I pulled my underwear up, skirt down, I gave myself a pat on the back for braving the wilderness and taking care of business old school.

I could totally survive the zombie apocalypse!

Smiling triumphantly, I looked toward the road. My car lights shone like beacons of hope, although I'd apparently wandered off at an angle while looking for the right spot to do my biz.

I pointed my Sketchers straight at the car, anxious to get back to safety now that I had zombies on the brain. But after only a few steps, my toe hit something and caught.

My body lurched forward. My palms hit gritty earth at the same moment my torso landed on a solid mass. A whoosh of air burst from my lungs at the impact, the gum flying out of my mouth along with it.

Dread oozed in through my pores and wrapped around my internal organs. No doubt, whatever I'd landed on didn't belong here. It felt like...

No, I wouldn't let my imagination run amuck this time. Bracing myself with my left hand, I lifted my phone with the other, pointing the screen downward. I touched the home button. The light from the screen shook as it reflected off a pair of pale blue eyes.

Pale, blue, lifeless eyes.

A zombie!

I scrambled off, tripping over its limbs as I tried to get as far away as possible. I may have screamed. It's hard to know if you're screaming on the outside when you're screaming so loudly on the inside.

When I reached the gravel, I went down hard. Skin ripped from the heels of my hands as I scrabbled over the rocks. I had to get to my car and I didn't care if I did it on two limbs or four.

Next thing I knew, I was sitting in the driver's seat, shaking, unsure how long I'd been there.

Had I blacked out? Maybe I'd fallen asleep driving and the zombie had been a dream. Actually, since it was just lying there, not trying to eat my brains, it didn't really qualify as a zombie. Not yet, anyway.

But this could still be a dream. Couldn't it?

Painful throbbing caused me to turn my hands over and examine them. My phone was still clutched in my fingers, a fresh crack jutting diagonally across the screen. The heel of my right hand and my entire left palm were scratched and bloodied.

According to the phone, only a few minutes had lapsed since I left the car. I couldn't have been here long.

Okay, this wasn't a dream, but I was fine. I was in control of my senses. And, unfortunately, the body I'd stumbled onto was no hallucination.

I dialed nine-one-one, closed my eyes, rested my forehead on the steering wheel, and answered the operator's questions until she figured out where the cops could find me.

When I finally heard sirens, I opened my eyes...

And saw the blood on my shirt.

∿

Nick Owen

I have to get out of this town.

That's pretty much what I was thinking every minute of every day. Even more so on nights like tonight, when mom called me over to her place to save her from yet another bogus threat.

This time, she'd been listening to town gossip about a group of Satan worshippers who were supposedly gathering in this part of the county to hold their rituals.

She called me a couple of hours ago, sounding both agitated and excited, because she was sure she saw someone in a black robe headed toward the old barn. I walked around the property for an hour and didn't find a thing.

Before the Satan worshippers, there was a bobcat at her back door, which turned out to be her neighbor's fat tabby looking for a second dinner. And a week before that, I was called over to investigate the gurgling sounds coming from her upstairs bathroom—"like someone chokin' on their own blood"—which I fixed by jiggling the toilet handle.

I was pretty sure she didn't believe she was in danger. More likely, she was addicted to the drama and attention.

Regardless, I was bone tired, and I was too damn young to be this damn exhausted. But mom wasn't the only reason I had to get out of this place. I'd come back to Bolo for all the wrong reasons and that never got you anywhere you wanted to be.

I needed to move on and let the useless sheriff deal with mom's nutty complaints. Wasn't like he had much else to do around here, except look for "foreigners," which is what he called anyone with an out-of-state license plate, and pull them over on trumped up traffic charges.

As I turned onto the highway, I was surprised to see the flashing lights of two county sheriff's cars on the gravel shoulder.

Huh. Sheriff Wade Strickland usually preferred to conduct his speed traps during the day and be home in time for dinner.

I rolled down my window as I eased up next to what I assumed was an accident. But there was only one civilian car on the scene and it didn't appear damaged.

"Hey, Nick," Deputy Daniel Scruggs called from between his car and the Honda. I stopped next to him, surprised to see his hand on the arm of a slim girl. Her hands were stuck behind her back like she was cuffed.

"What's up, Danny?" I asked, but my eyes wandered over to examine his prisoner more closely. She wasn't a teenager like I first thought, but an attractive young woman with long brown hair that flamed auburn as the red lights flashed through it. When I scanned her face, her eyes caught mine, holding me prisoner for several long seconds. A guy could drown in those big, round puddles of chocolate. She probably cried Hershey's kisses.

She wasn't crying, though.

Interesting.

In my experience, women got pretty emotional over being arrested. Men did too, for that matter.

Still, there was something about her that made me want to hang around and see if I could help her out. She had New York plates on her car and seemed to be all alone.

"Looks like we got ourselves a murder!" Danny smiled, his eyes widening on the word "murder" like they did when he announced he'd won fifty dollars on a lottery scratch-off.

He'd always been kind of a dumbass. When he was a kid, his nickname was "Goofy," surprisingly, not because of the way he acted, but because the odd shape of his eyes and protruding teeth made him look like the Disney character.

Nowadays, in uniform, he seemed even more cartoonish, if that was possible.

"A murder?" My eyes flicked back to the woman, automatically scanning her for evidence. Was that blood all over her clothes? The damp fabric clung to her female curves. I noticed how nice those curves were, even coated in some murder victim's blood, and felt a little creepy about it.

Damn, I need to get laid. But that had brought me nothing but trouble in this town.

"Caught her red-handed," Danny said.

His prisoner huffed out a loud breath and focused a conde-scending gaze on him. "*I* called *you*, dipshit."

I chuckled as I watched the glee drain from Danny's face. He tipped his head sideways toward her. "See, like most criminals, she has no respect for the law."

She rolled her eyes. "I had to remind your boss to put gloves on before he started collecting evidence."

Not surprised. Around here, calling the sheriff was only helpful if you had an intruder who could be chased away by the presence of police cars. Sheriff Wade Strickland and Deputy Daniel

Scruggs knew how to turn on the lights and sirens. Otherwise, they were out of their depth.

"You'd better just pray for a good lawyer, missy," Danny said to the woman.

A new expression crossed her face. Uncertainty? Fear, maybe?

My lips parted, ready to offer help. They were always willing to get me into trouble, saving damsels in distress. I squeezed them back together.

No more of that nonsense. I'd made myself a promise that once I was out of Bolo, I'd leave those bad habits behind. But why procrastinate? Tonight was as good a time as any to say *adios* to that addiction.

"Well, I'll see you later, Danny." I lifted my foot off the brake.

The woman's eyes met mine again and, for a second, I could have sworn she was asking me not to leave her out here with these morons. Then I reminded myself she and I didn't know each other. I was probably "projecting" my emotions onto her. At least that's what Gabe, my best friend and self-appointed therapist, would say.

"Yeah, see ya, Nick," Danny called as I gunned the accelerator and high-tailed it away from the crime scene.

No way was I getting involved in a murder case. Not after what happened the last time.

No *fucking* way.

CHAPTER TWO

Rika

The next morning, I was led into a bland, empty courtroom. The same deputy from last night unlocked my handcuffs and gestured to one of two ancient wooden folding chairs behind an equally ancient wooden table.

I was glad to sit down before anyone else got there. I'm not the fashionista type, but my jail uniform was pretty embarrassing.

Last night, when I got to the station, the sheriff insisted on taking my clothes as evidence. The top I'd miss, but it was a total loss, the blood unlikely to wash out of white cotton.

I didn't care about the skirt. It was one of the expensive designer separates Brandtt bought me so I could adequately represent him as his girlfriend.

In hindsight, I realized that after watching guys turn away from me in disgust all those years, I kind of liked the job of trophy girlfriend, at least in theory. But that position was wearing thin way before Brandtt fired me from it.

Anyway, I thought I was okay with losing the clothes until the sheriff replaced them with what could loosely be described as

Hello Kitty scrubs. Except the kitty faces scattered over the fabric were pixilated and missing one eye. Probably knock-offs that went so wrong, they couldn't be sold to pediatric nurses, the only people who should be wearing something like this.

To make matters worse, the deputy had taken it upon himself to over-bandage my skinned palms until all that was visible were my fingertips and thumbs. My feet were clad in a pair of pink flip-flops the sheriff had given me when he took my Sketchers.

On the up side, I felt pretty well-rested. After surviving on car catnaps for days, the puny jail mattress might as well have been a Stearns & Foster. I slept like a log, except just before I woke up when I had my recurring dream about being chased by a Twinkie.

After running in slow-motion for what seemed like hours, the Twinkie cornered me and was about to squirt me with its creamy filling. But just when I gave up, faced it, and opened my mouth to receive its gooey goodness, I woke up.

A Freudian psychiatrist would say my dreams are about sex, but I know for a fact they're all about the food. When I'm sad or stressed, there's nothing more comforting than a tummy full of carbs. I've known that since I was eight years old and my world crashed and burned.

The sheriff walked in. Actually, his big, round belly entered first, followed by the rest of him a couple of seconds later.

I hadn't noticed his hair last night, but in the bright lights of the courtroom, it was a shade of yellow typically found on canaries, or maybe lemons. Certainly not on fifty-year-old men.

After the sheriff, came a tall thin man with salt and pepper hair in a navy three-piece suit and bow tie. The two of them chatted for several minutes, the sheriff tilting his head toward me repeatedly. Then the suit sat down at the other table—the twin to the one I was sitting behind. I assumed he was the district attorney.

I felt like I was watching one of those movies where you're not quite sure about the genre. The sheriff and his deputy suggested this was a comedy while the D.A looked like serious business.

A dramedy, maybe?

A couple of other people ambled in and sat on the spectator benches. I wondered what I was supposed to do for a lawyer. Once arrested, I knew better than to say anything without an attorney present. But, even if I did know a lawyer, I couldn't afford to hire him. And, so far, no public defender had materialized.

A plain, middle-aged woman walked in and sat down at the court reporter's station.

Suddenly, the reality of my situation hit me full force. A tremor shook through me from the roots of my hair to my pinky toes.

Don't ask me how a court reporter could do to me what a sheriff, a pair of handcuffs and a jail cell couldn't, but my teeth began to chatter. My right eye twitched.

Maybe because everything since last night had felt completely surreal until this mundane woman in her cheap skirt suit and mousy brown hair showed up.

She was real. This was not a dream and soon a real judge would be sitting at the front of this real courtroom and...

And what? I was alone in an unfamiliar state and had no idea what was about to happen.

Wait, I was in Texas, the place where they executed first, asked questions later.

God, I could use a donut right now.

No!

I closed my eyes, took a deep breath and blew the craving out my nostrils, as my Jilly Crane counselor had taught me.

When I turned twenty and decided I had to change my life, the Jenny Craig Weight Loss Centers had been out of my price range, so I went with a cheaper competitor who Skyped with me from an undisclosed location.

Honestly, it was a relief that I didn't have to haul my butterball body to a strip mall and interact with the sure-to-be skinny bitch—*uh, counselor*—in person.

Over the next couple of years, the visualization exercises and mantras had worked. I'd dropped half my body weight and exceeded my goal.

One day at a time, sweet Jesus.

I was only religious when it came to eating, since logic and religion weren't very compatible. Instead of "There are no atheists in foxholes," I think the saying should be, "There are no atheists in weight loss."

A girl needs all the help she can get. I'd pray to a statue of Victoria Beckham if I thought it would help me drop a pound.

Breathe in.... Breathe out...

There, my craving had completely vanished.

When I lifted my eyelids, a round-faced Hispanic man in a black robe was coming in through the chamber door. Once he settled at the judge's bench, he opened the white box he'd carried in with him, and pulled something out of it.

"Danny, could you pass these around? I didn't get any breakfast this morning," he said. "My wife's still in Laredo taking care of her mom. Personally, I think my mother-in-law's milking this gall bladder operation for all it's worth. She's always claiming Belinda doesn't spend enough time with her."

Deputy Dan took the box, grabbed a pile of napkins from a side table, and headed straight for me. "Ladies first."

I peered fearfully into the familiar container.

Oh, my God! Donuts! I counted eleven left in the box.

Pink icing. White icing. Chocolate icing. Sprinkles. Three kinds of jelly. And that perennial favorite—glazed. I could almost feel the dough melting in my mouth.

Deputy Dan smiled and, with a flourish, laid a napkin in front of me as if we were on a picnic together and I wasn't the woman he'd accused of murder just last night.

My eyes flicked back to the donuts. One had always led to

two, then three, then the whole box. But not this time. This time, I'd choose one, the deputy would take the box away and everything would be fine. I reached in and selected the most perfect glazed donut ever created.

But weren't they all?

I nodded my thanks and made myself wait until he walked away. As he held the box out to the D.A., I bit off a chunk and chewed it very slowly, enjoying the feel of fresh endorphins swishing gently through my gray matter.

Carbs sweet carbs.

The deputy continued around the courtroom until everyone was holding a napkin with a doughnut on top. Just as I finished the last bite of mine, he returned and set the box on the table near me.

"I'll leave 'em here," he said. "You haven't had anything else to eat since we took you into custody last night."

Damn that scheming bastard! He'd not only left temptation inches away, he'd given me the rationalization I needed to eat more.

I tried to avert my eyes, but they kept flitting back to the box. All three filled doughnuts were still there, including one with a red substance peeking out the top.

Cherry, I presume? I thought flirtatiously. I had a tendency to treat carbs like they were a hot guy I was trying to pick up at a bar. Not that I'd ever had the courage to do that.

"All rise." Deputy Dan was now acting as bailiff. Everyone else stood, so I did, too. "Hear ye, hear ye, the court of the Honorable Gabriel Martínez is now in session."

Everyone sat down.

The judge looked at me and frowned. "Wade?" he said to the sheriff, "Where's her counsel? Didn't she request an attorney?"

"She can't afford one, and Gordy wasn't available," the sheriff replied. "Gout."

"Well, we may have to..." the judge's voice trailed off as he lifted his chin and smiled toward the back of the room.

I followed his gaze to a tall, broad-shouldered man dressed in a teal polo shirt and khaki shorts who'd just entered the courtroom.

He pulled a golf ball out of his pocket, held it up and jiggled it back and forth as if asking the judge a question. His biceps flexed impressively with the motion, which prompted me to run another scan of his body.

Typically, I was not a fan of golf attire, even the simple solid-colored shirt-shorts combo he sported. But I had to admit, if I were hiring models for a golf catalog, he'd be the cover shot.

"It's gonna be a few minutes before I can go, Nick," Judge Martínez said. "But meanwhile, there's something you can help us out with. We're in the middle of a bail hearing and the defendant needs counsel."

"Now?" the man replied. "Where's Gordy?"

"Gout."

The man shook his head. His medium brown hair was cut short, like he went to a barber instead of a stylist. Regardless, he was so tall and well-built, especially compared to the other men in the room, that he looked more like he should be playing a lawyer on TV than actually being one. In fact, with that body, he could also play a fireman, a Navy Seal, or pose as the hero on one those erotic romance novel covers.

I squinted, trying to see his face better. Was it my imagination or did he look kind of familiar? Probably wishful thinking since I'd never felt more alone.

"Damn it, Gabe!" he said. "I just came to pick you up for our golf game!"

Hm. His voice seemed vaguely familiar, too.

"It's just a bail hearing," the judge replied. "We'll be done in a few minutes."

Nick, as the judge had called him, inhaled and blew out a

breath so loudly I could hear it across the room. After a final, deadly glance at the judge, he crammed the ball back into his pocket and strode toward me.

The judge held a notepad and pen toward the deputy who brought it over and handed it to my reluctant attorney as he reached the table.

"Thanks, Danny." He looked at me. "I'm Nick Owen."

Wait, this was the hot guy who stopped by in the fancy black pickup truck last night. If he was an attorney, why didn't he tell me? It might have helped to have someone on my side at the scene of the crime.

Asshole!

He turned so his entire body was facing me, as if trying to block off some privacy for us. It worked. Between his impressive height and broad shoulders, I could no longer see the judge or the D.A.

As my brain tried to think of more expletives to call him, my body tingled under his frown. He had the most intriguing eyes. Not true blue. Not really green either. Ming? Or maybe Bondi Blue like that old iMac G3 my grandmother bought me years ago at a garage sale.

Since he was in a teal shirt, they were probably those chameleon kind of eyes that changed with their surroundings. And they seemed to reflect more than their fair share of light. The effect was kind of mesmerizing.

His gaze was momentarily distracted by my mummy hands before he shook it off and got down to business.

"Are you well-off?" His attempt at a private conversation had turned his voice husky—the tone a man might use while murmuring something sexy into your ear. It tickled down the sides of my neck causing my shoulders to give a little wiggle. But he was all business as he stared at me questioningly.

"Huh?" I lowered my line of sight from his eyes to his mouth so I could concentrate on what he was saying.

"Money-wise."

"Oh... No. I have a savings account, but it's only got about fifteen hundred dollars in it. There's that and whatever was in my wallet from yesterday—I mean, a few days ago, when my boss told me to leave."

He quirked his head curiously, then decided against asking for details and went back to his line of questioning. "And your family?"

"No money there, either."

"And you're not from around here?"

"No," I said. "I'm from L.A., mostly."

"Not that it matters right now, but what the hell happened last night?"

I sighed and began, "I had to go to the bathroom and nothing was open in this one-horse town, so..." I didn't want to get too graphic on our first date...um...meeting.

"Are you saying, out of the thousands of acres of land around here, you happened to pick the one spot with a dead guy on it?"

I started to nod, then shook my head. "I didn't pee *on* him. I just tripped over him on the way back to my car. And when I called the police, they arrested me."

He looked up at the judge, shrugged and half-nodded, half-shook his head.

"Go ahead, J.J.," Judge Martínez said to the other attorney.

"Your honor, we're requesting bail be set at a million dollars."

A million dollars? My eyes flitted to the donuts again. If bail was set at a million, I'd have good reason to eat the rest of the box.

Now I wasn't sure which outcome to hope for.

"You've got to be kidding me," Nick said.

"She's not from around here, therefore a flight risk and—"

"I'm requesting she be released on her own recognizance," Nick said firmly. "It's ridiculous for her to spend any more time in

jail just because she happened to be the one to report the body."
He glared at Sheriff Strickland.

I straightened my spine and added my "take that" look, but
the sheriff was only paying attention to Nick.

"You know I can't release her on her own recognizance,"
Judge Martínez said. "This is a murder case and she has no ties to
the community. Bail is set at two hundred fifty thousand dollars."

Two hundred fifty thousand? Might as well be a million. I reached
out and slid the box closer.

How many donuts do you get when your bail is set at a
quarter of a million dollars? My Jilly Crane counselor never
covered that.

"I don't guess you can get your hands on the ten percent—
twenty-five thousand—for the bail bondsman?" Nick asked.

Ignoring the insulting fact that he assumed I couldn't figure
ten percent of two hundred fifty thousand, I shook my head.
"No," I said. "Not even close."

Murder trials took forever. I'd be in jail for months...years...

I snatched the cherry-filled from the box and shoved as much
as I could into my mouth all at once. When I pulled the
remainder away, I knew my lips were covered with filling, but I
didn't pick up the napkin. If I left the red goo where it was, I'd
have something to enjoy later.

Nick gave me a strange look, then eyed the napkin before
turning back to the judge. "I'll act as her bail bondsman." He
shrugged.

"What the hell?" Sheriff Strickland cried. "You can't do that!
He can't do that, can he, Gabe?"

"Well, it is unusual..." Judge Martínez began.

"But perfectly legal in the state of Texas," Nick said.

"Okay," the judge replied. "And I'm ordering you to continue
as her court appointed counsel."

"*What?*" Now Nick was the one yelling. "You know I'm moving
away!"

"You've been moving away for the past two years. What firm are you joining in Houston?"

Nick's jaw tensed. He pursed his lips then mumbled. "I'm not sure yet."

"Do you have an address there?"

Nick sucked in an angry breath, which caused his chest to swell, filling out his polo completely.

Nice. After resisting the urge to poke at his pecs with my sticky fingertips, I let my gaze trail down to the middle of his shirt. Did he have a six-pack under there to match?

I squeezed my eyes shut. I should be worried about my murder case, not my hot attorney. But, really, as soon as the evidence was examined, they'd realize I wasn't the killer. This was a no-brainer. Within a couple of days, I'd be out of this mess, and I'd head straight home to L.A., like I should have in the first place.

Still...it wasn't right to leave half a doughnut unfinished, so I stuck it in my mouth before any mantras came to mind.

"Gabe, you know—" Nick began.

"I know you're the only attorney in the county qualified to try a murder case other than Mr. Boyle, here." He pointed to J.J., the D.A. "It'll take some time for them to process her out. We can still get nine holes in."

My new attorney expelled another loud breath and looked at me like I'd shown up just to screw with his life.

Gee, sorry for cutting into your golf time by being wrongly accused of murder, jerk.

He looked back at the judge, his expression defeated, which didn't bode well for my future.

"I'll pick you up from the jail in a couple of hours," he told me, then he turned and walked out of the courtroom.

CHAPTER THREE

Nick Owen

Gabe and I rode to the golf course in his Suburban. I didn't say a word all the way over. Just listened to him prattle on about how the women in his life were driving him crazy.

We both knew I was pissed off, but Gabe always assumed I'd forgive him. Normally, all I had to forgive was his and Belinda's attempts to fix me up with their legion of female relatives. But this time, he'd pushed our friendship to the limit.

I got out of the truck and let my eyes drift over what passed for a golf course around here. Old Mr. Baumgartner decided he wanted to build his own course on his family's land. He managed to get nine playable holes done before he died.

His middle-aged stoner son didn't care about golf, but figured he could make money off his dad's hobby. However, Lonny Baumgartner soon realized he didn't like spending time at the course, or doing any manual labor whatsoever.

The result was a course that tended toward sickly green on its best days, beige on its worst. Since collecting the money was too much trouble, Lonny set up a locked wooden box with a slit in the top where you could stick your check before you played.

My mind wandered to the Houston metro area, where a man could play on a different, lush green course every day for over two months without hitting the same place twice.

Maybe that's what I'd do. Forget the law. Travel the world on the pro golf circuit.

Except, now, I was stuck in Bolo as sole counsel on a damn murder case.

By the time we were standing at the first tee box, Gabe still hadn't said a word about what happened at the courthouse. As he pulled his driver from his golf bag, I couldn't stand it anymore.

"You know I don't take murder cases." I'd tried to say it casually, but couldn't keep the edge from my voice.

He rubbed an invisible spot off his club with a golf towel. "You were the youngest attorney in Texas to win three murder cases in a row."

Sure, throw that in my face. "I wasn't even lead counsel on—"

"On the first one," he interrupted. "But Anderson saw the jury wasn't buying what he was selling. The decision to have you question the last two witnesses and give the closing argument...that's what won the case."

"But—"

"And you were lead on the next two." He slid the tee into the soft ground and set his ball on it.

I hated to talk about my time as a defense attorney. Come to think of it, the past in general was no friend of mine.

"I was also lead on the one after that," I said. "The one I lost."

"Nobody wins every time," Gabe said matter-of-factly, but when he swung, he shanked the ball off to the left, a sure sign the guilt was eating at him.

"I lost the one that mattered," I replied.

"They always matter, Nick."

"Not like that one." I shook my head, still unable to accept the unthinkable outcome. "I don't know if the three I kept out of jail were guilty or innocent. They all had criminal records. They'll all be doing time again, sooner or later. But Johnny Chavez..."

"Didn't have an alibi. Had a motive."

"He was innocent. He didn't kill that girl any more than I did."

"He's got a lot of supporters in Austin and San Antonio," Gabe said. "And a good chance on appeal with a great firm defending him, thanks to that fund you started."

This was why I hated to talk about the case. No one felt the loss in their gut like I did.

"But, right now, he's a nineteen-year-old kid sitting in prison for a crime he didn't commit," I said. "He's the first thing I think of when I get up in the morning. Every night, I go over the case in my head before I fall asleep...what I could have done differently..."

"We're not gods, Nick. We're just people working within the constraints of the system we've got."

I yanked my driver out of my bag and teed up. "You know I want to get out of criminal law."

Gabe let out a long dramatic breath. "But my responsibility when I'm sitting on that bench is to make sure things are as fair as I can make them. J.J. has tried murder cases before. Who else around here is a match for him? Gordy Smythe? J.J. would eat him for lunch. And Wade... Well, you know."

Yep. I knew. Well, I didn't know for sure, but I'd heard the talk. There was a good chance Sheriff Wade Strickland was into some shady dealings. I'd heard talk of bribery. There had even been speculation the corruption had spread to the private lab the sheriff used to run forensics. That was the scariest rumor of all.

I swung and was pleased as my ball sailed straight up the fairway toward the hole. Gabe whistled through his teeth as he watched the textbook landing. At least something was going my way today.

"Look on the bright side," Gabe said as he slid his club back into his golf bag. "She's got to be the prettiest client you've ever defended."

"Huh." I gave him a sour look. "You know my track record in that area just gets worse every year. I've sworn off women for a while. Besides, she's off limits. I'm her attorney."

"Yeah, but maybe having her around will remind you you're still young and there are still a lot of possibilities out there."

It was true that I was younger than Gabe by nearly ten years. I just wished I could feel it, lately. I picked up my golf bag. "Gabe?"

"Yeah?"

"Does it not seem the least bit ironic to you that a month ago you informed me I had an unhealthy savior complex with women, and, today, you handed me a woman to save?"

"Yeah," he patted me on the back. "I guess that is pretty ironic."

"And pretty shitty," I added.

"And pretty shitty," he agreed as he went off to look for his ball.

∾

Rika

I'd heard of people killing themselves after being arrested. I always assumed it was because they'd done something terrible, been busted for it, and knew their lives were over. But I had a whole new perspective on jailhouse suicide now.

For the last two hours, I'd watched an elderly white-haired woman—Deputy Dan referred to her as "Ms. Tommy June"—painstakingly hunt and peck on my release papers using an ancient Selectric typewriter.

Yes, I said *typewriter*.

When that ordeal was over, I was moved to the chair next to Deputy Dan's desk, where I watched him take Ms. Tommy June's form and enter that same information into a turn-of-the-century

Gateway computer—also using the hunt and peck method—while staring into the oldest CRT screen I'd ever seen.

I imagined sinking a sword into my stomach and committing *seppuku*, also known as *hari-kari* to people who don't spend enough time on Wikipedia.

How could anyone stand to operate at sloth speed in this day and age? The inefficiency in this place was mind blowing. If my tablet-sized computer wasn't stuck in the backseat of my confiscated car, I could have done both their jobs in less than five minutes.

I closed my eyes and counted the ways.

One, type the information in using the keyboard, and proper hand position, of course. Two, speak into the microphone and let the voice recognition app fill in the blanks. Three, connect wirelessly to their system, pull up the form and write the answers longhand on my screen with the stylus. Four, use the advanced auto-fill app I'd written for myself—with a little help from a YouTube video—that would fill in every possible piece of personal information in the blink of an eye. Five...okay, maybe there were just four, but still, this...

Tap...long pause...tap...tap...

...was nuts. Maybe that short cut I took had somehow Doctor Who'd me back to the mid-twentieth century.

Worst of all, Sheriff Strickland had kept my cell phone as evidence. How long can a person be absent from social media before she's declared legally dead? It was torture sitting here doing nothing without my phone to pacify me.

I was bored. And I wanted another doughnut. Someone had taken the box away just before they led me out of the courtroom. But not before I'd grabbed a third one—chocolate icing with sprinkles.

I figured I deserved it. As hot as my lawyer was, he didn't exactly inspire confidence with his negative attitude and golf clothes.

He did inspire something else, though.

I allowed myself a moment to mentally re-examine Nick Owen. After all, I'd been an inmate for over sixteen hours, and inmates were supposed to be horny.

Hmm...tall. Six-three, maybe? Broad, thick shoulders. Strong chin. I've always felt the chin's importance was underestimated as a facial feature. In Hollywood, if you don't have a strong chin, you'd better be able to do comedy.

Nick had more than just a chin, though. His lips were what I called Goldilocks Lips. Not too thin. Not too thick. *Just right.*

And those eyes. Holy mo—

A door slammed, jarring me out of my mind's collection of Nick pics. I turned my head and saw him walking in from behind me.

"Got the papers ready, Danny?"

Deputy Dan poked one last key and the dot matrix printer roared to life. "Hey, Nick! Just printin' 'em out. You've got perfect timing," he said cheerfully.

Why did everyone act like this was just a typical day at work for them? I was under arrest for murder, for God's sake!

Nick reached over and pulled the first page from the printer. "And how are you doing Ms..." He snuck a peek at the form. "Martin."

"Martín," I replied testily. "It's pronounced Mar-teen. There's supposed to be an accent on the i." I looked up into his intriguing eyes and the anger drained right out of me. There was an underlying earnestness in his gaze even though his voice had been business-casual. "You can call me Rika."

I suddenly wished I hadn't eaten those donuts. Nick would like me better thin.

I slapped myself—mentally, of course—but I made sure it stung. From what the judge said, this guy might be my only hope, legally speaking. I certainly didn't need to complicate things by crushing on him.

He was studying the form again. "It says here your first name is Paprika," he said doubtfully. "Middle name Anise."

I cringed as I did every time my real name was spoken aloud.

"Those are cooking spices." His eyes flicked over and zapped Deputy Dan with an *Are you an idiot?* look. The tops of the deputy's ears turned pink. "This isn't a joke." Nick's gaze bore down on me like I was a child he was about to ground, and I knew how Dan felt.

Wait. He was in the wrong here.

"That's my name. My dad's a chef and my mom was a...free spirit type. But they pronounced it ah-*nees*, instead of *an*-iss. My dad had a Spanish accent and—"

He narrowed his eyes at me. "*This* is the name on your birth certificate?" Jeez, if he believed I'd given a fake name, maybe he believed I was a killer, too.

"It is," I said, narrowing my eyes right back at him. I'd been stranded in a tiny Texas town, stripped of my belongings, and accused of murder. And, if that wasn't bad enough, I was still covered in deformed cats while my unwilling attorney looked at me like I was a big fat liar.

It was the last straw. "I was named after fuc—"Ms. Tommy June leaned forward in her chair, her eyes big as DVDs. "...*freaking* spices, okay?"

He raised his hands to chest level, palms out. "Okay, Grumpy Spice. Simmer down." He pressed his lips together, but his eyes crinkled a little in the corners.

"Did you just combine a Seven Dwarves reference with a Spice Girls reference and a kitchen idiom?" I asked.

"I did," he replied.

Our gazes caught and locked as a thrill tingled down the back of my neck, splitting five ways, racing through my limbs and straight down my center. My thighs twitched.

He was *witty!* God, I was a sucker for a witty man, which

explains why, as a little girl, my first love was Jay Leno. But this guy was the whole package—smart, funny, and hot.

"Nicely done," I said, trying to appear unaffected.

I suddenly felt the need to examine his face more closely, and as I stared at his features, I realized they weren't quite perfect. Something about his nose. A slight quirk in the bridge as though it had been broken at least once.

Between that, the strong jaw and those captivating eyes, he hit the sweet spot halfway between Calvin Klein model and cowboy, which made him both witty *and* ruggedly handsome. He nodded a thanks as his expression broke into a full-blown smile.

Holy mother of Zeus!

I couldn't swallow now that I knew how truly beautiful he was. I stopped breathing until he turned away to grab a nearby chair and roll it over to face me. While he wasn't looking, I pinched my thigh hard forcing myself to jerk in a breath.

Once he sat down, I watched his long, thick finger skim quickly to the permanent address section of the form. Funny how something as simple as a finger can be arousing on the right person.

I glanced down at my boxy scrubs. Not that my arousal mattered one bit. He was way out of my league. He was *that* guy. The quarterback, homecoming king, girl magnet. He moved with the physical ease of the popular kids. An ease I'd never experienced.

I was the geeky, awkward fat girl who was ignored when I was lucky and bullied when I wasn't.

"Oh..." He chuckled. "Paprika Anise from California. That explains everything."

"Yeah, because Texas is so normal," I replied, angry now that I'd sorted him into the appropriate high school clique. His kind and mine were natural born enemies.

He ignored my moodiness and went back to reading until my stomach let out what can only be described as a howl.

"When'd you last eat anything other than donuts?" he asked.

"Yesterday morning, maybe?" The past few days were such a blur I couldn't be certain.

He frowned. "Danny, what the hell?"

The deputy startled. "Huh?" He was only a few yards away, but had been staring vacantly into space, unaware of our conversation.

Nick closed his eyes as if praying for patience. "Come on, let's go." He jerked his head toward the door and started walking as if I were a trained dog that would go wherever he commanded.

"Where?" I asked.

"I've got steaks marinating at my place."

Steaks? I hadn't eaten steak since just before I started my job as an E.coli tester, which had sort of ruined them for me. But I'd ingested no protein in the last thirty-six hours. I was starting to feel like one of those reality show contestants who had to eat whatever she could catch on some remote island off South America.

At the mention of steak, my mouth had started watering so fast I was afraid drool would leak out the corners. I stood and, as I followed Nick, his shorts tightened over his firm round ass with each step. Then, a little drool *did* leak out the corner of my mouth, but I reached up and slapped it away.

But wasn't it kind of weird for a murder suspect to go to her lawyer's place for dinner?

"I don't want to be any trouble," I said. "You weren't expecting company. Maybe you could just drop me off somewhere?" Although I was unsure how I'd pay for dinner or a place to sleep when all my credit cards were in the sheriff's possession.

"Nowhere to drop you," he replied. "And it's no trouble. I was planning to have Gabe—Judge Martínez—over for dinner after golf, but he's on my shit list now. Come on."

I shrugged and followed him out the door.

CHAPTER FOUR

Rika

Nick's house sat in an oasis of full-grown oak trees on enough acreage that I couldn't see any neighbors, even though the surrounding terrain was mostly scrub brush, squatty trees and cactus.

The house was fairly new and only one story, but it spread out lazily like a house that knew it had all the land in the world to lounge around on.

The truck's time and temperature panel said it was ninety-four degrees outside. I opened the door and stepped out onto the paved driveway. In the few yards between Nick's truck and the front door, sweat popped out on my forehead, just like it had when I left the police station. He opened the front door and I walked ahead of him into the much cooler house.

Brandtt's apartment was considered large for Manhattan, but the whole thing would have fit in Nick's massive living room.

It had the look of a lodge with a huge stone fireplace at one end and decorative wood beams in the vaulted ceiling. The couches were made from cream-colored leather, the oversized chairs upholstered in brown and cream with leather arm rests. The feel was surprisingly cozy for such a big room.

"I don't know why you'd want to move away from this place." I ran my fingers over the back of an armchair, grateful Nick had stopped at a convenience store and picked up large square Band-Aids to replace Dan's mummy bandages. I'd been so ready to rid myself of the deputy's handiwork, I'd changed them out on the way.

"It's not the house that's the problem," Nick replied.

I flip-flopped behind him as I followed, expecting him to elaborate, but that seemed to be all he had to say on the subject.

Once we were in the kitchen, he was even taller than he'd been before, which was impossible. Maybe he just seemed taller because the ceiling in this room wasn't as high as it had been in his living room and at the courthouse.

Or maybe it was because we were totally alone for the first time. A thrill managed to wiggle up my spine before I reminded myself why I was here.

I watched as he opened the refrigerator and pulled out a pan covered in foil. "Do you want some help?" I asked, not sure I could actually be of any.

"Nah. This is a one-man operation." He pulled out a chair for me at his eat-in kitchen table. I'd never seen anything like it. Clearly custom-made, the knotty wood of the table matched both a built-in bench on one side and the chairs on the other.

He opened the French doors and left them that way, apparently unconcerned about the price of his electric bill.

As he moved back and forth between the kitchen and deck, I felt awkward, like I was on a first date. Except for the fact that my "date" had basically been forced to agree to defend me for murder, post my bail, and take me in off the streets.

Okay, it was nothing like a date, except for the awkward part.

The upside was that I got to watch Nick bend over repeatedly as he pulled cooking pots out of the lower cabinets. While he went about his tasks, I became more and more aware of his body. His nicely formed ass, his strong arms, the definition in his calves...

When had I ever noticed a man's calves before?

He handed me a bottle of imported beer as he passed by, then went back outside and transferred a steak from the pan to the grill.

The sizzling sound made my stomach growl. I took a sip of beer as daintily as I could out of the bottle, hoping it would shut my gut up for a while.

He glanced over at me. "So, how are you enjoying our little town so far?" His tone was sarcastic, yet his expression seemed genuinely interested.

"I'm in denial about this whole thing." I traced my finger over the lines of a silver napkin ring on the table. It seemed like a weird thing for a bachelor to have. A straight one, anyway. "While I was sitting there watching Ms. Tommy June and Deputy Dan do my paperwork, I decided that getting run off the road last night hurtled me through a rip in the space-time continuum. Or maybe I'm a doppelganger of myself in an alternate universe."

He turned toward me. A slow grin crept over his face, warming his eyes. My heart did a *buh-bump* against my ribs that I was sure could be heard outside my body.

The smile went full-blown. His teeth were nearly as white as Brandtt's veneers. And Nick had one of those faces that changed from manly man to fun-loving and kind of boyish when he smiled.

Actually, Brandtt had possessed the same quality, but there was something contrived about his grin. Like he was doing it because he knew it made women swoon.

From Nick, the smile seemed appreciative—just for me— because of something I'd said.

"You're pretty smart for a hot chick." His smile said he was aware of the sexist nature of his statement but was enjoying teasing me.

I tried to smile back, but my lips only made it to half-mast. *Hot chick.* I wished I could see myself through his eyes. I shrugged. "Disconcerting, isn't it?"

He threw his head back and laughed. "I guess it would be to some people."

Did that mean he wasn't one of those people? Brandtt had found my geekiness downright annoying sometimes. I never blamed him because I was confused, myself. Men had started noticing me a few years ago, while I was losing weight, and I still didn't know what to do with that.

I'd spent most of my life as the polar opposite of hot. Although I'd been the new me for a while now, my self-image hadn't adjusted to the leaner body and I was beginning to wonder if it ever would. Most of the time, I still felt more like the Ugly Duckling than the swan.

Nick stirred a pot of beans he was rewarming on a burner next to the grill portion of his barbeque. He practically had a full outdoor kitchen a few steps from his indoor kitchen.

"You didn't fill in an employer on the forms at the station," he said.

I thought we'd shared a moment, but maybe the jokes and the beer were just supposed to lube me up to make his job easier.

Regardless, he was my attorney and I might as well come clean. "I had a job until a few days ago. I was an E.coli tester at a meat packing facility."

"Seriously?"

"Yeah. Why does that surprise you?"

He lifted his index finger. "Give me a minute." He closed his eyes. "Okay, I'm visualizing you in a white lab coat, hair in a ponytail, safety goggles... I can see it now."

When he opened his eyes and grinned at me again, I had to

smile back. I liked the idea of Nick visualizing me—I looked down at the scrubs—in *anything* other than this.

"What happened with the job?"

Back to business again. I blew out a disappointed breath. "My boss came in babbling about the FBI and money-laundering. He handed me a roll of cash as severance pay."

"Let's hope Wade's too lazy to check on that." He began moving the food from the grill to the table. "How'd you end up in Bolo from L.A.?"

"By way of New York."

"Wow. You need a new GPS."

"I need more than that," I admitted. "I followed my actor boyfriend from L.A. to New York when he got a new job."

Nick sucked in a deep breath.

"I know," I said. "But he begged me and... Well, anyway, when I got back to the apartment after losing my job a couple of days ago, all my stuff was waiting for me in the lobby. Brandtt had 'found someone new.' Like he was walking down the street that morning and tripped over her."

Nick sighed. "Yeah. I've had days like that... Did you say *Brandtt*?" He laid our plates and silverware on the table.

"Yeah. With two T's," I said. "I should have known."

He chuckled as he plopped a giant steak, a buttered baked potato and a ladle full of beans onto my plate. "Yep. I've been there too—Shellee, with three e's."

Was I crazy or did he and I really get each other?

Calm down, Rika. You've just been through a job loss, a break up and gotten cozy with a blood-soaked stiff. You can't possibly be in your right mind.

Plus, I didn't have a lot of experience with men. Zero serious relationships before Brandtt. I'd had a few really awkward dates with guys who asked me out after I'd lost a lot of the weight. The awkward part was caused by the fact that I wasn't used to making small talk with guys and I gave them short one-word answers followed by really long, really loud silence.

Brandtt had worked out because he loved to talk about himself so much, all I had to do was sit back and nod my head.

Anyway, the point was, I didn't know men and I certainly didn't know Nick. My body was just responding to his hotness.

And one day certainly wasn't enough to identify any red flags. After my last experience, I planned to vet future men a lot more thoroughly before getting into a relationship.

I looked down at the feast in front of me. It smelled fantastic. But this town probably didn't have so much as a Pilates class for me to work it off in. I shaved off a thin piece of steak with my knife.

"Anyway, I was feeling too humiliated to go straight back to L.A. and some friends have a condo for a month down on South Padre Island."

When I touched the slice to my tongue, I was sure I'd died and gone to Valhalla. It practically melted in my mouth. I swallowed and dug into the baked potato.

"Makes sense." He tore a man-sized hunk of beef off his fork with his white teeth. Did he have to chew so seductively? I wouldn't have thought sexy chewing was possible if I hadn't witnessed it personally, but Nick really had it down.

I forced myself to stop ogling him and we ate quietly for a few minutes. It was nice sitting in his kitchen, serenaded by the chirping of crickets. I'd almost demolished my baked potato when I looked up and found him examining me again.

"So, you're, what, Mexican-American?"

Red flag. What difference did my ethnicity make? I narrowed my eyes warily at him. "Colombian. My mom's parents came from there and my dad was straight out of Colombia."

Nick tilted his head back until he was staring at the ceiling. "Shit," he said.

Red flag! "What's that supposed to mean?"

"It means my job just got harder."

"Why?"

"About forty-eight percent of the people around here are run of the mill white folks. British, Irish, German descent, although most of them don't think much about where their ancestors came from. Another forty-eight percent are Mexican-American. I was hoping to stack the jury in our favor. Make them more sympathetic."

Oh. He was thinking ahead to the trial. I was having a hard time imagining myself on trial for murder. "What's stopping you if half the population is Latino?" I asked.

He shook his head. "There's no 'Latino' here. There are Mexicans, Whites, a couple of Vietnamese families that own the convenience stores and nail salon, and one black family. All any of them know about Colombians comes from old action movies about drug cartels. You can bet J.J. will remind them you're Colombian every chance he gets."

"Can he do that?"

"He'll find a way," Nick said. "Where are your parents now?"

"My mom died when I was eight." Would there ever be a time when that sentence didn't bring a lump to my throat? I was so young, no one told me the details and, even as I got older, it was the one thing I could never bear to google. What I did overhear was that she was abducted just after leaving a yoga class. I always found this fact ironically bizarre.

A yoga class. Did other people find yoga followed by abduction and murder as unfathomable as I did or did I focus on it because it was the only detail I knew?

"I'm sorry." Nick's eyes drifted away as if I'd refreshed an unwanted memory. "It's hard to lose a parent that young." He looked back at me. "And your dad?"

"He was forced to live in Colombia. He hadn't become a citizen yet. He had to go back and forth to Colombia to visit his sick mom several times. It was after nine-eleven and the government had started cracking down on immigration. The last time he went to Colombia, they wouldn't let him back in the country." Another lump. I swallowed hard. "Everyone decided it was best for me to live with my grandmother—my mom's mom—here in the States."

And I'd felt like an orphan.

"Have you visited him?"

"Yeah. Whenever he or my grandmother and aunts could get the money together when I was a kid. And, now that he's doing better financially, he flies me over a couple of times a year."

Nick looked away. "Damn it," he muttered.

Major red flag! "You'd rather I didn't see my father?"

He dropped his head and massaged the bridge of his nose, eyes closed, like he was thinking aloud. "You're genetically one hundred percent Colombian. You make regular trips to Colombia. You were driving toward Mexico when the cops found you with a dead body, and you were covered in blood."

"So?"

"J.J. will turn this into a drug mule scenario. It'll make a lot more sense to people around here than your story. They think vacations mean a few days visiting relatives in San Antonio or Corpus Christi. Most of 'em don't even go as far as Houston. They can't imagine this L.A., Colombia, New York, South Padre life you're living."

A wave of fear rippled through me. Was he telling me I could actually get convicted?

Not if he did his job. "Are you saying you're such a crappy attorney that you can't get an innocent person off a bogus murder conviction?"

His eyes suddenly changed color, from the pleasant dark teal they'd been since we entered his house to a stormy sea-gray. His jaw clenched and his fingers tightened on his fork. For a second, I thought he might stab me with it.

Instead, he stood and took his plate to the sink without a

word. After he rinsed it, he turned his back to the sink, gripping the counter on either side with his hands.

"You can fire me," he said. "The judge won't force you to keep me as your attorney if you don't want me." The expression on his face said he was hoping I'd do just that.

But I'd gotten a glimpse of my options in this town and the idea of not having Nick on my side freaked me the hell out.

I sucked in a calming breath and tried to keep my voice from shaking. "How many murder cases have you tried?"

"Four." His gaze dropped to the ceramic tile and stayed there.

"How many have you won?"

"Three."

Why did he look ashamed? Sounded like a pretty good record to me. "I don't want to fire you."

His lips parted just enough to allow a slow current of air to escape. Did he not want to represent me because a trial would keep him from moving? Waste his valuable time? Or was there something else?

I felt nosey asking too many questions, but shouldn't I know a lot more about a guy who'd be defending me for murder?

The doorbell rang, followed immediately by frantic knocking.

"Nick!" a woman's voice called. He strode out of the kitchen. I got up from the table and peeked around the door frame at the entryway.

As soon as he opened the door, a tall slender blonde dressed to the nines in a silky designer jumpsuit hurried in with an even blonder tiny dog in one hand, a bag of dog food in the other.

"I need a favor," she said breathlessly. She tossed her head to get her flowing locks out of the way. The top of her hair appeared less mobile, rising up high from the roots before swooping majestically down in layers, past her shoulders.

Nick glanced from one of her hands to the other. "No," He said. "No way."

"You're the only one she's used to," the woman said. Her

features were so perfect, she could have been a doll. "I'm leaving the country. Jacques is taking me to France with him." Her huge blue eyes sparkled with excitement. She set what I now recognized as a Maltese at Nick's feet and dropped the food by the door. "Thanks, you're awesome," she said convincingly. Cupping his jaw with one hand, she kissed him on the opposite cheek.

Nick pulled away. "I said—"

"Thanks, I owe you!" She backed up until I couldn't see her anymore. Unable to resist, I crept into the entryway behind Nick and peered out the door.

"Well," Nick called after her, "when are you comin' back?"

"I don't know. Jacques has a new job there."

"*What?*"

But it was too late. She took off—impressively fast in her high heels—and jumped into the passenger side of a flashy red sports car. Its tires screeched as it backed out of the drive.

"Shellee?" I asked from behind him.

"No." His face had tightened into an expression I couldn't quite read. It wasn't a good one though. "That was Megan...my wife." He stared after her as the car turned from his drive onto the main road.

He's married? "Your wife?"

"I mean ex-wife. The divorce happened so fast, I haven't quite..." His voice trailed off.

"I'm sorry." I really was sorry if he was pining over another woman. I wanted his full attention on me, um, my case.

"There's nothing to be sorry about. We were a disaster. I'm not sorry about the divorce, I just feel kind of..."

"Humiliated?" I offered up.

He turned and looked me in the eye, clearly surprised I'd been so blunt and probably not wanting to say or hear the word "humiliated" aloud. I tend to be blunt and blurty at times, a habit I'm sure I picked up from my grandmother.

I winced. "I know the feeling."

41

He tilted his head and thought about it for a moment. "Yeah, I guess you do... But *this*." He scooped the ball of fluff into the air and turned toward me. The dog's body was only slightly longer than his palm, but her glossy white hair hung down to her feet. A pink mini-Scrunchie sat atop her head, a long ponytail flowing out of it. "*This* is adding insult to injury." He set her down and grabbed the small bag of food.

As he walked past me into the kitchen, the dog turned toward the door and began barking. Actually, barking wasn't the right word for it. Ear-piercing yapping echoed off the walls until I could swear we had three tiny dogs in the house instead of one.

"Shit!" Nick said as he hurried back and swept her up onto one arm. "That sound makes me want to gouge out my eardrums."

I gazed at the poor little thing feeling kind of sorry for her. "I guess she didn't want to be abandoned either."

Nick gave me a look that said he didn't appreciate being compared to an abandoned dog. "I'm sure she didn't. She's one hundred percent companion dog and when her human leaves her sight she throws a hissy fit. I'm gonna take her out back and see if she needs to go potty."

I snickered.

He looked at me as if I was furthering the torture his ex had begun. "That's what Megan always called it."

"Okay." I pursed my lips in an attempt to squelch my smile as he walked out.

After a few seconds alone, I got bored—still no cell phone—and followed him. He was sitting on the steps that led from his raised wood deck to the vast green yard behind the house.

The dog was high-stepping, trying to find a place to comfortably squat in grass longer than her legs.

"I guess I'm going to have to cut it back down to an inch and a half again," he said without turning around.

"What's her name?" I asked.

He took in a dramatically deep breath and expelled it. "Gucci."

I tried to contain my laughter, but it came out as a snort. "Can't you just change it?"

"I doubt it. The dog is dumb as a box of rocks. It took Megan a year to get her to answer to this name."

Gucci finally gave up on trying to find a comfortable spot and squatted on the grass.

My mind veered back to the conversation we were having before she showed up. "Nick?"

He twisted around and looked up at me, using one hand to shade his eyes from the setting sun.

"You sounded really worried about a trial. Since I'm innocent, don't you think when they examine the evidence, they'll drop the charges and start looking for the real killer?"

He turned back as if checking on the dog, but the look on his face when I asked the question and the tension in his shoulders said something different. Like maybe there was news he didn't want to break to me.

Gucci came back to him and he lifted her onto the deck. She used her tiny black nose to sniff her way to the barbecue pit and lick at the wood beneath it with the tiniest pink tongue I'd ever seen.

Nick walked over and sat in one of the green patio chairs. He tilted his head toward the one nearest him and I sat too. My heart pounded faster. I felt the need to grip the armrests with both hands.

"There are issues," he said, "with the sheriff." I opened my mouth, but he wasn't finished. "And possibly the forensics lab he uses."

"What kind of issues?"

"Rumor has it the sheriff is dirty. The problem is, I don't know how dirty."

"If that's the case, why is he still sheriff?"

"He's an elected official," Nick explained. "If he does enough little favors for the locals, like fixing tickets, or driving drunks home instead of arresting them, it garners a lot of loyalty among voters."

"So, are you saying he'd try to railroad me just so he doesn't have to look at local citizens for the murder?"

"Honestly, I don't know what he'll do. It worries me Wade is so eager to close this case that he'd make such a ridiculous arrest. There could be more to it than just election concerns."

The chunks of cow I'd consumed came to life and flipped over in my stomach. "You mean he could be involved in the crime?"

Nick shrugged.

"And the crime lab might falsify evidence for him?" My voice pitched higher with the last question.

"Like I said, it's all rumor. The lab is fifty miles away, and small-town gossip can turn molehills into mountains. But it's happened before. Even big city crime labs have been found to skew results in favor of the prosecution."

All this time, the logical part of my mind had held my fear in check, telling me this was no more than a mistake that would be rectified at any moment.

I shook my head, trying to keep the word "railroaded" out of it. But there it was. I was being railroaded to prison by a crooked cop. Otherwise, why would he arrest me for reporting the body? Who dumps a body in the countryside, reports it and waits around for the police to show up?

Then I remembered who I was. Or, at least, who I'd wanted to be, before Brandtt talked me into leaving L.A. I sat up straight and pulled my shoulders back. "I'll just have to prove my innocence myself."

Nick narrowed his eyes at me as if trying to measure my level of sanity. "You?"

I nodded.

He opened his mouth like he was going to say something, but pinched his lips back together. I guess he figured he didn't want to argue with me after the shock he'd delivered. "Well, let's just see what evidence they come up with," he said.

It bugged me that he wasn't taking me seriously. So far in my life, the only man who'd really taken me seriously was my dad, and he hadn't been around nearly enough. I was pretty fed up with the rest of mankind.

"If the sheriff won't solve this murder, I *will* solve it myself," I said with determination I almost felt. "Besides, you said I was smart."

Nick stood from his chair. "For a hot chick." His eyes crinkled in the corners. The half-smile he blessed me with was of the teasing variety, causing a fresh crop of Texas sweat to burst through my pores. "Come on, let me show you where you're gonna sleep."

Sleep? I don't think so. But I got up and followed him into the house with Gucci close on our heels.

CHAPTER FIVE

Nick

For the first time in a long time, I didn't go to bed thinking about Johnny Chavez and the worst miscarriage of justice I'd been involved with.

Tonight, all I could think about was the woman who was sleeping on the other side of my house, thanks to Gabe. Well, Gabe hadn't told me I had to bring her home, but what else was she supposed to do? You had to drive two towns away just to get to a crappy motel I wouldn't put my worst enemy up in.

Fucking Gabe. The last thing I needed was another woman under my roof. She seemed pretty impressed with the house, though.

And I enjoyed impressing her just a little too much.

We'd had a really pleasant time at dinner. It was weird how, one minute, she felt like something brand new, the next, like I'd known her for years.

I chuckled, remembering the look on her face when I showed her the guest closet, half-full of Megan's clothes, and told her she could have them if she wanted them. She looked at me like I was nuts.

Megan's taste was pretty flashy, her dresses low-cut in the front and high-cut at the bottom. But I didn't think Rika would be so picky considering that, last night, she'd combined a flowy, feminine skirt with sneakers. I was no fashion expert, but even I knew that looked wrong.

I ended up lending her my smallest pair of drawstring sweat-pants and my UT "Hook 'em Horns" t-shirt. As oversized as they were on her, she looked pretty damned cute.

When she'd leaned forward earlier in the evening, the V-neck of her scrubs had opened up and, I swear, one of my eyeballs was trying to do the right thing and avert itself while the other was trying to score a peek.

But I couldn't afford to go there with her. In fact, I needed to forget she was a woman entirely, so I could focus on the pile of shit case my best friend had dropped in my lap.

A mix of adrenaline and acid washed through my stomach, leaving behind a persistent burn. I didn't want to be responsible for another person's life. And I couldn't shake the feeling that Wade Strickland didn't just *want* her to get convicted of this crime. He needed it.

Normally, Wade was as sexist as they came. The last place he'd look for a murderer was in the body of an attractive, petite woman. It was common knowledge that even the female "foreigners" could get out of a speeding ticket with a smile and an eyelash flutter.

What was behind this arrest? Was Wade involved in the murder? Was he getting paid off by some sort of organized crime ring? There were a couple of motorcycle gangs rumored to be smuggling drugs and guns through this part of the state to and from Mexico. Maybe Wade collected protection money from them. Or did he just want all this wrapped up in a bow so he could show it off come election time?

If we were in Houston, or San Antonio, or even Corpus Christi, I wouldn't have been worried about this lame case. I'd just put Wade and Danny on the stand and show them for the fools they were.

But, even though Gabe was as fair as they came, it was a jury who would decide Rika's fate, based on what they were told by a crooked Sheriff, using evidence processed by a possibly crooked crime lab.

Damn, I'd hated the look on her face when she'd asked me why I was so concerned. Until then, she'd seemed mostly flip about the whole thing, but, in that moment, I saw the fear in her eyes. I thought about the fact that she'd effectively lost both her parents when she was a kid.

She was twenty-four years old, for Christ's sake. She'd had enough bad luck already.

That's when I had the urge to get up off the step and put my arms around her. Tell her everything would be okay.

But I learned my lesson the last time, and I'd never make promises again I couldn't keep.

~

Rika

I awoke with my heart pounding, breathing fast like I'd been running from the Terminator. As I sat up, I tried to recall my dream.

The Twinkie was chasing me again. I remembered running through a door and locking it behind me. I breathed a sigh of relief. I was safe.

But then I turned and found a Hostess Ding Dong sitting on the couch facing away from me, watching a University of Texas football game.

Instantly aroused, I tiptoed to the back of the sofa and ran my tongue over his chocolaty coating.

Just a taste. That's all I needed...

Until I lost control and bit a hole in the top of him, sucking his creamy filling out before he had a chance to resist.

Another stress-food dream. But why the college football game this time?

I looked down at the Longhorn symbol on the t-shirt I was wearing. *Oh. Right.*

There was a light knock at my door.

"Yes?"

"I've got breakfast made," Nick called from the other side. "If you want some."

"Okay. Thanks," I replied, my voice still shaky from my erotic Ding Dong encounter. "I'll be there in a minute."

I jumped out of bed and ran to the adjoining bathroom. I was a mess.

Glad Nick had shown me the extra packages of toothbrushes in the cabinet drawer, I quickly brushed my teeth with the purple one I'd made mine last night and splashed water on my face. However, I couldn't find a comb or brush and my makeup had been impounded as evidence along with the rest of my belongings.

I ran my fingers through my snarled hair, but it stuck stubbornly up in front. I pushed on the top and it popped right up again as if it had been arranged that way with hair gel.

I'd experienced this phenomenon before when I inadvertently ran my jelly fingers through my hair during a carb fest. I leaned into the mirror and plucked a tiny red blob from my scalp.

Jeez! Had Nick noticed that last night?

Regardless, it was rude to let a homemade breakfast get cold. I turned away from the mirror, slipped on my flip flops and walked to the kitchen.

When I entered, Gucci ran toward me, barking until she reached my foot. She sniffed my bare toe, immediately lost interest and walked away. Pressing her tiny black nose to the kitchen floor, she snuffled every millimeter of one tile before moving on to the next.

Nick glanced at me, then did a double take. "You look great," he said without a smidgen of sarcasm in his voice.

After running my hand over my crusty hair, I glanced down at my baggy ensemble. I wanted to ask what, exactly, looked great about me, but a question like that could only make this situation more awkward.

I mean, I'd met the guy yesterday, I was wearing his clothes, and he'd cooked two meals for me in a row. We were living like a married couple—minus the sex—when we were little more than strangers.

Luckily, Nick was busy with breakfast because my eyes lingered on him a bit too long. This morning, he was in a pair of worn jeans and a light blue t-shirt that fit snugly on his impressive chest and shoulders.

Dressed this way, he looked younger than he did yesterday in the golf clothes. And I figured he must be a morning person because he also seemed in a better mood than he was last night, his eyes sparkling a lighter, happier blue than they had since I met him.

His feet were bare and there was a casual air in the room. Like we got up and had breakfast together every morning.

My stomach started to rumble. Whatever he was cooking smelled wonderful...and familiar.

"What did you make?" I asked.

"Bacon, potato, and egg *taquitos*."

Ooooh... My tongue orgasmed at the thought.

My grandma's next-door neighbor, Mrs. Ruiz was from Mexico. She and my grandma shared a love of cooking and often traded recipes and cooked together, so we were as likely to have Mexican tortillas in my house as Colombian *arepa*.

Nick handed me a plate with two soft breakfast tacos, or "fat wrapped in carbs," as my Jilly Crane counselor would call them.

I shouldn't eat this. I really, really shouldn't.

But how could I turn them down after all the trouble he'd gone to? That would be rude.

We sat across from each other at his kitchen table. Two cups of steaming hot coffee had already been placed there.

"It's Colombian," Nick said, nodding toward my mug. "I checked." His eyes crinkled in the corners even though his lips weren't smiling. It was the third time I'd seen that expression on his face. Tyra Banks called this "smizing," and, when Nick did it, it made me feel kind of melty inside.

No one would have guessed I was a fan of America's Next Top Model, but it was a favorite of mine as a teenager. The rail thin models would pose for the most beautiful pictures, then face the confessional camera and say the most idiotic things.

I'd sit and watch them while eating my Double Stuf Oreos and laugh, feeling superior to the beautiful people for sixty minutes a week.

Forcing my eyes off Nick's, I took a sip from my mug. "It's good." I bit into my taco. "This tortilla tastes homemade," I said, my hand covering my full mouth.

"Well, I can't take credit for that. Mrs. Hernandez sells them by the dozen at the bakery in town. She says I'm her best customer."

"Because you buy the most tortillas or for some other reason?" I flipped my eyebrows, then lowered my eyes, embarrassed at the flirtatious tone of my question.

"Hmm..." Nick appeared to give it serious thought. "She's about seventy years old, so I always assumed it was the former, but I could have sworn I caught her checking out my ass a couple of times."

I swallowed and smized back at him. "My grandma always reminds me she's old, not dead," I replied.

Nick chuckled and took a big macho bite of his taco. For the next few minutes, we focused on our food as Gucci tapped around under the table impatiently.

I couldn't help myself, I scarfed down both my tacos in record time, blissful warmth spreading through me with every bite.

We were just finishing our coffee when the doorbell rang.

I glanced down at my clothes again. "Are we expecting anyone?"

"I'm not," he said. "You?"

"I guess it could be the sheriff, here to arrest me for cattle rustling or raiding chicken houses, or whatever your criminals usually do around here."

He quirked his lips at me, then wiped them with a napkin and strode toward the front door.

"Hey, Nick." At the sound of the feminine Texas twang, I was off the bench and at the kitchen door in a flash. I wasn't sure why I felt so compelled to check out every woman Nick spoke to, but I didn't over think it.

Another long-legged blonde stood at the door, this one dressed in cut-off shorts, a red tank top and cowboy—excuse me —*cowgirl* boots.

"Oh...hi, BreeAnne." I thought I could hear a sigh in Nick's voice, but I didn't know him well enough to be sure.

"I've been tryin' to call you all morning."

"Really?" His voice sounded fake-surprised. "I guess I forgot to plug my phone in last night."

"Anyway, I was wonderin' if you could come look at my breaker box," she said. "My electricity isn't working. Couldn't even dry my hair this morning—look at it!"

I looked at it. It was beautiful blonde bedroom hair that soared up in the front, then cascaded down in soft layers, much like Megan's last night. I leaned to the side until I found my reflection in a decorative hall mirror. My hair was still standing at attention in front before swooping down—

Hey! That explained why he told me I looked great this morning. He had some sort of Lyle Lovett-pageant girl hair fetish! But I couldn't help thinking the look worked better on BreeAnne than it did on me.

I kind of hated her for standing in front of Nick looking so sexy while I was hiding in his kitchen wearing men's clothing, feeling fatter by the minute.

Nick sighed aloud this time. "BreeAnne...we've talked about this. You have a husband."

Her voice pitched up an octave into an extra-twangy little girl whine. "I know, but Wayne's out of town and I can't get an electrician to come by before Wednesday."

"BreeAnne..."

I wished he'd stop saying her name. I watched her tilt her head and push out her bottom lip. "Please, Nicky? The air conditioning hasn't been on for three hours and you know in this heat, by noon, I'll be sizzlin' like a slab of bacon."

I imagined her removing items of clothing from her sweat dampened body while Nick worked on her box. I was both jealous and turned on.

Apparently, it only took one night in jail to turn a straight girl bi-curious.

"Fine," Nick said. "I'll come by when I go to town in a little while."

"Thanks, Nicky!" She threw her arms around his neck, squeezing her full breasts against his chest.

He slipped his hands under her armpits and set her away from him. "See you later," he said as he shut the door. Leaning his back against it, he closed his eyes and shook his head slowly.

I made a move to get out of the kitchen doorway, but the swish of the voluminous sweatpant fabric gave me away.

His eyes met mine. "You see why I want to leave town now?"

I gave an apologetic shrug and nodded. "So, that wasn't Shellee either."

"Nope. That was my ex-wife, BreeAnne."

"Another ex-wife?" I blurted. "How old are you?"

Several seconds ticked by and I wasn't sure he was going to answer me. "Thirty-four," he finally said.

"And you've already been married twice?" Clearly, I was still in blurting mode.

He exhaled a loud breath. "Three times."

"*Three?*" I repeated, then asked, "Like Ross on *Friends* three times or Marilyn Monroe three times?"

He snorted as if he could almost find the humor in the situation, but not quite. "Trying to figure out if I'm just a fuck up or *seriously* fucked up?"

I shrugged and winced.

"Can't say for sure," he replied. "Gabe's working on it, though."

"Gabe?" I repeated. "As in Judge Martínez?"

"Yeah, he's sort of an armchair psychologist."

I supposed Bolo was too sparsely populated for each person to specialize in only one thing.

"Look," Nick said. "I need to go to town and see what evidence they have...and check on BreeAnne's electricity, apparently. If you want to go, we can stop by the store to get whatever you need."

"Sure..." I was about to say, "Let me change and brush my hair," but realized I couldn't do that until after I went to the store. "I'd appreciate that," I said instead.

"Come on, then." Nick did that annoying head jerk thing again.

But I guess I couldn't afford to be annoyed at the person who, not only held my future in his hands, but had also become the provider for all my basic needs.

Just like little Gucci.

I sighed and followed him out the door.

CHAPTER SIX

Rika

We pulled up in front of the grocery store and parked. I was still in Nick's sweat clothes, which were far better than looking like a crazy cat lady.

When we walked in, I went straight to the toiletries aisle. Shampoo, conditioner and a hair brush were my top priorities. Nick stood a few feet away, clearly not sure if he should act interested or pretend he wasn't watching.

"Good mornin', Nicholas!" said a female voice full of familiarity.

My head jerked up, but the jealous twinge disappeared when I saw the heavy-set, probably Hispanic woman pat Nick's cheek, a motherly twinkle in her eyes. Everything about her was round—her face, her body, her wire-rimmed glasses. Warmth radiated from her in a way that reminded me of my grandmother. I had the urge to throw my arms around her and ask her to make me some lunch.

"Hey, Ms. Tilly." Nick smiled affectionately. They hugged. I felt another twinge of jealousy, but wasn't sure if it was because

Nick was hugging her instead of me or she was hugging Nick instead of me.

Either way, I needed a hug. Or more carbs.

"Ms. Tilly, this is Rika. She's new in town." He held out an arm to usher me toward her. I stepped forward and took her outstretched hand.

"I know," she said sympathetically. She hung onto me, adding her left hand to the mix so my hand was completely engulfed in both of hers. "I feel terrible. If Wade had told me what was going on that first night, I would have been at the jail bright an early with a good breakfast for you."

Huh?

She released my hand as Nick asked her about a mutual acquaintance of theirs. They chatted while I grabbed hair supplies, including a package of black ponytail bands.

I wanted to replace my confiscated makeup, but Nick was paying my way. I couldn't nickel and dime him to death after he'd taken care of my bail.

I watched him as he laughed with Ms. Tilly at an inside joke. I hadn't quite figured Nick Owen out. He didn't bother to stop and help me the night I found the body. He was pretty pissed off at the judge for saddling him with me. Then he volunteered to pay my bail and took me in as if he'd known me for years.

In reality, all he knew about me was that I was an accused murderer. Wasn't he afraid I'd kill him in his bed, steal one of his trucks—he had a spare in the garage—and take off?

People lied to attorneys all the time. Shouldn't he be the least trusting person in town? Or at least in the top three or so?

After Ms. Tilly said her goodbyes and wandered off into another aisle, I approached Nick. "So, what's the story on—?"

"Matilda Strickland. Sheriff Strickland's wife."

"Seriously?" I asked.

"Yeah, you know how they say opposites attract? She's the

volunteer secretary at church, visits shut-ins. Never had any kids of her own, even though she wanted some. A lot of the kids in town call her Aunt Tilly. Of course, people who believe Wade is dirty say she's working herself to the bone trying to make up for his sins."

"Why would she stay with him?"

"Oh, he treats her real well," Nick said. "Not sure if it's because he loves her or because she's his best asset. I think she's what keeps him in office more than anything else. No one wants Ms. Tilly to lose her income."

"Yeah," I said. "I guess an awesome wife goes a long way in politics."

Nick frowned at the cart. "The cops took all your worldly possessions and this is all you need to replace them?"

I shrugged. "I can't get the things I miss most here. My laptop. My cell phone..."

"Yeah, it's hard to live without a cell phone," Nick agreed.

"It's a lot more than a cellphone," I informed him. "It's a Ginseng 300." I *loved* that phone.

"Ginseng?"

"Yeah, because it remembers everything. It's got twice the memory of anything else on the market."

"I've never heard of it," Nick said. "I get the feeling you're some kind of computer geek." He looked at me like he expected an explanation.

"I'm not a programmer or anything," I replied. "I just know HTML and how to jailbreak phones and a few other things I've picked up from all my time on the Internet."

"Really?" He tilted his head and narrowed his eyes as if studying me more carefully. "Girls like you are usually too busy with cheerleading or dance team or dating boys to learn how to do that stuff."

Girls like me? I was flattered he thought I qualified for any of those activities.

"I wasn't one of those girls," I admitted. "I didn't go out much. Didn't have a lot of friends."

He looked puzzled and opened his lips to ask more questions. But I couldn't go there. The idea of Nick imagining me a hundred pounds heavier made my stomach turn.

"Are we picking up groceries while we're here?" I asked.

Although he was surely too smart to be so easily distracted from his line of questioning, he let the subject drop.

"How do you feel about chicken?" he asked as he led the way to the meat department.

~

Nick drove out of the grocery store parking lot, just to pull into another lot thirty seconds later.

I noticed a clump of unusually large trees to the right of the lot, a wide empty field to the left.

A small plastic sign that read "Bar" jutted out over the door of an elderly building. The exterior might have been red at one time, but it clearly hadn't been painted in at least four decades, maybe more. The only newish item on the property was an industrial-sized metal dumpster at the far left of the lot, just off the pavement.

Nick glanced my way and chuckled. "Nice, huh? All we have to do after this is hit a couple of gas stations and you'll have had the grand tour of Bolo."

"Yeah, I can't say I blame you for wanting to move," I replied. "Whoever named the town did have a good sense of humor, though."

His brows drew together. "What do you mean?"

"I thought maybe it was named after the police acronym BOLO. You know, 'Be On the Look Out'? Because if you're not, you'll miss the whole town."

Nick chuckled and shook his head. "You're giving the town's

founders a lot more credit than they deserve," he replied. "It's named after the bolo tie."

I searched my memory banks for the term and came up empty. "The what?"

"You know, the string ties cowboys wore. It's the state tie of Texas."

"Texas has a state tie?"

"Yup."

Oh jeez. "So why are we here?"

"I figured LeeAnne could get you lunch while I go to J.J.'s office and see what evidence they have so far."

What the hell? "LeeAnne?" I repeated. "The one who came by the house this morning?"

"No, that was *Bree*Anne," he said.

"Are they twins?"

"No." His eyes drifted off like he was imagining that scenario. "I'd hate to think there was a carbon copy of either one of them running around." He shook it off. "It's kind of a generational thing around here. The oldest women in town have middle names like Fay and June, like Ms. Tommy June. My mom's friends ended up with Lynn, for the most part. Tammy Lynn, Terry Lynn... And the girls around my age got Anne. I have a younger sister named DeeAnne."

"So, BreeAnne, LeeAnne, and DeeAnne all went to school together?"

He shrugged and nodded.

"Where's your sister now?"

"She's living in Seattle. Mom drives her crazy, so I think she picked the farthest place she could to discourage visits." He turned off the motor. "LeeAnne owns this place. She makes a great hamburger."

I shouldn't have been hungry after the breakfast Nick made me, but, at the mention of a burger, my stomach started grumbling, reminding me it had been three whole hours since I ate. I hoped those were only vibrations I could feel and not actual sounds Nick could hear.

Damn. I was still wearing Nick's baggy hand-me-downs. The idea of sitting in a bar, eating my lunch alone while dressed like a secondhand football fan was depressing.

Besides, I didn't want Nick to leave me. I felt like I'd been dropped onto another planet. He'd become my security blanket in this wacky town.

"Can't I just go with you?" I asked, hoping I didn't sound pathetic.

"I think it's best if you don't. I'll be trying to get a read on what's really goin' on here and you'd be a distraction."

Did he mean I'd be a distraction for him or for J.J.? I wanted to believe I could be a distraction for Nick, unless he was referring to how silly I looked in his clothes.

He exited the truck, so I got out and followed him through the dull brown door at the front of the building. When I stepped inside, a musty scent filled my nostrils.

The place was dark with wood paneling covering the walls. Beer signs hung in seemingly random places, most with segments of neon burnt out. The floor was covered in industrial carpeting in deep red, dotted with unknown substances that had turned to gray or black putty over time.

I glimpsed a worn pool table through the doorway in a back room. The whole place looked like it had been assembled in 1970, then left to its own devices.

Nick must have seen the expression on my face. "I know what you're thinking. It's old, but the kitchen is clean as a whistle, I promise."

I'd always wondered why people assumed whistles were clean. Whenever I heard the expression, I always imagined a whistle full of the spit from a beer-bellied high school football coach.

"Hey, N.B." The woman approaching us was another blonde,

this one with the most extreme hair yet. Her style reminded me of a photo I'd viewed on the Internet back in my desperate high school days when I considered going blonde to distract from my exploding waistline.

I'd typed "famous blondes" into the search engine and there was Dolly Parton, champagne blonde with puffy bangs and long tresses and what seemed like a fountain of extra hair growing out the top of her head. LeeAnne's hair was performing that same trick.

"LeeAnne," Nick said, clearly annoyed with her already. "This is Rika. She's—"

"I know who she is!" LeeAnne said in a loud country twang.

"Of course you do," he said dryly. "Forgot where I lived for a minute."

"Ha!" She gave him a taunting smile. "You *wish* you could forget us, but you never will. You can take the boy out of Bolo, but he'll always bounce back, sooner or lat—"

"Anyway," Nick interrupted. "I was hopin' you'd feed Rika and entertain her while I take care of business. Put anything she wants on my tab."

LeeAnne placed herself between me and Nick, her back to him in an intentional snub. I'd been too distracted by the hair before, but with her so close, I couldn't help but notice the makeup.

Too much of it. Crimson lips, sparkly, bright blue eye shadow that competed with her sparkly bright blue eyes, and eyelashes that were most definitely false.

The makeup probably made her look older than she was, but there was no covering up the gorgeous genes she'd been blessed with.

Jealousy scalded over me, burning the skin on my chest. My hand jerked up automatically to rub it away.

LeeAnne was another conquest of Nick's, no doubt. She was totally his type and they were totally acting like exes. Her ample breasts were visible above the neckline of her scuba-tight t-shirt. "Barr's Bar" it read.

No wonder they didn't spring for a personalized sign. It would have been redundant. Besides, if LeeAnne ran around town like this, she was as good as a neon sign, since she'd bedazzled every letter on her shirt with tiny crystals. All in all, she was the walking definition of overkill.

"It's nice to meet you, Rika." She put an arm around me, propelling me along with her. "You can sit right here at the bar and talk to me while I supervise the lunch rush."

I glanced around the room. Two booths were occupied. One, by three middle-aged men wearing work shirts with their names embroidered on the left breast pockets. Another by a young couple whose toddler was jumping up and down on the cracked red vinyl seat.

Was LeeAnne saying this was the lunch rush? Or was she still expecting a lunch rush?

I decided not to ask. My short-lived time as a waitress had taught me you don't want to piss off the people who are handling your food. Instead, I sat down on the stool she'd indicated.

She turned toward Nick. Sticking her hand in front of his face, she flapped her fingers down in a waving motion. "Bye, N.B.," she said in a mocking tone.

"Why do you call him 'N.B.'?" I asked.

"Well, there's an interesting story about that—" LeeAnne began.

Nick stuck his index finger in her face. "We had a deal. Lurch over there would be behind bars..."

Wondering what kind of parents would name their kid "Lurch," I followed his finger as it pointed at the entrance to the kitchen where a young man stood, tall and thin with a long face and unfortunate short blonde bangs. Stoney-eyed, he seemed completely unaware anyone was talking about him as he carried a tray of clean mugs into the area behind the bar.

Okay, Lurch it is.

LeeAnne smiled mischievously. "You know I'm a woman of my word. I was just gonna say it was because of your first and middle names—Nicholas *Bernard*."

I snickered. I didn't mean to. He just didn't look like a guy whose middle name was "Bernard."

Nick smacked me with a quick glare, then put his hands on his hips and narrowed his eyes at LeeAnne.

"You never said I couldn't reveal your middle name." She batted her eyelashes at him innocently.

Hmm... Okay, so, there's something more to the N.B. nickname than his actual name. Maybe something sexual and embarrassing from when he and LeeAnne were together, assuming they were.

And it was something so annoying to Nick that he'd defended her creepy-looking brother in exchange for her silence.

Now I was dying to know. But maybe it was best I didn't. N.B. could stand for some icky lover's pet name, and I didn't want to imagine him in bed with her. Or any of those other blondes, for that matter.

What a man-slut.

Although I wasn't sure you could be considered a slut if you married half the people you slept with.

Wait, did I know for sure who his first wife was? Maybe it was LeeAnne.

I drummed my fingers on the bar, not liking the idea of them being ex-spouses any better than the idea of them being ex-lovers.

Nick huffed out a loud breath. "I'll be back in a couple of hours," he said to LeeAnne. "Try not to fill her head with your usual horse shit."

CHAPTER SEVEN

Rika

LeeAnne and I glared at Nick's departing back together. Did he imagine my mind was an empty vessel just waiting for someone to come along and fill it with whatever species of excrement they chose?

On the other hand, he mainly knew the worst things about me, like the fact that I'd followed an idiot actor across the country, worked unwittingly for a mob front, and somehow managed to get myself arrested for murder.

Okay, whatever.

Once Nick was out the door, LeeAnne chuckled, a mischievous gleam in her eye.

"What was that all about?" I asked.

"Oh, that goes way back," she said. "Here's a menu." She laid a laminated page in front of me.

There were hamburgers and cheeseburgers. Other than that —I swear to God—every single thing on the menu was fried. Chicken fried steak, fried chicken sandwich, fried seafood platter, French fries, fried okra, onion rings, fried corn-on-the cob, and for dessert, fried ice cream.

64

I ordered a burger, since Nick had recommended it.

LeeAnne and "Lurch" came back a few minutes later with my order—LeeAnne had taken the liberty of adding cheese—plus every side order on the menu for me to try. My eyes darted fearfully from one batter-dipped item to the next.

I read once that a fried seafood platter contained three days' worth of dietary fat allowance.

Calories don't count while under indictment for murder, the old Rika whispered in my ear.

I grabbed the fried something closest to me and tossed it into my mouth.

A fried cheese ball? Not bad.

"Rika, this is my little brother Dwight." LeeAnne gestured to the guy previously known as "Lurch."

I swallowed my cheese ball and smiled up at him. "Hi, Dwight."

Stone-faced, he gave me an obligatory nod, turned, and tromped back to the kitchen.

But I hardly noticed because the heavenly combination of fats, dipped in carbs, fried in fat had already sent endorphins rushing to my brain.

I grabbed the hamburger and took a Godzilla-sized bite. Clearly, fried cheese balls were a gateway drug.

"I heard that ol' jackass Strickland confiscated all your stuff," LeeAnne said, "even your money."

I nodded, my cheeks puffing out as I chomped. The fact that I'd literally bitten off more than I could chew didn't stop me from enjoying the meaty, bready goodness.

"So, I was thinkin'. Why don't you come work for me?"

Was she joking? I swallowed hard and took a couple of gulps of the Coke she'd brought me.

"Why would you want me to work here?" I asked. "You just met me, and I've been charged with murder."

"Oh, that." LeeAnne swatted the air dismissively. "Just last year, Wade Strickland arrested Dwight for a string of burglaries he couldn't solve. Does Dwight look like a criminal to you?"

Right on cue, Dwight walked by carrying a plastic bin, a three-inch spider tattoo visible on the side of his neck.

Instead of answering, I stuffed my mouth with French fries and widened my eyes. But LeeAnne must have followed my gaze. "He likes spiders," she explained.

"Arachnids!" Dwight yelled angrily. A vein bulged through a separation in his bangs. I checked the bar for possible defensive weapons.

Fork or butter knife?

"Yes, arachnids," LeeAnne said casually. "I always forget."

Dwight relaxed and moved on. LeeAnne turned back to me as if nothing had happened.

"The only evidence Strickland had on him was that the burglar drove a red pickup and Dwight didn't have an alibi 'cause he's alone a lot."

My mind stuck on the phrase "red pickup." After stumbling onto the body, I'd completely forgotten about my near miss with the truck. I'd ridden twice in Nick's truck. Why hadn't that jarred my memory?

Because it was a *red* pickup truck that ran me off the road.

I toyed with a French fry and tried to keep my tone casual. "I noticed Nick drives a pickup truck, too," I said. "Do a lot of people drive them around here?"

LeeAnne twisted her lips to the right and cut her eyes left in a thinking pose. "Well, almost all the men, of course, and some of the women. A lot of the moms prefer SUVs, though. More room for the kids and their fixin's."

"Fixin's?"

"Paraphernalia."

"But I guess there aren't many red trucks?" I tried again. "Is that why the sheriff thought Dwight was the burglar?"

"Oh, no. Lots of the young guys have red pickups," she said.

"Sheriff Strickland doesn't arrest people according to how guilty they are. Dwight has always been a loner and he acts kind of..." She looked over her shoulder at her brother, who was standing at a recently vacated booth, arranging the salt and pepper shakers, sugar dispenser and ketchup bottle in a straight line along the window. "*Different* than other people."

He sure did. In some ways, he was an ideal employee, performing every task to perfection. But I'd seen robots with more engaging personalities.

Of course, the only robots I'd spent time with were the charming ones in my Star Wars movie collection, but there was still something way off about Dwight's behavior.

"So, how about that job?" LeeAnne asked enthusiastically. "It would be cash under the table 'cause I don't want to deal with all that Uncle Sam employee bullcrap."

"Are you sure you need help?" I glanced around the near empty room. In truth, I was stalling for time to consider the pros and cons.

I needed a way to earn money so I wouldn't be completely dependent on Nick. A job would give me something to do and keep the boredom from driving me loony. Best of all, I could pump LeeAnne for information and try to figure out who the legitimate murder suspects were in this town.

"We're a lot busier after work and on weekends," LeeAnne said. "Mainly 'cause we're the only option. And you'd be great for business. Everyone in the county will want to come in and check out the Grey Widow."

"The what?"

"Well..." She leaned in, her eyes dancing with excitement. "The story that's going around is that you and the dead guy were coming through on a drug run to Mexico. But you were also lovers and into that *Fifty Shades of Grey* kinky shit. I think that part's on account of the handcuffs and other stuff the sheriff found in your car. Anyway, your lover went too far with his punishments and it pissed you off, so you decided to get revenge and you killed him."

I recalled the "Keeping the Love Alive" theme party Brandtt's friends had given us to celebrate our two-year anniversary as a couple. It was really just an excuse for them to gift us with absurd sex toys and drink too much champagne.

The fur-lined handcuffs were the tamest of the gifts. What else had Brandtt packed into my boxes?

"And now I'm the Grey Widow," I murmured. Wow, Nick was right. I could totally get convicted in this town.

And the downside to working at the bar was that people would be coming in to gawk at me like a chimp at the zoo.

Dishes clattered as Dwight stacked them in the kitchen, reminding me that working here might mean I'd be hanging out with the actual killer every day.

On the other hand, I could keep an eye on Dwight and collect any evidence of his guilt while letting the potential jury pool get to know me as a friendly waitress—and you'd better believe I was going to be friendly—instead of the infamous Grey Widow, kinky killer.

"Okay, LeeAnne, I'd love to take the job."

"Great! Now all we've got to do is get you out of Nick's ugly sweats. I've got lots of clothes I can lend you."

Panic fled through me as my eyes flitted over LeeAnne again, my gaze snagging on her blingy breasts. And could those shorts be any shorter?

If they didn't have the words "Hot Stuff" on the ass, I'd swear she bought them in the children's department.

"No, I couldn't LeeAnne. You've already been so nice. That would be too—"

"Baggy sweats don't get you the big tips, hun." She grabbed her purse from behind the bar. "Dwight!" she yelled. "Hold down the fort. I'll be back in an hour."

When I didn't budge, she curled her fingers around my wrist and pulled me out the door.

~

Nick

"You have a shit case," I said as I looked across the desk at J.J. in one of his many three-piece suits. I'd never even seen him with his jacket off, but I figured that would be like Dracula without his cape. "I'm surprised you're planning to prosecute."

I was sitting in his office, by far the most elaborate room in the plain one-story county courthouse. It was elaborate because when J.J. won the district attorney race, the first thing he did was fly his decorator down from Dallas.

All the locals who had reason to visit here couldn't stop talking about the fancy wall sconces, wainscoting and mock fireplace that you'd swear was burning real logs. The desk was mahogany, with a dark leather executive chair, expensive upholstery on the guest chairs, and all of it sat on a plush area rug.

The decor probably cost more than he'd make in a year as a county D.A., but he wasn't in this for the money. He'd made plenty in all those decades at his private firm in Dallas. He was here because retirement didn't agree with him and maybe for an excuse to have a fancy office again.

Of course, his pride and joy was the huge painting he'd had made from a photograph—J.J. flanked by both of the President Bushes, senior on his left, George W on his right—that hung on the wall behind his desk.

It was always hard to keep my eyes off of because, in the painting, W's face had come out looking a lot like that kid from those old *Mad Magazine* covers. Whenever I saw it, I wondered if it was painted by a lousy artist or by a talented one who was trying to make a political statement.

"She was covered in blood," J.J. said. "You better believe I'm prosecuting."

I tilted my head down slightly and gave him a stare that said he was forgetting the obvious. "She stumbled onto the body in the dark."

J.J.'s jaded black gaze danced with amusement. "And she's Colombian."

I didn't miss the triumphant gleam in his eyes. He lived for winning cases with the evidence—or lack thereof—stacked against him.

I was also pretty sure he was a sociopath and, in my opinion, sociopaths made the best attorneys because they didn't give a crap whether the defendant was innocent or guilty. It was all about the win for J.J.

Even though I'd been avoiding criminal cases since returning to Bolo, I got roped into two in which J.J. represented the state, so I'd had conversations like this with him before.

However, those conversations hadn't caused the blood to shoot up into my head like it was doing now. I told myself the change in my reaction was due to the fact that the other cases weren't murders like this one. However, a small voice in the back of my mind whispered that I might not be telling myself the truth. Or at least not the whole truth.

A mental picture of Rika's face hovered in front of me, so clear and sharp it blocked out J.J.'s stupid painting. Her big chocolate eyes peered up at me and the thought passed through my mind that I never wanted to see them cry—Hershey's kisses or anything else.

"She's American," I said, knowing full well he knew her nationality.

A grin spread over J.J.'s face. An evil one, but all his grins looked evil to me. "Not by the time I get through with her," he said.

My gut twisted. J.J. was famous for manipulating juries and

had about thirty years of practice at it. I wished, for Rika's sake, all the confidence I'd gained by winning three murder trials in a row hadn't been sucked out of me by the last one.

Maybe I needed to try at least once to appeal to whatever sense of justice J.J. might have tucked away in his otherwise empty heart. After all, as far as I knew he hadn't *officially* been diagnosed as a sociopath.

Leaning forward, my elbows on the arms of the chair, I asked, "J.J., you know she's innocent, don't you?"

He smiled at me again and my gut twisted a little tighter. *Sociopath it is.* "I don't know any such thing," he said.

"She's the one who called in the body."

"She wouldn't be the first person to commit murder, then call the police."

I blew out a disgusted breath. "But she might be the first to kill a man twice her size, go to the trouble of loading his body into her car and dumping it on the side of the road before calling the police."

"Who says she didn't kill him on site?" J.J. said, with a casual one shoulder shrug.

Anyone who'd looked at pictures of actual murder scenes knew how much blood came out of a dead body. J.J. definitely knew. He was probably counting on getting the jurors' heads wrapped so tightly around the fiction he created, they'd forget the facts I laid out for them—like how much blood a man loses when there's a sizable hole in his chest.

I leaned back in my chair, forcing my muscles to relax, keeping my face as unaffected as possible.

"Sometimes juries do listen to facts, J.J."

His eyes narrowed, his smile instantly gone. "You might as well hightail it to Houston, son," he said. "You're not going to win." He picked up a pen and punched the top of it on his desk as if punctuating his statement. "Not this time."

Damn. Now I knew I wasn't dealing with regular sociopath J.J.

Boyles. He'd just made it clear he was still angry about Dwight's trial.

He'd thought he had that jury eating out of his hand, convinced poor, weird loner Dwight was Satan himself. And, no doubt, they were enthralled by his version of events, but in the end, they surprised both of us and went with the facts. Nothing pissed J.J. off more than a jury who listened to facts.

I kept my mouth shut. There was nothing to be gained by rubbing salt in J.J.'s wound. He was the kind of man who only got better when you added fuel to his fire.

"Anyway..." he said, "my assistant's sent you everything by now. It should be in your emails."

I stood. All I needed was the evidence. No reason to hang around his office any longer than necessary.

"Oh, and counselor?" he said.

I'd made it to his doorway, but turned back toward him as he spoke. The edges of his lips were turned up as if he was fighting off one of his evil grins.

I raised my eyebrows and waited for it. Whatever "it" was, I knew it wasn't going to be good.

"You might want to pay particular attention to the chewing gum evidence." He chuckled. "I think you'll find that your client's in a *sticky* situation."

I gave him a half smile and a wave, my heart banging in my ears until I made it to my truck and pulled out my smart phone.

CHAPTER EIGHT

Rika

I sat in LeeAnne's vintage eighties black Trans Am for all of five minutes as she drove down the gravel road running behind the bar. At the end of it was a cozy white house with a pink-graveled cactus garden in front.

"A fan of succulents?" I asked as we walked toward the pink door.

"Huh? Oh, the cactus garden?" she said. "I'm not a huge fan, but it's a lot lower maintenance than grass, and Dwight and I don't want to spend our spare time doing yard work."

"Your brother lives here with you?"

"Yep." She unlocked the door. "My parents died in a car accident when we were young. They were both drunk." She shrugged. "My grandma died a few years ago. I came back here after my divorce. My grandpa died a few months later."

"I'm sorry," I said. I wondered if she found owning a bar distasteful after the way her parents died, but didn't say anything about it.

She took in a deep breath and shrugged again. "It's just been me and Dwight since then. At least they left us a way to make a living for a while." As she turned the knob, my eyes lingered on the decorative door wreath—heart-shaped, made from pink and white flowers. I wondered if Dwight objected to living in such a girly house.

Until I crossed the threshold and stopped dead in my tracks. I swallowed hard as I waited for my eyes to adjust from the bright sunlight to the dim interior. Surely I wasn't seeing what I thought I was seeing.

But no matter how much I blinked, they were still there, all over the walls—display box after display box, each containing a firearm.

"Well, come on," LeeAnne said. I took a few more steps, but stopped in the center of the room and turned around in a circle to verify that I was completely surrounded by weapons. There had to be at least two dozen guns in the living room. I caught a glimpse of several more through the doorway into the dining area.

"This is a lot of guns," I said as she dropped her purse on the blue fabric couch.

"Yeah, my grandpa was a collector. We've got antique pistols, foreign weapons, military stuff... Oh, and this one's my favorite." She pointed to a display box centered on the wall over an arm chair. "It looks like one of those big cowboy belt buckles, but, see that little pistol in the middle?"

I nodded, unable to move my mouth, even to close it.

"It's removable. You could actually pull it out and shoot some-body with it!" she said gleefully. "I mean, it only holds one round, but if you do it right, one's all you need." She nodded sagely. "That's what my granddaddy used to say."

My eyes jumped from the belt buckle gun to the two pistols on either side of it, to the long display box positioned above the sofa that held a gleaming rifle.

"The boxes slide open," she said, apparently mistaking my shock for interest. "If you want to see one up close."

"No!" I said too forcefully. "I mean...I'm good."

I followed her through a plain but functional kitchen decorated with more guns, into a hallway with a laundry nook on one side and a bathroom on the other. At the back of the house were three small bedrooms.

"That was my granny and papaw's room," she said, pointing to a closed door on the left. "I haven't had the heart to change it since they died." She breathed out sadly, then brightened. "But it's where all the really big guns are kept, if you want to take a look."

I shook my head. "Still good."

She pointed to the open door ahead of us. "That's Dwight's room."

I glanced inside. It was neat as a pin, bed made, covered with a dark blue spread, dresser top completely devoid of knickknacks or toiletries, or even pocket change. It would be an easy room to search for evidence if I could just get in there.

I took a step forward for a better look. Hanging on the wall over his bed were five different kinds of swords.

LeeAnne ushered me into her room, which looked like it hadn't seen an update since her teen years. The walls were bright pink, nearly the same shade as her shirt. The lovely white wrought iron bed had been decorated with clear Christmas lights, wound through the headboard.

Doesn't every classic antique need a little extra bling? The sheets and comforters were covered in pink roses.

LeeAnne sat me down on them and began rifling through her closet. From what I could see, her taste in clothing was a lot like Nick's exes', with shine and sparkle galore, except Megan did have more expensive taste.

In other words, style-wise, I was out of the frying pan and into the fire.

"Let's see..." Lee Anne murmured as she pulled out a red tank top and held it up in front of me. "You're more flat-chested than I am, so—"

"I'm a B-cup," I said defensively. That might not be big, but it certainly wasn't flat-chested.

"Oh, I'm sorry," she replied. "I just mean you're more petite. Your boobs are actually in perfect proportion to your waist."

Hearing the word "perfect" in relation to my body totally made up for the flat-chested comment.

Brandtt was constantly on special diets and exercise routines to try to get his body just a little more chiseled, and he always seemed convinced I needed to drop three more pounds. How he landed on that particular number, I never knew.

"I guess the cops didn't let you keep a push-up bra?" LeeAnne asked. Her expression said push-up bra confiscation would be the worst punishment of all.

"Uh-uh." I shook my head, hoping she wasn't going to find out what I did have on under Nick's sweats.

I was a preferred reviewer for a website that sells everything geek and, as such, regularly received free items to try out and report on. As it so happened, the day Brandtt broke up with me, I was trying their new latex Batgirl bra and panty set.

The good thing about it was that the two pieces were very easy to wash in rest area bathrooms and pat dry with paper towels. Since my boxes of belongings were packed by someone else and not labeled, this easy-care lingerie was especially advantageous for a long road trip and I planned to reflect that in my review.

However, if LeeAnne got a glimpse of them, everyone in town would surely have a description of my unusual unmentionables by dinner time.

It would be interesting to hear how they worked them into the Grey Widow scenario, though.

"*Jesus Christ Superstar!*" LeeAnne yelled.

I startled and nearly fell off the bed.

"It's like this was meant to be!" She was rummaging through the top drawer of her pink dresser.

"Last time I was at the factory outlet stores in San Marcos, I found a great deal on some cute bras. But when I got home, I realized the sizes were mismarked on the tags." She whipped out two bras, one black and one crystal-studded magenta. "They're thirty-four B!"

"Great!" I said, trying to match her enthusiasm.

"Somebody up there likes you!" She flung the bras onto my lap and went to her closet.

Hmm... Somebody up there cares enough about my boobs to trick you into buying bras for me, but doesn't care enough about my ass to keep it out of jail?

But LeeAnne was so excited, I didn't have the heart to say that out loud, so I opted for "Awesome!"

"Here, try these on." She held out a red tank top with "Luscious" written in sparkly script across the chest area and a pair of distressed denim short-shorts.

I opened my mouth to argue, but realized this was the chance I'd been waiting for.

"Okay," I said. I picked up the bras, snatched the clothes from her hands, and raced into Dwight's room yelling, "I'll just be a minute!" I shut the door quickly behind me.

I struggled into the black bra—bras are always harder to put on when you're in a hurry—yanked the tank top over my head and pulled on the shorts. Slipping off my flip flops, I padded softly over to the dresser.

When I tugged the handle of the top drawer, it was heavier than I expected. Real wood. Thick oak like my grandmother's. I pulled harder and it slid out, revealing the neatest sock drawer I'd ever seen.

Each pair was kept together by a clip, folded once, and arranged to overlap the previous pair at exactly the halfway point.

I reached in and ran my hand around the inside of the drawer, looking for a secret compartment.

"Rika?"

I jumped at the sound of LeeAnne's voice just outside the door. "Yes?"

"Don't mess around with anything in Dwight's room. He's real particular about his stuff."

Could she see me? "Okay," I called as my eyes scanned the room for cameras.

Silly. It was perfectly normal of her to warn me, considering her brother was such an extreme neat freak.

After searching the dresser, which contained only clothes, I turned to the tall chest of drawers at the foot of Dwight's bed. I opened the top drawer and found a brown padded envelope with "Tori's Tattoos" printed on the outside. Why would anyone get mail from a tattoo parlor?

When I reached inside, I pulled out a handful of spiders—temporary tattoo spiders exactly like the one on Dwight's neck.

So, instead of a real tattoo, he applies the same temporary tattoo over and over again? Weird.

"Rika?" *Crap.* I'd almost forgotten about LeeAnne.

"Yes?" I began opening and closing the rest of the drawers as quietly as possible.

"Are you okay?"

"Yeah, I had trouble with the bra clasp, that's all." That was sort of true.

"Need help?"

"No! It's okay. I've got it."

Holy shit! Every drawer I opened was full of Spider-Man collectibles.

Serial killers liked to collect things. But they typically preferred items that belonged to their victims—necklaces, rings, body parts...

Besides, there was no reason to think this murder was connected to others, not that I'd have a way to know if it was.

I knelt down and peeked under the bed. Clean. Not so much as a dust bunny.

I opened the closet, noting the Spider-Man costume hanging next to a bunch of button-down shirts. The closet floor was covered with carefully positioned shoes, each perfectly even with its partner.

Damn. If I had my phone, I could take pictures of the treads in case they matched shoe prints at the scene.

A memory flashed through my mind of the sheriff and deputy tramping all over the crime scene without taking so much as one photo before mucking up the dirt between the body and the road.

There wouldn't be any shoe prints to match against.

Standing on my tiptoes, I ran my hand along the closet shelf, expecting to encounter a layer of dust at the very least. It was completely empty and my fingertips came back clean.

When I opened the door, LeeAnne was standing on the other side of it, hand poised as if to knock. "I've never seen anyone take so long to change," she said.

I thought fast. "It's because of the other night." I turned my hands over so she could see my skinned palms. "When I landed on the ground, I think I sprained my index finger."

"Well, that's a shame," she said sympathetically. "But the important thing is, you look hot!"

She ushered me back into her room and pointed to the full-length mirror hanging on her closet door. "See what I mean?"

My eyes started a scan, but got wedged in my massive cleavage.

Holy cow! I'd been too distracted to examine the bra when I put it on, but it was clearly employing every method of boob technology available to womankind—underwire, padding, push-up, levitation...

Plus, now my breasts sparkled like a couple of disco balls.

I forced my eyes downward. My waist looked surprisingly small compared to my chest. My legs were longer than they'd ever been, but I guess that was because I'd never in my life worn shorts this short.

"What do you think?" LeeAnne prodded.

"I look..." my mind searched for the right word for this new shockingly sexual version of myself. My gaze was drawn to the word scrawled across my chest. "Luscious," I read.

"Damn right, you do!" LeeAnne cried, mistaking my literacy as self-validation. She turned and squatted in her closet. "What size shoe do you wear?"

"Seven and a half or eight."

"I knew it! We're sole sisters! Get it?" She placed a pair of red high-heeled pumps next to my feet. "Try 'em on."

Once I put the shoes on, the look was complete.

Completely slutty, that is. I looked like a prostitute. Not the real ones with track marks and greasy hair. The Hollywood version with shiny hair and a heart of gold. Still, I couldn't possibly go around like this.

"LeeAnne, these aren't..."

"The right size?"

"Uh...no..."

"The right shade of red? 'Cause I don't think they clash with the top even if they're not exactly the same."

"No, it's not the color."

She pushed her eyebrows together and peered up at me, completely baffled as to why I wouldn't want to wear spike-heeled dress pumps with denim booty shorts.

"They're...just not me," I said. "Maybe some sandals?"

"Sandals will cut your tips in half." I looked at her doubtfully. "It's bar science," she explained.

The longer I stared at myself, the more I could feel my IQ dropping. Still, I considered asking for a link to the scientific study correlating footwear and tips.

LeeAnne rummaged around a bit—she wasn't quite the housekeeper her brother was—and pulled a box from the back of her closet.

"We'll compromise." She whipped the lid off the box with a "ta-da!" flair. Inside, was a pair of three-inch wedge sandals in natural leather.

Once I put them on, I turned to the side to check out my profile. My ass was more prominent than usual, sitting high and proud, giving the boobs a run for their money.

I looked like one of those silhouettes off an eighteen-wheeler's mud flap, and I kind of liked it. If LeeAnne hadn't been with me, I might have pressed my fingers to my lips, and sung "poo-poo-pee-doo," as I popped my foot up behind me.

LeeAnne smacked me on the ass. "This is your money maker, right here."

"I thought that's what the push-up bra was for."

"You gotta get 'em comin' and goin'," she replied.

"More bar science?"

"You betcha." She held up a large Victoria's Secret shopping bag. "I put a wardrobe together for you while you were changing —stuff I think will fit you pretty well."

"Thanks." I was afraid to glance into the bag.

"If you'll just wait a minute, I'll drive us back," she said. "I've just got to change out of this thong. You know when you go to a dentist with one of those sadistic dental assistants who really gets up in there with the floss?"

"Uh-huh."

"That's what this thong feels like. I hope I shrunk my undies 'cause otherwise I grew my ass." She began working the button of her shorts.

"Okay, I'll just be out here." I hurried out of the room, closing the door behind me. Although LeeAnne seemed completely comfortable with me, I didn't feel we knew each other well enough for me to see her thong or what was underneath it.

I ambled through the kitchen, kicking the bag with my shins as I walked. Dwight must have been busy in here, too. It was outdated, but as neat as his bedroom.

The small appliances—blender, microwave, toaster oven, toaster, and sandwich maker—were lined up on the laminate countertop according to height. The white refrigerator was clean except for four spider magnets, exactly alike, centered in a straight row on the door.

When I reached the entrance to the living room, I kept my eyes down, still not on board with the idea of deadly weapons as home decor.

But if the zombie apocalypse hit while I was in town, all qualms are off. I'd be here in a flash.

Besides, I was pretty sure during a zombie apocalypse hypocrisy was no longer a thing.

A wastepaper basket sat on the floor at this end of the couch. It caught my eye because of the long flower stems sticking out the top.

Curious, I pulled up what turned out to be a bouquet of red roses, not nearly wilted enough to be thrown away. A lacy white ribbon was tied around the stems with a card attached. I flipped it over to the front.

You should never read someone else's personal card, I thought as I read the card. Honestly, if it had been inside an envelope, I wouldn't have taken it out, but it was just hanging there in the open, asking to be read.

I can't stop loving you, A.

Wow, what did this romantic guy do to piss LeeAnne off so much? But, as nice as she was, she was also pretty excitable.

I heard her door open and stuffed the bouquet back into the trash.

CHAPTER NINE

Nick

I was annoyed when I got back to Barr's and Rika was gone. Maybe more annoyed than I should have been, but I had reason to worry. She'd only been in town a couple of days and had managed to trip over a dead body and get herself arrested.

Then, when I realized who she'd left with, I was angry at LeeAnne. I couldn't put any logic behind the emotion, though. It wasn't like I owned Rika, just because I bailed her out of jail.

I guess I'd kind of liked the idea of being her only friend in town. But if that's what I wanted, dropping her off with LeeAnne was an idiot move. LeeAnne Barr was everybody's friend.

When I asked Dwight, he informed me that his sister said they'd be back in an hour. He checked his watch and told me they'd been gone "one hour and six minutes."

Dwight was clearly peeved about this time discrepancy. He was a very literal person and if you told him an hour, he expected you to be back in exactly sixty minutes.

At least there was no chance LeeAnne had taken Rika clothes shopping in an hour. I enjoyed an attractive woman in sexy clothes as much as the next guy, but LeeAnne's taste had always run a little on the trashy side for me.

I ordered an iced tea from Dwight, sat down at the bar and opened the email on my phone. After my meeting with J.J., his assistant sent me the photos of the evidence they'd collected so far.

A part of my brain had sprung to life the moment I'd walked into his office, excited to have something challenging to work on. Since I'd moved back to Bolo, I'd worked mostly on wills and contracts.

However, as eager as my brain was for a workout, the rest of my body had felt kind of sick ever since Gabe assigned me this case.

I barely knew this woman. She could be guilty. But when I looked into those big brown eyes, I believed every word she said.

Hell, even if she was guilty, I wanted to get her off...of the murder rap. Yeah, I wanted to keep her out of jail. That's all. Nothing more personal than that.

Wade hadn't come up with a definitive motive, or murder weapon, and had no explanation as to how a woman Rika's size could have moved the body on her own. Even if J.J. claimed she'd killed the victim where they found him, I'd realized I could probably dispute that with a doctor-witness and a bucket of red paint to illustrate how much blood should have been at the scene if the victim bled out there.

Regardless, I'd seen J.J. at work. He was a damn good attorney. So good, he could have been a con man. He could twist jurors' heads around until they were looking at everything back-asswards.

A sick feeling edged through my internal organs again.

Yes, I was a really good attorney, too. Juries in Austin seemed to respond well to my arguments. But J.J. had thirty years of experience on me, and the jury pool in this county sucked. I grew up here and still didn't understand how these goobers thought. It didn't help that, like anywhere else, the smartest people usually found a way to get out of jury duty.

The door creaked as it had ever since I could remember. I turned and watched LeeAnne strut in followed by...

I was aware of my jaw dropping, but couldn't seem to catch it in time. Rika had dumped my sweat clothes and replaced them with, well, not much.

Her *wares*—as mom would have called them—were on display. Hardware, like those legs. Slim and bronze with nicely developed calf muscles and tight thighs, as if she worked out regularly. Then there was the software, like those semi-exposed breasts that I couldn't peel my eyes off of.

Luscious.

Yes, they were.

I needed to do something fast or I was going to start having sexual fantasies about my client.

Look for something wrong with her.

Actually, she was a little on the thin side. If she put on five or ten pounds, she'd be irresistible.

She bent and set her shopping bag on a chair, giving me a clear view of her ass. I had the urge to take it with both hands and squeeze.

Damn, maybe she's irresistible now.

A warning ache in my groin prompted me to take a swallow of tea to cool myself down.

As Rika straightened and turned back toward me, LeeAnne flashed a triumphant smile. "Well?"

Old annoyances flared up. I couldn't let her feel so satisfied with herself. "It's worse than I imagined," I said. "You didn't take her shopping. You lent her your clothes."

Rika's eyes dropped to the floor. Guilt washed through me as I realized my knee-jerk reaction to LeeAnne had hurt Rika's feelings.

"You said not to mess with her head," LeeAnne replied. "You

didn't say anything about her body. Besides, she looks a lot better in my clothes than yours."

"Define better."

"Hotter."

"Well..." Attorney or not, I couldn't argue that fact. "Yeah."

Rika's gaze jerked up to meet mine. The corners of her mouth tried to curve up, but she fought them down. I could see the pleasure in her eyes, though, and it made me happy that I'd made her happy.

Wuh-oh. It's not your job to make her happy, shithead. It's your job to keep her from spending her life in prison.

"Did you get a look at the evidence?" Rika asked.

Damn. Why'd we have to meet this way, as attorney and client? Why couldn't...

My thoughts trailed off to nowhere. I couldn't imagine a scenario in which we would have met and hung out long enough for it to go anywhere.

There was also the undeniable fact that I didn't need to be hanging out with any woman. One of the reasons Houston sounded like a good idea was because it was the fourth largest city in the country.

Plenty of available hook-ups without taking the risk of running into them at the grocery store every day. A man could enjoy the sex and avoid the misery of being in a relationship.

What had she asked me?

Oh, yeah. Evidence.

I glanced at LeeAnne. I couldn't see her ears under all that hair, but I was pretty sure they were perked up like a Doberman's.

"Let's talk about it when we get to the house," I said.

"Why?" LeeAnne asked. "I won't tell everybody."

I lifted my eyebrows and gave her a "bullshit" look.

"Well..." she threw her hands up and shrugged. "I didn't say I wouldn't tell *any*body."

"Yeah, that's what I thought."

"Did you already do your other errand?" Rika asked.

"Huh?"

"Did you manage to *flip* DeeAnne's *switch*?" The double meaning was impossible to miss. Was she jealous? I couldn't help smiling at the thought.

"Not the way you mean, I hope, since DeeAnne's my sister."

Rika's skin deepened in color. Was she blushing?

Cute.

"*Bree*Anne..." she said with annoyance. "Whatever."

LeeAnne was watching us with way too much interest.

I stood. "Are you ready to go?" I asked Rika.

"Sure. Thanks for everything, LeeAnne." The two women hugged like they'd known each other for years. *Great.* "Oh, when do you want me to start?"

"Start what?" I asked.

"How about tomorrow night?" LeeAnne replied, ignoring my question.

"Okay," Rika said as she headed for the door.

"Start what?" I asked again as I followed her out. I didn't like the smug expression I'd seen on LeeAnne's face. Clearly, she felt she'd gotten the better of me somehow.

Rika gave me a "wouldn't you like to know?" smile and climbed into the truck.

Rika

Nick didn't look too happy when I told him I'd be working at Barr's. He didn't say much on the way home, but I got the feeling he might be thinking about more than my new employment status.

When we walked into his house through the door from the garage, Gucci tapped around at our feet, barking at us like we were intruders until Nick scooped her up. He said something about taking her outside and checking the oil in his trucks and disappeared out the door we'd come in through.

I wasn't sure if he was avoiding me because he was angry about the job or procrastinating about sharing evidence. Then I realized I'd only known him a couple of days. My grandmother always said, "Men are the simplest of all of God's creatures," so maybe he did just want to check his oil.

I took the bag LeeAnne had given me, walked into my bedroom and set it on the bed. Sucking in a deep breath, I looked inside.

Bling-bling-bling. A blinding array of shimmer flickered at me from the cotton t-shirts and denim bottoms.

My anxiety level spiked at the thought of wearing these clothes while waiting on customers at the bar. I'd never have picked out anything so flashy or sexy.

These clothes said, "Look at me!" I still wasn't comfortable with being ogled, not because I was a feminist—which I was, at least in theory—but because I was afraid of the leftover imperfections they'd find if they looked too hard.

When I started my "life change," as my Jilly Crane counselor called it, I'd thought the day would come where I'd see myself in the mirror and think, "That's it! I'm the perfect size now!"

Instead, every time I lost a jean's size, I'd only been able to enjoy the improvement for a few days. After that, all I could see in the mirror were the areas of imperfection that remained.

When I'd passed my—once unimaginable—goal weight and kept losing, my counselor told me that, while I looked great, under no circumstances should I continue getting thinner, and I obeyed.

But it was so confusing living in L.A., a city full of size zeros and twos. Then there was Brandtt and the "three more pounds" he was always bringing up.

I closed my eyes and fished around in the bag, grabbing an outfit at random. The top was a white mid-drift short-sleeve with the word "Saucy" in red sequins italics, a tilted bottle of Tabasco Sauce acting as an exclamation point.

I held it up in front of me. Depending on how low the bottoms sat on my hips, the t-shirt would bare between two and four inches of stomach.

I'd never even shown my stomach at the beach.

God, where did LeeAnne get these clothes? I really hoped this shirt was a promotional give-away because I hated to think she paid money for it. But she'd been so nice to lend me a job and a wardrobe.

Besides, Nick said I looked hot in her clothes. Well, he hadn't said it so much as agreed to it begrudgingly, but I was counting it, regardless.

I examined the tiny shorts. How was I going to walk out of the house in them? I wouldn't feel like myself at all.

Wait, maybe that was the key.

I recalled the conventions I attended as a teenager—Comic-Con, WonderCon, FanimeCon—costumed from head to toe. I'd meet up with other people I'd found online, free to interact with them because I didn't have to be myself.

Surely, I could just pretend LeeAnne's clothes were costumes and Barr's was just another convention.

HoochieCon here I come.

I sighed. If that didn't work, I could always revert to my childhood escape mechanism. My stomach turned as I recalled every miserable morning of middle school, when I had to trudge the gauntlet—the narrow aisle of my school bus.

Stares. Giggles. Not so inconspicuous whispers.

The humiliation was unbearable, so I'd started imagining I was surrounded by a force field. Not the invisible kind, but one in the shape and color of a burka, revealing only my eyes, so no one would know the identity of the poor misshapen girl waddling down the aisle.

While most of the other girls my age seemed to be shaped

like wooden fence planks or, in some cases, planks with nice round racks up top, I was shaped like an egg.

Not a goose egg or an ostrich egg. A *ginormous* Godzilla egg.

Unfortunately, the force field failed me at the worst possible moments. Like when someone on the bus decided to launch an open carton of chocolate milk at my head.

As I stood in the middle of the aisle, liquid streaming down the strands of my hair, the kind bus driver asked if I wanted to go back in my house and rinse it out. He even said he'd wait, which I knew was a big deal because parents often called the school district on tardy drivers.

I told him no, it was okay. I'd take care of it at school.

The truth was, I didn't want my grandmother to find out. She'd be heartbroken and angry, then she'd take some kind of action that would make everything worse.

Near the end of middle school, someone must have clued her in on what was happening, though. She suddenly decided I needed to be driven to school, saving me from ever setting foot on the high school bus.

She must have discussed the problem with one of my aunts who managed to rein her in, for once. That's what I assumed, at least, because she never gave a reason and I never asked questions. I was just grateful to be off the bus.

Setting LeeAnne's bag on the floor of my closet, I wandered out of my room, still in a gloomy memory-induced daze. At the turn in the hallway, the door popped open suddenly.

I screamed and jumped back. Nick let out a startled sound and retreated a couple of feet into the garage. Gucci skittered away from his heels, then scolded me with her high-pitched barks like a bitchy little bodyguard.

Nick and I relaxed as we laughed at ourselves. "You scared me!" I said.

"Back atcha. With a scream like that, you could star in horror movies."

He came in, Gucci racing in after him before he shut the door. "Both trucks are in good working order," he said as I followed him toward the kitchen. "Since you have a job now, you can use the One-fifty to get to work and back."

"Which one is that?" I asked.

"The black one."

"That's the one you like to drive," I said as we reached the kitchen. Plus, it had a fancy "King Ranch" emblem on the tailgate that I was pretty sure made it some sort of special edition. "I'll drive the white one."

"No," he said firmly. "That's an old Ranger I use for hauling dirt and picking up whatever my mom buys...or wants to get rid of."

After all he'd done, I was *not* taking his best truck. "I don't mind driving the older one. You've done enough for me, Nick. I don't want to take your favorite truck, too."

"You're using the black one." His hands were on his hips, his voice hard and bossy. Maybe I'd just figured out why he'd been divorced three times. "It's this year's model," he continued. "It's got all the safety features—front and side air bags, anti-lock brakes, stability control..."

Oh, my God.

Now I knew why three women had wanted to marry him. He was trying to hand all his safety over to me, just like that. That was *so* sweet!

But dwelling on the squeezing sensation in my chest felt the opposite of safe, so I changed the subject.

"Did you find out anything from the D.A.?" I asked.

"Yeah." He opened the refrigerator, pulled two bottles of beer from the door, and nodded toward the kitchen table while Gucci sniffled around on the tiles like a tiny vacuum cleaner. I guess if you weigh less than five pounds, every microscopic crumb makes a difference.

I sat on the bench side of the table, appreciating the solidness of the wall behind me. I'd never looked at evidence against myself before.

Nick picked up his laptop from the other end of the table and slid in next to me on the bench.

Did he notice I didn't scoot over and put space between us when his thigh touched mine? That would be the natural reaction, but my body just wouldn't budge. I wasn't sure if it had to do with my attraction to him, or the comforting feel of his thigh—nearly as solid as the wall—pressed tightly against mine.

The pleasant scent of Nick's light aftershave and manly soap combined into a soothing aura around me. My endorphins kicked in and I experienced a moment of certainty that everything would be all right.

He opened the laptop and clicked through to his email while I checked out his gear.

Pitiful.

His computer had to be five years old. If I remembered correctly, this model had about one-quarter the memory of mine and a really slow processor. Since he could afford something better, the only explanation was that Nick was a technological caveman. I tried to imagine him with a scraggly beard and long grungy hair.

Still hot.

A picture popped up on the screen. I gasped and clutched the spot where my pearls would have hung if I'd ever worn pearls.

And stopped breathing.

CHAPTER TEN

Rika

The dead man stared at me with empty pale blue eyes. Until a second ago, the memory had been dark and surreal.

With the exception of a few moments here and there, my mind had managed to treat this situation as if it were happening to someone else, and I was just an onlooker. I hadn't dealt with the emotions that should probably come with finding a man dead, then being accused of his murder.

I'd always been really good at stuffing my emotions deep inside, preferably underneath a pizza and a dozen cupcakes.

I knew emotion-stuffing was supposed to be bad for you, but did it really help to go around expressing your feelings?

It might have saved you from a hundred extra pounds and a decade of humiliation, said the Jilly Crane counselor in my head.

Okay, there's that.

"Did you ever see him before?" Nick asked as he stared at the picture.

"No," I whispered. This body had been a person. A live human. And, right now, his wife and kids could be searching frantically for him, hoping to find him alive.

My throat tightened, but I didn't want Nick to know how this was affecting me.

I needed him to share every helpful detail about this case and this town, since I might be the only person who could get myself out of this mess. I couldn't have Nick worried about upsetting me with details.

"They couldn't identify him?" My voice sounded surprisingly steady.

"Not yet. He didn't have ID on him. They're going to have to run fingerprints. Maybe dental records."

I stared at the victim's blood-soaked shirt—a long-sleeved button-down dress shirt. My eyes scanned along the sleeve to where the blood stopped at the elbow. Dove gray. Black leather belt. Black slacks.

"He's kind of dressed up for around here," Nick said.

"Yeah, like he was going somewhere other than the side of the road," I replied. "Cause of death?"

"Stabbing. Or maybe 'impaling' would be a better word. The medical examiner is having trouble being more specific about the murder weapon. He says it's likely elongated, pointed on the end, but over two inches thick, and four-sided. Also looks like the murderer twisted it around in there after he shoved it into the victim's torso, right below his sternum."

The cheese balls turned over in my stomach. I swallowed to assure myself they weren't coming back up. "To torture him? Or to make it harder to ID the weapon?"

"Your guess is as good as mine."

I ran the description of the murder weapon through my mind again. "Are you having a vampire problem around here?" I asked. It would be a shame if the victim were one of those nice, sparkly Twilight vampires hunted down by misguided townspeople.

Nick's brows jerked together. "*What?*"

"The weapon you described sounds a lot like a stake."

"Oh." Nick clicked to a copy of the coroner's report. "You're right it does. But the closest thing to vampires I've heard of around here is a group of Satan worshippers."

"Seriously?"

Nick shook his head. "It's a small town and there's not much to do other than get each other riled up and pass around interesting gossip. I'm sure it's just another crazy rumor."

I decided to google Satanic rituals as soon as I could get to a computer just in case there were any involving stakes.

On the other hand, Dwight had plenty of stabbing weapons at his disposal. If he'd twisted a sword back and forth while it was in the victim's chest, could the shape of the injury be misleading?

"What else have they got?" I asked, trying to stay as logical and removed as I could make myself. I didn't want to keep imagining that poor man with a stake—or a blade—twisting in his chest...or would below the sternum count as his belly?

It didn't matter. One was no less horrible than the other.

Nick clicked his mouse and my bloody clothes popped up on the screen.

My favorite top, an anime-inspired Lolita blouse I'd bought on eBay for thirty bucks. When Brandtt looked at it suspiciously, I told him it was Stella McCartney and he loved it.

I glanced at Nick. He was staring thoughtfully at the screen.

"If I'd staked a man through the chest, there might be blood on my shirt, but it wouldn't be soaked top to bottom," I said.

Nick gave me the same warm-surprised look he'd given me when I mentioned doppelgangers and the space-time continuum. I wasn't sure whether to be pleased that I'd impressed him or insulted that he assumed I wasn't a very smart person.

"True." His smile faded. "But other things will be harder to explain away."

A click of his mouse revealed a screen full of cash, fanned out so the denominations were visible. A pale pink Michael Kors handbag sat next to it.

Personally, I thought the pink was kind of washed-out looking, but Brandtt had been so excited when he gave it to me I felt obliged to carry it.

"Is that your purse?" Nick asked.

"Yeah," I sighed. "Totally not my taste, though." Truth be told, my preferences ran more along the lines of a backpack.

Nick looked at me like I was nuts. I guess it was pretty crazy to bring up handbag preferences in the face of a murder rap. But I felt better if I downplayed the situation. I needed to keep a cool head.

"And you were carrying three thousand dollars in it?" he asked.

"I don't know."

"You don't know?"

"Like I told you, my boss gave me a wad of cash as severance, and I got the idea I should leave while I still could. I figured I'd count it when I got back to my apartment, except when I got back, I didn't have an apartment, or a boyfriend, and I forgot all about the cash."

Nick's expression darkened. His gaze grew more intense. He seemed to be trying to use his Superman vision to see through my skull and into my brain.

He thought I was lying!

Righteous anger blazed through my veins. I stared back at him defiantly. "So, now my own lawyer doesn't believe me?"

"It doesn't matter what I believe. It's what I can convince a jury of that counts, and your story puts you in the middle of a crime ring right off the bat."

Asshole. Everyone knows "it doesn't matter what I believe" means "I don't believe you." Couldn't he at least pretend to believe me? I was his client after all.

His pro bono, freeloading client. But still...

Click. Next photo: A package of Uncle Amos Organic Sugar-free Gum. One stick was unwrapped, revealing its distinctive green color.

"They found this gum in your car."

"Yeah, it's my favorite brand," I said. "They sweeten it with stevia root instead of sugar."

"It's only sold on the West Coast of the United States," Nick said. "Nowhere else."

Why was he so interested in my gum? "I know it's only sold on the West Coast," I replied. "I had to ask my grandmother to send me a case when I found out they didn't sell it in New York."

Click. New picture: An already chewed piece of green gum. "This was found in the victim's mouth," Nick said. I was vaguely aware of him turning and watching my expression.

"He was from California?" I asked. What were the chances of that?

"Not sure it matters. We're screwed on this evidence either way." Nick lifted the beer bottle to his mouth and drained it like he was trying to soften the blow for himself.

Then the ramifications hit me. "If the victim's from the West Coast, the D.A. will say I knew him because I'm from L.A. If he's not, the D.A. will claim we must have been together because he was chewing my brand of gum."

"You really should have made him give the gum back before you killed him."

My gaze jerked up to Nick's, half-expecting him to be wearing a teasing smile. Instead, he was watching me intently again, gauging my reaction.

I clicked back to the photo of the victim. I stared directly into Nick's eyes, speaking slowly and deliberately. "I didn't know this man. I didn't share my gum with him. I didn't kill him."

After several long seconds, Nick dropped his gaze, focusing again on the dead man. "Okay," he said, nodding thoughtfully. "Okay."

I got the feeling he'd just decided to believe me, regardless of how bad the gum evidence looked.

"Hey wait!" I cried, causing the muscle in his thigh to flex

against mine. "I was chewing gum when I walked out there to..."
My mind flipped through a number of options before settling on
"relieve myself." I closed my eyes to bring my memory into clear
focus. "It flew out of my mouth when I fell on him."

"Are you saying the gum you were chewing flew out of your
mouth, straight into the victim's?"

"Well..." That did seem highly unlikely.

Nick massaged the bridge of his nose between his thumb and
forefinger. "Every time you open your mouth, you make my job a
little bit harder."

Ignoring his drama, I flipped back through the photos until I
reached the wad of gum. Since Nick's computer didn't even have
touch screen—*jeez*—I used the magnifying glass icon to enlarge
the gum.

"Look at this," I said. "There's some sort of foreign matter in
the gum." I clicked until the photo was as big as it would go.

"This has veins like part of a leaf." I manipulated the picture
until we were viewing the other suspicious matter up close. "And
this looks like a tiny piece of twig."

"Hm..." Nick said as he studied the photo carefully.

"You didn't think to look closer at random objects in chewing
gum?" I asked.

"I'm from Texas," Nick said with a teasing smile. "I know Juicy
Fruit and chewing tobacco, but I don't know what you granola
munchers like in your gum."

I chuckled, then turned my attention back to the laptop. "Not
sure what this means, though."

As Nick continued to stare at the screen, his smile faded. "I
do," he said solemnly. "It means Wade Strickland is one sorry
son-of-a-bitch."

Nick

Fuck.

As I stared at the close-up of the gum wad that was the only word my mind could form. *Fuck, fuck, fuck, fuck, fuck!*

"You think he—" Rika began.

"Yeah," I said. "I think that slimy old bastard looked at the pack of gum in your car, realized the gum near the body was the same stuff, picked it up off the ground and put it in the victim's mouth."

My blood turned ice cold as the words passed through my lips. My hands fisted at the very real possibility that Wade was faking evidence to try to pin this murder on Rika. Sure, I was suspicious of the arrest from the beginning, but this took it to a whole new level.

I'd always preferred to settle things with words, rather than violence, whenever possible. But not this time. This time I wanted to smash my fist into Wade Strickland's lying, cheating face.

Make that both fists.

If the man in charge of investigating this crime was falsifying evidence, what chance did Rika have?

Me. I was her chance.

Damn it.

Her soft hand curved over my knuckles, cupping my fist. Reflexively, my thumb moved up to caress the side of hers.

"Nick?" At the sound of my name, I met her gaze. "Whatever you're thinking, could you do it out loud?"

Her eyes were wide and questioning and beautiful in a way that surprised me every time I looked into them.

I sucked in a deep breath, then blew it out hard. "I'm thinking the sheriff committed murder and is trying to pin it on you." The image of Rika in an orange jumpsuit, hands and feet shackled as she was herded onto a prison bus, made my heart stop.

By being too chicken shit to get involved, I may have sealed her fate.

Why didn't I stop and check out the crime scene the night of the murder? I'd picked the worst possible time to overcome my savior complex.

"He's definitely an asshole," Rika said. "But just because he's fudging evidence doesn't mean he's the murderer."

At least someone was keeping a cool head. She was right about the "fudging," as she called it. There were all kinds of reasons Wade might want to railroad Rika—bribery, keeping arrest rates up, re-election...and maybe reasons I couldn't even imagine.

"How would you know?" I asked her, mostly because I wanted to know more about her.

She shrugged. "I read a lot of news articles online and google things I'm interested in like murders, kidnappings, police misconduct, etcetera."

She was full of surprises. Hard to believe a smart girl like her had gotten into such a stupid situation.

Girl.

I was torn about whether I wanted to think of her that way or not. Officially, she was a woman, but she was young, in her twenties. I was in my thirties, and kind of used up, with no business having any sexual or romantic thoughts about her.

So, thinking of her as a kid was a good thing.

Except I'd thought of Johnny Chavez as a kid. I'd gotten way too emotionally involved and maybe it clouded my judgement.

Maybe I should have advised him to take the plea deal. How many times a day did I think about the deal the DA offered when she thought she was losing the case?

But thinking of Rika as a woman might be worse.

She'd already gotten under my skin in a completely different way than I'd experienced before. A way that affected my body and my brain at the same time and I kind of liked it.

Shit.

Regardless, I needed to be straight with her. Not make promises I couldn't keep. Not this time.

"People here know Wade," I said. "And they know he's not perfect, but you're a stranger and when he gets on the stand and testifies..."

Her gaze left mine and her expression grew worried, but after a couple of seconds, she straightened and looked me right in the eye. "It's not going to come to a jury verdict," she said. "You won't have to prove me innocent because we'll know who the murderer is before that."

Was she delusional? I watched her, while working hard to maintain my poker face. I wanted to believe we weren't totally screwed, but I had to be realistic.

"And how do you think that's going to happen when the sheriff refuses to look at other suspects?" I asked.

"I'm going to investigate the murder myself."

I studied her expression for signs she was joking, but she'd said something like this before.

What the hell. I'll bite. "What makes you think you're qualified?"

"Well..." she fidgeted with her beer bottle, turning it round and round on the table. "I watch a lot of crime investigation TV."

I tried not to roll my eyes.

"And like I told you, I've read a lot of books and articles," she continued.

I'd learned after law school that reading about something was a lot different than actually doing it.

"And before I moved to New York, I worked for a private investigation firm in L.A."

That got my interest. I stared at her hard, trying to ignore the effect her big brown eyes always had on me.

Who was this person Gabe had gotten me mixed up with? E.coli tester-slash-private investigator? I didn't think she was guilty, but that didn't mean she wasn't nuts.

Hm. She'd quit making eye contact, which probably meant she was either lying or...

"In what capacity?" I asked.

"Huh?"

She'd heard me. Her ear was only a few inches from my mouth. "You worked for the P.I. in what capacity?"

Her gaze met mine and I could tell she was annoyed I'd asked. "Receptionist, *officially*..."

This time, I couldn't keep the eye rolling inside.

"But I'd started doing some skip tracing."

"Online?" I asked. "While you answered calls at the receptionist desk?"

"Yeah. And I made phone calls—"

"Then you turned the information over to someone else who went out in the field."

"Yes, but I was trying to become a private investigator," she said. "That's why I was doing all that research. It's just that my boss was a sexist old fart."

I couldn't help but laugh at that. She laughed, too, and her smile made me want to touch her cheek with my fingertips and guide her in for a kiss.

Damn. Back to business.

"You realize your computer skills aren't going to help you much in this situation?"

"Maybe not."

"And looking into this could be dangerous, considering how badly Wade wants to blame you for the murder," I said.

"I hear prison is pretty dangerous, too."

"Yeah." I couldn't argue with her there. I broke eye contact long enough to push away a mental picture of Rika behind bars.

When I looked at her face again, she was staring at me with a concerned expression I'd noticed on her before. What right did she have to be worried about me, given her current situation?

She closed my laptop, scooted out the other end of the bench and stood. I watched her walk to the fridge, open it, and pull out another beer.

"Anyway..." She opened the bottle and set it in front of me. "I have new evidence. Well, not new, since I guess it's been in my head all along."

I took a gulp of beer, hoping she really did have good news. I could use some.

"There was a reason I stopped where I did that night." She paced in front of the table. "As you know, all the businesses were closed in town and I really needed to go to the bathroom. I was just starting to consider the side of the road when I came around the curve." She turned back and paused in front of me. I sat forward, waiting, hoping...

But maybe she just had a flair for the dramatic.

"I saw a vehicle on the shoulder—my side of the road, facing me—for a split second before it jumped out in front of me, crossed over to the other lane and tore off in the direction I'd just come from. I had to veer off onto the gravel to keep from hitting it."

"So, you're saying you didn't pick that spot randomly. You were stopped there because of this vehicle?" Damn, I hoped she wasn't making this up.

"Yes."

"And do you have a description?"

"Kind of. I was too busy trying not to die to get a good look, but it was a red pickup truck."

"Is that it?" Red truck alone wouldn't get us very far.

Her eyes brightened as if a thought had just come to her. "No. It had something..." She touched her fingers to her brow as if that would pull the information forward. "Something on its side, right behind the cab of the truck."

"Something like a pinstripe?"

"More like a picture or an emblem. Round, I think. Or maybe the paint was chipped in a way that made it look like an image. It all happened really fast."

I was always suspicious of witnesses suddenly remembering something that wasn't in their initial statement. "How is it that you're just remembering this now?" I asked.

"Well, after falling onto the zombie—I mean, *body*—the traffic mishap flew out of my head. In L.A., you have a near miss like that every day on your way to work."

Well, the red truck was better than nothing. Maybe. If the jury believed it.

God, I didn't want to think about the jury.

"Any likely suspects in town?" Rika asked. "Someone you can imagine committing a crime like this?"

"Well, Wade's at the top of my list right now along with anyone who drives a red truck," I replied. "Could be drug runners passing through or a drug deal gone bad. And there's always the devil worshippers," I added sarcastically.

She shrugged. "As long as people around here believe in them, you could use them as an alternate theory at trial."

I liked the way that mind of hers was always working the angles. Made me smile. "I thought you said we weren't going to trial."

"We're not," she replied. Her chin was up, but I could see the doubt in her eyes. The more I watched her face, the more vulnerability I found in her expressions, despite her blasé attitude.

Savior complex. The phrase bounced back and forth in my head.

Okay, maybe Gabe was right. Maybe I needed women to be vulnerable, and I was projecting emotions onto Rika that she didn't have. She could be a sociopath like J.J. for all I knew, only with a hotter body. And prettier eyes.

Time for a new topic.

I stood. "I just remembered I have something for you," I said. I went out to the garage and grabbed the bag out of the back seat. When I walked back into the kitchen, I handed it to her.

She reached inside and pulled out the phone box. "Oh my God! A Ginseng, just like mine!"

"I figured you needed—"

She threw her arms around my neck. Before I had a chance to think it through, my hands were on her back, my cheek sliding against her silky hair.

She pulled me in tighter, her soft breasts pressed against my ribs, and I became aware of my little finger resting right below the small of her back.

If I moved my hand a few inches south, I could squeeze that nice round ass of hers.

She loosened her grip and I knew I had to release her or she might think I expected more for the phone than a hug.

I cleared my throat. "I programmed my number in there."

"Great!" she said. "Thanks! I can get the rest of my contacts off the cloud."

I still didn't trust "the cloud," personally. In my experience, clouds were here today, gone tomorrow, kind of like the women I married.

Rika sat down at the table, completely focused on the screen in her hand. It was as if I wasn't in the room anymore, which shouldn't have bothered me, but it did.

"I've got some stuff to do," I said. "I'll start dinner around six."

After a quick wave and an "okay," she was glued to the screen again.

I headed to my office to start trying to put together her defense.

CHAPTER ELEVEN

Rika

The next afternoon before work, I stood staring at myself in the full-length mirror that hung on the back of my bathroom door.

The t-shirt I had on was tight and yellow. A picture of bacon frying on a griddle graced the lower part of my torso. The word "SIZZLIN" hovered above it, right across my breasts in a fiery red font.

I guess LeeAnne figured this shirt made the clientele both hungry enough to order food and horny enough to leave a big tip.

Turning around, I looked over my shoulder at the word "HOT!" on my back. The pockets of the denim short-shorts barely covering my ass were embroidered with flames.

This was way too much heat for one outfit, but LeeAnne had gone to the trouble of folding each pair of shorts inside the shirt I was supposed to wear it with, and I didn't want to disappoint her.

However, the idea of tables full of customers watching my thighs jiggle as I walked away was terrifying. I took a few fake steps, keeping my head turned back toward the mirror.

Weird. I didn't see much jiggling.

I'd avoided viewing the backs of my thighs since junior high, preferring to keep them covered, even after I lost the weight.

Wait, did my ass look bigger with these high-wedged shoes on?

Maybe not bigger. Definitely more prominent. I was *sooo* not comfortable in these clothes.

I heard high-pitched barking and looked out the window. Gucci was at the very end of the grassy portion of Nick's back acreage, barking at a swaying bush a few yards away. Nick stood over her, arms crossed, shaking his bowed head.

As smart and hot as he was, there was definitely something wrong with him. He let his last wife stick him with her dog, and his second wife used him as a handyman.

Hm. I still needed to find out who his first wife was.

And why do you want to know so many personal details about him, Paprika Anise? My mind tended to call me by my real name when it was annoyed with me.

Because it only makes sense to know about the person defending you for murder, I told my mind. I waited to find out if my mind was going to call me a liar.

Gucci tiptoed daintily through the grass and squatted. I probably didn't have much time left.

I grabbed my phone and raced through the house to the garage, snatched the older set of keys off a hook on the wall and jumped into the white pickup truck. I pressed the garage door opener that was clipped to the sun visor, waited impatiently for the door to rise, then backed out.

I wasn't about to take Nick's black truck. I'd never driven a truck before and after all he'd done for me, no way was I going to be the one who put the first scratch on his One-fifty.

LeeAnne had asked me to come in around four-thirty today for a little training before what she referred to as the "dinner rush." After yesterday's lunch rush, I was doubtful she understood the meaning of the term.

It was only three o'clock, but I'd left early planning to visit a place I'd spotted the previous day called Dill's Dollar Store. The "D" in "Dill" looked like it had once been a "B," the dividing line of the letter semi-covered with white paint.

Bolo, Texas just might be the franchise knock-off capital of the world.

At the end of Nick's private road, I made a left turn. Another left a minute later put me on Zombie Road. That probably wasn't the official name of it, but since there were no signs in the vicinity telling me otherwise, that's what I called it.

I guess giving it a silly name was my mind's attempt at minimizing the impact of passing the place where I'd been chest-to-chest with an actual dead person.

However, it didn't keep a chill from jerking down my spine when I passed the remnants of the crime scene tape waving at me in the breeze.

Helloooo! Don't forget this is where you fell on the dead guy. Goodbyeyeyeye! You're going away to jail forever...

I turned left at the flashing light. The roads were as empty now as they'd been the night I arrived, except for one truck going by in the opposite direction.

A red truck.

I checked my rearview mirror. Something had registered in my brain as the vehicle passed. The same something I'd seen in that moment when the truck dashed out in front of me.

I jerked the steering wheel to the left, intending to make a quick U-turn.

Too fast.

My stomach lurched as the wheels on the left side of the truck levitated.

Holy crap! I was about to rollover! What had Nick said? Something about extra air bags? But not in this truck.

I was going to die and Nick would get to stand over my grave, shaking his head like he did over pea-brained little Gucci, saying "I told you so."

It felt like an eternity before the truck decided to settle on all fours again. As soon as I realized I wasn't dying, my determination returned. Unfortunately, the ditch on the side of the road prevented me from completing a U-turn, so I had to back up and try again.

Once I was turned around, I could barely see the red pickup in the distance. It hadn't made the right onto Zombie Road. It was driving straight ahead to parts unknown.

I mashed the accelerator, swerving right and left before getting the truck fully under control. This monstrosity didn't handle like my Honda Fit, that was for sure.

I sped up, even though I didn't have any business driving this fast. But there were no other cars on the road, and I didn't want to miss what could be my one and only chance to prove myself innocent.

The red dot ahead became clearer and clearer until it looked like a truck again. But what was I going to do if I caught it?

I should call someone. Nine-one-one? No, they'd probably route the call to Sheriff Strickland's office.

Nick.

I pressed the phone icon and nearly ran off the road. This loosy-goosy old steering system sucked. I touched "Favorites," hoping Nick had added himself there so I wouldn't have to scroll through my other contacts to find him.

Yes! He'd made himself Favorite Number One. After I hit his name on the screen, I noticed I was almost close enough to read the truck's license plate number.

Nick answered on the second ring.

"Hi, Nick...listen," I said breathlessly. "I've almost got the plate..."

The red truck sped up and I gunned the accelerator to catch

it. Nick said something I couldn't hear over the roar of the pick-up's motor.

"Okay, take this down..." I remembered you were supposed to call out names instead of the letters on license plates to avoid confusion. Years ago, I'd memorized the Los Angeles Police Department's phonetic alphabet, but now that I needed it, my mind was a blank.

First letter D... "Dumbledore!" I said.

"What?" Apparently, Nick was having trouble hearing me over the loud rumble of his pickup.

"Dumbledore!" I cried louder.

The truck in front of me sped up again, probably because I was riding his ass at seventy miles per hour. I sped up to stay within license plate range, my heart pumping like I was running uphill.

D, H... "Okay, it's Dumbledore, Hermione—"

"Rika!" Nick yelled. "What the hell is going on? Are you at Barr's?"

"Barr's? No!" Was he an idiot? "I'm giving you the plate—" I was forced to speed up once more. "Dumbledore, Hermione, Voldemort!" I said. "Dumbledore, Hermione, Voldemort!"

Damn! It sped up again and I still needed to get the numbers.

"Would you calm down and tell me what you're talking about?" Nick yelled. "Are you okay? Where are you?"

His words weren't really computing with me. The excitement of the chase had sent adrenalin shooting through my body, and my mind was focused on one thing only—getting the plate number.

"Dumbledore, Hermione, Voldemort!" I yelled again. "Just write—"

The red truck swerved left suddenly into the empty oncoming traffic lane. A split-second later, I saw why.

An animal was standing in the middle of my lane. But, since I was holding the wheel with my left hand, I automatically jerked right...

Into the ditch.

~

Rika

I was glad to find the lot in front of Dill's Dollar Store virtually empty so I could practice parking the old pickup between the lines. After three tries, I managed to herd it into a slot.

Luckily, the ditch I'd driven into wasn't particularly deep or steep, so I hadn't rolled over. The tires had ended up in mud in the bottom of the ditch, so it took me a few minutes of experimentation to get myself out.

Meanwhile, the armadillo I'd avoided hitting meandered over, pausing next to the truck as if surveying the damage he'd wrought.

But even if the armadillo was an asshole, I didn't want to see him get run over, so I honked until he skittered off into the ditch on the other side.

I was trying to keep a glass is half full attitude about the plate to avoid falling into a depression and eating my way through another box of doughnuts.

First, I'd seen the red truck again, which meant the owner of it probably lived around here. Second, I hadn't wrecked or died during the car chase, and, third, Nick now had a partial plate to work with. Surely he wrote the letters down after I called them out to him over and over again.

After getting out of the ditch, I'd tried to remember the names myself. I was pretty sure Hermione was in there somewhere and either Gryffindor or Dumbledore...maybe. Whatever. I'd find out later tonight when I saw Nick.

I got out of the truck and walked toward the store, which

seemed to be the closest thing this town had to a Walmart. And by closest, I mean one-tenth the size.

When I pulled the glass door open, the cowbell tied to the inside of it clanged. A chubby, thirty-something red-head in a blue Dill's Dollar Store smock smiled broadly at me from behind the only check-out counter.

"Welcome to Dill's!" Her green-gold eyes swept over me head-to-toe. "Can I help you find anything?"

"Maybe?" I said doubtfully as I scanned past the toys and makeup at the front of the store. "Do you have anything here I could wear to work out in?" I'd discovered Nick had an impressive gym on the far side of his gigantic house, a couple of doors down from his office.

"Somebody up there must like you!" she exclaimed.

That seemed to be the local consensus, despite the fact that I was facing a murder rap.

"We don't usually carry athletic clothes, but just this week we got a whole mess of 'em in!"

"Great!" I replied, proud that I knew what she was saying. After retrieving my contacts last night, I'd googled around and ended up studying a Southern Dictionary I downloaded onto my phone from Amazon. I now knew "a mess" referred to a quantity and could be used in place of phrases like "a bunch" or "a lot."

"They're at the back of the store in our Adult Apparel Department," the clerk informed me.

The Adult Apparel Department turned out to be four round hanging racks and a set of shelves. Although the *pickin's* were slim —why learn a foreign language if you aren't going to use it?—I found some gray shorts that looked like cut-off sweatpants and some solid black and solid white tank tops.

They were all one hundred percent cotton, but held a strong chemical odor I hoped would wash out. After combing the racks and shelves, I was pretty stoked to snag a pair of faux leather gym shoes in my size, and a few underthings.

When I took my stash to the front of the store, the redhead was still smiling. "I'm ReeAnne," she said.

Of course you are.

"You must be Rika."

"Yeah," I replied. "How did you know?"

"Well, you're driving Nick's pickup and wearing LeeAnne's clothes. She told me she lent you some, and, personally, I think they look better on you." She leaned across the counter and lowered her voice, despite the fact that we were the only two people in the store. "She's practically my best friend, but, honestly, they always look a little skanky on her...bless her heart." She did a quick head tilt to the left in conjunction with the last phrase that was probably meant to convey sympathy, false as it may have been.

I glanced down at myself. I didn't see how these clothes could look any less skanky on me—or anyone else—than they did on LeeAnne.

"Did you find everything you were looking for?" she asked.

Not exactly, but I'm grateful for what I can get nowadays. "Sure," I said cheerfully. "I'll take all of this."

As she rang up my purchases, I wrenched my phone out of my skin tight back pocket, proud I'd managed to find a way to pay for my own things.

This morning, after a call to my bank, they emailed me instructions and links to an app. I could now use my phone screen as a virtual debit card. That's why I'd chosen Edge World Bank over more well-known institutions. Their motto was "Always on the Cutting Edge."

When ReeAnne gave me the total, I punched my screen and held it out toward her. She looked at it, then looked back at me again, the smile never leaving her face.

"You're supposed to be able to scan it with your bar code gun," I explained. "It's a virtual debit card."

"Oh," she tilted her head and peered at me as if I were a small child. Her voice pitched higher. "You came here from New York City, didn't you?"

"Yes," I replied, trying not to act annoyed at her patronizing tone. "But this is supposed to work with any scanner."

"I'm sure you're right, but we don't have a scanner."

I looked around the strangely naked check-out area.

"Plus, we don't take plastic," she added. "Just cash or checks."

I sighed and stared sadly at the workout attire as my hopes of not ballooning back to my old self in the next few weeks disintegrated. Nick's dinner had been great again last night, but the chicken was basted with butter and coated in sweet barbecue sauce and served with Cajun rice *and* Pillsbury Crescent Rolls.

If I stayed on the Owen Diet much longer, I'd have to find a much larger woman to borrow clothes from.

"I'll tell you what," ReeAnne said. "I'll just put a note in the cash register, and you can come back and pay after you earn some money at Barr's."

"You mean just take the clothes without paying?" Was this a trick? When I walked out, surely alarms would go off and the sheriff would be there to arrest me again. No one ever, ever let you take store merchandise on the honor system.

ReeAnne chuckled and gave me that condescending look again. "You're working for LeeAnne and staying at Nick's. It's not like we don't know where to find you."

Good point. But still...

Had I encountered a tornado on my drive south? I felt kind of like Dorothy when she was dropped into Oz. Or maybe this was just what it was like living in a town so small everyone knew your business five minutes after you got there.

"Okay, well, thanks," I said as I took the plastic bag she held out toward me. "I'll be back as soon as I can to pay."

"I *know* you will," she said confidently. "See you around."

"I *know* you will," I said back.

~

I drove into Barr's parking lot to find Nick pacing in front of the door, his cell phone pressed to his ear.

When he saw me, he punched the screen and jammed the phone into his jeans pocket.

"Why aren't you answering your phone?" he said the second I emerged from the truck. I transferred the keys to my left hand, then wiggled the phone out of my back pocket and checked for calls.

Twenty-seven. All from Nick.

Punching through to the settings, I quickly found the problem. "My notification sounds were never turned on," I said. "I didn't know you'd called."

"Well, didn't you think I'd be trying to contact you after you called me in a panic, screaming gibberish?"

I glared at him. "I wasn't in a panic. I was excited. And I wasn't screaming." Well, maybe it sounded like screaming, since I was trying to talk over the loud truck motor.

Nick bowed his head and pinched the bridge of his nose. "You scared the hell out of me."

He was worried about me? That was so sweet! But, wait, had he said "gibberish"?

Uh-oh. "Did you get the partial license plate number?"

"What license plate number?"

"The one I was calling out to you over the phone," I said, "for the red truck."

Nick shook his head. "I couldn't make heads or tails of what you were yelling."

"It's standard operating procedure!" My voice pitched higher with frustration. "You call out names instead of letters so there's no confusion over "f" versus "s" and "b" versus "d.""

His brows jerked together. "Words like 'Adam' and 'Mary'!" He threw his hands out, palms up and half-shook his head at me.

"You said something about a plate, which made me think you were at work. After that..." He shrugged. "Gibberish."

"It wasn't gibberish!" I cried. "They're well-known characters from Harry Potter!" I waved my hands around as if holding an imaginary wand in each fist.

"Never read it," he said. "Never saw the movie."

"Movies" I corrected. "Plural." *What a Muggle.*

"How'd you even know it was the right pickup?" he asked.

I deep breathed, gathering all my patience as I explained, "When it passed by me, it had that same thing on the side in the same place, right behind the cab."

"But you still don't know what the thing is?" He was looking at me skeptically now. I didn't like that look one bit.

"No. I saw it out of the corner of my eye and my brain recognized the shape."

He blew out a loud breath and gave a "whatever" shrug. He thought I was wrong. Or nuts.

Asshole.

His eyes wandered to the white pickup. He moved back several steps to take in the passenger side. "Where'd the mud come from?"

"Mud?" I repeated innocently. I walked around to view the spatter. I raised my eyebrows in pseudo-surprise. "Weird."

He lowered his chin and peered at me as if he were a teacher looking over his spectacles at an incorrigible student. When I didn't answer, his eyebrows rose.

Let's get back to his screw up. "I can't believe you didn't write down the partial plate."

"*I* can't believe you already drove into a ditch." He stepped closer until I had to tilt my head back to see his face. "I'm glad you're okay, though," he said, his voice softer. His face held a tender expression.

My gaze was glued to his. I could see his hand reaching

toward me in my peripheral vision. My lips began to tingle. Was he about to...?

The keys were tugged from my hand. As I looked down, he fished another set from his pocket and laid them in my palm.

"Take the One-fifty home," he said as he walked to the driver's side of the white pickup and climbed in.

I watched him back up, then drive out of the parking lot, as I breathed a sigh of disappointment.

CHAPTER TWELVE

Nick

As I left the parking lot, my hands were tight on the steering wheel. I'd wanted to rest my forehead on my knuckles and chill for a few minutes, but Rika was watching from just outside the door.

Her frantic voice on the phone had kicked me into emergency mode. The only thing I could think to do after the call dropped was drive to town and look for her while pressing her name on my cell screen over and over again.

When she didn't answer and wasn't at Barr's, I thought she must have gotten into an accident. Except if she were in an accident, I should have seen it on the way to town.

Then crazy shit went through my head about her being killed by someone involved in the murder. I even imagined her being kidnapped by the Satanic cult before I mentally smacked myself back into reality, so I could decide on the next logical action.

I was about to start calling folks in the area to ask them to check the roads near their houses for signs of my old Ford Ranger when Rika drove in, healthy as you please.

Funny how fear can turn to anger the second you know a

loved one—or, um, someone you feel responsible for—is okay. Anger that they've scared the crap out of you for nothing.

But then Rika climbed out of the truck with her tiny shorts and her "SIZZLIN" breasts, and I was disturbed at the idea of her prancing around the bar in that get up.

There she was, all sexed-up in a bacon shirt, yelling and waving non-existent magic wands at me, and my dick reacted like I was watching a porn flick.

What the hell kind of fetish was that?

And now that the excitement was over, I was back to that gnawing in my gut that had been there ever since Gabe dropped this case on me.

Although the D.A. didn't have a whole lot to work with at this point, who knew what kind of so-called "evidence" Wade was going to pull out of his ass. I was pretty sure he'd already tampered with the gum.

And, God help us, if J.J. got enough dimwits on the jury. He might be able to score a conviction based on the gum and the fact that Rika wasn't from around here, therefore, suspect.

I turned right at the flashing light and saw the scraps of crime scene tape a minute later. I pulled off on the opposite side of the road to make sure I didn't disturb anything.

It hadn't rained since a couple of days before the body turned up, which is how I knew a ditch was about the only place my Ranger could have picked up the mud. The sunny weather also meant the crime scene hadn't been washed away in a downpour.

I stood and stared at it from a distance taking in the big picture. Pulling out my phone, I opened my email and checked the photos of the body again. As I paced slowly over the hard, dry dirt to where the body had been found, I looked back and forth between the foliage in the pictures and the real-life versions.

A part of me was hoping a ridiculously obvious piece of evidence had been left behind. Like maybe the killer's wallet had fallen out of his pocket with his ID in it, or a scraggly bush had managed to snag the swatch of underwear his mom had printed his name in.

At least then I could get out from under this dark cloud in my head and lose the stomach ache. And Rika would be free to drive home to Los Angeles.

And I'd never have a reason to see her again.

Wow. What was that sensation? Imagining this case over and done with should have felt like a weight off my shoulders. It shouldn't have caused a hollowed-out sensation in my chest. I couldn't possibly miss someone I'd only known a few days.

But, I had to admit, there was a big part of me that wanted to get to know her better. I liked having her around. She was smart in a geeky way, and chock full of surprises, something I wasn't used to in a beautiful woman.

Actually, I'd liked her since she'd said, "*I* called *you,* dipshit" to Danny the night she was arrested. I smiled at the memory.

But I couldn't let myself go thinking this was more than me being glad to have an intelligent, interesting person to talk to, which was a rarity around here.

I certainly didn't need any romantic entanglements. The ink was barely dry on my divorce, and I still hadn't figured out how I'd ended up married to Megan in the first place.

One day, I stopped to help a hot blonde with her flat tire. A few months later she and my mom were planning our wedding.

Not that I wasn't infatuated with Megan at first. I was. But while I thought we were taking the proverbial slow boat to China, she already had us there, riding one of those bullet trains to the alter.

And what was with my mom? I've heard of mothers who never like their son's girlfriends and throw monkey wrenches into his relationships whenever they can.

I could have used one of those moms. Mine liked my girl-friends too much. Way too much. Sometimes more than I did.

I wondered what she would think of Rika.

No. Rika was a client, not a girlfriend.

In fact, she was the reason I was out here sweating my ass off in ninety-five degree weather, staring at a whole lotta nothin'.

Recalling her description of the encounter with the red truck, I looked toward the highway, scanning the gravel shoulder on this side of it. Where would the truck have been parked? My eyes paused on an odd shape off to the left, near the road.

When I reached it, I squatted down to examine it without actually touching it. It was a latex glove, half-folded over on itself as if someone had pulled it off in a hurry. And, if I remembered correctly, it was a different color and thickness than the sheriff's department used.

Had the killer dropped it that night? Or maybe he thought he put it back in his truck and it fell out in the dark.

Rika had described being sprayed with gravel when the truck took off. Assuming the glove had fallen just outside the driver's side door, I paced forward to the approximate place the front tires should have been. The ground was nearly bald in two tracks parallel to each other, most of the gravel gone, dirt showing underneath.

When I walked toward the back of the imaginary truck, I found two more similar areas where tires might have gouged the gravel when they spun out. Studying the road next to where I stood, I noticed an unusual quantity of tiny rocks scattered in both lanes.

I switched my phone to camera mode and took photos of the road, the bald spots, the glove...

But if the glove was here that night, why was it still on the ground? Cops would consider a glove at a murder scene to be likely evidence.

The crime fighters in this county had zero experience investigating homicides that weren't of the most obvious kind. Every few years, a man shot his wife or vice versa over some stupid argument while under the influence of alcohol. The perpetrator confessed immediately. Case closed.

It wasn't like Wade and his deputies investigated murders every day.

But, come on, they could do better than this by watching a couple of episodes of Law and Order. Surely, they hadn't overlooked the glove.

If Wade were really trying to find the killer, it would have been bagged and tagged. If Wade were trying to stage a cover up, he would have gotten rid of it. Either way, it didn't make sense that it was still lying here.

My mind flashed back to the scene I'd encountered that night on my way back from mom's house. I tapped open the second email from the D.A.'s office containing the photos I'd deemed less important until now.

I flipped back and forth between them, studying the foliage and the bend of the road to be sure.

But there it was. Deputy Dan had parked his car directly behind Rika's Honda that night. And directly on top of the glove.

I hightailed it across the road to my truck, searching the small space behind the seat. I retrieved the plastic cover from a cheap rain poncho I kept in the cab. The packaging was still intact, except for the one side I'd sliced open to remove the poncho. It would have to do.

After rummaging around in the glove compartment, I found a pen. I went back to the latex glove and, using the pen, lifted it carefully into the plastic bag. If there were fingerprints or DNA traces left on it, I surely didn't want to disturb them.

And I wasn't about to turn this in to the sheriff's office. I'd have it messengered over to a private testing facility I trusted in Austin. Maybe something they found on it would point us in the right direction.

I breathed in a big hot chestful of hope. This case couldn't turn out like the last one. I couldn't watch another innocent person get put away. Rika, most especially.

My mind rewound once more to the sight of her, standing in Barr's parking lot, wearing LeeAnne's bacon shirt, waving imaginary magic wands while explaining Harry Potter to me.

In that moment, I felt like I saw the whole picture. A brave, determined, sexy woman who'd chased a possible murderer to get his license plate number. And the geeky, innocent girl inside with a passion for magical kids' books.

Even as we were arguing, I wanted to wrap my arms around her, slide my hands into those tight back pockets, and kiss her until her anger turned into something else completely.

But I also wanted to protect that innocent, geeky kid from harm. From the sheriff. From a bogus murder rap. Maybe from me, too.

I had a decade of life experience and bad decisions on her. As far as I knew, the only baggage she carried involved following her lousy boyfriend to New York. But everyone was entitled to one big screw up when they were young. And I was certain, smart as she was, she'd learn a lesson from it.

Unlike some of us, who just keep screwing up over and over again.

Even law school had been a bad idea. Sure, I'd graduated at the top of my class and turned out to be an excellent litigator. The partners in the firm called me "The Prodigy."

And, in theory, I'd always understood the adversarial nature of trials—that each side's job was to win. I guess I was okay with it during the first three trials, when I was defending young men with criminal records who just might have been innocent of murder that time... maybe.

But during the last trial, it hit me hard how nobody cared that my client was innocent. Not the D.A. Not the judge. Not my law firm.

Just me. Everyone else was playing the game.

When the verdict came in and I looked into the frightened

eyes of a teenager, tried as an adult, who'd be locked up with violent criminals for the rest of his life, I couldn't take it.

I went to the courthouse bathroom and threw up, dry heaving long after the contents of my stomach had emptied.

My mom had been trying to get me to come home to Bolo for years, her latest ploy being a self-diagnosed case of chronic fatigue syndrome. That was the excuse I used when I quit my job and came back.

And now here I was in Bolo, Texas, smack dab in the same boat I'd jumped out of in Austin.

Fucking Gabe.

~

Rika

"You think you can handle it?" LeeAnne asked after fifteen minutes of training.

I was pretty sure a monkey could handle this job. Barr's didn't offer fancy cocktails or a wine list. The clientele drank beer, whiskey, tequila, and either red or white wine, both of which poured straight out of boxes in the back, generically labeled "red wine" and "white wine."

When I was dismayed that there were only six plastic-covered menus in the whole place, LeeAnne explained she rarely saw new customers. Everyone came in knowing what they wanted.

"So far, it seems like easy money," I replied.

"Yeah, it's not bad compared to working at most bars or restaurants," LeeAnne said. "Too bad it won't be around much longer."

"Why is that?"

"Well, Dwight and I inherited the house and the bar free and clear. It makes us enough to get by, but as soon as one of those county building or fire inspectors gets around to us again, our days are numbered." She sighed. "We can't afford to rewire the electrical or do renovations."

I tried to imagine LeeAnne working somewhere other than Barr's and couldn't. "What would you do if you weren't running this place?"

Her gaze floated up as if she were watching her future on the ceiling. My eyes followed hers, but all I found was a charcoal-colored stain, probably old water damage. "I always thought I'd move to L.A. and become a stylist to the stars," she said.

My eyes flitted from her voluminous hair to her leather fringed cotton t-shirt that read, "100% Country Fried!"

I still wasn't sure if the phrase referred to her or the food.

"A stylist?" I repeated.

"Yeah, you know how all the celebrities have wardrobe stylists nowadays? The right stylist can take them from just being an actor to being a brand. I read that in *Star Style Magazine*."

Well, there was no denying that LeeAnne had branded herself. I glanced down at my chest. And me. In fact, I could honestly say I'd never felt more branded.

"But I fell in love and married an asshole," she went on. "Then my grandparents died and now I have Dwight to look out for." She glanced at her brother who was standing at the shiny steel counter in the kitchen, folding bar towels into perfectly uniform squares. "He doesn't handle change well, so I guess maybe I'll get my beautician's license and cut hair at my house or something."

Hair styling seemed as unlikely a profession for her as wardrobe styling. But when I thought about the hair I'd seen in this town, I decided she might be right on trend.

The door opened and four young guys came in, talking loudly and jostling each other. Although they were ethnically diverse—two white, one Latino, one black—all were tall and broad-shouldered.

"Hey, Ms. LeeAnne," they called before heading for the back room.

"Hey, boys," she replied. She turned back to me. "No booze for them. They may look big, but they're here for some after-football practice snacks and a few games of pool before they go home." She called after them, "And don't forget to tip your damn waitress this time!"

"Yes, Ms. LeeAnne," they sing-sang. They burst into laughter, clearly finding themselves hilarious.

"Thank God I don't have teenagers of my own," she said. "Most of 'em drive me bat-shit crazy." She watched through the doorway as one of the boys used a pool stick to poke another in the ass. "I went to school with their mothers."

That was impossible. "You can't be old enough to have a son in high school," I argued.

"Most girls around here get pregnant between sixteen and nineteen," she replied. "I'm almost thirty-four. Two of my high-school friends just became grandmas."

I grimaced.

"I know, right?" she said. "The last guy I slept with turned out to be twenty-four. My friend ReeAnne pointed out that he was closer to her son's age than ours. Made me feel like a pervert."

I chuckled, but wanted to make LeeAnne feel better. "You look great," I said. "I'd sleep with you."

LeeAnne gave me an odd look.

"If I were a lesbian, I mean. Well I guess we'd both have to be lesbians."

She snorted. "Okay, you go take the boys' food order. I'll get them their Cokes."

After I took down the orders, I walked to the kitchen and laid the ticket on the upper left corner of the metal table LeeAnne had shown me.

"Wrong!" Dwight shouted.

I jumped, nearly twisting my ankle in the high-heeled wedges.

"First ticket goes here!" he pointed to a spot on the table an inch from where I'd left the order.

Just as with LeeAnne and the arachnids, his reaction seemed over-the-top. He certainly seemed to have the temperament of a killer. However, I'd already asked LeeAnne what time she and Dwight came in today and they'd been here since ten-thirty.

I'd also checked his truck in the parking lot and it was a much deeper red than the one I was looking for. And it didn't have that special something on the side.

It drove me crazy to think I'd recognized the image on some level, but couldn't quite re-assemble it in my brain.

"Okay, Dwight," I replied. "I'll try to get it right next time."

"Okay," he said pleasantly, as if he hadn't scared the crap out of me a moment before.

When I walked back into the main room, a middle-aged Hispanic couple was coming through the door. The man was wearing a stiff red shirt with mother-of-pearl snaps, smoothed over a slightly rounded gut, and tucked into dark jeans that ended at a pair of red and gray cowboy boots.

His companion wore a casual, printed wrap dress that flattered her full figure. Her glossy brown hair hung straight to her shoulders then, curved under.

"Hey, Gabe," LeeAnne called. "Belinda! You're back!"

Gabe. I looked again. Yes, it was Judge Martínez looking very un-judge-like in his western after-hours garb.

The two of them came toward us as LeeAnne walked out from behind the bar and hugged Belinda.

"Rika," LeeAnne motioned me over. As I moved slowly in their direction, I tried not to look as anxious as I felt.

"Coach!" Someone yelled.

Judge Martínez looked toward the pool room and waved. "I'm going to go see my boys," he said to Belinda as he strode away.

"You know, he hasn't coached them since pee-wee football." Belinda was saying as I walked up. "And he's totally taking credit for the winning streak at the high school this year." She turned toward me. "You must be Rika."

I nodded, not sure how to act in a world where suspected felons hung out with their judges' wives.

"I heard you're having a rough time," she said sympathetically.

"Yeah," I replied as LeeAnne went to greet other customers. "I guess you could say that."

Belinda put her arm around my shoulders. A comforting warmth spread through me. "You'll be fine. Nick will take good care of you." Her lips quirked up in a mischievous smile. "And I see LeeAnne has lent you her clothes."

We cracked up together, then glanced guiltily toward LeeAnne.

Belinda seemed like someone I could relate to, and she was Gabe's wife, which meant she probably knew a lot about Nick. Maybe I could get some questions answered without going through gabby LeeAnne.

"Belinda, you know your husband made Nick defend me, right?"

"Mm-hm." She nodded.

How did I put this tactfully? "I'd like to know a little more about my attorney." I said. "Like, what's with the three wives? I'm mean at his age..." Okay, maybe that wasn't the most important information I needed to glean from Belinda, but that's what I was dying to know.

Belinda nodded again. "I know it sounds crazy, but Nick's a good guy. Gabe has a few theories." She glanced up and saw her husband headed our way. "Have you met Nick's mother?" She raised her eyebrows meaningfully.

Luckily, Gabe got pulled back into conversation, so I decided I'd better get to the important stuff while I had the chance.

"The other thing is," I said, "Nick seems weirdly under-confident for an attorney who's won three out of four murder cases."

She let out a disgusted snort. "And, of course, being a man, he didn't explain it to you."

"No," I replied. "And, several times, he's seemed really stressed. Like he actually thinks I'll get convicted."

Belinda's voice dropped to a near whisper. "He's a great attorney," she said sadly. "But he's heartbroken."

"About his divorce?"

"You'd think, but no." She glanced back and saw her husband coming. LeeAnne was also headed back towards us from the other direction.

"We'll have to talk more another time," Belinda said. "Gabe hates it when I gossip, even though I get most of my gossip from him, especially since I've been leaving town so much."

"LeeAnne," Gabe said as they both reached us. "I'm starving to death and my wife refuses to feed me!"

"Huh!" Belinda huffed. "I drove in all the way from Laredo today, and he expected me to get the groceries and cook for him after I cleaned up the mess he made in the kitchen. *Que loco!*" She directed the last two words to me, warmth radiating from her smiling face.

The Spanish sent a flood of homesickness through me. I wanted Belinda to take me home in her pocket and keep me safe until all this was over. I wanted my *Lita*.

A wave of guilt replaced the homesickness at the thought of my grandmother.

I'd been putting off calling her, but we hadn't talked in several days and she was going to start worrying.

I checked the time. Eight o'clock. Perfect. She always played dominoes with her friends on Saturday evenings.

Lita owned a cell phone, but it was never charged, so she operated from her land line. I could leave her a message without getting the third degree.

Ducking down the back hall and into the bathroom, I hit the call button, crossing my fingers that she wasn't hosting the game this week. Her phone rang six times, then clicked over to her twenty-year-old answering machine.

"Lita?" I said. My parents had referred to her as my "*abuelita*"—little grandma—from the time I was born. I could only manage the last two syllables when I started talking, and I'd never added the first two back in.

"I'm with friends down in Texas. I'm going to spend some time here, then I'm coming back home. Brandtt and I broke up. I may not pick up calls right away because I don't want the phone to get wet. Just wanted you to know I was okay. Love you!"

Another wave of guilt washed through me, but I fought it off with the fact that I hadn't lied...technically.

I was in Texas with friends, sort of. LeeAnne had lent me clothes and Nick had me staying at his house. That was pretty friendly.

I knew when she heard the part about the phone getting wet, she'd assume I'd gone to South Padre Island like I'd been considering previously. But, it was true I didn't want the phone to get wet, which could happen. I was in a bar. So, I would just turn it off and put it in LeeAnne's office for the night.

Still guilty.

But what good would the truth do anyone? My grandmother would be beside herself with worry. She'd immediately call my dad and my aunts, and everyone would be frantic to help, but there was nothing they could do. My dad couldn't even get into the country.

Not telling was definitely for the best. I ran to LeeAnne's office and put my phone in the desk drawer she'd shown me, shut the office door and got to work.

~

"I told you you'd be good for business," LeeAnne said several hours later. "We've had three times the customers as last Saturday."

"Great!" I said with pretend enthusiasm. "And Dwight is amazing. I thought all those food orders would be too much for him, but he's like a machine."

"Yeah." LeeAnne's expression darkened. "That's Dwight." She handed me the check I'd been waiting for. I forced myself to walk past the host of inquiring eyes and deliver it to the table.

The whole night had been creepy. Normally, people went to an establishment like this to interact with friends or family or meet other patrons.

Tonight was clearly all about me. Families, couples, groups of older women—they all came in and spent much of their time gawking at me.

I wasn't sure which was worse, the idea that they were sizing me up as a possible stone-cold killer or the moments when I slipped back into high school mode and was sure they were discussing the size of my ass or pointing out lumps of cellulite on the backs of my thighs.

I kept flashing back to the first day of school—every year throughout junior high and high school—when I walked into the classroom to take my seat and all eyes were riveted to my super-sized body.

On the plus side, the night might have been good for my image. I was as friendly as I could be, and several of the women who came in told me I was much too nice to be the Grey Widow they'd been hearing about.

But not everyone. Some people had already decided I was guilty before they came in. I could see it in their eyes. They held their hands over their mouths and whispered about me to their companions.

The weirdest moment of the night had been when Sheriff Strickland came in alone and took possession of the back booth.

As he alternated between draft beer and whiskey shots, he watched me...constantly.

Unfortunately, I couldn't tell if he was hanging around to keep an eye on his murder suspect or getting trashed because he felt guilty about the way he'd treated me.

Around midnight, the place slowed down. All the diners were gone, along with many of the drinkers. A few people were still playing pool in the back room and several serious drinkers sat alone at the bar or the tables.

I took a quick bathroom break and saw that Dwight had already started to clean up. He was in LeeAnne's office operating an old brown vacuum cleaner that must have been purchased when the bar first opened.

Electrical tape was wrapped around the cord in three different places, duct tape on the zippered bag.

The machine stopped suddenly and I watched Dwight lift it and slam it down on the floor. It popped back on and he continued his vacuuming.

That sucked. I hoped my presence here earned Barr's at least enough money to replace that crappy old machine.

When I went out front again, I was surprised to see Matilda Strickland coming through the door. "Thanks for calling me," she said to LeeAnne.

LeeAnne tilted her head toward the back booth. Ms. Tilly's eyes followed the gesture, resting sadly on her husband, slouched over his mug.

But when she noticed me, she smiled warmly. "Rika, how are you?" she asked as she gave me a gentle hug. It should have seemed weird, considering who she was married to, but, from her pillowy body, a hug felt like the most natural thing in the world.

"I'm fine," I replied. I felt the need to reassure her, so she wouldn't worry. "LeeAnne's been really nice."

"I'd expect nothing else." She reached up and gave LeeAnne's hair a motherly caress. "Her heart was always in the right place, even when she was a little girl." Her gaze drifted to the back booth again. "Unlike some people, who need help staying on the straight and narrow."

Obviously, she knew her husband. But I had a feeling he didn't tell her everything. Like how he was falsifying evidence to send me to jail.

I opened my mouth to say something. Maybe she could give him a good talking to. Straighten him out on my behalf.

But, she clearly loved him and I couldn't stand to make her feel worse about him than she already did.

Not tonight, anyway.

Besides, if he was willing to fake evidence for a murder trial, this was probably way too big to be cured by wifely intervention.

"Well..." Matilda looked back and forth between us. "Make good choices." Her eyes said, *Not like I did.*

"Let me know if you need help getting him to the car," LeeAnne replied.

As it turned out, Wade Strickland was still ambulatory—barely—and he didn't put up a fight. When he saw his wife, he pulled himself up and fell back onto the booth seat. He tried a second time and managed to remain standing while Matilda wedged herself under his arm. They walked out of the bar, his body leaning heavily on his wife's sturdy shoulders.

"That's what I'd still be doin' every night if I'd stayed married," LeeAnne said angrily. "That asshole stole the best years of my life. And the greedy bastard would have taken more if I hadn't put a stop to it."

She stared off into space, her brow furrowed angrily at someone I couldn't see.

"The best years of your life are still in front of you, LeeAnne," I said.

Her face jerked toward me as if she was surprised I was there. Or maybe surprised she'd made her statement aloud.

"Yeah, sure," she agreed as she hustled off toward the kitchen.

CHAPTER THIRTEEN

Rika

I was fast asleep when the knocking began. I jumped up from my cot and peered through the bars. Skimming past the long row of cells, I could just make out the door.

"Rika!" a voice called in a familiar Spanish accent. More knocking. "Paprika!"

"*Papi!*" I cried. "*Papi!* I'm here!"

As the knocking continued, I pulled violently at the iron bars, but they didn't budge.

"Rika." The voice was different this time. That wasn't my father!

My eyes popped open. Bright sunlight flooded through the wood blinds in the window.

I was in Nick's house, not a prison. I pressed my hand to my chest, trying to slow my racing heart. "Yes?" I called, then cleared the frog from my throat. "Come in."

The door opened. "Time to get up," he said. He was wearing black athletic shorts topped with—be still my heart—a faded blue cotton Nike muscle shirt, damp and clingy like he'd just worked out.

"Did I sleep all day?" I sat up. "Am I late for work?" LeeAnne was kind enough to give me a job and practically treat me like family. I certainly didn't want to look like I was taking her for granted.

"No, it's Sunday. We need to get ready for church."

"Did you say church?" I blinked at him. He really didn't seem like the churchy type.

He inhaled and the lines of his chest pushed through the shirt fabric.

Nope. Those pecs did not belong in a house of God. They'd fit in a lot better over at Magic Mike's.

I propped up on one elbow. As my body shifted, my thighs rubbed together, reminding me I'd slept in only my t-shirt and underwear. The thought of being so scantily clad only a few feet from Nick's hot body kindled a spark of yearning *down there.*

"Yeah," he began. "Everybody goes to church around here and you have a public image to build."

"You really think it will make a difference?"

"It works for the average politician," he said, leaning casually against my doorframe. "At least until he's caught accepting a contractor's bribe while an intern toots his horn for him under the desk."

I couldn't help laughing. "I don't think it's ever happened exactly that way. Nice imagery with the intern and the horn, though." I narrowed my eyes. "Interesting how you had it right there on the tip of your brain. Like you'd given it a lot of thought."

"Yep," he said with a chuckle. "Back when I was considering running for office." His lips curved into a full-on smile that sent a thrill down my back.

Oh yeah. Church. "How much time do I have?"

"Depends on where you want to go. Bible Church service starts at ten. Catholic mass is at eleven."

"Which one do you usually go to?"

"I don't usually go to church."

"But you just said everybody goes."

He shrugged.

I picked up my phone and checked the time. "The first service starts at ten and you woke me up at six forty-five?"

"I wasn't sure how long it takes you to get ready. Every woman I've ever lived with has been high maintenance." His voice dropped as his gaze shifted to the window. "High maintenance. High drama."

Yeah, the big swoopy hair alone could take hours to perfect.

"I guess that explains why we've known each other for four whole days and you haven't married me yet."

His eyes met mine as he burst out laughing. Warmth filtered through me at the thought that I'd managed to snatch him back from his negative thoughts.

"Besides," he said. "I thought you'd want time to wash the country fried out of your hair."

I lifted a piece of hair to my nose and sniffed. The smell of day-old seafood platter assaulted my nostrils, making me feel kind of nauseated, yet really hungry at the same time.

As if reading my mind, Nick said, "Tell you what, after I take a shower, I'll make you some breakfast. How about pancakes?"

No sexier words had ever been spoken. I imagined Nick, his hair damp from the shower, walking toward me in nothing but a towel, a platter of syrup-soaked carbs balanced on one hand.

I nodded, a dreamy smile most certainly on my face.

He turned to go.

"Wait," I said. "I don't have anything to wear." I pinched the top of my "SIZZLIN" shirt between my forefinger and thumb to illustrate the problem. And the stuff Megan left behind in the closet wasn't any more appropriate for church than LeeAnne's clothes.

"Oh..." Nick thought for a moment. "I may have something." He left and came back seconds later holding a hanger. On it, was a long-sleeve, boat-neck dress in an animal-print inspired fabric, the brown and black spots falling somewhere between leopard and giraffe in size and shape, dropped generously onto a cream background.

Normally, I wasn't a big fan of animal print, but this designer version in high-quality material was animal print done right. I liked it.

My enthusiasm was dampened, however, when I realized how Nick must have obtained the garment. "Megan?"

"BreeAnne. She bought it online, then decided the print was too much for her...or something." He gave an *I'm only a guy. What do I know?* shrug.

I could see how a pattern like this might be overwhelming on a blue-eyed blonde, but on me...?

I took it from him and lifted the tag that hung off the back, hoping it was my size.

Eight hundred ninety-nine dollars! And it wasn't even a ball gown. Jeez, I'd thought Brandtt's taste was expensive, but this was nuts. I dropped the tag like it was a hot ember.

Nick nodded. "I know. They tell you their favorite sports are football, baseball and basketball until you marry them and find out they're shopping, shopping and more shopping."

Despite his rueful tone, he didn't seem particularly concerned about the expenditures. Or the cost of defending me while needing to pay his personal expenses, come to think of it.

"Nick?" I didn't want to pry, but... "You haven't mentioned other clients and you're defending me for free."

He held up a hand to stop me. "There's nothing to worry about," he said. "I can defend you, whatever it takes."

"But—"

He huffed out a breath like I was making him do something he hadn't wanted to do. He walked to the foot of my bed. "Look out here." He pointed out the window above me. I got up on my knees, careful to yank the bedspread around to cover my ass as I shuffled closer to the glass.

"Okay..." I looked past the perfect green lawn to scan the scrub brush and stubby trees.

"See that thing way out there that's moving kind of like a rocking horse?"

"Yeah." My eyes focused on a metal object bobbing up and down in the distance.

"That's an oil well." He said it as if he wasn't convinced having an oil well was a good thing. "It's not the only one, but my investments are diversified now, anyway."

I stared out the window, unsure what you said to a man upon finding out he had an oil well. "So, you didn't load up the truck and move to Bever-*lee*?"

He chuckled. "Swimmin' pools... movie stars?"

I really liked how we were on the same page humor-wise, even for a *Beverly Hillbillies* reference.

He was so close, staring down at me with appreciation in his gorgeous eyes. They were Dodger blue today and I suddenly had the urge to hit a home run.

The room grew hot. I felt awkward and fidgety, like I'd just accidentally made eye-contact with the high school quarterback. The nerves under my skin prickled. I couldn't handle the anxiety. I had to break the tension. "Okay, get along little doggie so I can wash the bar off."

"Yeah." He turned to leave. "Right now, you smell a little too much like LeeAnne for comfort."

Hmm... LeeAnne. I didn't like the idea that Nick so familiar with her smell. What was the deal between those two, anyway?

I narrowed my eyes shrewdly as he shut the door behind him. In a town that loved to gossip as much as Bolo did, I was sure I could find out.

~

As Nick drove me to church, I felt like I'd finally lucked out, wardrobe wise. His ex's cast-off dress looked like it was designed with me in mind, and the high-wedged sandals LeeAnne had given me actually went well with it.

I'd never required a ton of makeup, but I'd still been happy to find an unopened tube of red lip gloss in the bathroom. Maybe BreeAnne had bought it to go with the dress and never needed it. Or maybe it was Megan's lip gloss, since she seemed to have a habit of buying things she never used, as evidenced by the dozens of clothing items in the closet with tags still attached.

It looked to me like Nick's wives had really taken advantage of his generosity. Maybe even married him for his oil wells until they found a new diversion.

I didn't get it. What kind of idiot would throw back a guy like Nick?

Fickle flakes.

Did they break his heart? Nick didn't deserve that kind of treatment. I slid my eyes to the left to sneak another peek at him. I wasn't the type to get excited over men in uniforms and that included business suits—the uniform of the corporate conformist.

Except Nick didn't look like a corporate drone in his tailored charcoal suit. When he'd slipped the jacket on over his crisp white shirt, he'd looked like a leading man, straight off the red carpet of a movie premiere.

When he turned the steering wheel, my eyes caught on his hands. So masculine. So powerful. What would they feel like on my body? I imagined his right hand leaving the wheel, resting confidently on my thigh. Sliding up underneath the hem of my dress. As his finger hit the sweet spot, I shivered.

Nick glanced over. "Are you cold?" Before I could decide on an answer, he turned the thermostat knob to the right and flipped the fan from three to two.

Great. The last thing I needed right now was less air conditioning.

Nick turned into the Bolo Bible Church parking lot, and my mind reset to the task at hand.

Suddenly, I was hit with a case of nerves. After the last few nights, I knew people would be staring at me and judging me, but at least then I had a job to keep me busy. Today, I'd just be sitting or standing or kneeling, or whatever Protestants did, there on display.

Nick parked and got out of the truck, but I was too anxiety-ridden to move. He came around and opened my door for me as hot air rushed into the cab. I hoped he didn't think I'd purposely waited for him to help me out the door. That was so 1960.

He looked at me expectantly. I stared back at him, momentarily hypnotized by his penetrating blue gaze. "The seat belt's going to have to come off," he said. "Kind of a prerequisite to getting out of a car."

I blew out the breath I'd forgotten to exhale previously. "It may be the only thing holding me together," I confessed.

Nick placed a hand on my upper arm. It was even warmer than the outside air. He squeezed. "I've got you," he said.

At that moment, there was no question in my mind. Nick would look out for me. Nick had my back.

I wished he would have my front, too.

"Yeah, um, okay," I said as he leaned across me, reaching for the buckle.

I sucked in the scent of freshly washed manly man and had to fight the urge to tip forward and sink my teeth into his earlobe. Sure, it was just an ear, but it was Nick's ear, naked and handy.

I got out and we wove through the parking lot. As we walked up the steps of the church, I felt his hand on the small of my back.

Uh...wow. I wanted to lean my head on his shoulder and slip my arm around his waist, but I made conversation instead.

"This is the only hill I've seen around here," I said, as if I cared about the topography of Bolo, Texas.

"The church sits on a man-made hill." Nick gestured to the large red brick structure topped with a white cross. "They brought in thousands of pounds of dirt just so it would sit up higher than the Catholic church across the street."

"'Cause that's what Jesus would do?"

"Exactly." We chuckled together and my anxiety fell away. "Plus, the locals get to claim they have the only basement for hundreds of miles. Elevation's too low for them in these parts."

"They actually brag about a basement?"

"In case you haven't noticed, there's not a lot to crow about around here."

The sanctuary was mostly empty when we walked in, since we'd gotten there early, before Sunday school let out. Nick said this was good because we could snag a prime spot halfway up the rows of pews, next to the aisle, where everyone would see us.

Just as we got to the row Nick had chosen, a female voice called his name and two women came walking from the front of the aisle. One was Matilda Strickland, the other was that Southern cooking lady, Paula Deen.

"Did you see the flower arrangement your mom donated for this week's services?" Ms. Tilly asked. "Isn't it lovely?"

Okay, so maybe that wasn't Paula Deen with her. She was definitely younger than Paula. But she had Paula Deen's hair on steroids. Platinum, layered, teased up high on top and fluffed wide on the sides. The women around here sure knew how to maximize their hair volume.

"Lovely!" Nick replied. His enthusiasm was just convincing enough to satisfy the older women, but just ironic enough to tell me he didn't give a crap about floral arrangements. "Hi, mama," he said to Paula's twin.

His mother planted a palm on each of his cheeks. "There's my handsome boy!"

I watched Nick take in a slow breath like he was fighting for control. He reached up and pried his mother's hands off his face.

"Rika, this is my mom, Tammy Lynn."

"This is Rika?" she replied. "Such a tiny little thing to be a—" She stopped herself, apparently not willing to say the word "murderer," at least not in the house of God. "Uh, to be having such a hard time," she continued. "Bless your heart!" She took my hand and patted it.

I smiled what was probably a sickly smile at her, unsure how to respond to such over-the-top fake sympathy.

"Nick!" She grabbed her son's arm. "I was trying to call you all day yesterday! Didn't you get my messages?"

Nick pulled out his cell phone and pretended to check. I say "pretended" because I could see his screen and all he did was tap his settings icon and turn the notifications off.

"Nope, no calls," he said. "I think I need a new carrier. Been missing a lot of calls lately. Too bad I signed that contract."

Liar, liar, pants on fire.

"Anyway," Tammy Lynn said. "I need the plants and potting soil I bought at Juanita's to be picked up and brought to the house."

"What about the landscaping service I pay for every month?" Nick asked. "Why aren't they doing it?"

"It's really more of a lawn service, and whenever I ask them to do something extra it takes weeks for them to get around to it."

"Mom, I've got a murder tri—"

"I'm sure you can find a few minutes for the woman who suffered through thirty-six hours of labor for you to come into this world."

Nick lowered his chin and stared down at her skeptically. "When I was a kid, it was twelve hours of labor," he said. She peered up at him, widening her baby blue eyes until I thought they'd burst out of their sockets. Nick's shoulders dropped. "Fine. I'll take care of it."

"Oh, and bring your tools. I've got other things that need fixin' around the house."

"I didn't doubt that for a second," he murmured so only I could hear.

Suddenly, a loud noise echoed off the walls. I glanced around and found the sheriff in the second row on the far side of the church. His head had lolled back on the top of the pew and his mouth hung open, emitting a grinding snore.

"Want me to thump him on the top of his head, Ms. Tilly?" Nick asked hopefully.

She laughed. "Nope, I recently purchased an app for just this situation." She pulled out her cell, glanced around to make sure the sanctuary was still empty, and touched an icon on her screen.

The phone screamed to life, the sound of sirens splitting the air. Her husband bolted from his seat as she turned the sound off. His head jerked right and left as he patted his hip, searching for his gun, which he didn't find because he'd traded his uniform in for an ugly brown suit.

Matilda smiled at us conspiratorially. Her husband saw her across the room. "What happened?" he asked.

"I don't know." She shrugged innocently. "You must have had a nightmare."

So, Matilda Strickland wasn't a doormat. She had her ways of dishing out a little retribution for the embarrassment her husband caused her.

I liked her even better now. Besides, she had a really cool cell phone for a woman who was practically my grandmother's age.

Church goers started to arrive. Matilda and Tammy Lynn went off to greet them.

"Her cell phone totally kicks your cell phone's ass," I said to Nick.

"What?" He pulled his phone out again. "This is an iPhone!"

"An iPhone 3G," I said with disgust. "It can't have more than sixteen gigs of storage and it doesn't even have LTE."

"How would you even know that?"

"I googled the specs when I saw what you were using. You try doing that on your phone and see how long it takes you."

A door near the front of the sanctuary opened and a sixty-something man stepped through, turned and closed the door quietly behind him. He sucked in a slow, tired breath, then made his way toward us.

His cheap black suit was too big, giving the impression he was melting away in it as he moved. When he neared, my eyes were drawn to his hollowed-out cheeks. His eyes were dark and blood shot, ringed by charcoal-colored circles.

"Nick Owen," he said with forced joviality. "What a surprise. Don't think I've seen you here since the last time I married you."

Ouch.

Nick pushed out a chuckle I was sure he didn't feel.

The man's eyes shifted to me, then back to Nick. "Planning another wedding?"

Nick's jaw tightened, but otherwise his face remained impassive. "Reverend Jenkins, this is Rika Martin, my client."

"Martín," I corrected. "I'm Rika Mar-*teen*."

The reverend's black onyx eyes met mine. A chill slid down my back. Neither of us reached out to shake hands, and I was good with that.

"Glad you could make it," he said, not looking the least bit glad. Wasn't he supposed to be happy when a murderer came to church? I could be here to repent my sins for all he knew.

But without another word, he drifted toward the open sanctuary doors, where church members were streaming in.

"That was...well, *weird*." I said.

"Yeah." Nick watched Reverend Jenkins walk away. "Every time I run into him, he seems a little more distant and several pounds thinner."

"Do you think he's sick?"

"Not the way you mean. News like that usually travels at the speed of light around here. I get the feeling it's more a disease of the soul."

"I guess that's the worst kind for a man of the cloth."

"Yep," Nick said as he gestured for me to sit down. "The very worst."

~

Nick

I was glad when the service was over, although bringing Rika turned out to be a pretty good idea. People made it a point to come greet me as an excuse to get a good look at her, which is what I was counting on.

I hoped her big brown eyes would look as innocent to everyone else as they did to me. And I wanted them to see just how petite she was—too small to kill a man and drag his body in and out of her car.

It didn't hurt that she came across as a little shy with crowds and seemed genuinely appreciative of compliments from the ladies. Like she was surprised every time.

Kind of scary that she was that good an actress. No woman could be as attractive as she was and not know it by now.

The most disturbing moments, though, were the ones when I had to watch her interact with the male members of the church. Older ones who shook her hand then held onto it about ten seconds too long. And young ones who flirted openly with her.

The irritation that jangled down my nerves each time was unsettling. I had to keep unfisting my hands and reminding myself this was a good thing. Men don't want to convict a woman they'd like to date. And Rika needed all the positive word-of-mouth she could get.

Of course, I had to sit through one of Reverend Jenkins dull sermons to make this happen. He'd been here for over twenty years and, in my opinion, had started phoning in the job. And he certainly dumped too many tasks on Ms. Tilly, who wasn't even paid for her work.

As Rika and I exited the church into the bright mid-day sunshine, I realized my hand was on her lower back again. While that might be appropriate behavior with a girlfriend or wife, I didn't understand what was triggering the reflex with Rika.

Maybe the fact that she was in my care until the trial was over. Regardless, once my palm made contact with her spine, I had a hell of a time peeling it off.

"I feel like that went okay." Rika's words sounded more like a question than a statement. She turned her big hopeful eyes up at me and I wanted to curl my fingers around her shoulder and pull her against me.

Just to reassure her, of course.

"Uh, yeah." I cleared my throat even though it didn't need clearing. "The women wanted to be your friend and the men wanted to..."

"What?" she asked as if she really didn't know. Could she possibly be so oblivious to how appealing she was to men? I was used to women who knew what they had and used it for all it was worth, and I didn't like not knowing whether she was playing me or not. "To, um, do what men always want to do, I guess."

She raised her eyebrows in surprise, then jerked her head suddenly to the left.

"I... I think..." She made a beeline through the row of parked cars nearest to us, pausing to let a Range Rover pass before zeroing in on a red Dodge Ram in the next row.

"Oh, my God!" she said, walking up behind it. "I think this is the plate." She went around to the driver's side of the pickup and stopped near the cab. "This is it! She pointed at the symbol painted on the side, pulled out her phone and took a picture.

She went back to take one of the license plate as I moved in to get a closer look at the shape, custom painted on the side. Sort of an open-ended horizontal oval with an oval dot inside.

"What is this?" I noted the changes in the thickness of the line and the stems that poked out on the right side of each oval.

"I think it's a gamer symbol." Rika stared into her phone as she walked back toward me. "It looks really familiar."

"Like, for a video ga—?"

"Halo!" she said triumphantly. "It's the Halo symbol."

"How can you be sure?"

"I googled it." She held her phone out toward me jiggling it back and forth tauntingly. I took it from her hand. She'd searched "video game symbols," and the image on the truck was an exact replica of one of the first search results.

All around us, car doors slammed as church members left for home. "We'd better get away from here and watch to see who gets into this truck," I said.

We went over and stood next to my One-fifty, pretending to chat while we waited. When I spotted the lanky body, topped with curly orange hair, my heart dropped into my gut.

"Damn," I muttered as the revelation sunk in.

"Do you recognize him?" Rika asked excitedly as he hit his remote and got into the Dodge.

"I do," I replied. "But the news isn't good."

CHAPTER FOURTEEN

Rika

After he assured me he knew where the suspect lived, we climbed into Nick's truck. The excitement of finding the probable murderer practically had me bouncing off my seat.

"Seat belt," Nick said.

"Holy mother of Zeus!" I cried. "That was such a good call, having us go to church today!" I tried but couldn't steady my shaking hands enough to buckle up. Nick wrapped his fingers around mine, and the mechanism clicked together.

What was it with me and seat belts today? Not that it mattered. Nothing mattered but the fact that I'd identified the pickup truck from that night. Soon, I'd be cleared of murder charges and then maybe Nick and I could—

His statement finally pushed its way through my adrenaline rush and into my brain. "Wait. When you say it's not good news, do you mean because he's a badass, and I could be in grave danger until he's arrested?"

"I wish," he said as he backed out of the parking space.

"Hey!"

"No..." He huffed out a frustrated breath. "I mean, if that were the only problem I'd find a way to keep you safe."

I twisted my body toward him. "So, what's worse than me being in grave danger?"

"You finding the truck that dumped the body and still going to jail."

"What?" My hand flew to my chest. "Why?"

"What you just witnessed is one of those miracles of modern science the fertility doctors are so proud of. That was either JimBob, JoeBob, or BillyBob McGwire."

"Seriously?"

"Hey, I didn't name 'em. Anyway, we know that one or more of the triplets burglarizes houses in this and surrounding counties. But that's all we know."

"What about the truck? The victim's DNA could be in it."

Nick shook his head as he turned onto Main Street. "We'd have to get the sheriff to request a search warrant. Even if he did, we wouldn't be able to prove who dumped the body. Whenever one of them is suspected of a crime, he says it must have been one of his brothers. Eye-witness testimony doesn't help because they look just alike and vehicle ID's don't help because they live together and claim to drive each other's trucks regularly. They've never even been arrested because there's no way to know which one to arrest."

I racked my brain for a way around this monkey wrench. "So, the only way to catch them is to sort out their fingerprints because DNA is the same in identicals, but fingerprints are different."

His eyes sparked with appreciation. I loved it when he looked at me that way. "That's right," he said. "I'd ask how you knew that, but I'm pretty sure you'd tell me you googled it."

I validated his assumption with a self-satisfied grin, then got back to business. "Everyone seems to know everything about everyone else around here. What's the word on the street about the McGwires?"

"No one knows jack shit about them and don't think that doesn't drive the busy bodies in this town crazy. The triplets made pretty good grades in high school. Of course, some people claim they each specialized in a couple of courses, like math and Science or English and Spanish, and took each other's tests. They didn't participate in sports or clubs. Ate lunch only with each other. Even the girls who dated them aren't sure they were dating the same one the whole time. Both parents were dead by the time they were nineteen, so it's just the three of them living out on their property. They keep the road to the house gated. No trespassing signs everywhere."

"So, bottom line is, the guy driving the truck today is not necessarily the guy who was driving it the night of the murder."

Nick pulled up to the stop light and turned to me, his head tilted. "See, that's the part that never rang true for me. A man's truck is kind of a personal thing. I have trouble believing they don't each want to drive their own."

I narrowed my eyes at him. "You can believe they'll share their girlfriends, but not their trucks?"

"Well, women come and go, but your truck—"

"*Really?*" I shook my head. Men sucked.

"...is something you can count on," he finished quietly as he made the left turn.

I thought about his statement for a moment. From what I'd seen, the women in Nick's life counted on him, to put it nicely. His wives spent his money and kept expecting him to grant them favors, even after they left him. The one interaction I'd witnessed with his mom gave me the impression he was supporting her financially and was still expected to be at her beck and call for manual labor.

Belinda had asked if I'd met his mom. Now maybe I knew

why. It seemed to me that at least two of Nick's wives had been just like her.

"One more thing about the McGwires," Nick said, snapping my mind back to the matter at hand. "No one's ever accused them of anything other than burglary—breaking into homes and businesses when the owners aren't home. That's a far cry from committing murder." He turned onto Zombie Road.

"Are you saying you think, in the middle of the night, a McGwire just happened to be hanging out a few yards from the body?"

"No. I'm saying there's a good chance someone else is involved. Maybe he didn't kill the victim. Maybe he just dumped the body."

I sighed and let my head fall back. "But there's no reason for him to give up the real murderer if he doesn't think he can be convicted of involvement in the crime."

"If we could even figure out who 'he' is." Nick slowed as we passed the scraps of crime scene tape, still stubbornly clinging to the bushes.

There has to be a way. "Do you know a private investigator in Texas who can run the plate?"

"I'm planning to call him first thing in the morning," he said. "Do you have any ideas on how we can use the owner's name once we get it?"

"No." Right now it seemed like the McGwires had covered all their bases. "But it can't hurt to know which one bought and registered it."

"Yeah, that's what I was thinking," Nick said.

We were quiet for the rest of the ride.

Once we got home, Nick made lunch from last night's brisket leftovers. I was hesitant to ingest more bread, but the sight of his tender beef slices brushed with Hickory brown sugar barbecue sauce, nestled in a soft sour dough bun was irresistible. Besides, with all he was doing for me, it would be pretty bitchy to start making dietary demands.

Of course, with no scale in my bathroom, I was convinced I'd been gaining a couple of pounds a day since I got here. Every night before I fell asleep, I pinched the skin at my waist, trying to measure the thickness between my fingers compared to the night before.

Today, after we finished our sandwiches, I went to my room and changed into workout clothes—black sports bra, black tank, gray cotton gym shorts. Once I had my athletic shoes on, I looked in the mirror and was glad to see my old self again.

It had been a while. Way before LeeAnne started styling me, I'd let my relationship with Brandtt push me farther and farther away from my own style.

Although, throughout my adolescence, I'd had no choice but to wear whatever I fit into, once I started losing the weight, I became a t-shirt and jeans kind of girl. When I wanted to crank it up a notch, I'd pull out one of my colorful hippy-ethnic skirts and a peasant top.

My grandma always said I reminded her of my mom when I wore those clothes. I liked it when she said that and was satisfied with my simple, inexpensive wardrobe.

My excuse for letting Brandtt push me into the latest designer fashions was that he worked in the entertainment business. Looking just right was part of his job and, as his supportive girl-friend, it should be part of mine, too. But, now, I was two years older and wiser than when I met Brandtt. If I wasn't forced into an orange jumpsuit after all this was over, I was going to do *me* again.

And I was going to forgive myself for being foolish about Brandtt. My grandmother always said everyone makes mistakes.

It's the people who don't learn from them who deserved to be eaten by the dogs.

That may sound harsh, but she had a really rough childhood that may or may not have involved packs of marauding wild dogs. I was afraid to ask.

By the time I'd tied my shoes, the brisket had settled like a log in my stomach. I'd have to wait a while on the workout. As much as I hated gaining weight, I hated barfing even more. I could never hack it as a bulimic.

Once I located my package of ponytail bands, I slipped one on my wrist and went looking for Nick. If he was going to stuff me like a turkey, the least he could do was entertain me while I waited for my food to go down.

I heard the familiar yapping and found Gucci staring intently at the door to the garage, barking so hard, her tiny front feet left the ground with each syllable. I picked her up and opened it, certain Nick was on the other side.

When I stepped through, my lungs seized and I couldn't seem to get enough oxygen. But it wasn't the muggy Texas air that shut down my respiratory system. It was Nick.

He stood on the bed of his truck in the driveway in the midst of various tools and yard equipment wearing a pair of dark Levis, well-worn cowboy boots, a cowboy hat and...

Gulp.

No shirt.

His golf shirts and t-shirts had not done him justice. Without the coverings, his torso radiated power and his shoulders seemed even broader.

And when he lifted items from the truck bed—be still my hammering, oxygen-deprived heart—his pecs flexed with every movement.

Holy mother of Zeus!

Nick had what I referred to as a full-blown *man-rack*, not to be confused with man boobs, since a man-rack was one hundred percent muscle. I wanted to climb up into the truck and press my palms against that steely rack.

Finally, I peeled my eyes from his chest—intending to stop objectifying him—but my eyes slid down to his six pack...

He bent to rearrange some items and when he stood again, his jeans inched down.

Make that an eight pack.

I'd thought the gym at his house was a little much in a private residence, but, clearly, it was worth every penny.

Lightheaded, I was in danger of passing out and crushing poor little Gucci under my Nick-crazed body. I forced myself to breathe, but did it quietly so as not to alert him to my peeping.

This might be creeper behavior, but I needed to ogle him just a little bit longer. I felt like a chest virgin, as if I'd never seen a shirtless man in real life before.

Brandtt had worked out at least a couple of times a week and was always aware of his food intake. He couldn't quite decide if he was vegetarian or paleo or low-carb, depending on what his actor friends were into that month. But, next to Nick, Brandtt would look protein-deprived.

Nick was...

Nick was a *man*.

One thought emerged in my brain, its font popping bigger and bigger until it crowded out every other thought, every other feeling I'd had previously toward Nick.

I want that. *I want that. I Want That...*

I. WANT. THAT.

I wanted to place my palms on his damp pecs and slide my tongue over those incredible abs and unbutton his jeans with my teeth.

The fantasy threatened to fall apart at that point because I had no reason to believe my mouth was talented enough to undress a man. I always felt a little clumsy with Brandtt and usually had to give up and let him unbutton his own jeans, and that was when I was using my fingers. I'd never even had the urge to try it with my teeth.

I rebooted and imagined Nick flipping the button loose just before I pulled the zipper down with my teeth.

Yeah.

I could feel the sweat emerging from the pores on my torso under my shirt, on my forehead, on the skin where my thighs were pressed against each other... I didn't care if he was sweaty or I was sweaty as long as we made more sweat together.

My eyes fell closed as fantasy Nick whipped my t-shirt off and pressed his slick body against mine.

Oh. Yeah.

"Yap. Yap-yap!"

My eyes flew open.

Apparently, when she realized I wasn't moving her closer to her human, Gucci decided to get his attention herself. She totally sucked as a fantasy wing woman. I set her down on the concrete and she pitter-pattered to the truck as fast as her tiny legs would carry her.

Nick looked up from his work and smiled at me. The picture shirtless, smiling Nick made was so beautiful, my lungs shuddered.

"Sorry," Nick said. "Was she bothering you in there? I was afraid to bring her out. She tends to get underfoot."

"It's okay. I'll watch her." I was glad for an excuse to stay out here with half-naked Nick.

He picked up a huge, tightly wound garden hose and laid it on his forearm. Every muscle in his arms flexed with the exertion.

I leaned against the doorframe for support, now aware of every nook and cranny on my body.

"I've been meaning to take this extra-long hose to my mom's," Nick said as he laid it next to the leaf-blower. "I don't need two of them." My eyes darted to the fly of his Levis as I wondered where he kept the other one.

Jeez, say something, nerdo. "That's a lot of stuff you've got in there."

Hey, I didn't say it had to be brilliant.

"Yeah, once mom gets me over to her place, I never know what she'll come up with for me to do."

He looked like he was about finished up, so I walked over and picked up Gucci, who'd been staring worshipfully at him from just behind the truck. But who could blame her?

He hopped off the tailgate and lifted it, locking it into place. When he turned around, his eyes trailed leisurely down my body to my sneakers, then back up again until he met my gaze.

"You look..." I could see him considering and discarding several words. Unfortunately, I couldn't see what those words were. "Normal," he finally finished.

Normal? What did that mean? Had he noticed my weight gain? He'd described me as a "hot chick" a few days ago. Now I'd deteriorated to *normal*?

"Normal," I repeated involuntarily.

"Yeah, you've been wearing other people's clothes since you got here. LeeAnne's wardrobe is..." He shook his head as if he found her fashion choices unfathomable.

I was relieved he was just talking about the clothes. "Are hers any worse than the cyclops cat scrubs the sheriff gave me?"

He tilted his head as if recalling me in my jailhouse attire. "Lucky for you, you look good in anything."

The sentence wrapped around my heart and squeezed so hard my chest ached. For so many years, I'd desperately wanted to look good in *something*. And now I didn't care if anyone else thought that statement was true, as long as Nick believed it.

Calm. Down.

I pressed Gucci tight against my chest as I tried to steer myself back to reality.

That was probably an offhand remark Nick had made to

dozens of women—the three he'd married certainly, and a bunch of others I didn't even know about.

"Do you want to go over to mom's with me?" he asked.

Did I? I really needed to work out, but I hated the idea of being so far from Nick's chest—I mean, Nick—for several hours.

When I didn't answer right away, he said, "Probably a bad idea. My mom would talk your ear off, and you'd be bored and—"

"I'll go." I was suddenly desperate not to be left behind. "I'll go with you."

"Okay. I just need to put a shirt on."

The word *nooo* nearly escaped from my mouth before I caught it.

"I learned my lesson the last time I went to her house." He opened the door and kept talking so I followed him down the hall. "I wore a short-sleeved shirt because I was just supposed to spray a couple of wasps' nests, and I came back with my arms all scratched up from trimming her tree limbs."

When I got to the doorway of his bedroom, I wasn't sure what to do, but he was still talking as he walked into his master bath, so Gucci and I stepped into his room. Wow. I'd never been in a bedroom with such high vaulted ceilings.

And the flat dark wood headboard rose at least twelve feet from the floor to the place the ceiling would have been if it wasn't vaulted. Near the top of the headboard were built-in lights that cast a very soft glow over the bed. Much lower, were built-in his and hers reading lamps. The bed was arranged on the diagonal, which kept the room from looking too mammoth to be cozy. The other dressers and shelves were all made from wood, designed in the same minimalist style.

It was hard to understand why Nick would want to leave a gorgeous place like this. In here, I could almost forget about Bolo completely. Of course, it was possible one of his wives decorated the place.

Stupid wives.

I saw the "bleh" face I was making in the mirror of the dresser. It was not pretty.

"My mom doesn't have much of a filter..." Nick was saying from the bathroom. I heard water running and imagined him splashing it on his face, his neck, and his steaming hot torso.

Maybe he's the one who needs the SIZZLIN shirt.

"And she's not the most..." I strained, waiting for him to finish the sentence, but he didn't seem to know how. "Just don't take anything she says too seriously." He chuckled as he came out of the bathroom, toweling himself off. He grabbed a light blue denim shirt from the closet and pulled it onto his shoulders.

Sigh. He should walk around in unbuttoned denim shirts all the time.

"And don't believe anything she tells you about me."

She? Oh, yeah, we were talking about his mom.

"What?" I smiled mischievously at him. "That's the whole reason I'm going!"

He chuckled. I whispered a silent goodbye to each beautiful muscle as he buttoned his shirt. For one crazy moment, I wondered what he'd do if I stepped over to him and pressed my lips to his. But never in a million years would I have the courage to find out.

"What should I do with Gucci? " I asked instead.

"Bring her with us," he replied. "Mom gets a kick out of her."

We walked toward the front door, but Nick halted suddenly and pulled out his phone.

"I've got an email." He tapped a couple of times, then peered intently at the screen. "The victim's name is Avery Cook. Have you ever heard of him?"

"No." I shook my head for emphasis. "Is he from around here?"

Nick scrolled down as I tried to get a look at the email. "Not from around here. From Dumas. It's a town way up in the Texas panhandle. At least ten hours away."

I blew out a relieved breath. "Thank God he's not from New York or California."

"Yeah." Nick frowned at the phone. I was sorry he'd gotten the email today. Life had felt so pleasant for a couple of hours. It had seemed normal for us to be living in this house together. He'd looked carefree and happy.

But now, he'd been reminded of the real reason I was lurking around him and it had sucked the enjoyment right out of him.

Jeez, why was I always worried about his feelings when I was the one up on murder charges?

Still, I touched my fingertips to the wrist of his free hand. "Not today, Nick," I said. "Let's just go." I smiled hopefully.

Although his lips didn't turn up, his eyes smiled back at me. His wrist turned over. His fingers grasped my hand. Then, his thumb rubbed back and forth on my skin as he stared down at it.

Confused, I peered down at my hand to see what he was trying to rub off.

Nothing. I checked his expression. *Intense.*

Was he comforting me back? Or was this something more? Whatever it was, it was sending rogue tingles up my arm. I put all my concentration into keeping them from crossing the shoulder barrier because if that happened my body would fall into a tingly, tumbling free for all.

He frowned at his thumb and released me.

"Yeah," he said. "Let's go."

CHAPTER FIFTEEN

Rika

A couple of hours later, I was sitting on Nick's mother's deck thinking I'd already learned a lot about Tammy Lynn Owen, despite only spending a few minutes with her.

Nick had stopped by Juanita's house—which doubled as a plant nursery—on the way to his mom's house. However, she'd picked out so many potted plants, shrubs and trees, not to mention the sod and four—*yes, four*—fancy birdbaths, that we had to make a second trip.

He didn't seem surprised when she hadn't paid for any of it and simply wrote out a check and loaded everything onto the truck.

Once we made it back and Tammy Lynn had a glass of iced tea in my hand, she couldn't wait to show me all her son had done for her.

"I didn't want one of those square decks," she said as we walked out the back door. "Everybody has square decks." Her eyes drifted to the deck's edges which curved in a perfect semi-circle. To achieve this effect, Nick had to cut the boards with precision, each a little smaller than the one before it.

"And we couldn't find pre-made Roman pillars that matched the ones on the front of the house perfectly, so Nick had to make these for me, too."

I examined the pillars that were holding up the roof on the covered half of the deck. Swoopy designs were carved into the tops and bottoms. I was no wood-working expert, but they looked like a real pain in the ass to make. I nearly pointed out that no one would ever be able to examine her front and back pillars side-by-side, but the work had already been done, and I didn't think she'd appreciate the observation.

She gestured toward the white decorative fence that curved around the sunny half of the deck you could step down to from the covered half. "He even made the mini versions for the railing."

Sure enough, after every four slats was a mini Roman pillar, carved just like the big ones.

"Of course, I designed the whole thing."

"Of course." I gave her the best smile I could, considering what I was thinking. She really seemed to take advantage of Nick. But maybe he enjoyed all this physical labor. Like a hobby or something.

I watched as he set a giant pot containing a new bush on the ground near the edge of the yard, then came back a few seconds later with a shovel. He stared at the old shrubbery for a moment and pointed the shovel into the ground. When it didn't sink in, he propped his boot on it and forced it into the dry earth. The back of his shirt was already blotched with sweat.

He didn't look like he was enjoying himself one bit, unlike his mother, who was smiling as she looked on.

The more I watched him slaving in the ninety-bujillion degree heat, the more I wanted to rescue him. Bring him into the shade. Take off his shirt—for *his* comfort of course—and give him my iced tea.

"He's such a good son," Tammy Lynn said.

"He sure is," I replied, trying to keep the annoyance out of my voice. On the other hand, if toiling in the hot sun would have gotten me my mother back, I'd gladly have done it. Every fucking day. But I couldn't imagine her requiring it of me.

"His daddy died when he was ten." Her smile faded. "He's been my big man ever since. He's taken real good care of his sister and me."

Was his mom saying that when her husband died she'd expected her ten-year-old son to take responsibility for her—a *grown* woman—and his little sister?

I felt sick to my stomach. I hadn't realized Nick had lost a parent so young. It did grow you up faster in a lot of ways, but, at least I was still allowed to be a kid. I wished I could run over to Nick and throw my arms around his sweaty body.

"Gucci, Gucci, goo!" Tammy Lynn snapped her fingers as Gucci ran to her, looking up at her expectantly. Tammy Lynn broke off a piece of cookie from a plate on the patio table. She held it in the air over Gucci's head as the tiny dog twirled round and round on her hind legs. When she lowered the treat, Gucci snatched it and ran away to enjoy her cookie in private.

"Where is it you're from?" Tammy Lynn's full attention was suddenly on me. My skin prickled with discomfort.

"Los Angeles," I said.

"No..." She shook her head. "Where are your people from? Mexico?"

"My mom's parents and my dad all came from Colombia."

She tilted her head and blinked at me, her interested, yet bewildered, expression reminding me of the one Gucci usually wore. "I guess I've never met anyone from Washington D.C. before."

Now I was the one confused. I stared into her wide eyes until I puzzled out her meaning. "Not *District of Columbia*." I tried not to sound condescending. "Colombia."

"Oh... Is that in Mexico?"

Was she kidding me? "It's in South America."

"But we're in South America."

I waited for a punch line. Nick had a good sense of humor, after all, but his mother's expression was serenely serious.

"No, we're in *North* America."

She threw her head back and cackled like I'd just said the funniest thing ever. "Honey, I don't know what maps you've been looking at, but Texas is about as south as it gets in America."

Wow. Although Nick appeared to have inherited his mother's eyes, he had to have gotten his IQ from his dad. I wondered if men who married trophy wives ever considered the fact that they were playing genetic Russian roulette with their future offspring's intelligence.

Normally, I wouldn't have left it at that, but I just didn't see how I could educate Tammy Lynn on the entire Western Hemisphere in one afternoon.

In lieu of response, I sipped more iced tea.

After a few awkward moments, she patted my hand. "Don't worry, sweetie, I used to be bad with geology, too."

I swallowed my tea the wrong way and went into a coughing fit. After patting my back, Tammy Lynn brightened and asked, "So, did your parents teach you to speak Colombian?"

Uh... Maybe there was a reason ten-year-old Nick had to take care of his mother. But I still didn't want to embarrass Nick's mom by telling her there was no such language as Colombian. Not because I wanted to be friends with Tammy Lynn, but because a part of me hoped we'd be in each other's lives...

I shook the crazy thought out of my mind.

"Yeah," I replied. "I speak a little." Liar's guilt wedged at the bottom of my throat. Was it right to knowingly leave an ignorant person ignorant? I washed the lump down with a gulp of iced tea. "Nick sure is working hard," I said, hoping to move the conversation away from me.

She gazed out at her son as he transferred a bush from the pot to the hole he'd made for it. "He's such a good boy." She shook her head. "Shame he's not married."

Here was my chance to get the four-one-one on Nick's love life. "But he was, right?" I attempted a facial expression that combined mildly curious with sympathetic.

"Yes, and I don't understand what happened." Tammy Lynn sipped her tea thoughtfully. "The last two seemed perfect for him. They were both pageant girls like me." She turned her head and tilted it just so, like she was demonstrating her pageant pose. "I can always tell a pageant girl right off the bat. They have a certain poise and sophistication."

And the hair. Don't forget the hair.

I nearly chuckled at my secret thoughts until I realized I had neither poise nor sophistication, and Nick's mom had probably decided I wasn't pageant-slash-Nick material "right off the bat."

"Either of them made a perfect daughter-in-law."

Did she mean perfect *trophy* daughter-in-law?

"I'll never understand why they didn't work out."

Maybe because they were selfish whores? Or was I just jealous because they'd gotten to jump right into Nick's arms while our relationship was strictly look but don't touch. I considered the options for a moment.

No, they were definitely selfish whores.

"And the first wife?" I held my breath, hoping I didn't hear LeeAnne's name. She was my friend and I didn't want to have to imagine her with Nick.

"*Her?*" Tammy Lynn swiped her hand through the air like she was swatting at a fly. "Trash."

I cringed as my mind scanned through LeeAnne's tacky wardrobe.

"They were barely eighteen," Tammy Lynn continued. "She told Nick she was pregnant and he insisted on doing the right thing. I didn't trust her for a second. I told him to ask for a paternity test, but he believed every word she said."

"So, it wasn't his baby?" I wondered how long Nick had raised the kid before finding out it wasn't his.

"What baby? They got married and poof!" She spread her fingers in the air. "No baby!"

A lie that big would explain why Nick was so annoyed by LeeAnne.

I took a deep breath for courage. "Does she still live around here?"

"No, thank the Lord. She took off after high school. Haven't seen her since."

So LeeAnne and Nick hadn't married each other. I let my breath out all at once and Tammy Lynn gave me a strange look. *But they could still be ex-lovers.*

Damn. There was no guarantee Nick's mom would even know about that.

I wanted to stay on this topic, but Nick was coming our way drenched in perspiration.

Wow. I'd never seen a man who could wear sweat like Nick Owen could. I watched a drop trickle down his neck onto his collar bone and disappear into the V of his shirt. I wished I could follow it down.

As he climbed the steps, he removed his hat and swiped at his forehead with his sleeve. "I could use some of that iced tea," he said.

"Sure thing, Sweetie." Tammy Lynn stood. "I'll getcha some."

As soon as she disappeared through the door, Nick propped a foot on the top step and leaned in, his hand resting on his thigh.

"Here's the deal," he said. "After you see me plant one more bush and set out the bird baths, you're gonna get a migraine or have female problems or whatever will require you to go home."

"To L.A.?" I teased.

"Look..." He swiped at his forehead again. "If you don't get me out of here soon, I'm going to have a heat stroke, and it's fifty miles to the nearest emergency room. I'll come finish in the morning when it's not pushing a hundred degrees."

Nick's relationship with his mom was pretty strange. I'd heard of mamas' boys, but they were usually living in their moms' basements, mooching dinners, and getting their moms to do their laundry. This was the complete opposite.

"Can't you just say you need to leave?" I asked.

"Not without a lot of sighing and guilt-tripping," Nick replied. "She's not a bad person, but she hasn't done a minute of manual labor in her whole life. She's just...clueless."

Or a complete narcissist. But I figured you couldn't tell a guy that about his mom.

"Sure, Nick," I replied. "I've got your back."

And any other part of your anatomy you want me to take possession of, my body whispered. Luckily, my brain was still in control of my lips.

He smiled as his incredible eyes shone with something that looked very much like affection.

And that was all the reward I needed.

CHAPTER SIXTEEN

Rika

I was glad weeknights were slow at work. In the days since we found the truck and learned the name of the victim, I'd been having trouble remembering the simplest orders, the only kind there were at Barr's.

So far, the only new information we'd obtained was that JimBob McGwire had both purchased and registered the red Dodge Ram. Supposedly, the sheriff was looking into the victim's activities, but we already knew he couldn't be trusted, so Nick contacted a private investigator to be sure we learned everything we could.

Meanwhile, I had no idea what to hope for. If Avery had a record of involvement with drug or gun running or human trafficking, it would fit right into the Grey Widow scenario. If he had no criminal record, I wasn't sure where that left me.

Would J.J. Boyle claim I picked him up as a hitchhiker on my way through Texas and murdered him? What would my motive be? Perhaps, scorned by Brandtt, I was retaliating against men in general.

Maybe there were a few more unsolved man murders

between here and New York they could pin on me. I made a mental note to have Nick request to examine my old phone if necessary. Maybe there was a way to use my navigation app to prove my route from New York didn't take me through the Texas panhandle.

I came to, unsure how long I'd been standing in the middle of the bar, staring blankly at the neon Miller Lite sign on the wall. LeeAnne was in her office, which made me the lone waitress at the moment. I hustled to the game room, where the only two customers were playing pool.

"Another round?" I asked as I collected empty bottles.

"Sure, sweet *thang*," the taller one drawled. The mustachioed forty-something man was kind of ruggedly handsome in a smoked-too-much-drank-too-much Marlboro Man sort of way. But when he'd walked in, I noticed his cowboy hat didn't have the same effect on me as Nick's did.

His bald, pot-bellied friend, not wanting to be left out of this threesome, took a step toward me. He pointed his cue stick at my chest. "I like your shirt." He wiggled his shaggy eyebrows up and down.

"Thanks." I lifted the stick away with one finger and scooted out of the room. The last thing I wanted was to be reminded of my attire for the evening. The top read, "You bring the Crisco. I'll bring the HEAT!" The shorts were embroidered with "Hot, Fresh" on one back pocket and "Buns" on the other.

I sighed and summoned my burka force field.

When I walked back into the main room, Reverend Jenkins was coming through the door. He was wearing slacks and a polo shirt, no jacket, and should have looked more relaxed than he did all suited up on Sunday.

He didn't.

"Here for dinner?" I asked.

"No, I'm, um, meeting someone." He lifted the Bible he held as if that told me all I needed to know. Moving past me to the game room, he glanced around, then came back and sat in the corner booth at the back.

Since he hadn't answered me about dinner, I wasn't sure if I should follow him and try to take an order or leave him alone.

But maybe this shouldn't be about him. Maybe this was my chance to pump him for information about his parishioners. Perhaps if he knew who the killer was, he'd at least drop me a hint.

I sauntered over to the table, super casually. "Can I get you something to drink while you wait?"

He glanced up, but didn't make eye contact. Did that mean he knew something and felt guilty that he couldn't tell me?

"I don't drink," he said.

"Everyone has to drink something," I replied jovially. "Otherwise, we'd shrivel up like raisins. Iced tea? Water?"

"A glass of water would be fine." He sounded like he was just trying to appease me. But my eyes caught on the open Bible he held tilted up on the edge of the table. The words "Holy Bible" were currently upside-down.

What does it mean when a minister comes to a restaurant-bar, doesn't want to order anything, and pretends to read his Bible?

Hm.

When I returned with his water, I said, "I guess you've got the inside scoop on what's happening around here with all the confessions you must listen to."

"You must be Catholic," he said as if he didn't approve. His eyes remained on the pages of his inverted Bible. "Protestants don't need an intermediary. We have a direct line."

Since he wasn't looking at me, I tilted my head side to side as I repeated his words in a childish voice in my mind.

I hadn't sat through a mass since I moved out of my grandmother's house, but, still, his holier-than-thou attitude rubbed me the wrong way.

"Oh, like Pagans and Wiccans!" I said fake-amicably. "Don't they deal directly with their gods or whatever?" Personally, I had little knowledge of, and nothing against Pagans or Wiccans, but I figured he wouldn't appreciate the comparison.

I was right. His gaze jumped up to meet mine for the first time. Stoney charcoal irises ringed in red, where the whites should have been.

I couldn't look away as the icicle of fear slipped down my spine. Surely a killer's eyes were no more sinister than his.

The door squeaked and I was released from Reverend Jenkins' ghoulish gaze. A beefy gray-haired man entered wearing a white t-shirt under denim overalls, a red ball cap and bright red Nikes.

The only people I'd seen dressed like this in the past were toddlers. Seeing a six-and-a-half-foot man in an OshKosh B'Gosh style ensemble made my brain twitch.

He headed straight toward us, ordered a draft beer from me and sat down across from the minister. By the time I served him and got back behind the bar, LeeAnne had emerged.

"Hmph. That's interesting," she murmured.

I leaned in closer. "Who is that with the reverend?"

"Grady Fitz. Officially, he's a farmer. Has land a few miles out of town."

"And unofficially?"

"Bookie. Loan shark. And he does some moonshining on the side, but that's mostly a hobby. His parents migrated here from Kentucky. Says he doesn't want to lose the 'culture of his people'."

I laughed. "So, what do you think he's doing with the minister? Turning over a new leaf?"

"Not likely. Reverend Jenkins has a gambling problem." She shrugged and dipped her head to one side. "Which probably means he's short on cash, so he could be placing a bet, borrowing money, or both."

"Why meet in a public place?"

"Around here, wherever you go, somebody's going to catch you together or see your car going down a certain road you have no reason to be going down. This way, he can pretend he's counseling Grady."

I remembered what Nick said about rumors in this town. "You don't think Grady could actually be in the market for spiritual guidance?"

"Do I look like I just fell off a turnip truck into a cabbage patch yesterday?"

Taking a page from LeeAnne's book, I grabbed a bar towel and pretended to wipe down the already clean counter while stealing glances at the back booth. Five minutes later, a thick envelope appeared on the table, although I didn't see who put it there.

"Sweet thang?"

Dammit. I hustled to the game room, took an order for onion rings and cheese balls and rushed back, only to find the envelope gone. But, either way, Reverend Jenkins was up to no good. Could his money problems be bad enough to pull him deeper into a life of crime? Would he kill to keep his secrets?

I remembered his cold gaze. Out of everyone I'd met in this town, he was the one I'd be most afraid to meet in a dark alley.

Once the exchange took place, Grady paid for his beer and left. The reverend followed a few minutes later. I felt like I'd missed an opportunity, but I guess it was naive to think one or two criminals were responsible for all the gambling, loan sharking, *and* murders around here.

I made a sweep through the game room. My customers were ready for Sweet Thang to bring them their check. I headed back to the main room to total it up, but my feet stopped almost before my brain fully processed what I saw a few yards in front of me.

Bright orange hair. Thin freckled face. Long lanky body sitting on a bar stool.

A McGwire.

My eyes dipped to his hands as his fingers drummed impatiently on the counter.

No way could I get this lucky. I instructed my feet to play it cool and keep walking. Making a beeline for the front door, I stepped out and scanned the parking lot.

Dwight's red Toyota pickup.

LeeAnne's Trans Am.

Nick's black One-fifty—he'd outmaneuvered me by hiding the keys to the Ranger.

A silver king cab pickup with an "If you ain't country, you ain't shit" bumper sticker on the back window.

Damn. Maybe it's the wrong brother.

But, even if the pool players came together, there should be one more vehicle. I stepped to the corner of the building and checked the parking spaces around the side.

Ding, ding, ding! The red Dodge Ram was parked haphazardly on top of a line, taking up two spaces, not that it mattered at Barr's.

I jogged over to it and tried the handle on the driver's side.

Locked.

The passenger's side was locked, too.

I peered into the bed of the truck. Nothing suspicious. Just a bunch of empty beer and soft drink cans.

But I had the body-dumping vehicle right here in front of me and the possible murderer sitting inside. There had to be something I could do.

I considered what Nick had said about a man's truck being a personal thing. The only set of multiples I'd known fairly well were the identical twins at my junior high. They were inseparable, yet, I witnessed two different screaming fights between them, both over one twin borrowing the other's sparkly blue hair Scrunchie.

Everyone needs something that's all their own, I guess.

As my brain assembled the next steps of my plan, I dashed in the back door of the building.

"Dwight, where are the garbage bags?" I asked.

"Storage room, bottom shelf." He paused only a moment to answer, then went back to washing dishes. I was surprised he didn't ask why I needed a garbage bag when the current one wasn't full or why I was coming in the back door. But this was Dwight I was dealing with and he lived in his own world most of the time.

I found a trash bag and a pair of rubber gloves, pulling them on as I hurried out to the truck. After climbing into the bed, I started shoving the cans into the trash bag as fast as I could while checking over my shoulder in case the triplet decided to leave suddenly.

When I was done, I went inside through the back door and hustled the bag into LeeAnne's office. After removing the gloves, I sauntered back behind the bar, surreptitiously swiping at the perspiration on my forehead.

McGwire was still on his stool, taking a pull off the bottle of beer LeeAnne must have served him.

"LeeAnne?" I said casually.

When she turned, I tilted my head toward the kitchen. She followed me through it to the storage room. "What's up?"

"The guy at the bar. He drove the red truck here—the one I saw at the scene on the night of the murder."

"Oh, my God!" she said, her eyes wide.

"I need your help."

"Sure. Anything."

"Do you know who he is?"

"One of the McGwire triplets. Nobody knows who's who, so, if we ever see them, we just call them 'Mac.'"

"Do you think he knows who I am?"

"Hard to say. The triplets mostly keep to themselves. They don't seem to trade gossip with anyone in town." She made a face that told me not trading gossip was a character flaw in her book. "They don't even speak to other people at church, except for 'hi' and 'fine'."

Hm...I needed to get inside that truck one way or another. "Do you think he'd find me attractive?" I asked doubtfully.

LeeAnne chuckled. "He's a man, isn't he? Don't you ever look in a damn mirror?"

I wished it was as simple as that.

"Besides," she said. "You're wearing any man's two favorite things." She formed a shelf with her hand and held it under my breasts as if they were on display.

"Okay," I said. "The guys in the back room need their check. If you can take care of that, I'm going to offer McGwire some free shots. You can take them out of my pay. When I get him to leave the building with me, can you grab his bottle and anything else he touches and put them in a plastic bag?"

"Fingerprints?" Her blue eyes sparkled with excitement. "Anything else I can do?"

"I don't know yet. I'm going to see if I can get him talking about himself and get into his truck to look for evidence."

That reminded me I'd need something to put the evidence in. I glanced around, then pulled a gallon-sized Ziploc out of its box.

After trying to fit it into the tiny front pocket of LeeAnne's shorts, I gave up and stuffed it in the back between my shorts and underwear.

"Does it show?"

LeeAnne examined my ass, stuck her hand down my pants, and smoothed out the wrinkles in the plastic. At that moment, Dwight walked in. I tensed, wondering how we would explain LeeAnne's hand down my pants. I wasn't sure I trusted him with the truth.

He strode past us, picked up a bottle of bleach from a shelf on the back wall and went back to the kitchen, seemingly unaware of our presence.

"There ya go," LeeAnne said. "Can't tell a thing." She came around front, hiked my bra straps up and tugged the neckline of my shirt down, exposing as much cleavage as possible. She stepped back. "A couple of margaritas and I'd do you myself."

After giving her a *wish me luck* look, I took a deep breath and went back through the kitchen, smiling widely as I approached McGwire.

"Can I get you another one?" I asked seductively, I hoped. I leaned on my forearms directly in front of him, since I had more faith in LeeAnne's push-up bra than I did my own seduction skills.

His gaze caught on my cleavage for a full three seconds before moving to my eyes. "I haven't seen you around here."

"I could say the same," I replied with a head tilt I hoped read as flirtatious. I should have practiced in the mirror before I came out here. I had zero practice at flirting.

"Yeah." One side of his mouth curved upward. "I guess it's been a while since I was in here." He dangled his bottle, tipping it back and forth to show me it was empty.

I got him another, twisted the cap off and placed it on a cardboard coaster.

"Thanks," he said before taking a swig.

Swallowing the last remaining saliva in my mouth, I gave him the fake-sly grin a girl at my high school always used on the guys. She was voted Football Sweetheart by the team, so I figured she knew what she was doing.

I leaned on the counter again. "Can I tell you something?" I glanced around like I was about to impart top-secret information.

"You can tell me anything, baby."

I squelched the urge to ask him not to call me "baby," and stayed on task. "I have a thing for red-headed guys," I whispered. "Practically a fetish."

"Is that so?" His chest puffed out as a Cheshire Cat grin spread across his face.

This was actually working! Clearly the authorities hadn't used the right tactics against these McGwire boys in the past. All they needed to do was ply them with alcohol and borrow one of LeeAnne's push-up bras.

An unwanted image burst into my brain—Sheriff Strickland in a push-up bra and low-cut t-shirt.

I threw up a little in my mouth.

Focus, Paprika!

"Yeah, I think it's a Viking thing." I trailed my finger down the neck of McGwire's bottle. "Vikings are hot."

By the look in his eyes, I was afraid I'd played that card too soon. He was about to suggest we get out of here.

Rookie mistake.

"Can I buy you a shot?" I asked before he could say anything.

"Sure!"

Who didn't want a free shot? Except me, of course. I couldn't handle more than one glass of wine. The one and only time Brandtt talked me into a shot, I spent a half hour in the ladies' room hurling my guts out.

Several shots later, McGwire's eyes were glassy and he'd grown a lot more talkative. Unfortunately, he'd been talking about hunting for the last half hour and my beginner acting skills were being taxed to their limits as I tried to look like I cared how many "points" the last buck he killed had on its antlers. How was I going to turn this conversation in the right direction?

A plop sounded, prompting McGwire to pull his phone from his pocket. "My stupid brother," he slurred. He tried to roll his eyes, but found it too difficult to lift his lids that high. "Thinks 'cause he's five minutes older than me, he gets to keep tabs."

This could be my chance. As he typed a slow reply, I pretended to check my phone, but turned the voice recorder app on instead.

"I know what you mean." I set the phone on the counter. "My sister's a real pain. Bosses me around and takes my clothes without asking." This was a complete fabrication. I was an only child. But how would a criminal from Bolo, Texas know that? I poured him another shot. "She even took off with my car once and didn't bring it back for a couple of days. Do your brothers do that to you?"

"Huh!" He lifted his chin defiantly. "They wouldn't dare. I mean, we have each other's backs and all, but they know I'd beat the shit out of them if they ever laid a hand on Missy."

Oh, great. He'd clearly lost track of what we were talking about. "Missy?" I repeated, trying to banish the annoyance from my tone.

"My pickup. She's a Dodge Ram SRT-10." So, Nick was right. They didn't drive each other's trucks. I now had a McGwire on tape identifying his truck and claiming he was the only driver. But I was missing one key piece of information.

"You sound like a badass," I said. "I have a thing for bad boys."

"And redheads," he reminded me, punctuating the phrase with a burp.

I tried not to wrinkle my nose at the recycled beer odor permeating the air between us. I dipped my chin coquettishly and leaned in closer. "I heard LeeAnne call you 'Mac.' Is that short for something else?"

He waved his hand around as if dismissing the name I'd just said. Before I knew what was happening, he grabbed my fingers, pulling me toward him until his lips rested against my ear.

"JimBob," he murmured. "That's the name you'll be screaming when I stick my—"

I pulled back and faked a giggle, not wanting to hear the rest of that sentence. A shiver of revulsion skittered down my back at the thought of bumping boots with him. And not in a million years could I imagine yelling "Oh, *JimBob!*" in the heat of passion.

Wait. The recorder couldn't have picked up his name. He'd spoken too quietly. LeeAnne could testify that he came in and that she collected the fingerprints, but I still needed him to say his name out loud.

"So, your name's JayBob?" I asked innocently.

His brows jerked together, forming two deep furrows. "Jim-Bob!" he yelled. "Are you deaf?"

"Sorry," I said, widening my eyes vacantly. "I didn't mean to make you so mad... *JimBob.*" I murmured his name in the huskiest voice I could muster.

He waved his hand around like he was swatting mosquitos. "As long as you get it right when it counts, baby."

I realized he hadn't bothered to ask my name all night, but I'd heard a name wasn't necessarily a sexual prerequisite for men.

JimBob threw some cash on the counter. "Let's get out of here."

Fear-tinged adrenaline streaked up my spine. This was my big chance.

Big chance to get murdered.

But I pictured myself behind bars, and my courage returned. "Okay. Just let me tell the boss." I went to the other end of the bar, where LeeAnne had been wiping and watching.

"What's happening?" she asked excitedly.

"Bag the bottle and glasses like we talked about. When we get to his truck, I'm going to send him back in for my purse so I can search the cab."

"You don't have a purse here."

"Just stall him for a while, then tell him you can't find it."

"Okay..." She pressed her lips together and glanced behind me at JimBob. "You be careful."

I nodded, took in a deep breath, turned and smiled broadly at JimBob. "Let's go!" I said.

CHAPTER SEVENTEEN

Rika

When JimBob pulled the door open, I was glad to see the moon was nearly full. Barr's had no parking lot lights. Only one small bulb on each side of the building under the eaves.

In my rush to get the cans earlier, I hadn't noticed the outdoor illumination one way or the other. However, working inside the cab of the truck would be more difficult. At least with the moonlight, I wouldn't have to do it in pitch dark.

As soon as we were out the door, JimBob flopped his lanky arm around me. My shoulder groaned at the impact. His body appeared so scrawny compared to his height. I hadn't expected his limbs to be so heavy.

Tendrils of fear uncoiled inside me as I considered how much bigger and stronger than me he actually was. And a guy who would commit murder—or even dump a body for a murderer—didn't have a lot of scruples.

He staggered and tilted my way, causing me to stumble under his weight before we regained our footing. I'd succeeded in getting him really drunk, which had worked great for extracting information. But now that we were alone, would it make him more pliable or more dangerous?

"Here she is!" He stretched his arm out toward his truck with the finesse of a tipsy game show model. "Missy." He whispered her name worshipfully.

"She's beautiful," I replied as he fished clumsily in his pocket. He finally retrieved his keys, lifting them triumphantly over his head as he hit the remote, unlocking the doors.

"Score!" I said.

"Okay, I will." He propped his hands on the cab, trapping me against the truck.

Oh, God. If he kissed me, I didn't think I could keep from throwing up a little in *his* mouth. I flipped around and pretended I was trying to get the passenger door open.

He made the best of it, kissing the back of my neck, which, luckily, was covered by my hair, so I couldn't actually feel his lips on my bare skin. His palm cupped my ass, fingers squeezing.

Was that the crinkle of a Ziploc bag I heard? I had to do something before he discovered I was packing plastic.

"Oh, damn!" I cried, the falseness of my voice ringing in my ears.

Please be too drunk to notice.

"What is it?" he asked as I turned to face him.

"I left my purse inside. Could you go and get it for me?"

"Nah." When he shook his head, the muscles in his neck were so loose, it looked like his noggin might just flop off and roll away. "You can get it after." Apparently, we were supposed to do the deed right here in the parking lot.

"But I have something special in there."

"What?"

What, indeed? What could be worth the trip for him?

Condoms? He might say he had some in his truck.

Handcuffs? He was a criminal. He might have an aversion.

An oatmeal cookie? No, I was the one having anxiety induced carb cravings right now.

"It's a surprise." I crossed my fingers behind me for luck.

He glanced at the building. "But it's all the way across the parking lot." He sounded like a small child who didn't want to clean his room.

"Not far for a big Viking warrior." I batted my eyelashes so desperately my lids hurt. "I'll wait in the truck."

Turning toward Barr's he thrust a fist into the air as if holding an imaginary sword. "Argh!" he said as he walked away.

Was he confusing Vikings and pirates? I shook my head, jumped into the cab and watched until he disappeared around the corner of the building.

As I tugged the Ziploc out of my shorts, I realized I didn't have any gloves. Maybe I wasn't so good at scheming on the fly.

My eyes caught on a small plastic Dill's Dollar Store bag that had been abandoned on the floorboard. I grabbed the end of it and flopped it inside out over my right hand.

Instant glove!

Sliding to the driver's side, I flipped the sun visor down. Several pieces of paper were filed in the elastic band. I pulled them out and put them into the Ziploc.

Next, I opened the console between the seats. JimBob seemed to be using it as a trash receptacle. I found store receipts, junk mail, and an empty can of chewing tobacco. *Yuck.*

Otherwise, the truck cab was disappointingly clean. The glove compartment held only an owner's manual and an insurance card. I left them where they were.

I glanced back toward the bar. The coast was still clear. Whatever LeeAnne was doing to keep him in there was working, but I wasn't sure I needed the extra time. This truck didn't even have a back seat like Nick's did. I flipped around to peer into the space behind the seat.

A baseball bat...and a shotgun.

Fear shuddered through me as I turned forward, trying not to think about the weapons at my back. I ran my hand along the base of the seat next to the door, looking for a way to push the seat back in case some evidence had made its way underneath.

Instead, my fingers brushed against paper, thicker than the receipts were printed on. I pulled it out and held it next to the window.

By the moonlight, I could make out typed lines of random letters—like part of a word search—that had been doodled and scribbled on in colored pencils by a child. The scrap I was holding had been torn off, so it was hard to say how long the original page had been, although it was narrower than a typical sheet of paper.

I placed it into the Ziploc and slid the Dill's bag off my hand, dropping it back onto the floor where it had been.

When I checked over my shoulder, JimBob was emerging from around the corner, even wobblier than when he left.

I looked down at the Ziploc. I'd neglected to plan where I was going to put it once it was full of evidence.

After verifying there was no hiding anything in my cleavage, I considered stuffing it into the back of my shorts again. But there was no guaranteeing I could get away from JimBob before he managed another ass grab.

Squeezing all the extra air out of the bag, I sealed it and shoved it down the front of my shorts. The denim shifted forward, causing the back seam of the shorts to wedge deep in my butt crack.

Ouch.

Worse, when I looked down at my crotch, I appeared to have grown an oddly-shaped package. I wished I'd left the can of chewing tobacco in the console. All I could do now was hope JimBob was too sloshed to notice.

After scooting to the passenger's side, I opened the door and got out. "Hey! You're finally back," I said. "Did you find it?"

"Find what?"

Yep. LeeAnne had kept him occupied with more free booze.

"Well, I'd better go look for it, then." I turned to leave, but his fingers captured my wrist. He yanked me toward him, pinning me between the side of his truck and his body. His thigh pressed against the tobacco can, causing it to dig into my pelvis, but he didn't seem to notice anything amiss.

His palms came up to squeeze both my cheekbones, holding my head in place as his mouth came down on mine.

I clamped my lips together like a clam as his beer and whiskey-scented tongue tried to gain entrance.

Using all the strength I had in my fingers, I peeled his hands off my face and pushed him away.

He staggered backwards. "What the hell is wrong with you?"

"I...I'm...allergic to alcohol," I blurted out. It was almost, sort of, true. "Even a trace will send me into anaphylactic shock." Okay, that was a total lie.

JimBob stood there, swaying, watching me as if his brain needed a few extra seconds to absorb what I'd said.

"That's okay," he said. "We don't have to kiss."

And he was back. One hand on my breast, the other on my ass.

Now what?

If I pushed him hard and ran for it, would some drunk-guy animal instinct cause him to chase me and take me down like a jaguar on a baby deer? His legs were wobbly, but twice as long as mine, and LeeAnne's wedges weren't designed for sprinting.

If I made it inside, would he be angry enough to come after me with his shotgun before LeeAnne could lock the door? There was every reason to believe he was capable of very bad things.

Something long, skinny, and hard dug into my stomach.

Ick.

He swept my hair back, bent down and fastened his lips to my neck.

Ick. Ick. Ick.

Insects burst from my pores and crawled in random patterns across my skin. My hands slid between us, searching for the ideal push point on his chest, preferably one that would send him sprawling to the ground and give me time to escape. But one of his ape-like arms was wrapped around my back. The other hand grasped my thigh, then rubbed the front of my shorts.

Uh-oh.

"What the fuck is that?" He pulled back and squinted at my crotch. "Are you a dude?"

Since when did a can of Skoal and a bunch of receipts feel like a penis?

It didn't matter. He was going to be pissed whether he thought I was a man or he found out I'd rummaged through his truck.

I drew my thigh back the little bit I could and thrust my knee into his groin. The move didn't have enough momentum behind it to deliver a death blow, but it must have stung because he jerked back and covered his crotch protectively. "Ouch!"

"Gee, I'm sorry," I said as I took a couple of sidesteps toward the bar. "It was a knee-jerk reaction." *Literally.* "I'm just really sensitive about the, um, *unusual* shape of my vagina."

That should get rid of him.

"Really?" He stepped toward me. "Can I see it?"

What?

He grabbed my upper arm with one hand as his other hand reached for my hoo-ha. *Holy crap!*

My mind formulated a plan a split second before my body executed it. I pushed at his chest with both hands while hooking my foot around the back of his ankle. He fell backwards onto the pavement.

I cringed as the words "the bigger they are, the harder the fall" zipped through my mind. Hopefully, all that alcohol cushioned his fall.

"Hey!" he yelled.

"I'm sorry," I said, and I kind of was. "Another knee-jerk reaction. I'm going to seek counseling." I turned toward the building.

"Wait," he called as he pushed himself off the ground.

"Rika!" LeeAnne's voice rang out.

"Yes, LeeAnne?" I was already edging toward her.

"Someone's on the land line for you. She says it's an emergency."

"An emergency!" I called over my shoulder to JimBob as I walked faster. "It could be about my grandmother!"

"Well..." JimBob sounded peeved. "Are you coming back?"

"I doubt it, if it's an emergency." I gave him a little wave. "Sorry. See you later." I could almost touch the building. A shuffling sound caused me to turn my head back once more. It looked like JimBob was planning to follow me.

"We're closed now," LeeAnne said. "But, tell you what, I'll bring you a free bottle of beer if you'll call someone to drive you home or sleep it off in your truck. You've had too much to drive."

JimBob let his ass drop to the bumper of his truck. "Yeah, okay."

As soon as LeeAnne and I were inside, I turned and threw my arms around her. "Oh, my God!" I said. "Has anyone ever told you you're the most awesome friend ever?"

She chuckled as she reciprocated, patting my back in a comforting rhythm. "No," she said. "Can't say that they have."

Nick

I was sitting in my media room, trying to watch one of those late-night talk shows that's supposed to be funny. Actually, I usually found it pretty funny, but not tonight.

Tonight, I couldn't seem to focus on the monologue. Couldn't stop drumming my fingers on my knees or scratching a non-existent itch on the back of my neck. Eventually, I had to stand up so I could stop annoying myself with my own fidgeting.

I checked the cable box. Eleven-fifteen and Rika still wasn't home. Barr's usually shut down early on weeknights. Most residents of Bolo were tucked into their houses by ten o'clock. I paced to the front foyer and looked out the window.

It had been over forty-five minutes since I'd texted Rika to let her know I'd saved a plate for her from dinner in case she was hungry. A completely unnecessary text, since I saved something for her every night. The message was just an excuse to check on her.

She hadn't responded and every minute I didn't hear from her bumped my stress level up another notch.

Maybe my imagination was running away with me. If so, I'd come by it honest, considering my mom was convinced she had devil-worshippers in her backyard. Maybe there was a certain age where the crazy gene kicked in and I'd just hit it.

I'd started by thinking about how there was likely a murderer, or murderers, running around town and Rika was driving home alone in the middle of the night.

She wasn't used to driving a truck around, and I'd already learned she had no qualms about chasing down a possible killer alone. Worse was the idea that the killer could decide to go after her, if he thought she knew too much.

I pulled my phone out again and tried to compose another casual text, but nothing came to mind except "HELLO! Would you please reply so I don't think you've been kidnapped and murdered?" I erased that text and put my phone away. She was probably driving home by now, and I didn't want to distract her with it. Maybe I should just call Barr's to see what was going on.

But LeeAnne would answer and make a big deal out of it and tell everyone in town I was checking up on Rika like a jealous boyfriend.

Shit. I'd had a bad feeling in my gut ever since Gabe dumped this case on me. That bad feeling was occasionally interrupted by really good feelings when I was in Rika's presence, which made the bad feeling even worse later on.

I felt responsible for keeping her safe. I was definitely responsible for keeping her out of prison and it weighed on me nearly every minute of the day.

Gucci was tapping around my feet, looking up at me with tiny expectant eyes. Even though I liked dogs, not in a million years would I have chosen a four-pound Maltese who dropped to three pounds whenever she decided the brand of dog food in her bowl wasn't special enough for her highness.

Basically, she was my diva ex-wife's Mini-Me.

I sighed, then picked her up and took her out front, grateful for the excuse to be a few feet closer to wherever Rika was. I watched the hairball sniff around the flower bed like a professional dirt connoisseur for five full minutes before squatting. Actually, she wasn't doing anything any other K-9 wouldn't, but, for some reason, Gucci tended to come off silly and pretentious like her original companion.

Who you married.

I rolled my eyes at my dog. At my ex. At myself.

If I wasn't careful, they were going to stick that way, like a demon-possessed teenager in a horror movie. I chuckled at that thought, but, a second later, I was back to worrying about Rika again.

Was she my latest project? The new woman I had to save?

Definitely.

Was it my fault this time?

Definitely not. Not my fault. Not my choice.

So why was I so concerned about a woman I'd known for a few days? Although, whenever we were in a room together, it felt like longer. In a good way.

An eternity later—or possibly just ten minutes—headlights

appeared at the end of the drive. I breathed out a long sigh of relief.

Once my truck came to a stop and the driver's door swung open, Gucci made her move. She charged toward the truck, barking as if she didn't recognize it from the hundred times she'd seen and heard it pull in.

When Rika's foot came out, it would have been a direct hit if Gucci hadn't skittered out of the way. She was the dumbest dog I'd ever met, but she sure had the skitter down. I guess moving fast is a requirement when you're seven inches tall.

Rika got out of the truck with the keys and a plastic baggie in one hand. She reached into the truck bed with the other and pulled out a black garbage bag.

"You'll never guess what I brought home with me," she said enthusiastically.

"My guess would be trash..." I squinted at the clear plastic. Was that a Skoal can in there? "And more trash."

"You're right!" She flashed me a smile, both mischievous and triumphant that caused a sharp twitch in my groin area. "And you've never been more wrong!" She lifted the bags like they were trophies.

I was so distracted by what seemed like extra cleavage tonight, it took me a second to notice she was standing near the door with her hands full. I shook off my temporary paralysis, walked over and opened the door. She breezed in, Gucci at her heels.

Once we were inside, Rika handed me the garbage bag like she was presenting me with a hole-in-one plaque.

Shaking the bag, I heard the unmistakable rattle of aluminum cans. "How am I wrong, exactly?"

"Be careful!" She grabbed the bag from my hand. "I have shot glasses in there with the cans." She laid her treasures down gently on the coffee table in the living room and we sat on the couch.

Every drop of relief at having her home began to drain out of me as she told me about her night.

When she informed me she'd hatched a plan with LeeAnne to get McGwire's fingerprints and find out his name, every muscle in my body tensed at the thought of the danger she'd put herself in.

Before I could point out the foolishness of her scheme, she pulled out her phone and I found myself listening as she flirted shamelessly with McGwire. That's when a pack of wolves took up residence in my belly and started using my gut as a chew toy.

By the time she got to the part where JimBob McGwire pushed her up against the truck and planted his lips on her bare skin, my head nearly blew off my neck.

What the hell was she smiling about? I wanted to take her by the shoulders and shake some sense into her, then find McGwire and smash his mouth through the back of his head.

Still smiling. Like she was proud of herself for getting that creep to paw her. I couldn't take anymore.

I stood up before I knew what I was doing. I think the words "Are you freakin' *nuts*?" came out of my mouth, and I definitely didn't use my inside voice. Her smile faded, but I couldn't help adding, "You could have gotten yourself killed!"

The stupid part was that I wasn't imagining her being murdered when I yelled at her. I was imagining her getting cozy with JimBob McGwire.

"But I was just—" she began.

"You were *just* in a deserted parking lot alone with a killer!" I paced the room, rubbing the back of my neck. That pesky itch had intensified to a burn.

"You said he probably wasn't the killer."

"Well, what the fuck do I know?"

I still wasn't picturing her dead. All I could think about was McGwire's hands and mouth in the places I was dying to put mine.

She's your client, not your girlfriend. She's your client, NOT your girlfriend.

I deep breathed as I tried to get the words to move from my brain and absorb into my reluctant body.

She stood and put her hands on her hips, her feet planted wide like Wonder Woman. "I'm trying to solve the murder." She raised her voice to match mine. "It's not like *you're* making any efforts to catch the killer."

Ouch. She thought I wasn't taking good enough care of her and it stung. I'd always tried my hardest to take care of the women in my life. Not that any of them ever appreciated it. Why did I expect Rika to be any different?

"It's not my job to catch the killer." I stepped toward her. "It's my job to get you off. What good will it do to get you off if you're dead?"

She snickered.

"*What?*"

"Nothing." It was hard to tell with her, but I could swear her face had deepened in color like she was blushing. I replayed my last statement in my head.

I'd said something about getting her off. Was she thinking of the other meaning of that phrase? Was she imagining us together?

Damn, I wanted her to imagine that.

In my mind, I closed the space between us. Yanked that silly t-shirt off over her head. Unbuttoned her shorts and slid my hand around back, over her beautiful round...

She was staring curiously at me. Maybe because I'd morphed from angry breathing to no breathing in a matter of seconds. I sucked air into my confused lungs and laced my fingers together so my hands couldn't do anything without permission from my brain. For extra insurance, I sat back down on the couch.

"Let's see about that evidence," I said.

CHAPTER EIGHTEEN

Rika

Nick agreed to have the truck evidence, along with the glove he said he found at the crime scene, tested for fingerprints at a private lab before turning it over to the sheriff. But first, we had to take all the scraps of paper into Nick's home office and make copies.

Being alone in this room with him felt more intimate than anywhere else in the house. Maybe because it was so masculine with its mahogany desk and dark leather couch. Or maybe it was because this was the one room I couldn't imagine his wives spending time in.

The copying was taking longer than it normally would have, since the only gloves Nick could find in the house were the big rubber kind meant for cleaning toilettes, not handling thin pieces of paper.

The scanner light flashed and Nick lifted the lid, then picked the receipt up carefully from the glass and laid it on the adjacent work table.

"Why the couch?" I asked.

"Huh?" He turned to look at me and I was captivated by his

eye color *de jour*. The office lighting was brighter than the living room and he was wearing an army green t-shirt with a yellow logo, turning his eyes to a sea green with gold sprinkles I'd never noticed before.

They were mesmerizing.

At moments like this, it seemed especially strange that I lived in his house, shared meals with him, gazed into those eyes on a regular basis, but wasn't supposed to touch him.

Oh. He was staring at me expectantly. I quickly rewound the conversation and picked up my train of thought. "You have a desk chair, two club chairs for guests or clients or whatever. Why do you need the couch back here?"

Nick glanced at where the couch sat against the same wall as the copy machine. "That's my mulling couch."

"Your mulling couch?"

"Yeah, whenever I need to mull something over, I lie on that couch."

I tried to imagine him there. I'd never seen him in a reclining position. Would his hands be at his sides? On his stomach? Cushioning his head?

"Maybe I need a mulling couch," I said.

He plucked another receipt from the baggie. "Tell you what, when all this is over, I'll buy you one." The statement stirred a strange mix of emotions. I kind of liked the idea of having something to remember Nick by. Something he bought just for me, even though the idea of having to remember him instead of seeing him every day made me a little sad. On the other hand, I didn't want to be another woman in his life he needed to placate with presents, but still...

"What kind of couch do you think I'd like?" *Silly.* My mouth had taken over before my brain had a chance to shut it down. I was testing Nick like a teenage girl tests her boyfriend. A girl's lawyer should not be expected to predict her taste in home furnishings.

"Hm..." Nick tilted his head as if trying to imagine. "I wonder what Harry Potter sits on?" he mused. "Or maybe you'd rather have the captain's chair from the Starship Enterprise."

Wow. How did he know me so well already? He lifted his brows for confirmation and it was all too much. His nearness. His teasing, knowing eyes. The unmistakable scent of Pillsbury Crescent Rolls clinging to his clothing.

My hunger pang was overshadowed by searing heat that originated in my chest, spreading like wildfire over my skin.

I closed the short distance between us, my chin tilted upward. His brows squeezed together, a question in his eyes.

I was ready to answer that question. For better or for worse. My lips were parted and tingling, but he was so tall, my wedges weren't quite enough to reach him. Disregarding the fact that he didn't come down to meet me, I strained on the balls of my feet, determined to reach him.

He seemed frozen in place. Not leaning in toward me. Not shifting away.

But his tongue slipped out and wet his lips. His breathing accelerated. I lifted my hands from my sides, anticipating the way his pecs would feel in my palms.

It was happening. I—geeky, awkward Paprika Anise Martín—was making it happen. Right f-ing here. Right f-ing—

Yap! Yap, yap, yap!

I startled and jumped back. When I looked down at the source of the commotion, Gucci was staring up at me, an accusing look in her tiny black eyes.

Could that little blonde bitch have known I was about to horn in on her territory? Or was she working undercover for the state legal ethics board?

Wordlessly, Nick closed his mouth, turned to the machine and got back to work.

I hid my hot face from him by pretending to examine the last receipt he'd copied. Gucci came round and planted herself between my feet and Nick's.

Moment lost.

~

Once we finished in the office, we took the copies we'd made back to the living room to examine them.

I'd seen several true crime investigation shows in which the killer had neglected to dispose of receipts from the day before the murder listing items like guns, duct tape, and shovels. We didn't get that lucky.

Most of JimBob's receipts were for beer, chewing tobacco, and lottery tickets. Several had *Mary Queen* stamped on the top. I couldn't believe what I was seeing, but Nick confirmed that the restaurant still used an old-fashioned ink pad and rubber stamp for every receipt.

"Whatever you do, don't eat their food," he said. "That fryer hasn't been cleaned since before they lost their franchise license."

I was still reeling over the rubber stamp. That and the ancient office equipment at the police station. I shook my head. "I hope I can get back to my own century when all this is over."

"You and me both," Nick replied.

"I guess you might already be on your way if it weren't for me." I said. "I'm sorry I screwed things up for you."

"Nah." Nick gave a quick think-nothing-of-it head shake. "Gabe was right. I hadn't really decided what to do next." He looked kind of disturbed by the admission. It must suck to go to school all those extra years for something you find out you don't want to do.

Seeing Nick unhappy gave me an icky feeling in my chest. I scanned the table for a distraction.

"So, what's this?" I pointed to the colorful scrap of paper I'd found between JimBob's truck seat and door.

"Looks like a part of a word search some kid doodled all over in colored pencil."

"That's what I thought," I said. "But do the McGwires have kids?"

"I've never seen them with any."

"Are there any kids missing?"

Nick laughed. "You think the McGwires are running a child slavery ring here and nobody noticed?"

I shrugged. "You don't seem to know much about them."

"Yeah, but people around here are pretty good at keeping up with their small children."

"I guess that makes sense," I said, chuckling at myself for overlooking such an obvious point.

While Nick warmed the dinner he'd saved me, I focused on the color copy of the word search, mainly because it was the only halfway interesting item I'd confiscated—that sounded better than "stolen"—from JimBob's truck.

Every letter in the word search was circled individually in red, blue, orange or green. In the left margin were primitive doodles of a house and a tree, and flowers almost as tall as the house. That, along with the smattering of red hearts in the right margin, made me pretty sure the artist was a little girl.

The thought of JimBob McGwire as a father of a small child made me grimace.

"Everything okay?" Nick asked as he opened the microwave door and set a plate inside. Nick usually seemed aware of my facial expressions, even when he was supposed to be doing something else.

Still watching me for signs I might be the killer? Or was it something else? I sure wanted it to be something else.

He was staring at me expectantly.

"Fine," I replied. "Just random passing thoughts."

He nodded, extracted the plate and stirred the mashed potatoes around before sticking it back in the microwave.

Looking down at the puzzle, I wondered if finding the words in it would give me a clue as to where it came from. Maybe it was a page from a word puzzle book sold at Dill's, and ReeAnne would remember who she sold it to. Or maybe one of the teachers handed it out at school and would recognize the doodle artist's handiwork.

I was grasping at straws. There was no reason to think this scrap of paper had anything more to do with the murder than the Skoal can or the Mary Queen receipts. But there was nothing much I could do until the fingerprint information came back, so why not?

As I jogged to Nick's office to grab a pencil, I realized it was the only exercise I'd gotten since I'd been here.

Every night, after becoming concerned I was pinching more fat between my fingers than the night before, I promised myself I'd get up and work out the next day. But I kept accepting Nick's offers to take me with him on his errands and to his mom's house. He wouldn't even let me help once we got there, which might be for the best considering I knew nothing about gardening, farming, or carpentry.

When we got home from the errands, I needed a nap because I'd worked late the night before and would need to work again that night. At least that's what I told myself. But, in the back of my mind, I was afraid I'd fallen into my old habit of using food to comfort myself, then being so lethargic from the carbs, I couldn't drag myself onto the treadmill.

As I sat down at the table, Nick laid a meat and potatoes-scented plate in front of me. As usual, the portions were more appropriate for a linebacker than a five-foot five—okay five-foot four and a half—female.

Nick had pre-sliced my steak for me. He'd been cutting my meat since the third night I stayed here. I'd seen how important meat preparation was to him, whether grilling, baking or frying, and I'd become convinced he didn't like the way I'd butchered his masterpieces.

Maybe I'd been cutting against the grain instead of with it, or vice-versa. *Whatever.* I kind of liked my meat pre-cut, anyway. Less time before it got to my mouth.

I speared a slice as Nick started emptying the dishwasher. "Nick?" I said after I swallowed the bite.

He paused, clean silverware in hand, and gave me his full attention. "Yeah?"

I needed this to sound casual. No way did I want him to know about my previous life as a blimp.

"I've been eating a lot since I got here. I could use a workout buddy, or maybe a drill sergeant."

"A drill sergeant?" He drew his eyebrows together in what appeared to be concerned confusion. "The last thing you need is a boot camp. You look..."

I watched him consider and discard adjectives, just as he had the first time he saw me in my new gym clothes. I nearly sprained my brain trying to read his mind.

"...fine."

Fine? Really? He was an attorney, for the love of Zeus! A trial lawyer. And the best he could come up with was "fine"?

"Besides, it's not like you couldn't stand to gain a few pounds."

It's not like you couldn't stand to gain a few pounds. What did that mean, exactly? The sentence looped round and round in my head.

Was he saying I was too thin? I'd googled "ideal weight" dozens of times in the past few years, never quite satisfied with the range of answers I found. How could one hundred seven pounds and one hundred forty-eight pounds both be healthy weights for my height?

Did other women naturally know how much they should weigh? Or did their eyes dart directly to problem areas whenever they looked at their bodies in the mirror like mine did? When it came to body image, I was constantly befuddled, and stupid Nick wasn't helping any.

I let the subject drop and concentrated on the word search again. I found the words "camel" and "donkey," which were certainly there intentionally. But I also found words like "move," "job," "bed," "bad," "won," and "far," any of which could have been inadvertent. I was almost certain "fart," and "crap" were unfortunate accidents. But without the puzzle's title and word bank portion of the page, it was impossible to know anything for sure and would be hard for ReeAnne or a teacher to recognize.

Just for kicks, I listed out the letters circled in red, then those circled in blue and so on. I treated each color as a word jumble, changing the order over and over to see if anything coherent materialized.

It didn't.

I laughed at myself. What was I thinking? That a pint-sized criminal mastermind was composing secret codes in her spare time at preschool?

I needed to get some sleep. Maybe tomorrow would bring me some real clues.

The next night, I found myself driving home around nine-thirty, despite the fact that it was a Friday. LeeAnne said business was slow due to a rodeo kick-off dance in the next county. According to her, it was especially popular with local married couples, mainly because it gave parents an excuse to get away from their kids.

As I turned at the flashing red light, I pondered the kid thing. I was still on the fence about having them someday.

From what I'd seen, as soon as a couple got married, everyone they knew with children started bugging them about having a baby. Meanwhile, these same people were desperately trying to get away from the kids they had every chance they got.

Hm... Having a baby is like giving birth to your own kidnapper.

Still, the thoughts of coupledom and kids somehow slippery-sloped my mind into a big pile of Nick. I hated to accept that I had a thing for my lawyer. It seemed pathetic and cliché. Kind of like thinking you're in love with your therapist.

And if I considered it scientifically, this little crush was probably about proximity or pheromones. Or a psychologist would probably say it was a result of the judge putting the idea in my head that Nick was the only one who could "save" me.

Ick.

There was no getting around the fact that I was the girl who followed an idiot actor across the country. And maybe my Jilly Crane counselor was right and I did it because I didn't have a dad around to make me feel valuable to men and my weight had stunted my love life. So, when a handsome prince deemed me worthy of his attentions, the fairytale was irresistible to me.

Maybe all that was true, but I was *not* a girl who needed to be rescued.

I'd always had a job. At fourteen, I started my own online tutoring service, and each year as I learned more, I made more money per hour.

Pre-cal and calculus were gold mines. I saved money and bought my own used car. And, although my grandmother wouldn't let me pay rent, by the time I was eighteen, I was buying most of our groceries.

What was my point? Oh, yeah. I didn't want to be rescued. Well, I did want to be saved from jail, but I didn't want to be like all of Nick's other women who seemed to expect the world from him.

From what I could tell, his wives wasted a lot of his money then left. And boy was his mother a piece of work.

My lips tightened at the irrational annoyance I felt toward all

Nick's women. But it seemed really unfair that his bitchy wives had gotten to be with him, something I'd probably never get, considering I was a) his client and b) not a blonde with the never-ending legs of an NBA player. Oh, and I almost forgot c) not beauty pageant material.

Nick could have any woman he wanted, at least for a while. Why would he ever choose me?

I'd been forced on him. It was important to remember that fact. I certainly didn't want to fall into the nerdy girl trap of thinking just because the quarterback was nice to me, he was having the same impure thoughts I was.

As I neared his drive, a terrible thought struck me. He wasn't expecting me home this early. What if he had someone over? I couldn't expect him to let that eight-pack go to waste just because he'd offered to put a roof over my head.

And surely, he wasn't used to going weeks without sex. What if I walked in and found yet another blonde draped across his lap?

The mental picture triggered the carsick area of my brain and my stomach responded with the appropriate nausea.

But I was already turning into his drive, so I had no choice but to face whatever Friday-night floosy Nick might be entertaining in our—uh, *his*—home.

As I pulled up to the garage, I noticed there was no extra vehicle out front, although, he could have picked his date up and brought her home with him. In fact, knowing Nick, he met a beautiful stranger at the grocery store, and they were now in his bedroom, enjoying the first night of their honeymoon.

Asshole.

I came in through the garage and walked around the main part of the house, my eyes narrowed suspiciously. No one in the kitchen, the living room, or the back yard. The place was eerily quiet.

But surely Nick was here. His Ranger was sitting in the garage.

Unless the floosy picked *him* up.

Now I had to know exactly where Nick was and what he was doing, even if it was none of my beeswax. I passed through the foyer to the hallway on the opposite side of the house.

Nick had told me I was welcome to the gym, the media room, and the laundry room, and he'd more or less invited me into his master bedroom the first day we went to his mom's, but I still felt kind of guilty skulking around this part of his home at night.

I peeked into the open door of his master bedroom. *Nothing.*

The gym. *Zilch.*

The laundry room. *Nada.*

Thinking I heard something behind the closed media room door, I sidled up to it, pressing my ear to the cool wood.

I heard a man's voice. Was that Nick?

Another voice replied and the liquid in my veins turned to bloodsicles.

It was a woman's voice! *The Friday night floosy!*

CHAPTER NINETEEN

Rika

Before I could consider my actions, my hand grabbed the knob and turned it. The door opened and just as I'd imagined, Nick was sitting on his plush sectional couch with a blonde sprawled across his lap.

Well, maybe not just as I'd imagined, since the blonde quickly jumped to her feet and started barking at me.

Nick's head jerked around, his expression surprised, and maybe embarrassed or guilty, I wasn't sure since I hadn't seen this precise combination on his face before.

Is he watching porn?

I checked the screen.

Not porn.

Nick searched under Gucci for the remote control as I watched him curiously.

His somewhat frantic attempt to find the remote made me check the TV again. "Is that *The Notebook?*" I asked.

Now, his expression was definitely embarrassed.

"I wasn't watching it. I was just flipping through the channels when you came in," said the man who wasn't quite sure where he'd set his remote.

"Is that a tear in your eye?" Okay, maybe that was a mean thing to point out to a big macho Texan, but Nick had gotten to witness my life turn into one embarrassment after another—every time I got dressed for work, for instance—and it was about time the tables were turned.

He quickly jabbed his finger into the corner of each eye checking for moisture, while using his other hand to switch the channel to a baseball game.

"So..." I dropped down on the other end of the sectional. "Is this what you always do on Friday nights? Sit around watching *girlie* movies?"

His eyes on the game, he replied, "Not always, but it's come to my attention that going out has brought me nothing but trouble."

"And wives," I added.

He gave me a grave look. "And wives."

Gucci yapped twice.

"And dogs."

"Just one dog." He pushed Gucci's butt down into a seated position and she shut up.

"For now," I said.

Although Nick's lips held steadfast in a firm line, his eyes crinkled a little at the edges like he was tempted to laugh. It was a nice expression.

I sighed. Nick had a lot of nice expressions.

Hellooo! Nerdy girl!

Oh, yeah. No fantasizing.

I hopped up off the couch so suddenly Nick's face jerked toward me and Gucci jumped up and started barking again.

"I'm going to change out of my hoochie clothes," I said. "I think I'll finally take a turn on your treadmill."

He smiled. "Aw, just when I was starting to fatten you up."

I froze and stared at him, his words repeating in my head.

He narrowed his eyes as if examining my expression. "Rika, you know I'm being ironic, don't you? I was just teasing you."

I reminded myself to breathe. "Sure." I plastered a fake smile on my face. "That's what we do. Tease each other. See you later."

As I headed for my room, the word "fatten" echoed through my head. His off-hand jokes about my weight were confusing and distressing to me. Meanwhile, he kept stuffing me with bread every chance he got. Dinner rolls, crescent rolls, garlic bread, and even tortillas wrapped around the breakfast tacos and fajitas he made. As if the carbs weren't bad enough, I thought I saw him pouring bacon grease into the cornbread.

Why wasn't there a *mother fucking* scale in this *mother fucking* house?

I changed clothes quickly, determined to spend a couple of hours in Nick's gym before I went to bed. But when I got to the foyer, he was headed my way.

"I have to go to Mom's," he said. "She's in a panic, convinced she's seen people in grim reaper robes headed toward the old barn."

I remembered the barn being pretty far back from the house. "Can she really see that far in the dark?"

Nick shook his head. "There's never anything really wrong at her place, but if I don't go over there now, my phone will be ringing all night."

I totally forgot about my workout. "Can I go?" The idea of taking off with Nick on a crazy adventure in the dark seemed like fun.

"Really?"

"Sure, I love a good snipe hunt."

"Maybe you should stick around then, 'cause mom loves sending people on them. Well, me, at least."

I smiled a little inside. I couldn't wait to get away from Bolo, but I sure liked the idea of sticking to Nick. Uh...*with* Nick.

Not that that was okay either.

But Nick was standing at the entrance to the hall holding the door to the garage open, and I couldn't resist walking through it.

～

Tammy Lynn was all drama when we got to her house, convinced she had Satan-worshippers in her own backyard. However, it didn't keep her from sticking a platter of cookies under my nose and insisting I try one. I held my breath to avoid their aroma and escaped out the back door with Nick.

The night was dark and peaceful, except for the chirping of the local cricket choir. Nick kept the flashlight focused on the path in front of us as we traipsed toward the barn. It was even farther from the house than I remembered, and I kept having to swipe at the sweat as it seeped out from my hairline.

Although the temperature dropped into the high seventies at night, the humidity rose, turning the entire outdoors into a sauna.

Nick looked ahead at the barn and sighed. "I'm thinking my sister had the right idea."

I slapped at a bug on my neck that turned out to be a trickle of sweat. "You mean moving far away?"

"Yep."

"I haven't been here long, but your mom does seem to harass —I mean *call on*—you a lot."

He chuckled. "Yeah, it was a relief all those years I was away at college and law school and working in Austin. I mostly forgot what it was like being around her. Since I've been back, I feel kind of..."

"Used?"

I hoped I hadn't overstepped with my observation. We walked on in silence.

A minute later, I became aware of a sound that definitely wasn't crickets. I grabbed Nick's arm but he'd already halted.

"I heard something," I whispered.

"I saw something," he said at the same time.

The low murmur began again as my eyes homed in on a pale flickering light barely visible through the spaces between the old barn boards. Nick turned off the flashlight, and we moved forward in unison as stealthily as cats. When we reached the closed barn door, we hunched down and peeked through the slats.

This cannot be happening. What was going on inside the barn was so unbelievable, I actually pinched myself to make sure I wasn't dreaming.

By the light of several candles, I counted thirteen robed, hooded figures arranged in a circle, twelve in black, the thirteenth in deep red. The hoods hung past their foreheads, obscuring their features.

Nick looked at me, his eyebrows raised halfway to his hairline. I widened my eyes to convey what both of us were thinking: *Satan Worshippers! Tammy Lynn was right!*

The one in red stood at the far end of the barn, holding something snowy white—like a small bundle of laundry—in his arms. He was murmuring in Latin.

Unholy shit!

"Lucifer," I whispered. "He said 'Lucifer.'"

"You speak Latin?" Nick asked.

"No, but he said, *Loo-see-fair-ee,* which is almost exactly like the Spanish word, pronounced *Loo-see-fair,* but spelled like 'Lucifer' in English."

Nick narrowed his eyes at me as if deciding whether I knew what I was talking about or not. That pissed me off. By now, he should have known I wasn't like his ditsy ex-wives.

"I thought lawyers learned Latin in school," I snarked.

"We learn *ad litem* and *pro bono*. They don't teach us devil worshipper Latin."

We watched as Red Robe passed the bundle to the black

robed figure on his right who began chanting in Latin. With his index finger, he made a sign in the air over the bundle.

"What is that?" Nick asked. "The sign of the cross?"

I'd spent too many Sundays at mass with my grandma to get this one wrong. "No way. That was more like a star." My brain searched for the most logical explanation. "A reverse pentagram?"

Nick grimaced.

After a minute or so, the bundle was passed to the next person, who began the same ritual. A movement caught my eye and my gaze jumped back to the first devil worshipper.

"What's Red Robe got in his hand?"

Nick pressed his face harder against the boards, squeezing his left eye closed as he peered through the gap with his right.

"Shit!" he whispered, almost too loudly. "It's a dagger!"

As I found a better knothole to peek through, I tried and failed to hold my left eye shut. Regardless, the glinting object certainly looked like a dagger.

I swallowed hard as fear prickled the back of my neck. "I think this would be a good time to get your gun," I said.

Nick scowled at me. "Just because I'm from Texas, you assume I have a gun?"

"Well..." I shrugged. When I turned back to the knothole, the bundle was being passed again. The fabric shifted and I saw...*skin?* I grabbed Nick's arm. "It's a baby!"

"What?" He peered hard through his knothole. "Holy fuck!" He stood suddenly and I followed suit, unsure of the plan but ready to back him up. He turned away from the barn.

"Where are you going?" I grabbed his arm, but he shook me off.

"I'm going to get my gun."

Sure, it was a good idea when *he* said it.

"Wait," I said. "What if they try to hurt the baby before you get back?"

Nick glanced in the direction of his truck. "I think I have plenty of time to get there and back before it makes the circle. If I don't, scream like a horror movie victim." That wouldn't be too hard considering I was pretty sure I was in a horror movie.

Nick ran off toward the truck. I was glad I'd heard him on his treadmill a few times since I'd been staying at his house. I'd hate to have to choose between giving him CPR and saving the baby.

I resumed my position at the knothole. Still, no faces were visible in the flickering candle light, just black holes where faces should have been. Goosebumps rose on my skin and my stomach flip-flopped in my belly.

Was it my imagination or were the proceedings moving more quickly now? As if the robed figures were tired of the ritual and just wanted to get it over with.

My muscles tensed as the baby was handed off faster and faster. What kind of sorry Satan worshippers were these, anyway?

In what seemed like no time, the bundle was in Red Robe's hands again.

I glanced back and saw Nick running toward me, half a football field away. Red Robe murmured more Latin over the baby. Then he stepped behind a makeshift altar—a sheet of plywood held up by two saw horses—and laid the infant down on it.

That couldn't be good.

Oh, my God. Oh, my God. Oh, my God.

What could I yell that would thwart a baby-sacrificing devil worshipper? Words mixed and swirled, jumbling around in my head. Red Robe raised the dagger in both hands.

"*Expelliarmus!*" I screamed.

CHAPTER TWENTY

Rika

The dagger dropped from Red Robe's hand. I jumped up and opened the barn door as Nick ran up, his shirt soaked through, sweat pouring down his face.

Apparently, it was a lot easier to run at your own pace in a climate controlled house than full-out in a sauna.

Nick waved the pistol around the circle. "Put your hands up!" he managed between gulps of air.

I was hurrying over to get the baby when Red Robe started to say something as he took a step forward, knocking the baby off the altar.

"*No!*" I dove in as the bundle fell.

My reach landed just shy of the baby.

For a moment I couldn't move. Couldn't breathe. I waited to hear a cry, but the bundle lay silent and unmoving in the dirt. Nausea filled my stomach, my body preparing to regurgitate the horror it was about to witness.

I crossed myself automatically, even as the logical side of my brain told me it would do no good.

Hands quaking, I reached for the blanket and lifted the edge away.

I grabbed the baby and held it up by its foot. "It's a doll." I stood, suddenly aware of the smelly barn dirt coating the front of my body.

Nick, pistol still at the ready, took a hard look at the doll. He swung the gun right and left, threateningly. "What the hell is going on here?" he shouted.

"Don't shoot, Mr. Nick," someone yelled. All the Satan worshippers began talking at once as they pulled off their hoods.

I scanned their faces and realized we were surrounded by a bunch of teenagers. I recognized several of them as the high school football players who came into Barr's after practice. The one in the red robe looked vaguely familiar even though I didn't think I knew him.

"What the...?" Nick lowered the gun as he gazed around the circle at the frightened expressions. "What the hell are you kids doing?" He shook his head, then looked pointedly at Red Robe. "Gabriel Martínez, your parents are going to..." His voice drifted off as if he was trying to imagine what the punishment was for devil worshiping in the Martínez house.

Gabriel Martínez. Gabe Junior. He looked like a thinner, younger version of his dad, the judge.

"Please don't tell on me, Uncle Nick! My parents will ground me until I go off to college. We were just goofing around. You know there's nothing to do around here. I heard you used to drag race on the weekends when you were my age. This is a lot safer than drag racing." He looked at Nick accusingly. "Or at least it was until you showed up and pointed a gun at us."

Maybe Gabe Junior should consider a career in law like his old man.

Nick held up a hand and the kid stopped talking. "Where'd you get the weapon?" he asked, clearly not willing to let some kid win this argument, even if he did call him "Uncle Nick."

"It's a cosplay dagger."

"A what?"

I hurried over to Nick and murmured in his ear. "Cosplay is when people dress up in costumes. Sometimes they wear them to cons—"

He shook his head slightly and frowned to let me know he had no idea what I was talking about.

I tried again. "Cons are like Star Trek conventions, but for anime, manga, comic books and video game characters."

Nick walked over and lifted the dagger from the dirt. "It's rubber."

"See," Gabe Junior replied. "We weren't hurting anybody."

"Please don't tell our parents," someone cried. Others chimed in with the same frantic request.

Nick sucked in a frustrated breath and expelled it loudly. "Take off those damn robes," he said. "I'm starting a fire in the barrel behind the barn and you're going to burn every last one of them. You've got half the county believing we have devil worshippers around here."

The kids removed their robes and filed out in front of us. The smallest Satan worshipper—a skinny, flat-chested girl in a Bellatrix Lestrange t-shirt—stopped in front of me.

"That was really cool." She gazed at me admiringly. "You said it, and the dagger fell right out of his hand."

"Um..." I glanced at Nick, who'd knitted his brow into a puzzled expression. "Thanks."

Not wanting to explain her comment to Nick, I made a show of shaking the dirt off my shirt as I followed the kids outside.

~

Nick

By the time we finished at the barn, we were beat. Worse, our clothes had also collected a chemical smell because I'd neglected to anticipate the odor of melting synthetics.

I helped Rika into the truck. Once the excitement was over, we realized she'd skinned her elbows diving for the baby.

She didn't really need my help getting in the truck, but I felt responsible for her injuries. I should have figured out what was going on here a lot sooner.

Growing up in Bolo, my friends and I spent half our time at the cemetery, scaring the crap out of each other. It didn't take a genius to guess the town Satan worshippers were just a bunch of kids screwing around on a Friday night.

I yawned as I walked to the driver's side of the truck. Teenagers were freakin' exhausting. I'd never been gladder I didn't own one. Seemed crazy to think that if my first wife—of five months—had actually been pregnant like she claimed, I'd have a sixteen-year-old.

As old as I thought I felt sometimes, I still felt way too young to have a teenage kid. Thank God I dodged that bullet.

I used my cell to call Mom and tell her there was nothing to worry about, pulled myself into the cab and buckled up. I looked over at Rika, covered chin to thighs in dirt.

The night had been ridiculous, but I couldn't help thinking we'd made a pretty good team. And there was something I'd wanted to ask since we busted in.

"Hey, what was it you yelled at the kids?"

Her eyes jerked my way, then shifted to the floorboard. "*Expelliarmus*," she said sheepishly.

"Ex what?"

"*Expelliarmus*. It's a disarming charm from Harry Potter."

I tried to stifle a chuckle. "A good choice, I guess. It certainly disarmed Junior."

I couldn't keep the laughter out of my voice. I'd told her to scream and, of all the things she could have screamed, she picked a Harry Potter spell. That was one of the cutest, geekiest, most heroic things I'd ever witnessed.

Rika was not your run of the mill hot chick, for sure.

She folded her arms in front of her and pressed her lips together. As funny and sarcastic as she was, I'd noticed she could be pretty sensitive at times. I hadn't quite figured out her triggers and certainly had no clue about the reasons behind them.

In other words, I was no Gabe.

"Hey..." I reached over and grasped her dirty chin, turning her face toward me. Her eyes said "drop dead," but I couldn't help thinking each new expression was cuter than the one before. "You were pretty heroic tonight."

"Yeah," she said sarcastically. "I saved a doll from being rubbered to death."

She wasn't giving herself enough credit. I waited until she made eye contact again so she'd know I was serious. "As far as you knew, you stayed behind with a barn full of armed devil worshippers, then called attention to yourself to save a baby. You didn't know they weren't dangerous." I dusted the dirt off her chin with my thumb. "And Addie thought you were the coolest."

I smiled at her and she quit fighting it and smiled back. Warm layers of satisfaction unfurled in my gut. I sure liked making her smile.

Our eyes were padlocked into a gaze neither one of us wanted to break loose from. I liked those big eyes of hers. They were intelligent, undeniably feminine and, just now, they were pulling me into their chocolaty depths where I thought I could drown a happy man.

Before I knew it, my fingers were sliding up the side of her face. My palm cupped her jaw. Her eyes widened in surprise, then her lids lowered in what looked like a sultry invitation. As I started to lean toward her, her mouth opened slightly, and I could almost feel her soft, full lips against mine.

My seat belt caught and I couldn't go any farther.

Holy hell. If it hadn't stopped me, I would have kissed her. My client. My twenty-four-year-old client. I was an asshole.

I decided to be grateful for the divine intervention, even if I normally didn't believe in such a thing. The seat belt had no reason to catch. The motor wasn't running. My foot wasn't on the brake.

That's when I remembered the belt had malfunctioned a couple of times, weeks ago, and I'd meant to take it by the dealership and get it fixed.

Whatever. Whether it was the man upstairs or the ghost of Henry Ford, somebody did me a favor.

Except it didn't feel like a favor because for a second there, I thought I was finally going to get a taste of Paprika Anise.

CHAPTER TWENTY-ONE

Nick

Sunday morning, I listened at Rika's door about two dozen times, waiting to hear the shower kick on.

I'd put off this news as long as I could, telling myself I didn't want to ruin her weekend and there was no point in stressing her out sooner than necessary.

That was part of the reason. The rest was that I didn't want to say what I had to say aloud because then it would be real to me, too.

The brick that had settled in my stomach a couple of days ago grew weightier as I walked to the kitchen to make breakfast.

To soften the blow, I was making buttermilk pancakes and bacon. Bad news always goes down better with a mouthful of pancake that's been slathered in butter and drizzled with real maple syrup. At least I hoped it did.

Maybe I should have gone for doughnuts instead. I could still see her in her crazy cat scrubs, red doughnut filling coating her lips. The scene was simultaneously disturbing and hot. Every time I thought of it, I imagined leaning down and sucking the jelly from her mouth.

It hit me that if I'd given in to that impulse in the first place, my problems would have been solved. Gabe wouldn't have assigned her case to me, and she and I could be...well, something other than attorney and client.

Of course, I might have lost my license to practice, but that could have been a relief.

I was flipping the pancakes on the griddle when Rika came into the kitchen with her hair half blow-dried, the scent of her shampoo momentarily replacing the smell of bacon. She was wearing one of the over-sized t-shirts I'd lent her in lieu of a robe. It hit her mid-thigh, making me wish I'd lent her a smaller shirt.

Still, my dick twitched and grumbled in my jeans. I'd been getting a lot of complaints down there lately. Her living with me had been both fun and frustrating, often at the same time.

"Hungry?" I set the bacon on the table and went back to the griddle.

"Starved," she said as she sat down. "But I'm starting to feel guilty about you cooking for me every day."

The truth was I enjoyed cooking. It was a simple form of science, at least the way I did it. Just measure the ingredients and follow the cooking instructions.

And unlike trying murder cases, as long as you abided by simple food handling guidelines, the worst possible result was a burnt rib eye.

"Nothing to feel guilty about," I said as I slid a pancake onto the platter. "You're my guest."

"More like a squatter." She uncrossed her legs and used her toe to stroke Gucci, who'd been sniffing around the table prematurely for crumbs.

My eyes darted to the hem of the shirt, which had crawled up another inch since she sat down. Normally, I didn't try to eyeball my client's underwear, but a guy only had so much control over his eyes in a situation like this.

"It's not like you would have invited me to stay here if I hadn't been forced on you," she said.

I wouldn't? That was hard to believe when I couldn't keep my gaze from constantly flicking to her toned bronze thighs. An image flashed through my brain—those legs wrapped around me, her heels digging into the small of my back.

I scorched the edge of my thumb on the griddle.

Ouch!

I pulled it away, resisting the urge to blow on it. Luckily, she was still playing with Gucci and didn't seem to notice.

"You never know." I lifted the edge of each pancake in the stack with a spatula and shoved in a pat of butter. "If we'd met some other way, maybe..."

What was I doing? I shouldn't be speculating about an alternate universe where I was picking Rika up and bringing her here for something other than legal counsel. "Maybe we would have been friends," I finished.

In my peripheral vision, I saw her shoulders drop, her gaze shifting to the table.

"Anyway," she said. "I should probably do some of the cooking."

"Can you cook?" I walked over and set the platter on the table.

She shrugged. "I'm sure I could google it."

I chuckled. I liked her can-do attitude, her penchant for research, and her interest in all kinds of things. Made her interesting to talk to. It also made me feel like I'd spent too much time around a particular type of woman.

On the other hand, I liked being Rika's sugar daddy, which was kind of at odds with the other stuff I liked about her.

Whatever. I wasn't going to analyze it. That was Gabe's job.

"Why don't we just stick to what works for now? You've got plenty to do. I hear you're a pretty good waitress."

"Where'd you hear that?" she asked.

"LeeAnne." Since Rika hadn't made a move toward the food, I lifted a pancake with the spatula. "How many do you want?"

"I...um..." Her eyes were glued to the pancakes. "I think I'll just have a slice of bacon."

Great. She didn't like pancakes.

But she wasn't staring at them as if she didn't like them. The look on her face was more like a sailor fresh off the boat in a titty bar. Like she was dying to have carnal knowledge of one, but didn't think she was allowed to touch it.

It wasn't the first time I'd seen that look on her face and it often left me confused as to whether or not she enjoyed my cooking. At least until she suddenly grabbed a fork and started shoveling it into her mouth as if she hadn't eaten for days.

This time, though, she just kept staring.

"When did you see LeeAnne?" Her gaze met mine and I tried to decipher her expression.

"A couple of days ago. I went to the store while you were napping and ran into her there."

Her eyes dropped again and she nibbled her bacon. She seemed to be giving my answer more consideration than it warranted.

"Are you sure you don't want a pancake?" I tried again.

"No thanks."

Okay...

There went my plan to get her high on maple syrup before I dropped the bomb. I took a deep breath.

"Rika," I paused until she made eye contact. "We start seating the jury for your trial tomorrow."

∾

Rika

I blinked up at Nick, not willing to comprehend his sentence. "What?" I half-whispered.

"Tomorrow we'll be choosing the jury for—"

"*Tomorrow?*" I was no longer whispering. "It's supposed to take freaking forever for murder trials to—*tomorrow?*"

"Yeah, listen..." Nick held out his simmer down hand. "I think it's better to do this right away. Actually, it was Gabe's idea. He couldn't say it in so many words, but last time I saw him, he kept talking about the constitutional right to a speedy trial and I realized—"

"We can't have a trial!" I yelled. I couldn't believe he'd actually requested a quicker trial date. I stood and glared down at him. "We haven't solved the case yet!"

Nick sighed. "Rika, there's not much chance of solving the case."

Not with that attitude.

"You don't know that." I paced to the French doors and back again. "We haven't even gotten the fingerprint results back yet!" I lifted my hands, wiggling my fingers to illustrate my point.

He stood and grasped my hands in his, pulling them down between us. "Even if all the fingerprints belong to JimBob McGwire, that just proves he's the only one driving that truck. It's a far cry from proving he murdered the victim. Or that he was even involved. But we can use your testimony about his truck to instill reasonable doubt in the jurors' minds."

I yanked my hands away. "The fingerprints were only one step," I said. "I can't believe you're giving up this easily. You just want to get me out of the way so you can move on with your life!"

The muscles in Nick's face tensed as his irises turned storm cloud gray right in front of my eyes.

"I'm *not* giving up!" He'd finally lost his cool and I got perverse satisfaction from the idea that his stress level was up there with mine now. He put his hands on his hips and glared at me. "I'm doing my job. Right now, they have no hard evidence against you. Other than the gum and the fact that you found the body, it's just a wild tale."

I shook my head. "It's always going to be just a wild tale because that's all there is."

His hands dropped to his sides. The anger seemed to drain from him all at once. He closed his eyes and when he opened them said, "Not exactly."

"What?"

He peered deeply into my eyes. His eyes had gone even darker now and it was freaking me out. "Can you sit down?" he asked gently.

Oh no. Not sitting down news.

But I followed his lead and sat back down at the table.

"I heard from Danny that the sheriff is sending items from your car to be DNA tested."

"Why?"

"To show the victim was in your car. Which may mean Wade has planted DNA evidence on those items, considering what he did with the gum."

My heart stopped. "Holy mother of..." I didn't have enough air in my lungs to finish the expletive.

I'd kind of figured throwing the gum into the victim's mouth was just a spur of the moment, opportunistic thing. But it made sense that someone who wanted me convicted badly enough to fake one piece of evidence might be desperate enough to fake more.

"Look, the lab the county uses is really backed up. It takes weeks, sometimes months, to get DNA results. So..."

"Speedy trial," I said.

"Yeah." Nick exhaled a long breath and I knew he wasn't any more eager to go to court tomorrow than I was.

My eyes dropped to the platter. *Screw you, Jilly Crane.* This could be the last time in my life I tasted real homemade pancakes.

Sliding one onto my plate, I lifted the bottle of syrup and

drenched the pancake in sticky liquid. I folded it into thirds with my bare hands and chewed through it like a beaver.

Nick's eyes widened as I repeated the action two more times. Then I got up without a word and left the table.

∿

I pulled Nick's One-fifty into the parking lot of Saint Anne's Church, directly across the street from the Bible church we'd visited last Sunday. St. Anne's was by far the smallest Catholic church I'd ever seen, both in square footage and height, which made sense, considering the size of the population here.

Glancing around, I noticed a couple of cars in the parking lot. According to the sign, mass was already over for the day. I hoped the doors were still unlocked.

The truth was, I kind of freaked out after Nick gave me the news. Before this morning, my murder trial had seemed vague and far off. Between enjoying my time with Nick, working at Barr's and trying to solve the murder, I'd been able to put the trial out of my mind for the most part.

Actually, I'd pretty much convinced myself I'd find the killer and there would be no need for a trial at all. So, after I fled Nick's kitchen without so much as rinsing my plate, all I could think of was how much I needed my grandmother.

But I still couldn't bring myself to call her when she'd be powerless to do anything but worry. So, in a moment of desperation, I threw my—aka BreeAnne's—dress on and took off for the nearest Catholic church, the place I went with my Lita every Sunday of my childhood.

Not this particular church, of course, but it was as close as I could get to the sanctuary where I was always safe from the heckling and bullying that was a part of my everyday life back then.

As I walked toward the front door, I felt pretty hypocritical. I hadn't been to mass or confession in several years, mainly because I couldn't find anything about religion for my logical brain to hang its hat on.

Yet, as soon as shit—I looked up at the cross carved into the front door—I mean, *stuff* got real, here I was.

No atheists in foxholes?

I closed my eyes and sighed. Really, all I wanted to do was sit in a pew and look up at the stained glass and pretend my Lita was by my side.

At the top of the steps, I took a deep breath and pulled on one of the handles. The door swung open. As I stepped inside, I couldn't see a thing.

Reflexively, I put my fingers to my eyes and rubbed my lids, opened them and realized I just needed time to adjust from the bright daylight to the dim interior.

As the door closed slowly behind me, it emitted a *creeeeak.*

Gulp.

Church hadn't been this creepy when it was full of people and my grandmother was holding my hand.

From the small foyer where I was standing, I could see all the way through to the huge crucifix attached to the front wall of the sanctuary.

The place was deathly quiet. Although, in a church, I guess you're supposed to think of it as "peaceful."

I took a few steps forward and paused. The whole point of coming here was to calm my fears, not give me a fresh case of the heebie-jeebies.

I shook my head. This was a bad idea. But as I turned to go, my eyes caught on a tall brown table that held a floral arrangement, a small statue of the Virgin Mary, and two piles of papers.

One was a stack of bulletins from the day's mass, but it was the other one that captured my interest. I stepped closer, lifting one of the pages to make sure I was seeing what I thought I was seeing.

A word search! Clearly meant for children, it was printed in large letters like the partial I'd found in JimBob's truck. The title at the top read, "Bible Word Search #48."

I scanned the word bank and the bottom half of the puzzle to see if it was the same one.

No "donkey" or "camel." Not even a "crap" or a "fart."

This was silly. How many word puzzles were there in the world? Besides, JimBob didn't even come to this church. And, really, I was only focusing on the children's puzzle because I didn't have real clues to investigate.

"May I help you?" My head jerked at the unexpected sound, and I came face-to-face with Severus Snape.

I gasped audibly.

Steadying myself with the edge of the table, I eased my breath out slowly. Okay, he wasn't actually Snape. But if you told me they were brothers, I wouldn't argue the point. Same dark eyes. Same dour expression. *Same black frock?*

Oh. This frock was topped with a white collar.

"I'm Father Heinrich," the man said in a German accent that scared me even more than his face. "I'm sorry..." His voice was hard, cold. "But you missed mass." His eyes bore into me accusingly.

"Yes, um...I'm sorry, too." I lied. I cringed inwardly, waiting to be struck by lightning before remembering I didn't believe in that stuff anymore.

Old habits die hard.

Father Heinrich bared his teeth at me. Well, maybe it was supposed to be a smile, but it looked artificial and didn't reach his eyes.

I wanted to go running back to the safety of Nick's house. When I heard the paper crumple in my hand and glanced down at it, my wits returned. "Do you have these all the time?" I lifted the puzzle for him to see.

"Yes. We change them out every week. Something to keep the little ones busy during the mass."

I dug my phone out of my purse and pulled up a photo of the paper fragment I'd taken from JimBob's truck. "Is this one you've given out before?"

He peered down at my phone screen. "It's possible. I don't pay much attention. There are sites online where you can download Bible word puzzles. I just make copies and set them out."

So, it was possible the word search had come from here, but how would it have gotten into JimBob's truck?

"Do the McGwires ever attend mass here?" I asked.

Father Heinrich nodded. "Two of them were here this morning. They come pretty regularly."

"Do you ever see all three at once?"

"No, but I haven't been here long. I'm only aware there are three of them because people talk, you know."

Weird. Why would triplets who did everything else together attend two different churches? "Do you know which two have been coming?"

"I'm afraid only God knows the answer to that question." He held out his hands, palms up and lifted his eyes skyward, a pretty melodramatic move for such a basic conversation.

So, two brothers were likely Catholic, one protestant, presumably JimBob. Or, they could be shuffling back and forth one or two at a time. But what would be the point in that?

"Instead of trying to invent evidence against my parishioners, perhaps you should just confess, Miss Martín." Creepy crawlers skittered down my back at the sound of my name coming out of his mouth.

His eyes bore into mine as if he was examining my dark, murderous soul. Guilt washed through me.

Wait a minute! I was innocent!

"Confess?" I repeated, in case he didn't hear what had come out of his own mouth. I glanced toward the confessional booths along the side wall.

"To the police. You should confess and take a plea deal. It would be a shame for you to spend the rest of your life in jail."

What was wrong with this picture? I folded my arms and tilted my head, staring at him every bit as hard as he was staring at me. "Shouldn't you be encouraging me to confess my sins to you?"

"I see no repentance in your eyes," he replied. "What good would it do for you to confess if you feel no remorse?"

My chest swelled with righteous anger. "I feel no remorse because I'm fu—*freaking*—innocent!" I snapped.

His eyes remained level on mine, hardly blinking, like he was trying to psych me into a confession. Why would he want me to confess to the cops so badly? He was supposed to be concerned with my eternal soul.

I thought about the Reverend Jenkins across the street. What the hell was wrong with the reverends around here? Maybe Bolo was the place bad ministers were sent to be punished.

"I'd expect a man of the cloth to be above local gossip," I said.

"I've found most gossip is rooted in truth."

That was it. He was calling me a murderer and a liar after I'd come here for comfort in my time of need!

Since my Hermione Granger wand was back in L.A. at my grandmother's house, I lifted the Ginseng Nick had gotten me, flipped on its tiny flashlight and beamed it right into Father Heinrich's face.

"*Densaugeo!*" I cried.

I didn't wait around to see if his teeth grew to Bugs Bunny size, but I liked to think they did.

CHAPTER TWENTY-TWO

Rika

The cowbell sounded as I entered Dill's Dollar Store. ReeAnne, who was arranging a patriotic t-shirt display, turned and smiled at me. As I smiled back, I realized she was probably just excited to get to tell her friends about her latest Grey Widow run-in.

"Hey there, Rika," she called.

"Hi, ReeAnne. I'm here to pay up, but I want to look around a little first."

"Have at it," she replied cheerfully and went back to her work.

I headed toward the nail section and was relieved to find a manicure set. It was one thing to eat Nick's food and sleep in his guestroom, but no way was I asking to borrow his toenail clippers.

While I was there, I decided to search for a more conservative nail polish for court. LeeAnne had insisted on painting mine dark red one day when there were no customers in the bar.

I kind of enjoyed it at the time, but now I was afraid the color would make it easier for jurors to imagine me with blood on my hands.

Nick had already texted me to make sure I was okay. And to inform me LeeAnne had dropped off court clothes for me—what she referred to as "funeral clothes." I just hoped they were more head-of-state funeral clothes as opposed to the sparkly Liberace version.

After picking up some cheap sunglasses to temporarily replace the ones Sheriff Strickland took away with my car, I headed to the checkout stand.

"This stuff, plus whatever I owe you for last time," I said as ReeAnne approached.

"Sure *thang*." She began ringing up my new purchases. "How's it going for you over at Barr's?"

"Great," I replied. "LeeAnne's been really nice."

ReeAnne's eyes widened and she leaned in. "Can you believe the dead guy turned out to be her ex? She's always been just awful at pickin' men, bless her heart." Her head dipped to the left, pseudo-sympathetically, with the last phrase.

"Wait. What?" Surely I misheard. "The dead guy is who?"

"LeeAnne's ex-husband Avery. Nobody else around here recognized the name because she met him when she moved up to North Texas. I went up to visit her once, though."

My head reeled, trying to make sense of this new information. Did Nick know the victim was LeeAnne's ex? Surely LeeAnne knew the identity of the body by now. LeeAnne knew everything that went on in this county.

"How did you hear who the victim was?" I asked.

"Danny told me his name when he came in the other day and I recognized it." She shrugged. "Weird coincidence that Avery ended up dead in Bolo when he lived in the panhandle his whole life, as far as I know."

"Yeah," I said. "Weird."

I grabbed my bag and my change and took off for Nick's.

$\sim$

After charging through the house like a crazy person, I found Nick in the backyard, watering plants. I marched across the thick green lawn until I was a couple of feet behind him.

"*What. The. Fuck?*" I yelled.

He turned and I lost my train of thought. He was wearing his jeans, cowboy hat, no shirt ensemble, holding his extra-long hose in his hand. Trickles of sweat were using his abs as a water slide.

Nick frowned at me. "Are you still upset about the trial starting tom—"

"*The trial?*" His stupid question caused my anger to reignite, full force. My hands flew up in the air. I was now talking with them like my grandmother and aunts did, but the action was beyond my control. "No, I'm not upset about the trial. I'm infuriated that you didn't tell me the dead guy was LeeAnne's ex guy! You knew, didn't you?"

Nick hung his head to one side, closed his eyes and sighed. "Yeah, I knew." He lifted his lids and I was struck mute by the soulful blue shining back at me.

Maybe I should have done this via text message.

"I got a full report about him from the private investigator a couple of days ago," he said.

Several seconds ticked by as hot Latina blood—which, apparently, is a real thing—scalded my middle, flowed through my limbs, and scorched me all the way to the tips of my toes. It charged up into my neck and I thought my head would blow off.

I forced myself to breathe deeply as I pried my gritted teeth apart. "Why didn't you forward the report to me?"

"Avery Cook had never been arrested for anything, but the authorities feel certain he was involved in criminal activities, mainly because of the people he's been associating with all over the state," Nick said, way too calmly. "After what you did with JimBob, I was afraid you'd run off half-cocked and try to question those associates."

Whatever guilt Nick had felt initially for withholding information was gone from his expression. Now, his face said, *I'm the big, smart man who's got to save this silly girl from herself.*

Asshole.

"Is this what you normally do?" I asked in a low half-growl. "Hide key pieces of evidence from your clients?"

"No, not normally, but—"

"Let's get something straight." I pointed a finger at his chest. He was lucky it wasn't a gun. "You're not in charge of me. I'm not your mom, your sister, or your girlfriend."

"*True...*" He reached up and used the side of his hand to push my finger away slowly, like he was trying to disarm an insane person without spooking her. "If you were my girlfriend, you'd be sleeping in an entirely different part of the house."

My mind flashed to Nick's extra-tall bedroom with its extra-large bed and, somehow, a shot of half-naked Nick and his extra-long hose got superimposed into the scene.

I waited for his mischievous grin to emerge, but he wasn't laughing and his eyes were one hundred percent serious as if he could imagine a scenario where I would be... where we'd be...

Damn it! Was he trying to distract me by flirting? Probably. His type had that tactic figured out before they finished elementary school.

I shook off the effects and glared at him. "You didn't even tell me the victim was my boss's ex!"

"I figured she'd tell you if she wanted you to know."

"If she *wanted* me to know? Why would she want anyone to know? It makes her a suspect!"

Nick shook his head. "LeeAnne didn't do it," he said as he walked to the outdoor spigot and turned off the water.

I followed him. "How can you say that for sure?"

"I've known her all my life," he said as if that was that. "She didn't do it." He held his arm up in an L-shape and began winding the hose around it.

This time, even his impressive guns couldn't distract me from the subject at hand. "You've known a lot of people around here all your life and there's a good chance one of them did it! And don't you think it's kind of weird LeeAnne hasn't mentioned to me that she was married to the man I'm accused of killing?"

I followed him up the deck stairs. He put the hose down and sat in a chair.

I wasn't ready to sit.

"Not really," Nick said. "It was a tough time for her. I heard Cook was pretty abusive."

For a moment, I felt bad for LeeAnne. She didn't deserve to be abused. She'd given me a job right off the bat. She'd lent me clothes. She'd been nothing but nice.

But what if all that niceness came out of guilt because I was arrested for a crime she committed? Or, worse, a way to keep me close and keep tabs on what was going on?

"That makes her more of a suspect." I sat down in the other chair, turned, and looked Nick in the eye. "Him being abusive. A bad marriage. It makes her a suspect and everyone is just ignoring that fact."

"No one's ignoring it," Nick said. "Wade's asked her to come in for questioning tomorrow."

"Wade? As in Sheriff Wade Strickland, the man who arrested me for reporting the body?"

"Rika..." Nick said on a sigh. "LeeAnne's not a murderer."

He was looking at me with gentle blue eyes as if he wished he could produce a killer for me and put my mind at ease.

But what did I know about him or any of the people in this town? What was this weird relationship he and LeeAnne had, where he acted like he hated her, but stuck up for her behind her back? How did I know Nick was really trying to get me out of this murder rap?

All the people in this town had known each other for years— Gabe, Wade, J.J., Nick...

I didn't get to choose my attorney. Gabe assigned one to me.

How did I know they weren't *all* involved in the crime somehow? This entire town could be a crime syndicate, and I could have been the unlucky outsider who literally stumbled onto their criminal escapades.

Shit! What have I gotten myself into?

"Hey," Nick tugged gently on a strand of my hair.

"Hm?" It was all I could manage without blurting out the thoughts that were raging through my head.

"I've got meatloaf in the oven and I was about to make home-made mac and cheese. Want some?"

I wanted to tell him I wasn't hungry, march away, and shut myself in my room so he could sit alone and do some serious thinking about his lies of omission.

My stomach yowled at the threat of missing one of Nick's dinners.

I shrugged. "I guess so."

Besides, I hadn't met a problem that couldn't be relieved—at least temporarily—by a few mouthfuls of macaroni and cheese.

Nick

I yanked the second pillow out from under my head—the one I'd shoved there just a minute before.

I flipped from my right side to my left, a tactic I often used when I wanted to switch off a particular subject that was nagging at my brain.

It didn't work.

Rika...jury selection... trial... Rika on trial for murder...

Truth be told, this wasn't the first night I'd laid here obsessing over her, but none of them had been as intense as this. In fact, a few of those thoughts had been downright pleasurable.

Not tonight.

Tonight, my brain bounced back and forth between the look

of betrayal in her eyes when I told her the trial was starting, to wondering how I was going to seat a halfway intelligent jury while J.J. tried to pack the box with idiots.

Knowing I was the one person responsible for keeping Rika out of prison sent molten iron pouring into my stomach, every single time. Since the trial was scheduled a few days ago, I felt like I was lugging an anvil around in there.

She'd wanted to solve the murder herself. I had to admire that. But it was pretty naive.

Not that she wasn't smart enough, but to solve a crime you need evidence or a witness or, at least, a police force that's not working against you.

From the day Gabe assigned me this case, when I wasn't trying to act calm in front of Rika, I'd been making notes at all hours of the day and night. Notes on the evidence and lack thereof. Notes on the slipshod way the sheriff was handling the case. Notes on every conceivable angle J.J. Boyle could use to make Rika look guilty.

I kept a legal pad next to my bed for when I woke up during the night with a new idea I needed to get down on paper.

Those notes were all typed and organized and sitting on my desk, despite the fact that I wouldn't need them tomorrow and would certainly have new ones in the next few days before the actual trial.

This time couldn't end up like last time. I didn't have the intestinal fortitude to watch another innocent person go to jail. Rika of all people.

I didn't know how it happened, but she'd really gotten under my skin. Sometimes I didn't want her to go back to L.A. almost as badly as I didn't want her to go to prison.

I'd promised myself I'd never, ever tell her that. I'd made a mess of my life. She was young and beautiful and, most importantly, smart. She could do a lot better.

If I could just get her out of this murder rap, she'd have a great life, and that's all I could ask for.

I turned onto my right side again and took in a deep relaxing breath.

Relaxing, my ass. Who was I kidding? I wasn't falling asleep anytime soon.

I threw back the covers, walked to my office and picked up my notes.

CHAPTER TWENTY-THREE

Rika

I stood behind the bar watching as the finalists' names were called in the costume contest.

It didn't seem fair that after two grueling days of jury selection, I had to spend another working at Barr's Fourth of July picnic. And although I appreciated LeeAnne lending me more-or-less appropriate clothing for court, I couldn't muster up the same gratitude regarding the costume she lent me for today.

In what universe did I belong in a Dolly Parton costume? Over a giant foam rubber-filled bra, I was wearing a white fringed western top with pearly snaps and white stretch bell bottoms. A platinum blonde wig topped off the ensemble, one so voluptuous, it made me about five inches taller.

I asked LeeAnne why she didn't go as Dolly, since the costume made a lot more sense with her skin color. She said normally she did, but she wanted to shake things up this year and dress as Britney Spears.

When I reminded her the costumes were supposed to be country western singers or southern heroes—don't ask me why on Independence Day—she informed me that Britney was from Louisiana.

Hm. Okay.

I was glad the evening was almost over. The picnic and games held on the large field next to the bar were done. As soon as the costume contest was finished, everyone would get into their cars and drive to the next town where a professional fireworks display was held each year.

It seemed like nearly all the locals had been here today, including Father Heinrich, who'd glared at me all day from his fancy deck chair with built-in umbrella.

Sheriff Strickland and Ms. Tilly were there. I noticed he didn't drink much when she was around to keep an eye on him. If only she'd been with him the night he was picking gum up off the ground and sticking it into a dead guy's mouth, I might not be on trial for murder.

That thought evoked a strange mix of emotions, considering I only met Nick because I was arrested. The idea of never knowing he existed produced a hollowed out feeling in the base of my throat until I gulped it away.

Deputy Dan came to the picnic with his mom, who he still lived with. Nick and Tammy Lynn sat with Gabe and Belinda until Nick—who was apparently too cool to wear a costume—bowed out early to go home and work on the case. He ended up driving Ms. Tilly home because Sheriff Strickland had to answer a call about a burglary.

The day was a hectic one for me, which was probably a good thing because I was so busy hustling food trays back and forth between the kitchen and the picnic area, I didn't have a lot of time to worry about my trial.

And now I was just exhausted and wanted to hit the sheets.

I took a few more glasses into the kitchen where Dwight stood in his Spider-Man costume—the only costume he would ever wear, according to LeeAnne—loading the ancient dishwasher.

When I returned to the main room, an all too self-assured J.J. Boyle was accepting the blue ribbon for his Colonel Sanders costume.

They sure had a loose definition of "hero" around here.

After the applause and congratulations, people began to clear out surprisingly fast. LeeAnne and I gathered up the remaining dishes and took them into the kitchen.

I'd been trying not to think about the fact that she still hadn't said a word to me about her ex.

When I was with LeeAnne, it was hard to think of her as a killer, but sitting in court yesterday and the day before, it had really eaten at me.

Could we truly ever know what another person was capable of? Not all killers looked like killers, not even all serial killers. I mean, sure, Charles Manson was a no-brainer, but Ted Bundy was so dreamy, Mark Harmon played him in the movie. And my grandma loved Mark Harmon.

"Rika?" I jumped at the sound of LeeAnne's voice.

"Yeah?" I replied as my hand pressed my heart back into my chest.

"Sorry if I startled you. Are you going to see the fireworks?"

"No," I replied. "I'm just going to head home...I mean, to Nick's."

She chuckled at my Freudian slip. My face heated. I always assumed I had too much pigment in my skin for people to know when I was blushing. Or, at least I hoped.

"Anyway," she went on. "Dwight really wants to go see them, so I was wondering if you'd close up."

"Sure." I couldn't possibly say "no." I'd never seen Dwight act as happy as he had today in his Spider-Man costume and, if a fireworks display would top off the night for him, I didn't want to stand in his way.

"Okay, thanks," LeeAnne said. "When we leave, just get the key from my desk and lock the front door. Oh, and check the game room for any trash people may have left around and take the trash bag out to the big garbage can. Dwight's already set it on the rolling cart outside the kitchen door... along with the vacuum cleaner." She sighed. "We had it so long, it was like part of the family, but it's dead as a doornail now."

I wasn't sure what the appropriate statement here was—*I'm sorry for your loss?*

Luckily, LeeAnne kept talking. "Then all you have to do is lock the back door with the same key and roll the cart over next to the dumpster. We don't want to draw the varmints closer to the building."

"No problem," I said. I'd helped LeeAnne and Dwight go through the closing process several times.

"But you don't need to dump the big trash can into the dumpster," LeeAnne added. "Just leave the cart next to it and Dwight will take care of it in the morning."

"Got it," I said.

When the last customer left, thirty minutes later, I went to LeeAnne's office. I sat down at the desk, opening and closing two of the three drawers, but finding no key. I hesitated to open the bottom drawer, since it was the one where she kept a gun.

When I did, I was surprised to find it completely empty—no key, no gun. I hoped no one had snuck in on my watch and stolen a firearm. However, LeeAnne kept her office unlocked all the time as if she had no worries about gun theft whatsoever.

As I shut what I thought was the last drawer, I realized there was one more—a skinny one right below the lip of the desk. I opened it and froze.

What was that noise?

It had sounded exactly like the squeak the front door made every time it was opened. Or was it the drawer?

I couldn't be sure. And, since I wasn't the murderer, the real killer was running around loose, maybe still in this town.

I snatched up the key, not bothering to close the drawer, and tiptoed down the hall to the kitchen. Seeing no one there, I dashed in, transferred the key to my left hand, and grabbed one of the large chef knives Dwight used for chopping.

Holding the weapon to my chest as I prowled around the place didn't make me feel one iota better. I was in Texas. What were the chances an intruder wouldn't have a gun?

Or a chainsaw! I instantly regretted my horror movie addiction. I'd seen every Texas Chainsaw Massacre movie—old and new—multiple times. They'd been scary fun in the moment, but I never took the fear home with me because I lived in big cities far, far away from Texas.

My stomach turned as I remembered a scene from Texas Chainsaw Massacre 2, when Leatherface took a fresh bloody face he'd cut off a dead person and placed it on the live female DJ he'd abducted from the radio station.

I didn't want a dead person's face on mine. And I certainly didn't want to *be* the dead face.

I shuddered as I skulked through the doorway into the main room. I whipped my head right, then left, but saw no sign of anyone. It was quiet as a cemetery.

Shuffling backwards into the hall, I pushed the doors open to both bathrooms.

They were empty. I headed back to the main room. As I emerged from behind the bar, I peeked around it to make sure no one was crouched up against it on the other side.

A crash sounded and I jumped three feet into the air, thrusting the knife out in front of me, threateningly.

Oh. That was just the old ice machine dumping a new batch of ice.

But there was still one room left uninspected. The game room. As I crept toward it, I decided that if the intruder hadn't come in armed, he could be waiting on the other side of the doorway with a pool cue.

When I reached the doorway, I ducked, thinking he'd be trying to whack me in the head. While he was thrown off by my fancy ducking ploy, I would stab upward and get him under the chin.

The room was empty.

I expelled the breath I was holding, just as relieved at not having to stab someone as I was at not getting a pool stick to the head.

Whew. Okay. I was being silly. I walked calmly to the front door, locked it and pushed on it a few times to make sure the deadbolt had caught.

I went to LeeAnne's office and closed the small drawer. It squeaked...just like the front door.

I'd been a silly, silly girl.

After I picked up the last couple of beer bottles and wiped down the bar top, I pulled the trash bag out of the kitchen garbage can and tied it.

When I walked through the kitchen and opened the back door, the cart was waiting there, just as LeeAnne had said. It was kind of like those luggage carriers bellmen put your bags on in hotels, except this one held the poor dead vacuum cleaner and a much larger garbage can than the one in the kitchen. I stuffed the trash bag into the top of it, then paused and looked around.

The parking lot was empty. The adjoining field where the picnic was held had been cleared of all remnants of human activity. No cars passed on the road, probably because nearly everyone in town had left for the fireworks.

Until I landed in Bolo, I hadn't realized how accustomed to noise I was.

Real noise. Horns honking, car motors, sirens... My entire life had been spent surrounded by man-made sounds.

As I locked the back door up tight, I wondered if I could ever get used to such peacefulness. Not that I'd necessarily have to. I mean, unless Nick and I somehow ended up together.

Jeez! Just stop it, Rika. He was forced to be your lawyer and he's a nice guy. End of story.

I glanced over at the dumpster at the edge of the parking lot and began pushing the cart toward it. I needed to keep my thoughts planted firmly in reality. This garbage was real. My murder charge was real. A relationship with Nick was—

Boom. Ping.

I looked around, trying to figure out what I'd heard.

Boom. Ping.

There it was again. And a dent that wasn't there a moment before appeared on the pole, right above my index finger.

I glanced around. I thought I saw movement in some oak trees to the left side of the parking lot near the road. Was someone shooting off fireworks?

Boom.

Something hot grazed the side of my thumb as it dawned on me I was being shot at.

Suddenly panicked, I jumped behind the garbage can. It was only made of plastic, but at least the shooter couldn't see me. From that position, I tried to pull the cart forward, but pulling it from the side caused it to move all wonky, the back end turning toward me until it did a one-eighty. This device was clearly designed to be pushed from the back, not pulled from the side.

I went with it, flipping it around and around, careful to stay behind it as shots rang out and metal dinged around me.

When the cart and I finally made it to the dumpster, I huddled behind the large metal receptacle, trying to decide my next move. If I stayed behind the dumpster, would the shooter give up and go away, or come in closer for the kill?

Moving around the back, I peeked at the parking lot to remind myself how far away Nick's truck was.

It was parked facing the empty field, fifteen, maybe twenty, yards away.

Not far at all when you're strolling leisurely to your car after a matinee. But when you're running for your life from a determined killer, it might as well be a football field.

Two things I was sure of. One: I needed to get to the truck and drive out of here. Two: If I tried to get to the truck, I was going to die.

Something trickled down my forehead. Was I hit?

I reached up to touch my scalp and felt...the wig. I'd completely forgotten I was wearing it. Pulling it off, I wiped the sweat from my forehead.

I was about to toss it away when an idea hit me. A stupid, crazy idea.

But the only one I had.

CHAPTER TWENTY-FOUR

Rika

I pulled the heavy trash can off the cart, but left the vacuum where it was. Taking the wig off my head, I balanced it on top of the vacuum handle. The weight of the hair caused it to slide to one side and fall to the ground.

Shit!

I turned to the garbage can and dug around until I found what I was looking for. A full bag of hamburger buns we'd been forced to throw out today, due to mold. I removed the twist tie and used it to fasten the wig to the vacuum handle so it hung from the top.

I paused for a moment, listening. The shooting had stopped. What did that mean? Was the shooter searching for me with a rifle scope? Coming closer to find me and take me out at point blank range? I imagined my blood spattering the side of the dumpster.

Focus, Paprika!

Grasping the sides of my shirt, I yanked the snaps open, stripper style. As quickly as I could, I hung the shirt on the vacuum cleaner bag and resnapped it. I was down to my bra and stretch pants but, for once, I would have gladly appeared naked in public if that's what would keep me alive.

I checked my handiwork. There was no way a vacuum cleaner pretending to be Rika dressed up as Dolly Parton would work for long, even in the dark parking lot. I only hoped it would provide a distraction for the few seconds I needed to run to the passenger side of Nick's truck. If I was right about where the shots were coming from, the truck would hide me from the shooter.

I pulled the truck keys from my pocket. Summoning every last drop of strength, I pushed the cart, hard, back toward the building, then turned in the opposite direction. As I got to the back side of the dumpster, a barrage of gunfire told me my plan was working.

So, I ran.

I think I ran faster than I'd ever run before, yet it felt like I was moving in slow motion, hoping my dirt-sucking twin would keep my potential murderer's attention for a few seconds longer.

When I was within a few yards of the pickup, I remembered to click the unlock button, but as I did, the wedged bottom of my shoe hit the ground at an angle. My ankle twisted and there was a teetering, flailing moment before I found myself sprawled out, face down on the pavement.

I pushed myself up, half crawling, half running, until I slammed against the side of the truck. I slid down, resting my back against a tire as I skimmed my hands over my body to make sure I wasn't hit anywhere important. To calm my exploding heart, I told myself if necessary, I would simply make a tourniquet out of my bra, or seal the wound with the duct tape I'd seen behind Nick's seat.

There was no blood that I could find, but I was pretty sure I had bruises from the fall, along with the twisted ankle.

Quietly, I pulled the passenger-side door open, and crawled onto the floorboard. Once I got the door closed, I dragged myself up into the driver's seat, keeping my head low.

I needed to get out of here.

I looked down at my hand expecting to find keys, but they weren't there. I felt around on the seat as my mind replayed the last couple of minutes, including the one when I fell and the keys flew out of my grasp.

Nooo! I scooted back to the passenger side and peered out the window. There were no keys that I could see anywhere near the truck. By now, the shooter was probably trying to figure out if I'd run back to the building, gotten in the truck, or run off into the field somewhere. I couldn't get out and wander around looking for keys.

Please, God, let me get out of this alive!

Okay, the original saying was true after all. There are no atheists in foxholes. I just hadn't understood before because I'd never been pinned down under enemy fire. I looked over my shoulder and saw the wig and, once snazzy, fringed shirt, both riddled with holes.

That was supposed to be *me.*

And it was still going to be me if I didn't think of something fast.

My phone vibrated in my back pocket. I pulled it out and was relieved to see Nick's name on the screen. I pressed it and said, "Nick?" breathlessly into the phone.

"What's wrong?" he asked, alarm obvious in his voice.

"I'm alone at Barr's. Someone's shooting at me in the parking lot. I made it to the truck but I lost the keys."

"Stay in the truck. I'm on the way back from mom's. I'll be there in less than two minutes," he said. "I have an extra key with me."

"Okay, thanks." The phrase seemed completely inadequate for this situation. Wait, if Nick was coming here, he could get hurt. "No, Nick. Never mind," I said. "It's too dangerous. I'll think of something."

"Stay the hell there!" he yelled. Then, in a slightly calmer tone he added, "Stay in the truck. Keep your head down. I'm almost there."

Seconds later, he squealed into the parking lot and pulled up next to me. When I saw the passenger window of his Ranger glide down, I tried to open mine, but it wouldn't go down without the key in the ignition, so I opened the door.

"Here's the key," he called. He threw it towards me.

Shit! The key seemed to be flying at me in slow motion. I flashed back to those miserable days in P.E. when I stood at the back of the volleyball court praying, "Don't let the ball come to me! Don't let the ball come to me!"

Did he still not understand what a big nerd I was? I worked out, but I did *not* engage in actual sports. I especially didn't engage in sports that involved catching things that were flying in the air at me. I'd never been able to catch a ball. How could I possibly catch a key?

I thrust my hands out wildly and...

Caught the key.

I stared down at it in disbelief.

Gunfire rang out, jarring me back into action. My rear window shattered.

"Fuck!" Nick cried. "Stay as low as you can!"

I glanced toward him to verify he was taking his own advice. He was scrunched way down, the top of his head nearly even with the back of the seat.

I stuck the key in the ignition and started the truck. My phone rang. Nick.

"Listen. On three we drive forward." This would put us onto the dirt field, but I knew from the day's activities it was hard and dry. "Then veer left back onto the pavement so you can leave through the driveway. If you don't you'll end up in the ditch. Got it?"

"Yeah," I said.

"I'll stay next to you and block 'em 'til we get to the driveway.

When we do, you go in front of me and hightail it home. I'll be right behind you. Ready? One...two...three!"

We both drove into the field then swerved left, like a couple of synchronized swimmers, if the synchronized swimmers were driving trucks on dry land while being shot at. So maybe it wasn't much like synchronized swimming, but I was surprised at how in sync we were.

Shooting had restarted as soon as we took off. I heard glass breaking and turned to check on Nick. His driver's side window was blown out.

"Nick!" I screamed, then realized his head was still on his body.

He slowed and I raced ahead of him, screeching out of the driveway and onto the main road to the sound of pings that seemed to be hitting the side of the Ranger. Nick peeled out behind me.

When I got to the turn, I ignored the red light. I didn't slow down enough and just missed plowing into the grand historical home on the corner, however, I did take some of its lawn with me.

A glimpse at my rearview mirror confirmed Nick was behind me. I turned right onto Zombie Road and headed for his house.

As we drove up to the garage, he must have hit the remote because the door slid up and we both pulled inside. The second both vehicles were parked, the door closed behind us. I took off my seatbelt, but sat for a moment, deep-breathing, feeling grateful to be alive.

Nick came over and opened my door. I immediately covered my naked mid-drift with my arms, not wanting him to see any muffin top that might be bulging above my Spandex pants.

"Are you hurt?" Nick asked as he examined me by the light of the cab. After scanning the front of my body, he slid a hand down my back, then up my neck to my hairline.

"I'm okay," I said as his fingers tried to probe through the bobby pins that had held my hair up under my wig. "It's just a nick on my thumb and my twisted ankle," I said. "I'm not sure how actresses run around in stilettos on TV. I couldn't even do it in wedges."

Nick slid an arm under my knees, another behind my back and lifted me out of the truck. I'd seen this done on the soap operas I watched as a teenager. It looked so romantic and I tried a number of times to build a fantasy around the concept. Except whenever my fantasy guy lifted me, he'd grunt from the weight of my hefty body. His knees would wobble and he'd start to drop me.

That's why, when Nick lifted me out of the truck, I held my breath and listened hard.

No grunt. I wrapped my arms around his neck as he carried me through the garage and the house like I was as light as a feather.

Within a few minutes I'd gone from being in mortal danger to feeling incredibly safe in Nick's arms and I didn't want to let go.

"Damn, it's good to be home," I said as I rested my cheek on his strong shoulder.

But it really wasn't the house I was thinking about.

∾

Nick put me down on the couch, saying something about getting me bandages. I hobbled quickly to my room, threw on a tank top and washed my hands, taking extra care with my thumb.

I'd been incredibly lucky. My wound was little more than a scratch on the outside edge of my thumb pad. No one would ever guess it was a bullet wound.

But I flashed back to how close my hand had been to my head at that moment and my insides shuddered.

I realized I was still limping around in the wedges, so I took them off and paced to the living room in bare feet, testing my ankle. It was throbbing, but not broken and I could get around on it. The rest of my body was sore from fleeing for my life, and the fall I took in the parking lot.

Nick came in with a tube of Neosporin, Band-Aids, a roll of bandages, and a bag of frozen corn. He sat down on the heavy square coffee table and lifted both my feet onto his lap.

"What are you doing?" I asked, trying to pull them back. If my feet were ever going to make contact with Nick, I wanted them to be freshly washed and pedicured, not dusty from a day spent working a picnic and running for my life.

Nick laid his hand on my lower shins, keeping my legs where they were until I relaxed them. "I need to compare your ankles to see if one is swollen," he said.

"I already looked." I replied. "It's not swollen."

Nick ran his fingers around my ankles like he was taking some sort of measurement. It tickled. I managed to stifle the giggle, but my body jerked.

He caught the movement and his eyes smized at me mischievously. "I'll be the judge of that," he said.

The look was hot, the statement annoyingly macho. It was confusing being around Nick.

"Why should you be the judge of my ankle?"

He held my foot between his thumb and forefinger, rotating my ankle as he watched it. "What sports did you play?" he asked.

Crap. Sports...sports... I racked my brain for an answer. I'd never played a sport in my life.

"Tennis." It was sort of the truth.

His gaze met mine. "Really?" He lifted his brows, his beautiful eyes peering at me with interest.

They mesmerized me instantly and I came clean. "On computer," I admitted.

Laughter rumbled up from his chest. He shook his head as he pressed the bag of corn to my ankle. "*That's* why I should be the judge."

"What sports did you play?" I asked in a snotty tone, but I really just wanted to know more about him.

"You name it. I've tried it."

Oh, I could play this game. "Curling," I said. I gave him a *take that* look.

"What?"

"Curling," I repeated triumphantly. "It's an Olympic sport. Google it."

The look he gave me caused warmth to spread from my chest up to my cheeks. It was the same look of surprise and appreciation he'd blessed me with the day I talked about doppelgangers and the space time continuum, and a few other times since.

"I'll rephrase," he said as if he were in court. "I've played a lot of sports, but I spent the most time on baseball and football. My dad put me on the peewee teams when I was five. I ended up choosing football in high school."

As he spoke, his thumb caressed the skin just above my ankle. It felt nice, but I couldn't help wondering—if Nick and I had gone to high school together, would he have been one of the guys who looked past me as if I didn't exist? Or one of the assholes who murmured hurtful words and snickered as I walked by? As I saw it, those were the only two options.

"What part did you play on the team?" I asked.

He tilted his head and narrowed his eyes as if trying to decipher a foreigner's English. "You mean what position?"

"Yeah."

"Quarterback."

There it was.

My heart sank into my stomach. But it was important that I got it through my thick skull—and a few other parts of my body —that Nick and I were not birds of a feather and, therefore, could not flock together. Or participate in any other activities starting with the letter F.

That fact was especially important to keep in mind now,

when the simple caress of his thumb sent a zip-a-dee-doo-dah all the way up to my hoo-ha.

Ugh. Even worse. Nick was inspiring me to compose geeky sex rhymes.

Better just rip off the metaphoric Band-Aid now. "Homecoming king, too?" I asked.

He glanced around the room. "Have you been going through my high school yearbooks?"

Sigh. Just as I suspected.

I visualized the cold of the frozen corn moving up to numb my calf, my inner thigh, my hoo-ha.

As I moved my feet from his lap to the floor, I answered his question with a shake of my head.

"Then how did you—?"

"The way you walk," I said. "The way you stand. The way you exist in time and space. Like, 'Of course I belong in this moment,' and 'Of course people are happy to look at me...know me...' etcetera."

His shoulders straightened, his face hardening. "You make me sound like a pompous ass."

I snorted. He didn't get it. "No," I said. "You don't need to be. You get to be what nature made you and it's enough...more than enough."

I wasn't sure why I was sharing this information with Nick, except maybe this was the first opportunity I ever had to explain it to one of his kind. They didn't understand how lucky they were. Even Brandtt wasn't one of the chosen few, having lived his high school years with braces and acne, waiting for a growth spurt that didn't come until he was eighteen.

"You don't have to try to be a particular thing," I went on. "Or change your appearance or the way you act because you're already the thing other people want...or want to be."

Nick narrowed his eyes and looked at me hard. I could see

him running my words through his formidable attorney brain, trying to extract a meaning impossible for him to comprehend.

"But you're..." One of his hands came up and made a gesture that told me he was referring to my face, my body. Implying I was one of those people, too.

"No," I interrupted. "I'm not... I wasn't...any of those things."

His lips parted and I knew he was itching to argue the point, except he wasn't completely sure what we were talking about.

I didn't care to pursue this conversation further. Nick seemed to view me as something other than what I felt I was. I'd be leaving soon, and I wanted him to keep that version of me in his memory banks, assuming he thought about me at all once I was gone.

He uncapped the Neosporin and reached for my hand and I was relieved he seemed to be letting the subject drop.

But as I looked down at the scratch on my thumb, a floodgate opened in my mind and the night's events came rushing through. I flashed back to how close my hand had been to my head when I was hit. Then I thought about the Dolly costume, shot to shreds.

Someone was shooting at me tonight. Someone was trying to kill me. Me. Personally.

My insides began to shudder. As I stared at my hand, it started shaking like I was in the middle of a seven-pointer on the Richter scale. My thumb twitched wildly.

I was having the same kind of delayed reaction I'd experienced in the courtroom that day when the court reporter walked in.

Nick's eyes jerked up from my hand to my face. He looked startled. "You're pale," he said.

A high-pitched sound that could only be described as a hysterical giggle trembled from my lips at the thought of someone with my coloring being pale.

"I'd better get you to a hospital."

I realized I'd stopped breathing and forced myself to inhale a shaky breath.

"No," I said. "I'm not injured. It just sunk in that I could be dead right now."

When I looked down, I wondered if my body was really shaking this much or if my eyeballs were spasming, creating an optical illusion.

Nick jumped up and left the room, returning quickly with a blanket and heating pad. He arranged the blanket over my shoulders and plugged in the heating pad. When he offered it, I grabbed it and held it to my middle.

He finished putting the Band-Aid on my thumb, moved to the couch and sat right next to me. Draping one arm over the blanket, he squeezed me against the side of his body. He used his other hand to rub the heat back into my exposed forearms.

As my body warmed and my breathing normalized, I felt kind of ridiculous. Who comes through a dangerous encounter acting completely normal then suddenly loses it?

Oh. There wouldn't be a need for words like "delayed reaction," "flashback," and "post-traumatic stress disorder," if everyone processed their emotions immediately and completely.

My eyes locked on something else Nick must have brought into the room on one of his trips because it wasn't usually on the coffee table—a box of tissues.

Huh. I guess I should be crying right now.

I should have been hurt that someone thought my life was worth so little—possibly someone I'd actually met. Or I should have been crying relieved tears because I wasn't lying dead in Barr's parking lot with Deputy Dan standing over my shirtless body.

The thing was, I hadn't cried in a long, long time. I didn't cry when Brandtt broke up with me. I didn't cry when the other kids snickered at me in high school. I didn't cry on the junior high bus when I was hit by chocolate milk or whatever else some kid decided to throw at me that day.

I did cry when my mom died. I cried a lot. Day after day for months. When my dad wasn't allowed back into the country after his mother's funeral, I cried again. But in secret, every night before I fell asleep because I knew my grandmother was trying her hardest to be mother and father to me, and I didn't want to make her feel like she was failing.

I cried every night for what seemed like forever. Then one night, I didn't cry. And I hadn't cried since. Even those times when I visited my dad in Colombia and my heart broke at having to leave without him, I didn't cry.

I still felt things in my chest, in my throat...but it was like I'd run out of my lifetime supply of tears. Or maybe I'd gone so long at this point that my body had just forgotten how to do it.

Regardless, being incapable of crying bothered me, so I tried not to think about it often. It wasn't normal, especially among my Colombian family and the Mexican friends of my grandmother, who were often at our house. Sometimes I thought there should be a children's book about me—*The Latina Who Couldn't Cry*.

I looked down at my thumb again and another shudder jerked through me.

"Rika," Nick said quietly. I'd never heard his voice so gentle. It caused a strange sensation in my chest, one I wasn't sure was good or bad, considering all the other sensations rattling around inside me at the moment. "Rika, look at me."

I turned and looked up into his face. His eyes were a deep, dark blue tonight, maybe because of the black t-shirt he had on. Regardless, his look was so intense and so beautiful it took my breath away.

"I've got you," he said as he squeezed the side of my body tighter against his. "I won't let anything happen to you."

I rested my head on his shoulder, and for the next few minutes, we sat quietly as I matched my breathing to his.

Then, almost as suddenly as it began, my fear receded and my brain kicked into gear.

I straightened. "Did you see anything?" I asked. "A vehicle?"

Nick shook his head. "There was nothing parked on the shoulder. You may have noticed all those oaks near the shoulder on that side of the parking lot. LeeAnne's grandparents planted them years ago.

"There's an old dirt road in between them that was the original entrance to their property. It ran up next to the house and back to the old barn way before they thought of building the bar. Once the bar was built and the parking lot was paved, they cleared a new road directly behind the bar and that's what everyone's used to get to the house ever since. I think whoever shot at you was on the old dirt road, using the trees for cover."

As he talked he was staring straight ahead. I turned to look at his profile. Something in my peripheral vision caught my attention.

"Your ear!" I cried. But it was worse than that. Behind the gash at the back of his ear was a line cutting horizontally along his scalp. "Your head!" I yelled. Several small blobs of dried blood clung to the graze.

The nausea came on fast. My hand flew to my mouth and, for a second, I thought I was going to hurl.

I wasn't one of those people who was overly squeamish, fainting at the sight of blood, especially such a small amount of blood. What sickened me was the thought that, while my close call had been on my thumb, Nick's had been on his skull.

"I'm fine," Nick said calmly. "We're both fine."

But he'd almost not been fine. It hit me that his plan to get me safely out of the parking lot had put him between me and the shooter. My heart beat harder in my chest as I realized I had a lot of feelings about that fact.

I hated it because he could have been killed. I loved it because never in a million years would I have imagined a man using himself as a human shield for me.

I also hated that I'd been this damsel in distress who needed to be saved. But I loved that he didn't even hesitate to come to my rescue.

"I'm sorry," I whispered. "I almost got you killed."

Nick removed his arm from my shoulders and pressed our palms together folding his fingers around my hand. "You've got nothing to be sorry about," he said. "You weren't the one doing the shooting." His voice was so warm and reassuring, I wanted to crawl up inside him and live there like one of those alien parasites.

But this was no time to check out. "Do you think JimBob realized I took evidence from his truck and came after me?"

Nick shrugged. "It's possible, but I'm wondering about the timing. Yesterday afternoon, I added your name to the witness list."

I tossed the heating pad onto the coffee table and turned toward Nick, my right leg bent on the couch, my left foot on the floor. "Who would see the witness list?"

Nick released my hand as if the touch was no longer appropriate now that I wasn't dying of shock. That sucked. I started pulling the bobby pins out of my hair so it would look like I had better things to do with my hands than hold his anyway.

"Gabe, J.J., and whoever J.J. shares the information with," he replied.

"Like Sheriff Strickland?"

"Probably."

"So, it could have been JimBob or the sheriff shooting me."

Nick took a deep breath. "Or if JimBob was dumping the body for someone else, that person could be getting worried about the trial."

Great. "In other words, our suspect list still consists of everyone who was on it in the first place."

"Well," he said. "I think we've ruled out Satan worshippers."

We sat silently for a moment as I ran the night through my mind in reverse.

Before Nick came, someone was shooting at me. Before that, I was pushing the cart out to the dumpster—a job Dwight did every single night.

Did it mean something that the one night I took the cart out, I was nearly killed?

I tried to remember who else was left in the bar when LeeAnne asked me to close up, but it had been such a busy day, I was a little fuzzy on that detail.

Maybe it wasn't important. The shooter knew I'd have to come out sooner or later.

For the first time tonight, I noticed Gucci tapping around impatiently at Nick's feet. Had she barked when we'd come in like she usually did? I'd been so consumed by the shooting drama I hadn't noticed. Nick hadn't either.

"I think you'd better take her out," I said.

"Huh?" Nick looked like I'd jerked him out of deep deliberations. "Who?"

I pointed at Gucci.

"Oh." He glanced her way, then his eyes did a quick scan of me. "Are you gonna be okay?"

"Yeah," I smiled weakly at him. "One brush with death is all I had planned for tonight."

He chuckled, even though we both knew it wasn't funny, scooped Gucci up and headed for the kitchen.

I went back to recalling the night's events.

Hmm. Before LeeAnne asked me to close up, I'd spent the day working the Fourth of July festivities in the ridiculous Dolly Parton costume. Before that, LeeAnne had brought the costume to work and insisted I wear it, despite the fact that she'd originally said she had a Crystal Gayle costume for me, which would have made a lot more sense. At least Crystal was a brunette.

When I asked LeeAnne what happened to that costume, she insisted being Dolly would ensure bigger tips, even if the hair color was crazy on me and boobs were clearly fake, because people got a kick out of the "enormous titties," as she called them.

But there was something else that had scratched at the back of my brain this afternoon, something I didn't have time to process because I was so busy. What was it?

I scanned backward and forward several times until my mind snagged on that something.

Speakers outside at the picnic playing country music. A song...

I Can't Stop Loving You.

A file opened in my mind as if I'd clicked it with an intracranial mouse.

CHAPTER TWENTY-FIVE

Rika

I heard the back door open. I jumped up, ignoring the pain in my ankle, and met Nick in the kitchen.

"It's LeeAnne!"

"What's LeeAnne?" Nick asked as Gucci sniffed around my feet for crumbs from the food I wasn't eating.

"The shooter tonight," I said excitedly. "And the murderer!"

Nick's eyebrows rose in an *Are you crazy?* expression.

I talked fast, counting off each point on my fingers. "One: LeeAnne and Avery Cook were in a marriage that involved domestic violence. Two: The day LeeAnne took me to her house, I saw fresh roses in the trash with a card that said, 'I can't stop loving you,' and it was signed 'A,' which means he was still after her."

After the last piece of information, Nick's eyebrows came back down. His face held a concerned frown like he was seriously doubting my sanity.

I ignored him and went on. "Three: Two days after the murder, LeeAnne mentioned her ex and said he would have taken more of her life if she hadn't, quote, 'put a stop to it.' Four:

Today, she insisted I wear a costume that might as well have been a neon sign. Five: She asked me to close up alone for the first time...*tonight.*"

I'd used up all the fingers on my left hand, so I started on the right. "Six: LeeAnne has a bujillion firearms to choose from in her house. And seven: After LeeAnne left tonight, the gun she always keeps in the bottom drawer of her desk at the bar was gone!" I scanned my memory for more incriminating evidence.

Nick blew out a frustrated breath. "We've talked about this. It wasn't LeeAnne," he said, like that was that.

"It wasn't LeeAnne?" I yelled. I noticed I was waving my hands around like a sign language school dropout, so I fisted them and glued them to my hips. "That's all you can say? 'It wasn't LeeAnne'?"

I took a step toward him, but stopped because any closer and I'd have to bend my head back to look up at him. That wouldn't exactly put me in the power position. I wished I still had the wedges on, even with the twisted ankle.

"It wasn't LeeAnne," Nick repeated. He shrugged his shoulders, palms turned toward the ceiling and shook his head at me, clearly annoyed by how unreasonable I was being.

Asshole.

"With my *normal* hair," I pulled a hunk of my hair forward for emphasis, "in the navy blue Crystal Gayle dress I was supposed to wear, I would have been hard to see in that parking lot. But LeeAnne suddenly changed her mind and decided I had to be Dolly Parton... ME!"

Using both index fingers, I pointed to my espresso-colored face and widened my dark brown eyes at him to remind him how ridiculous that costume was on me. "She couldn't have made me a better target if she'd dressed me up as a disco ball!"

Nick was shaking his head again and I wanted to strangle him. He clearly had a blind spot when it came to big-haired blondes and now that my life was in danger, it was really pissing me off.

"I don't know what this weird relationship is you two have," I went on, my hands flailing in the air again. "And I don't care if you screwed her back in the day or whatever. You're my lawyer now and—"

Nick looked at me as if I'd said something perverted.

I gave him my death stare. "*What?*"

"I'd never sleep with LeeAnne." He seemed kind of disgusted by my accusation.

Relief filtered through me. I wasn't one step closer to solving the murder. I just really didn't want him to have a thing for LeeAnne.

I mentally rolled my eyes at myself. *Stop thinking of Nick that way. He wouldn't want you. You're not a big-haired, big-boobed blonde. You're certainly not "pageant girl" material.*

Lowering my hands to my sides I asked calmly, "Can you explain why you're so sure it's not LeeAnne?"

"LeeAnne's got a heart of gold," Nick said. "She literally gave you the shirt off her back."

He was scowling like he was disappointed in me and it stung.

"Besides," he went on. "We were shot at by a rifle tonight, not LeeAnne's grandpa's six-shooter she keeps in the bar. Not to mention the fact that target practice is the Barr family hobby. Her granddad put a rifle in her hands when she was six. She can knock the whiskers off a prairie dog at a hundred yards."

Eek. I hoped that was just a saying. I'd hate to think LeeAnne made a habit of knocking whiskers off prairie dogs, whatever those were. Surely they needed their whiskers for something. I made a mental note to google it later.

"Bottom line," Nick said, "if LeeAnne wanted you dead, you'd be dead."

I tried to decide if I was more relieved to have reason to think my friend LeeAnne might not be trying to kill me or disappointed that my seven fingers of facts added up to zilch.

I wasn't convinced, but my evidence against her was completely circumstantial, so I move on. "In that case, don't we have to rule out the sheriff, too?" I asked.

Nick snorted. "Wade can't hit the side of a barn at twenty paces. No sense of aim whatsoever."

I felt like the facts were just taking me in circles. No one could be ruled out, but no one could be ruled in, except JimBob.

"Can we sit down and talk?" Nick asked.

Uh-oh. This stand-up conversation was bad enough, I didn't want anything to do with a talk that required sitting. But I sighed and sat down at the kitchen table anyway.

Nick walked to the refrigerator, grabbed two bottles of beer, opened them, and set one in front of me. He pulled out the chair across from me and settled into it.

I watched him stare at his bottle for a minute or so before he finally spoke. "One of the reasons I added your name to the witness list yesterday was because I got the reports back on the fingerprints. They're all the same—the receipts, the cans, the glasses from Barr's. Even the glove I found at the crime scene."

My torso jerked forward and I nearly knocked my beer over. "Oh, my God!" I said. "JimBob is the only one using that truck!" I thought about the glove. "JimBob dumped the body." My voice was quiet with the shock of it.

Despite the fact that I'd assumed the person driving the red truck disposed of the body, it was very different than knowing I'd been up close and personal with the perpetrator. My skin crawled at the idea that the same hands that had tried to explore my "deformed" crotch had pulled Avery Cook's corpse from the pickup and thrown it out on the ground.

Nick continued in a level tone, not seeming nearly as affected as I was, but I guess that was to be expected. JimBob hadn't been all up in his business.

"Normally, attorneys are hesitant to put the defendant on the stand in murder cases," Nick said. "In your case, for instance, you might have to answer questions about your employer in New York who has a criminal record, as it turns out."

Crap. I could imagine what the jurors would think of all the "I don't knows" I'd have to answer about my last job. Nick was clearly afraid they wouldn't believe I was just an E.coli tester.

"But," he continued, "you're the only one who can testify about the red truck with the Halo logo at the scene of the crime, and you and LeeAnne can testify about JimBob that night at the bar. Then I'd probably be allowed to enter your recording into evidence."

"Okay..." I said, sensing he had something more on his mind. Something he wasn't as sure about.

His eyes had grown dark with concern. "Now that you're being targeted, I think we need to be a little more proactive."

Proactive sounded good to me. "What do you have in mind?"

"I was thinking we could lure JimBob to the truck dealership with some sort of prize offer. I know someone with the Texas Rangers office. Since Wade could be involved in the crime, I think I can get their cooperation."

"But why would the dealership owner agree to run a sting on one of his own customers?" I asked.

"Because I'm a better customer," Nick replied.

I thought about this for a moment. "All you have is one new truck and one really old one." I watched Nick's gaze flick toward the French doors and stay there. "Unless you bought cars for Megan and BreeAnne."

LeeAnne wasn't the only one who could hit the bullseye. I caught the half-grimace Nick tried to hide. In lieu of an answer, he chugged his beer.

Jeez. I hoped he hadn't bought Megan that fancy little sports car her boyfriend was driving her around in.

"A *really* good customer," Nick added.

My mind shifted gears and I sighed sympathetically. "You bought one for your mom, too."

He nodded, lifted the nearly empty bottle to his lips while splaying his first two fingers as he drained the last drops.

Two for his mother. Maybe she had to have a car every time a wife got one.

"Anyway..." Nick's tone said we were done with that conversation. "We can offer JimBob a cruise or something for test driving a new model. It's a crap shoot whether he'll show up or not. If he does and we get his fingerprints on something while he's at the dealership to prove it's still him and not one of his brothers, we'll lay out all the other evidence, and he may roll over on the killer, assuming it's not him. Maybe agree to a plea bargain and confess if it is."

My mind was racing. Trials were a slow-moving pain in the backside, but solving murder cases was a whole different animal. And now Nick was onboard.

Yay!

"It doesn't have to be a crap shoot," I said.

"How's that?"

"Pax. It's a huge gamer convention in Seattle... Actually, I think they've expanded to other locations now, but since it's bogus anyway, we might as well send him to the original. Offer him airfare, hotel and tickets. Anyone with a video game symbol custom painted on his truck won't be able to resist."

The darkness lifted from Nick's face as his gaze turned bright blue. How did he do that? The corners of his eyes crinkled before the full-blown smile took over his face.

I swooned.

Okay, I'm not really sure what swooning is, but I'm pretty sure I did it. I loved it when he seemed impressed by me. It made me feel all light-headed and melty inside.

He lifted his bottle in toasting position so I lifted mine, too. "Pretty smart for a hot chick." He clinked his bottle against mine.

Heat spread through my entire body. His gaze was warm and approving and bedroom appropriate all at the same time. I couldn't think of a thing to say, so I just smiled back at him and gulped down my beer.

~

I woke up at seven the next morning, even though the trial wasn't scheduled to start until one to give the good citizens of Bolo the chance to recover from their Independence Day revelry.

My heart was racing. I'd been having a nightmare. I closed my eyes again, and attempted to replay the mental images that had me so shaky.

I saw myself, hoisting my heavy body up the steps of the junior high bus. As the door closed behind me, I noticed there was no driver, just seat after seat filled with chattering kids. My heart pounding, I searched for an empty spot.

There was only one, all the way at the back of the vehicle.

As my hand tightened on the strap of my backpack, all noise ceased and every eye onboard turned to stare at me. I sucked in a shaky breath and moved forward.

Suddenly, I was being pelted with food—a peanut butter sandwich, chicken nuggets, jelly doughnuts, a slice of pizza...

But instead of shielding myself or trying to get away, as each new edible hit me, I tried to capture it and stuff it into my mouth. I swallowed as quickly as possible, not bothering to chew if I didn't have to, knowing if I let one morsel hit the floor, something disastrous was going to happen.

I turned and realized the bus was moving fast toward a high curving freeway bridge. There was still no driver, but I knew I was operating the vehicle remotely and I had to keep eating or we wouldn't make the turn on the curve and we'd go hurtling off the side to our deaths. I ate faster and faster until I was choking on the food and that's what woke me up.

It was one of those dreams that sounds stupid if you try to describe it to someone, but is incredibly stressful while you're in the middle of it.

My Jilly Crane counselor was always quoting psychiatrists who claimed the elements in your dreams were not literal, but symbolic of other stressors in your life.

She'd probably say I was feeling overwhelmed at the idea of the murder case against me, and the food represented evidence or something. If she only knew just how far I'd fallen off the wagon lately, she'd...

What could she do? Mantra me to death? She was likely in another state, maybe another country. And she'd never been wrongly accused of murder as far as I knew, so screw her!

Still, I mentally scrolled through the food I'd been scarfing down since I landed in Bolo—tons of red meat, fried everything, and the carbs...

I reached down, placing my thumb at my belly button, my index finger two inches below it. I pinched.

Holy mother of Zeus! It was happening again! I was getting fat!

After falling into this alternate universe where I was the Grey Widow, working at a bar in hoochie clothes and contemplating a life behind bars, I'd somehow managed to let myself believe it didn't matter so much what I ate. As if the extra weight would just melt off magically once I got back in my car and drove over the county line.

I scrambled out of bed, pulled all my clothes off and stood in front of the full-length mirror. How far gone was I?

As usual, I couldn't tell. No matter how much weight I lost or how much I worked out, my stomach never really looked flat.

And I always thought my ass might be too big compared to my boobs. And that maybe my thighs were too thick. How thick should thighs be, anyway?

Whatever.

I took a shower, blow-dried my hair and put on my Batgirl bra and panties. I needed to feel like a superhero if I was going to get through my first day of trial.

I caught a glimpse of myself in the dresser mirror and paused. Could I have gained weight while I was in the shower? I could swear I looked wider.

Hurrying back to the bathroom, I checked the full-length mirror again. Not as wide.

This was like living in a carnival fun house. Which mirror was I supposed to believe?

There was only one way to solve my dilemma and it was with a scale. Even if Nick didn't care about his weight, he'd had two wives. Hadn't one of them left a scale behind?

I heard Gucci barking. The motor of the One-fifty cranked. Nick must be making a quick run to the grocery store as he often did early in the morning.

As my mind flipped to its previous topic, I realized that if there was a scale in the house, the most likely place for it was the master bathroom—the one room I'd never been in.

I had at least thirty minutes before Nick returned, which was about twenty-eight more than I needed.

I opened the door to my bedroom, ignoring Gucci as she stood in the foyer, peering forlornly at the front door.

Hurrying to the vast master bedroom, I entered the adjoining bathroom and...

Wow! I stopped short.

The bathroom was Texas-sized and rustic gorgeous with his and hers round copper sinks, a huge oval wood bathtub, the wall behind it tiled in tiny stones of cream and various shades of brown. The shower was made of stone tiles with copper fixtures.

Who needed the rest of the house? I knew a lot of people in New York who'd be happy to live in this bathroom.

As my eyes scanned the room, I almost missed the scale sitting on the floor between the tub and shower because it was wood, or at least wood colored, and blended in with the rest of the decor.

I approached it feeling both relieved to find it and afraid of what it would tell me.

Taking a deep breath, then exhaling it in case my internal air registered on the scale, I stepped on.

I watched the digital readout change its mind several times before it finally froze on a number.

According to Nick's scale, I was five pounds heavier than when I'd left New York.

I stepped off, let the read-out go dark, and stepped on again.

No change.

Holy mother of Zeus! I'm losing control again! Any minute I'll resume my natural Santa Claus-like shape!

What were those Jilly Crane mantras again? In my current state of panic, they were swirling around, jumbled in my head.

Calm the fuck down!

Okay, that wasn't one of the approved mantras, but it was all I could come up with. It helped a little. My mind settled on a plan.

I just needed to spend a couple of hours in Nick's gym before it was time to go to court, and I'd be back in the groove. Work out every day and cut down on the carbs again and I'd be fine.

But what if I went to prison? They probably served the inmates cheap carby food at every meal. Would there be a gym?

In the movies, the prisoners were always working out in the prison yard with giant dumbbells.

Great. I'd have gigantic arms to match my ginormous ass.

The sound of a sharp intake of breath caused my face to jerk in the direction of the doorway. Nick was standing two steps inside his bathroom, sort of frozen in motion, his chest bare, his t-shirt in his hand as if he'd just taken it off.

His eyes were the only things moving, sliding down my body, lingering on my Batgirl breasts, before skimming all the way down my legs to my toes. When his eyes met mine again, I found they'd deepened to a mysterious dusky gray.

He didn't say a word.

My face heated and my eyes shifted away from his. I was mortified.

Nick had walked into his private bathroom and found his chunky client standing there in ridiculous super hero underwear. What was he supposed to say?

This proved to me, beyond a shadow of a doubt that there was no man upstairs because, if there were a God and this had to happen, surely, he would have made it happen five pounds ago.

After several seconds of stunned silence, during which I watched his pecs rise and fall with his heavy breaths, Nick's lips parted.

"Nice underwear," he said in a husky voice.

I glanced down at my silly Batgirl lingerie. "I didn't buy them," I said defensively. "I'm testing them for a website...an online store." I grabbed a towel from a rack near the bathtub and wrapped it around my body.

"They're...nice," he repeated. His voice was quieter than I'd ever heard it—practically a whisper—yet it held a dangerous quality, and every muscle in his chest and arms was taut.

Was he angry?

"I'm sorry for being in here," I said. "I was looking for a scale. I thought I heard your truck drive away."

He started to speak again, but his voice came out hoarse. He cleared his throat twice, his eyes never leaving my towel. "Some guys came over from the dealership. I left them a message last night. They just delivered us loaner trucks while the others get fixed."

"Well... I'm sorry," I repeated. "I'll just get out of your way." I stepped off the scale and started to leave, holding the towel in an iron grip.

But as I tried to pass him, his hand reached out and grabbed my arm.

No, not grabbed.

He'd touched his fingertips lightly to my upper arm, but the effect was the same. I stopped dead in my tracks is if he were holding me there.

I looked down at his fingers. His hand was so much more masculine than Brandtt's.

The air grew thick around us. My body began to shake. I forced my eyes up to meet his. Electricity jolted through me as if he'd zapped me with a magic wand.

I couldn't move. I thought I heard a sizzling sound in the space between us. His lips parted like he was about to say something, but no sound came out.

Without permission, my body turned so it was facing him. I heard myself whisper, "Nick..."

Suddenly, one of his hands curled around me, sliding up my spine. His fingers wove into the hair at the base of my head and pulled it back as his lips came down on mine. He must have dropped the t-shirt because his other hand cupped my jaw, his thumb caressing my cheek.

When he thrust his tongue into my mouth, I experienced a full body shiver. He rewarded my reaction by going deeper, pressing into me so forcefully, I felt it in my chest.

I melted into his hard torso as his arm tightened possessively around my back.

Holy mother of Zeus. Never in my life had I experienced a moment of such pure unadulterated passion.

I forgot about holding onto the towel. I slipped my hands up his chest, my palms gliding over his shoulders. The towel shimmied down my body and landed on the floor at my feet.

As I pressed harder into him, the button on his jeans scraped the skin just above my belly button. Something long and hard had swelled to life and was digging into my abdomen.

Oh, yes! If I could just have Nick, it would be worth getting arrested and standing trial. Hell, it would be worth getting shot at.

He pulled his head back a little and his lips left mine. I was afraid the kiss was over, but he tilted his head the other way, controlling the position of mine with his strong hand. Then he came back in for more, his lips hard, his tongue thrusting into me over and over until I felt the pressure between my thighs.

I squeezed the muscles in his upper arms and slid my hands higher, toying with the short hairs on the back of his neck. Then I took over the kiss, driving into him, showing him how much I wanted this...

Wanted *him*.

He groaned and cupped my ass, pulling me harder against him.

I couldn't wait any longer. I slid a hand between us and fumbled with the button of his jeans.

Suddenly, Nick's entire body went stiff. His lips stopped moving on mine. His fingers slackened in my hair.

Then, he released me, practically thrusting me away, panting as he steadied himself on the corner of the bathroom counter.

"Fuck," he said.

Yes, that's what I was hoping for, but maybe not the way he meant it right now. Confused, I reached up and wiped my mouth with the back of my hand, wishing I was still wearing the towel.

Nick crossed over and eased down to sit on the edge of the bathtub. After massaging the bridge of his nose for several long seconds, he looked up at me.

"Paprika..." He murmured my real name with such tenderness, I couldn't hate it anymore. "That can't happen again."

The rejection crashed hard in my chest. My mind went where it always had. What was wrong with me? Why didn't he want me?

My eyes darted to the mirror to check the size of my thighs, and to look for traces of the stretch marks I was so obsessed with.

I'd rubbed every special cream or lotion I could find on them from the moment the weight started to come off, finally having hope that a man might see me naked one day.

And they'd worked surprisingly well. Even Brandtt the perfectionist had insisted he couldn't see them. But I was still convinced I could see tiny silver lines on what must be my otherwise resilient skin.

"I... Okay..." I said shakily.

He must have seen the look on my face because he stood and started to reach out to me, but fisted his hand and forced it down to his side instead.

He swallowed hard. "You're my client," he said. "It's unethical..."

"Yeah, okay, I know..." I mumbled.

Was it too much to hope that a man like Nick would be so overcome by passion for me he'd forget he was a lawyer? Forget I was his client? Forget I was a murder suspect?

Okay. Maybe that *was* too much to hope for, but it didn't stop the humiliation from burning over my skin. I would have given anything to be with him. He, on the other hand, was more interested in preserving a law license he didn't even want to use.

Regardless, why kiss me then push me away?

"Rika?" he said gently and I felt his voice in my chest.

"Yeah, sure," I mumbled. "Won't happen again."

And I left the bathroom, half-tripping over Gucci as I fled.

CHAPTER TWENTY-SIX

Rika

I was sitting in court in a tight-fitting charcoal blazer and matching skirt.

Because of the one-button design, I was sure when LeeAnne wore it, the lapels were forced apart by her abundant chest, emphasizing her favorite assets. But since I was smaller up top, her jacket looked fairly demure on me.

The skirt could have used a couple more inches of fabric at the bottom—for both trials and funerals, in my opinion—but I was sitting behind the defense table when the jury came in, so no biggie there.

Nick sat next to me in a dove gray suit, tailored perfectly to his body, looking even hotter than I'd seen him before, which was saying a lot.

Despite all the concerns he'd had about this case from the beginning, today he appeared cool and collected, the picture of confidence.

Meanwhile, I was craving a giant chocolate-chocolate chip muffin—or three—and trying not to fidget.

When J.J. Boyle walked in earlier carrying a briefcase in one hand, a paper grocery bag in the other, I'd hoped the bag was filled with snacks for us all to enjoy. But if it was, they were for later because he'd left it sitting on the prosecution table, untouched.

I fantasized about a first day of the trial after party with a cake and sugar cookies with frosting, plus a variety of chips to balance out the most important food groups—salty and sweet.

"All rise," Deputy Dan said, this time before the judge entered the room. "The court of the Honorable Gabriel Martínez is now in session."

Judge Martínez came in from his chambers, his hands devoid of doughnuts, his robe blacker than it had been at my bail hearing or even during jury selection.

Or was I just imagining that?

After everyone sat down, Judge Martínez glanced at the jury, the court reporter, J.J., then at Nick and me as if making sure everyone was present.

"Mr. Boyle?" he said. "Do you have an opening statement?"

"Certainly, your honor." J.J. stood and tugged once on the bottom of the vest to the navy suit he wore.

He turned and walked with measured steps, stopping only a couple of feet in front of the jury box.

"Ladies and gentlemen of the jury," he began. "A man...is *dead*." He paused for five full seconds to let the last word sink in.

My brain flashed back to the moment I shined my screen light on Avery Cook's face and looked into his pale dead eyes.

"A young man of thirty-five, still in his prime," J.J. continued. "Not a perfect man. A man who made some mistakes." His voice rang out clear and passionate and true, and the building suddenly felt more like a church than a courtroom. "But a good-hearted man..." J.J. released a heavy breath as he bowed his head. "A Texas boy, born and bred."

His voice shook on the words "Texas boy" as if he were

fighting back tears. Several of the female jurors started blinking faster. One lifted a tissue to her eye.

Holy mother of Zeus! J.J. was good. He was, like, a minute into his opening statement and already bringing jurors to tears. Even I had a lump in my throat. By the time the trial was over, I might be ready to convict myself.

No wonder Nick was worried. J.J. wasn't some run-of-the-mill country lawyer. He was one of those "if the glove don't fit, you must acquit" super lawyers.

I slid my eyes over to check Nick's profile. His face revealed no emotion. I figured that was better than the raw fear that was probably showing on mine.

I looked down at the table and inhaled slowly to calm my heartbeat.

"Through the course of this trial," J.J. continued, "I will reveal to you how this poor Texas boy was tempted into a life of crime by the defendant, a sultry Colombian of American birth, experienced beyond her years."

Wow. Nick called it on the Colombian thing. J.J. managed to work it in right off the bat. I had to admit, though, I was kind of flattered by the idea that I had enough "sultry" power to turn a good man bad.

J.J. paced over and stood next to the prosecution table. "She used the skills she's honed in places like Los Angel*eze* and New York City and Medellin, Colombia, to draw poor Avery farther and farther into her dark world. A world, not only of crime..." he reached into the bag on the table and pulled something out. "But perversions of the flesh, as well."

It took my brain a moment to understand what my eyes were seeing as J.J. carried the item he'd taken from the bag toward the jury box. When I realized what it was, I gasped.

About the same time, several female members of the jury gasped, too. Mouths dropped open in shock and hung that way, as if some of the jurors had lost the ability to control their jaw muscles.

This was because, in his right hand, J.J. Boyle was holding a black, two-foot long, double-headed dildo.

I hadn't seen it in a while, but I recognized it as one of the gifts Brandtt's stupid friends had given us at the "Keep Love Alive" anniversary party. It had been sitting in a box with the other stuff in the back of the closet since that night.

Whatever possessed Brandtt to pack it in my belongings instead of leaving it where it was or throwing it away, I didn't know. Maybe he was being considerate, thinking I'd need all those sex toys now that he was out of the picture.

My face heated as the jurors' eyes flicked from the huge dong, to me.

Jeez, Louise!

When we'd opened the gift, I wasn't even sure if it was meant for two people to use simultaneously or for one person to stick into different orifices at the same time.

I still wasn't sure, come to think of it. I'd been afraid to google the subject and see things I could never unsee. And I certainly didn't want to ask about it and give away how inexperienced I was. Brandtt's worldly-wise friends would have teased me mercilessly.

My eyes locked with a middle-aged woman in the jury box, the only African-American juror. Was it somehow racist that the huge phallus was black instead of another color? I cringed at the thought that the jury now believed I was a murdering, perverted, racist. And what must Nick think of me now?

He was out of his chair. "I object, your honor. That...um, *thing* hasn't been entered into evidence. The prosecution is trying to inflame—"

"Sustained," Judge Martínez said. "Mr. Boyle. Put that thing away and approach the bench."

J.J. did as he was told, his face the picture of innocence as he headed to the front and peered up at the judge.

Judge Martínez was speaking quietly, so I squinted, trying to see his lips more clearly.

When I was ten, I went through a phase in which I decided I would become an expert lip reader. I'd never perfected the skill, but I was pretty sure I saw the word "antics" come out of the judge's mouth.

Yeah, J.J., we don't want to see any more of your antics.

I started to glare at his back, but remembered the jury could be watching, so I tried to re-assemble my innocent expression.

Then I wondered if my innocent expression looked fake to the jurors. It felt fake to me, even though I knew I was innocent.

I sighed. Being on trial for murder was really hard.

"The jury will disregard the...um...props in the District Attorney's possession," Judge Martínez said as J.J. walked back to stand between his table and the jury box.

Yeah, right. Like any of us could possibly scrub that from our gray matter.

Undaunted, J.J. continued his opening statement, which starred me as a criminal mastermind who'd duped a poor innocent Texas boy into a life of crime and degradation.

When Avery realized the damage he was doing to society, he decided to come clean and inform on me to the cops, so I gutted him.

J.J. Boyle had missed his calling as a fiction writer. The jurors were enraptured by his story, which was probably a thousand times more intriguing than what actually happened.

By the time he finished his statement, I was sure I was going to prison. I wondered if Texas prisons had the standard orange uniforms or black and white stripes.

Maybe they'd have those hot pink ones I read about. I was pretty sure I could rock hot pink. I remembered the article was about male prisoners in Georgia.

Damn it. I was going to spend the rest of my life dressed like a piece of citrus fruit making not-so-sweet love to whatever linebacker-sized lesbian decided she was into short-ish Latinas.

I wondered if I needed to pretend I was Mexican-American instead of Colombian so I would be accepted into a prison gang.

I hoped they wouldn't require me to get a prison tattoo. I didn't have tattoos, but if I got one, I'd want it to be a full-color scene from Alice in Wonderland. Or maybe a black and gray Hermione Granger, clearly the most competent of the three main Harry Potter characters.

Regardless, I didn't think my prison tattoo artist would be qualified for my choices and they certainly wouldn't help my prison cred any.

"Mr. Owen?" the judge said, snapping me back to the present. "Would you like to make an opening statement?"

I swallowed hard, turned, and looked at Nick.

～

Nick

By the time J.J. sat down, my innards—as my grandpa used to call them—felt like they'd gotten twisted around each other and were being held that way with duct tape. For only the second time in my life, I was nauseated in a courtroom.

The first time was when the jury brought back the guilty verdict on Johnny.

As I stood, I glanced down at Rika. Her head was tilted up to look at me, her big chocolate eyes filled with fear. And maybe a little hope. Hope that I could save her from Wade and J.J. and a life in prison.

How many times had I sworn I would never be in this position again? Never another murder trial. Never a case where the stakes were high for someone I cared about.

The sick in my stomach rose into my throat, but I couldn't let the jury see Rika's attorney toss his cookies before he'd even given his opening statement.

"Counselor?" I heard a faraway voice say. Sounded like Gabe's voice. My head was spinning and I was concentrating on breathing deeply and swallowing hard until I could speak without losing control of my digestive system. "Nick?"

I jerked my eyes up to meet Gabe's stare. I could have sworn in that moment he was sending me a telepathic message. Something about how I was a kick ass attorney and had won three murder trials in a row.

Apparently, that was what I needed. I took one more deep breath, placed my left hand on Rika's shoulder and squeezed reassuringly.

This was both for her and for the jury. We were better off if they saw her as someone fragile, in need of my protection. J.J. had done everything short of calling her the "Grey Widow" outright.

I paced toward the jury box and scanned the faces of the jurors, who'd clearly been affected by J.J.'s words.

"Wow," I said, glancing over my shoulder at J.J. "I think that's a word we can all agree on after Mr. Boyle's tale... Just, wow!"

I threw my hands out in front of me and shook my head.

"With a tale like that, Mr. Boyle could be a screenwriter in Hollywood. That story had it all—sex, violence, murder, and an evil temptress to lure an innocent young man into her sinister dealings."

My nausea was fading, my mind suddenly sharp. "However, that story has absolutely nothing to do with the facts of this case." I glanced toward Rika for effect. I shouldn't have met her hopeful gaze because the stabbing sensation in my chest nearly threw me off track.

"And it has absolutely nothing to do with the person sitting at that table." I gestured toward Rika, this time careful not to look into her face.

"The story you just heard is the one the prosecution thinks you want to hear. He thinks you want it to be true so you can tell it over and over at your backyard barbecues for years to come. I have more faith in you than that." I paused, my eyes sweeping over them again. "I have faith that you wouldn't want to send an innocent twenty-four-year-old girl to jail just so you could tell that story."

I noticed the subtle change in postures. In their eyes.

I was making headway.

"The *true* story of the defendant is a different one entirely. The *true* story is about a girl born into a modest suburban neighborhood where she had what she needed growing up, but not a lot more...like many folks around here. A girl who lost her mother at the tender age of eight. And when her Colombian father was not allowed to stay in the country, he made the gut-wrenching decision to leave her in the care of her maternal grandmother because he thought she'd be better off in the United States. Because he thought she'd be *safe*."

The jury was with me. I had their undivided attention. It was up to me now to pull all the sympathy for Rika out of them I could. I needed them to want to believe in her.

"The *truth* is that, despite these heartbreaking setbacks, the little girl made good grades and as soon as she got old enough, took a part-time job to help her grandmother. She never got into trouble. Never got arrested..."

I took a deep breath, hoping I didn't lose them on the next part. "The biggest mistake she ever made was following her boyfriend when he asked her to leave the suburbs and join him in New York, where he had a better job. A year later, when they broke up, she decided to join some friends on South Padre Island before having to face her family back home and tell them about her failed relationship."

I glanced over at Rika. She looked so small, sitting behind the thick wood table. It was hard to imagine anyone would think she was a killer. But the next part of the story was the hardest to believe.

"The *truth* is that Miss Martín drove for days until the night she got to Bolo, needing a snack and a bathroom and found everything closed. She took the short cut she was told about onto the old highway, where she was run off the road by a red pickup. At that point, she decided to heed nature's call and tripped over the body—a body likely deposited there by whoever was in that truck.

"The *truth* is that Miss Martín did her civic duty and called the authorities, and when she did, was arrested at the whim of a sheriff looking for an easy way to close a case." I turned toward the gallery and gave Wade—who was sitting on the front row— an accusing stare.

"The *truth* is that there's no connection between Miss Martín and Mr. Cook, and there's nothing in Miss Martín's past or present to indicate she's capable of committing any crime.

"The *truth* is that the sheriff's department mismanaged the crime scene then refused to investigate the real leads in this case. And the *truth* is that if you convict my client based on the wild tale concocted by Mr. Boyle, you'll be sending a message to her father that he was wrong to entrust his daughter to the good people of the United States of America. That we don't care enough about justice to ensure the safety of the innocent from the tyranny of incompetent, uncaring officials."

I paused long enough to scan the box, looking every juror in the eye once again.

"Don't let *that* be the *truth*."

As I turned and walked toward Rika, I noticed the look on her face had changed. The fear was gone. Her eyes glowed bright and warm with something I couldn't quite identify. But for a split second, that look was all I wanted. All I needed.

Then J.J. called his first witness.

CHAPTER TWENTY-SEVEN

Rika

Driving the loaner truck to work that evening, I couldn't help mentally rehashing my very stressful day in court.

After opening statements, J.J. called Sheriff Strickland to the stand and asked him to tell the court what had transpired that night. J.J. would stop him periodically and ask questions to "clarify" the situation—also known as: make Rika look guiltier.

That's when I learned I didn't seem upset enough when the authorities got to me the night of the murder. The sheriff described me as "cold." Later, Deputy Dan got on the stand and described me as snotty and uppity.

I wanted to scream at them that maybe their *twenty-seven-minute* response time was plenty for a fat, bullied orphan girl like me to process my feelings and compartmentalize them, like I'd been doing since I was *eight fucking years old!* But I figured if I did, I might be confirming Deputy Dan's assessment of me.

I remembered watching a true story about a woman in Australia in 1980, who told the authorities a dingo had eaten her baby. She was put on trial and convicted of murdering her infant, her demeanor suspect because she was so calm and stoic throughout the ordeal.

She spent three years in jail before proof was found that a dingo did, in fact, eat her baby.

My take-away from that story and the first day of my trial was that women are required to be weeping, hysterical messes when shit goes down or we risk getting accused of causing said shit.

Oh, and that men were fucking assholes.

I thought of Nick, making out with me in his bathroom then sending me away without finishing the job.

In that instance, he was a *non*-fucking asshole, which seemed even worse at the time.

He'd done a good job of cross-examining the sheriff and deputy, though, asking them a lot of questions that made it clear they'd messed up the crime scene and hadn't really considered other suspects.

As I watched the jury members' faces, I couldn't be sure what they were thinking. For all I knew, they might still have visions of giant black dildos dancing in their heads.

I was jolted by the sudden thought that I could be convicted of murder *within a few days*. My mind had set the trial results way off in the distance, even during jury selection. But things were going pretty fast.

I decided right there in the courtroom, I couldn't sit around and wait to be convicted. I had to do something.

And that's why, after I turned right at the stoplight onto Bolo's main street, instead of going straight to Barr's, I made another right into the Dill's Dollar Store parking lot.

As the bell on the door clanged, announcing my arrival, I was glad to see ReeAnne behind the counter. After we greeted each other, I walked around the store, picking up necessities I didn't really need right now, and hurried back to the counter.

While ReeAnne rang up my purchases, I started a "casual" conversation.

"Did you have fun at the picnic?" I asked.

"Sure," she said. "But I enjoy any holiday I don't have to work."

"What about the fireworks? Did you go see those?"

"Hell, yeah!" she replied with more excitement than I thought fireworks deserved. "They're the best part of the Fourth of July!"

I guess entertainment is pretty scarce around here.

I pretended to examine a nail polish display to the right of the counter as I asked, "Did you and LeeAnne hang out together there?"

She stopped punching buttons on the antique cash register and looked at me. "LeeAnne didn't go to the fireworks," she said.

"You mean you didn't see her there?"

"No, I mean, she didn't go. If she'd gone, I would have seen her because everyone we know from high school goes to the same place. An old high school friend of ours has his insurance office across from the Meady town square. We all take our deck chairs and watch from the roof. LeeAnne doesn't make it every year, but when she does, that's where she goes."

I looked down at the polish I was holding, pretending to check the name of the color.

Crimson.

Like the blood on the murder victim, LeeAnne's ex.

Like the blood on my thumb after I was shot at.

Like the blood on Nick's ear.

"Why did you think she was at the fireworks?" ReeAnne asked.

"Um..." What should I say? "She left early." I shrugged. "Must have been a miscommunication."

ReeAnne cocked her head to one side. "She left early and didn't come to the fireworks?" she said. "That's weird."

I shrugged again and handed her a twenty-dollar bill.

LeeAnne has some explaining to do.

~

I left Dill's determined to confront LeeAnne about where she really was on the night of July fourth, but the moment I walked into Barr's and looked into her clear blue eyes, I had second thoughts.

She'd already heard about the shooting, since Nick had to report it, and expressed concern about both of us. She seemed so damn authentic, and forthright, and straightforward and a bunch of other synonyms for "honest" that were probably listed on Thesaurus.com.

What if she'd simply decided she wanted to see the fireworks from another angle this year? Or Dwight wanted to be closer to the action than the roof of a building?

I decided I needed to give LeeAnne the benefit of the doubt for at least a few more hours while I checked out her story.

The restaurant was fairly busy tonight, with an equal combination of dine-in and take-out orders.

I struck up a conversation with everyone I saw—which I'd learned was totally normal in Bolo, anyway—and asked them whether they attended the fireworks display. About two-thirds had.

Then I worked in a question about whether they'd seen Dwight and LeeAnne there. No one had.

By closing time I'd had enough. When the last customer left, I was ready to have a serious chat with LeeAnne. But before I did, I downloaded an app on my phone that allowed me to schedule texts. I composed one to be sent to Nick in fifteen minutes if I didn't use the eye scanner to unlock my phone and cancel.

It said,

I'm confronting LeeAnne. She wasn't at the fireworks display. If you're receiving this pre-scheduled text, she's probably killed or incapacitated me by now.

That sounded pretty scary. Or pretty crazy. Oh well, I'd probably be dead if he read it, so why not go all the way?

I added, *All I ask is that you stand up at my funeral and say "You were right. I was wrong," to my dead body.*

My aunt, *Tía* Margo claimed that was all a woman really wanted to hear from her husband, and I thought I wouldn't mind hearing it from Nick either, especially after the LeeAnne arguments we'd had.

"LeeAnne, can we talk?" I asked immediately after the last customer walked out.

"Sure, sweetie."

Damn. I wished she hadn't called me "sweetie." And if that wasn't enough, she knitted her brows, her eyes full of what looked like genuine concern.

I broke eye contact, afraid hers would convince me of her innocence before I asked the first question.

Anxiety gnawed at my stomach and I wished I'd gotten myself a basket of French fries and carbed up before I started this, but it was too late now.

I turned and walked to a booth. LeeAnne followed and we slid in across from each other.

"Why haven't you said anything about the dead guy being your ex-husband?" I blurted out.

Smooth move, Paprika.

LeeAnne looked startled, then several other emotions crossed her features too quickly for me to identify them.

"I was kind of hoping Nick wouldn't tell you," she replied.

What? "Don't you think it's something you should have told me?" My hands lifted of their own accord, ready to help me get my point across. I tucked them into my lap, since I needed to maintain control. Not only did my hands react to my emotional state, but my emotional state could be further intensified by my hands waving around.

They reminded me of my cousin's dog. He wagged his tail

when he was happy, but if you stopped his tail from wagging, he immediately looked unhappy. The happiness-tail wagging response went both ways. That's kind of how it was with me and my hands.

"I'm sorry," LeeAnne said, her voice quieter than I'd ever heard it. "My marriage isn't something I like to advertise. I just—"

"There's a difference between advertising," I cut in, "and sharing information with the innocent accused killer of your ex, who you pretend is your friend." Hands or no hands, I couldn't keep the angry edge from my voice.

She jerked back like I'd slapped her. "Of course, I'm your friend!"

I ignored the wounded look in her eyes and said, "And you proved it by withholding important information from me."

Her eyes filled with unshed tears, causing prickles of regret to stab at the skin on my chest. I rubbed the spot with my fingertips.

"Nick and Wade knew and if I thought I had information that would help your case..." Her voice faded out in a very non-LeeAnne way. "I'm sorry," she said in a near whisper.

The loud and proud woman I'd known for the last couple of weeks seemed to shrink in front of my eyes. I felt awful I'd caused her to look that way.

"Rika," she said. "The two years I was married to Avery were the worst of my life...scary...humiliating..." Her eyes drifted off as if she was reliving those scary humiliating moments right here in front of me. "I never thought I'd be that woman," she said. "The one who stayed after her man hit her, then believed him when he promised it wouldn't happen again."

A big ball of guilt formed in my belly, and rolled around in there, searing my stomach lining.

None of this means she didn't kill him, my brain said to my stomach. *Or that she didn't shoot at you.*

"LeeAnne," I began again, *sooo* not wanting to ask this question. "Where did you go when you left here last night?"

She blinked at me, her eyes shifting back and forth, and I knew she was trying to decide whether or not to stick with her original story.

"I know you weren't at the fireworks display," I said, so we could dispense with that option.

Her eyes widened, her brows rising in surprise.

"I've asked around," I added. "And you took your gun."

The meaning of my questions seemed to dawn on her all of a sudden. She blinked and looked me in the eye. "Are you thinking I *shot* at you?"

"You lied to me," I said. "I'm not sure what to think."

Her shoulders dropped and she exhaled a big breath. "You're right. I've been lying to people for a long time."

CHAPTER TWENTY-EIGHT

Rika

I stared at LeeAnne, waiting for an explanation, bracing myself for her to confess that she tried to kill me.

"We were over in Juniper, about twenty minutes from here," she said. "There are plenty of witnesses. And I always take the gun with me and put it in the glove compartment when we're not going straight home."

I watched her expectantly. Maybe I had to accept her statement about the gun because I'd always left before she did until last night. But no way was I taking her word that there were alibi witnesses at some vague place in a town I'd never heard of.

She glanced around as if to ensure we were alone. Dwight was in the kitchen cleaning up.

Lowering her voice, she began, "No one knows this, but when Dwight was little, my grandparents took him to the doctor. They were the ones who really raised us, since our parents were the partier-druggy types. Kind of came and went as they pleased."

She pressed her lips together and shook her head slightly, clearly still angry at her no-good parents.

"Anyway, I overheard my grandparents talking. Dwight was

diagnosed with Asperger's Syndrome. But my grandparents were pretty old-school. They decided not to tell anyone about it. Didn't want people to think there was something wrong with him, I guess. They even seemed to convince themselves he'd just grow out of it."

Asperger's Syndrome explained an awful lot about Dwight's lack of people skills and obsession with spiders and swords. If I remember my googled articles correctly, he fit the description to a T.

LeeAnne glanced toward the kitchen again. "As you can see, he didn't. Instead of knowing the truth, everyone around here thinks he's just a creepy loner. And since my grandparents died, it's been hard. I love him, but sometimes..."

The guilt ball in my stomach inflated to basketball size. LeeAnne always seemed so upbeat. How did I miss that she was dealing with so much?

Everyone she counted on was dead and she was responsible for not only the bar, but a brother with a major developmental difference that she'd been expected to keep secret all these years.

"I'm really—" I began, but she cut me off with a sweep of her hand and a think-nothing-of-it head shake.

"I found a group for autistic and Asperger's adults and one for their family members that meets at the same time over in Juniper. Fourth of July night, they were having a party and Dwight wanted to go."

I didn't know what to say. LeeAnne had been so kind to me since the day we met, and I was starting to feel like a self-involved bitch. The basketball in my stomach filled itself with lead.

This only means she didn't shoot at you last night! my brain yelled at my stomach.

That was true. If she were the killer and JimBob dumped the body for her, who's to say he wouldn't snuff me out for her? It was awfully convenient, how soon he'd shown up at Barr's after I identified his truck. Maybe he and LeeAnne were playing me somehow, knowing I wouldn't find any real evidence in his truck. Making me think she was on my side.

I turned this thought over in my mind, trying to determine whether or not letting me search that truck could be to their advantage. No good reason for a ruse like that came to me.

"LeeAnne?" I said.

"Yeah?"

"I saw the flowers in your trash the day I went to your house —the ones from Avery. You had to know he was coming to town. He was dressed like he was trying to impress a date."

LeeAnne shook her head. "He called to see if I got the flowers and tell me he was coming to see me. I told him the flowers were in the garbage and if he came near me, I'd take out another restraining order on him."

"And what did he say?"

"He laughed, like I'd just told him a joke and hung up. So, yes, he may have been planning to see me before...whatever happened happened, but I never saw him or spoke to him again."

The only way to disprove what she was saying would be to get Nick to request her phone records. But Nick was convinced LeeAnne was innocent, despite the fact that he acted like she annoyed the hell out of him. What was that all about?

"Okay," I replied. "But there's one more thing I need to know."

"Shoot," LeeAnne said. Then she winced at her choice of words considering that I was recently shot at in her parking lot. "Sorry," she said. "I meant, go ahead."

"I need to know what this weird relationship is between you and Nick."

"What does that have to do with the murder?"

"I have to determine whether my attorney is looking out for my best interests or not."

"Nick?" LeeAnne cried. "Oh, my God. He's one of the best guys I've ever known and a great lawyer. Way too good for Bolo!"

"See," I threw my hands out toward her. "That's what I'm

talking about. When you're in the room together, you act like you can't stand each other, but you defend each other a hundred percent when you're not."

LeeAnne laughed as the sparkle returned to her eyes. It bugged me that the sparkle was because of Nick.

"Does he really stick up for me?" she asked.

"Completely," I said. "Now spill."

"If I tell you, you can't tell him I told you."

"Scout's honor." I held up three fingers, not knowing for sure if that was the right amount since I was never any sort of scout. But I figured LeeAnne wasn't either.

"Okay," she began. "When we were kids, Nick sort of protected me. Like I told you, my parents weren't really around. My grandparents were busy with the bar, plus they had to look after Dwight. It was like Nick noticed no one was really looking out for me and took the job on himself." Her eyes drifted off for a moment. "He's always been like that."

I slid my forearms forward on the table, impatient to hear the rest of the story.

Her eyes found mine again and she went on. "We spent a lot of time playing in the field next door with other kids from around here. If anybody so much as looked at me sideways, Nick would act like he was my dad, even though he was less than a year older than I was."

She leaned back, uncrossing then recrossing her legs under the table. "So, the summer after third grade for me, fourth for Nick, these older boys started coming around, trying to pick on us."

She jerked and straightened her spine. "One of them was JimBob McGwire's dad, come to think of it! Angus McGwire. He was tall for his age and a son-of-a-bitch. Used to call me 'rich girl,' cause my family owned the bar.

"Anyway, one day, at the end of summer, my grandma had gotten me clothes for school and I had a brand new More Sparkle

Barbie lunch box. Barbie had a sparkly wand and shimmery accessories and it wasn't even from a garage sale like a lot of my stuff was, so I brought it out to show my friends."

Of course, a More Sparkle Barbie lunchbox was LeeAnne's prized possession. She'd sort of turned herself into More Sparkle Barbie since then.

"The big boys showed up that day—four of 'em. One—Roger somebody who doesn't live around here anymore—took my lunchbox away. When I grabbed for it, he twisted my arm behind my back and I screamed. Nick saw what was going on and took up for me. After he got me loose, he laid Roger out with two punches to the face."

This revelation triggered a couple of different reactions in me. A young Nick sticking up for LeeAnne against four other boys was sweet and heroic and made my insides feel mushy.

The fact that Nick had taken big Roger down with two punches kind of turned me on, which I found disturbing.

First, because I'd thought I was above that sort of cave woman thinking. Second, because we were talking about Nick as a kid and I didn't want to feel like a pervert.

On the other hand, Nick was an adult now, so I probably wasn't a pervert, but had likely voided my feminist card by getting so excited over a guy stepping in and fighting a girl's battle for her.

"What about the other three guys?" I asked.

"Well, they all circled around Nick, and I was afraid they were going to hurt him bad. I ran into the bar, used my shirt as a basket and carried out three of the balls from the pool table. When I got back, Nick was taking a beating from the bigger boys, so I used the only ammunition I had."

I tried to imagine how she could stop a major fight with billiard balls. "Did it work?" I asked, still not sure what "it" was.

She nodded. "Hit one on the nose, one just above his eye, and one on the temple. I always did have pretty good aim." She shrugged. "Although, truth be told, I was aiming to hit them right between the eyes. They just kept moving so much..."

She leaned back against the seat as if the story was over.

"That still doesn't explain why you and Nick act like arch enemies."

"Oh," she shook her head. "Sorry. Forgot what you asked."

She leaned in again and rested her forearms on the table.

"Once the story got around, it was mainly about how scrawny little LeeAnne Barr saved Nick Owen's ass with the billiard balls. The older kids started calling me 'Balls.' They'd be like, 'Hey, Balls!' Kind of got me some respect with the big kids and the nickname trickled down to the younger ones. Unfortunately, the one they gave Nick did, too."

"Which was?" I could feel my eyebrows climbing up my fore-head in anticipation.

"No Balls, or N.B. when adults were around."

I was instantly angry on Nick's behalf. "But that's not—"

"Fair," LeeAnne finished. "I know. They just thought it sounded funny. Nick had been angry with me right off the bat for getting involved. Claimed he had things under control. No boy around here wants to be saved by a girl. But after the nicknames started, he was really pissed off at me.

"That name followed him through the rest of elementary and junior high. But on the first day of high school, a kid said it to him and made the mistake of shoving past him. Nick laid him out with one punch."

A quiver wiggled through me at the image of macho one-punch Nick Owen.

Damn it! I might as well move into a cave.

"Wait," I said. "If he hates it so much, why do you still taunt him with it?"

"Honestly, I was really hurt that he didn't appreciate what I did for him. In my mind, he'd saved me and I'd returned the favor. He didn't thank me and started scowling at me all the time, so I taunted him. I guess it became a habit."

"Jeez," I rolled my eyes at her. "You're adults now. Don't you think you can let it go?"

LeeAnne straightened again, pressing her lips into a stubborn line before saying, "I'll quit calling him N.B. the day he thanks me for saving his ass. Or apologizes for *being* an ass, either one."

I rolled my eyes so hard this time, they almost stuck that way, just like my Lita said they would.

"This whole town is nuts," I said.

"You got that right," LeeAnne replied. "But if you live in a nut house, you have to be a nut or get eaten by the squirrels."

I ran that analogy through my mind a few times, trying to decide if it made any sense.

Whatever. "Okay, thanks for the talk, LeeAnne."

"Anytime, sugar."

I grabbed my keys from behind the counter and left.

"The prosecution calls Dr. Charles Hess," J.J. said, his voice ringing out clear and confident.

As I watched the medical examiner being sworn in, centipedes crawled around in my stomach.

I'd heard other people got butterflies. Not me, and the flutter of butterfly wings sounded pretty damned pleasant compared to the creepy crawly sensations I was experiencing.

I closed my eyes and relived those moments, a half hour ago, as we walked from the truck to the courthouse. Nick's hand was pressed to the small of my back every second until we reached the defense table. It warmed me and made me feel protected from the eyes of the people who'd gathered in the halls and the gallery of the courtroom to see the Grey Widow.

I wished I could feel the comfort of some part of Nick's body touching mine right now. But I knew he couldn't so much as hold my hand or the jury might decide I'd used my mystical Colombian female wiles to mesmerize him like I had poor Avery.

My eyes popped open. Several jurors were looking my way. Did it seem strange to them that my eyes had been closed? What did they think I was doing? Praying?

Praying would be good, since most people around here went to church. Unless they wondered why I would need to pray before the forensic testimony. An innocent person would be confidently awaiting it so she could be exonerated.

I forced my eyes back up to Dr. Hess who was settling into the witness chair. His hair was white, his pale face full of wrinkles, but his eyes were bright blue.

At J.J.'s prompting, Dr. Hess gave his testimony about the condition of the body.

His time of death window meant that Avery Cook had been killed less than two hours before I found him. The jury members, as well as the rest of us, were able to view the bloody body on the projector screen provided by the prosecution.

When J.J. asked about the murder weapon, the slide switched to a drawing of what it most likely resembled.

To me, it still looked like something I'd use to stake a not-so-sexy vampire. (I say a not-so-sexy one because everyone knows you let the sexy one turn you so you can live forever with him and have his vampire babies.)

However, Dr. Hess said no wood splinters or metal fragments were found in the wound and a wooden stake surely would have left splinters.

Once they were finished with that topic, the prosecution clicked to a slide of the chewed wad of gum. I felt Nick go tense beside me, although his face revealed no emotion.

"Can you tell us what we're looking at now, Dr. Hess?" J.J. asked.

"This is a wad of chewing gum," Dr. Hess replied.

Duh-uh.

J.J. switched to a slide of the Uncle Amos gum sticks from my car, one of them unwrapped to reveal the color.

I'd seen this same slide yesterday during the sheriff's testimony.

"Dr. Hess, did your laboratory perform tests comparing this gum found in the defendant's car, as Sheriff Strickland testified yesterday..." He switched back to the wad. "And *this* gum?"

"Yes, we did."

"And what were your findings?" J.J. raised his brows as if he didn't already know the answer.

"They're the same."

"Same unusual brand?" J.J. confirmed.

"Yes."

"Same flavor?"

"Yes."

"And where was this wad of gum found?" J.J. glanced toward me and Nick, his eyes smizing, but not in a good way. It was an evil smize. I wondered if Tyra Banks would call it *e-smizing* or make up an entirely different word for it.

"I found it inside the victim's mouth," Dr. Hess replied.

Several jurors' eyes widened, and I heard gasps followed by whispers behind me in the gallery.

"No further questions for this witness your honor," J.J. said. This time, he turned and grinned at Nick triumphantly.

I heard Nick take a deep breath before he stood, then, as if he was taking a relaxing Sunday stroll, he walked over to the computer that sat on the edge of the prosecution table and tapped on some keys.

The photo of the gum wad enlarged once, twice, three times. Nick looked up at the projected image and hit the button two more times until the image was the size of a bowling ball.

"Dr. Hess," he said, a friendly—and super-hot, I might add— smile on his face. "When you were inspecting this gum, did you happen to notice anything *extra* imbedded in it? Anything you might find unusual?"

"Yes," the doctor said. "I did."

"Can you show us these irregularities on the screen?"

Dr. Hess, clearly my kind of geek, pulled a laser pointer from his pocket and aimed the beam at the screen.

"There's one piece of foreign matter here," his laser drew an imaginary circle around something tiny but hard-looking in the upper right corner of the gum. "And a second one here." He pointed out the green fragment lower down.

"And did you or anyone else in your lab ascertain what those irregularities are?" Nick asked.

"Yes. This one is the tip of a thorn from a mesquite tree." Dr. Hess gestured with his pointer again. "And this is a portion of leaf from the same type of tree."

"So, the wad of gum found in the defendant's mouth contained plant debris not typically present in this brand of gum or any other that you know of." Nick recapped. "Is that correct?"

"Yes," Dr. Hess replied. "That's correct."

Nick glanced at me, his eyes smizing—the good kind of smizing, not the J.J. kind--and three things hit me at once.

One, Nick was a good lawyer and a confident one, now that he was standing in front of a jury.

Two, he didn't hate this job as much as I was led to believe he did.

And three, he was really hot when he smized. Sure, I'd seen him do it before, but when a man was as good looking as Nick, it would probably take years before I was immune to the smize-shock, if ever.

I realized I was getting turned on in the middle of my own murder trial.

The ever-horny Grey Widow scoping out her next victim.

My eyes shifted to the jury to see if that's what they were thinking, but all eyes were on Nick who'd begun talking again.

"Dr. Hess, in your opinion, would a person continue to chew gum after it had debris in it?"

J.J. jumped out of his seat. "Objection, your honor!" he said. "The witness is only an expert on the actions of dead people."

"The *actions* of dead people?" Nick repeated.

J.J. threw him a dirty look.

"Sustained," Judge Martínez said. "It hasn't been established that Dr. Hess is an expert on gum chewing."

Nick seemed undaunted. "Are you a gum chewer?" he asked the witness.

"Yes, I am." Dr. Hess nodded.

"How long have you been chewing gum?"

"Since I was a boy," he replied. "About forty years or so."

"Objection!" J.J. cried.

"To what?" Judge Martínez asked.

"I see where he's going with this, your honor, and the witness is not a professional gum chewer."

Several members of the jury chuckled.

"Overruled. Go ahead counsel." He nodded to Nick.

"Since you've been chewing gum for forty years," Nick went on, "you're probably as expert on *non-professional* gum chewing as anyone else, wouldn't you say?"

"Yes," the doctor replied. "I suppose so."

"Would you, personally, continue to chew gum after it had debris in it?"

"No."

"And why not?"

The doctor half-shrugged. "Because it would be disgusting." He grimaced.

Nick nodded in agreement. Then he placed a finger to his lips thoughtfully. "Is there any way to tell for certain that this wad of gum was in the deceased's mouth at the time he was killed? As opposed to being *placed* in his mouth..." Nick glanced at Wade. "After he was dead?"

"No way that I know of," Dr. Hess replied.

"So, just to be clear, you agree it's possible the gum was placed into the victim's mouth after he was lying dead on the ground?"

"Well..." the doctor appeared to be considering his answer carefully. "Certainly, it's possible."

Nick strolled to his right, toward the jury box. "Which scenario sounds more likely to you, Dr. Hess?" Instead of looking at the witness, Nick propped both hands on the jury box railing, facing the jurors. "That the victim continued to chew debris-filled gum while he was still alive? Or that someone picked up the wad of gum Miss Martín lost when she fell and placed it in the victim's mouth later?"

"Objection!" J.J. said.

"Withdrawn," Nick replied. "No further questions."

CHAPTER TWENTY-NINE

Nick

I was lying on the couch in my office, mulling over the day.

Rika was getting ready to go to work at Barr's, and I was planning a celebratory nap as soon as I'd finished my mulling.

The jury was with me today. I could feel it. Especially when I'd challenged the gum evidence.

The best part was, by the time Gabe called recess, J.J. wasn't making eye contact with me anymore. And since Gabe had something else on his schedule for tomorrow, I had a long weekend to gloat and work more on Rika's defense.

J.J. would probably be resting his case Monday or Tuesday, so we also needed to use the time to go over Rika's testimony.

But all in all, things felt pretty damn good.

My eyes were already closed, so I let my mind drift off to my happy place—a beach in Hawaii, where I wasn't licensed to practice law and I could just sit and drink beer and listen to the waves.

When I opened my eyes, Rika was standing over me, wearing a bikini top and a grass skirt, two fruity-looking cocktails in her hand.

This had been happening a lot lately—Rika invading my

happy place, my mulling, my dreams. And every time, for a split second I was really glad to see her until I remembered I was her lawyer.

The part that made my chest tighten, though, was when I realized, for the umpteenth time, that I wouldn't be good for her, even when the trial was over.

I hadn't been good for my other wives.

Honestly, I just wanted to put my marriages out of my head and forget they ever happened. Surely, the first one shouldn't count. I was eighteen and lied to, for Christ's sake.

The other two...well, Gabe kept insisting I rehash that shit with him so it didn't happen again.

But hell, I don't know. They were both beautiful women who needed me in one way or the other and I felt responsible for helping them. Then it turned out that they liked everything I liked. It was really easy to be together. A lot easier than being alone.

I didn't actually remember proposing to BreeAnne or Megan. Suddenly, there was all this talk of marriage—mostly by my girlfriend and my mom—and it didn't seem like a bad thing.

But after we were married, instead of enjoying golf and watching football with me, they got angry when I tried to enjoy them.

They also accused me of not listening to them or paying enough attention to them. And they were right, I guess, but at some point, it seemed like they stopped saying anything interesting. Eventually, I wondered if they ever had said anything interesting or if I was just taken in by their looks and their easy going ways until they weren't so easy going anymore.

Lately, Gabe had been insinuating that I was somehow reliving my relationship with my mom in my marriages, which was just gross. If I had to explore that theory in order to have a good relationship with a woman in the future, I'd rather just pass on all of the above.

The truth was, nothing had really, truly seemed okay since my dad died. But that was years ago and what good did it do to dwell on it?

Maybe that explained all these inappropriate thoughts about Rika and me, though. When she'd told me her mom had died when she was eight and she'd lost her dad soon afterward, it had picked at the scab I'd been wearing all these years. I knew what it was like to lose a parent. How it changed you.

But why did it seem like she was doing so much better than I was? I mean, she had followed a jerk boyfriend across the country, but she was twenty-four and not yet divorced so she was still way ahead of me at her age.

My computer pinged from my desk.

Since Rika and Gabe wouldn't leave me alone on my island to nap, I decided to check the message.

I sat in my desk chair and clicked to my email. On the subject line of the new message were the words "NEW EVIDENCE." I read through the email as my heart sank into my stomach. Still in denial, I read it again.

Shit!

I grabbed my cell from my desk and dialed Wade's cell. He didn't pick up and I didn't leave a message. Instead, I called the sheriff's office. When I found out Wade wasn't there, I asked for Danny.

"Deputy Daniel Scruggs," he answered, his voice full of self-importance.

"Hey, Danny, it's Nick."

"Hi, Nick, how's it going?"

"Fine," I said, trying to keep the acid out of my voice. "I need you to do me a favor."

"Sure, name it."

"I need you to patch this call through to Wade, but don't tell him it's me," I said. "I have a surprise for him." If he were here in person, the surprise would be a punch in the face, but I wasn't telling Danny that.

"Cool!" Danny said. "I love surprises!"

God, what a dumbass.

Thirty seconds later, I heard Wade's voice saying, "Strickland."

"What. The. *Fuck?*" I said.

"Who is this?" he asked, but we both knew he was stalling.

"What's this shit about new evidence?"

I heard Wade suck in a stilted breath. "Oh, that? You knew it was likely to happen when you insisted on such a quick trial date."

My left hand came up to rub the burn from the back of my neck. "This is bogus and you know it."

"I don't know any such—"

"Damn it, Wade, why are you doing this?" I asked. "I've known you most of my life. You have your faults, but I never thought you were a murderer. Are you a murderer, Wade?"

He gasped before he said, "Me? The new evidence suggests your client's the murderer."

"Not to me, it doesn't. To me, it suggests that you're mixed up in some nasty shit that either has you killing a man or helping to cover up the crime."

"Well, it looks to me like that little Latina hussy you've got living with you has pulled the poncho over your eyes."

My hand squeezed the phone hard. "You call her that a second time, and the third time you'll be doing it with no teeth," I said. "Sheriff or not." I ended the call and tossed the phone onto the desk.

Rika

When I pulled into Nick's driveway, my lights shone on a silver-gray pickup truck.

Hm...company. The only company we'd had since I'd been staying at Nick's were his ex-wives. I hoped I wasn't about to encounter wife number one.

But Nick had texted me at work and asked if I could get away early. Surely he wouldn't have called me home early just so I could meet another ex.

I slid past the silver truck and parked the loaner One-fifty in the garage. By the time I got to the door separating the garage from the house, Nick already had it open. He was still in his white dress shirt from court, the sleeves rolled up. This look warmed my body in a way I had no explanation for.

"Perfect timing," he said. "They just got here."

"Who?" I asked. But Nick had me by the elbow, propelling me toward the living room. When I got there, I stopped dead in my tracks, my eyes darting back and forth, unsure who to gawk at first.

"Rika, this is Michelle Vargas and Cody Young. They're from the Texas Rangers Division."

Michelle Vargas was a dark-haired, dark-eyed Latina like me, but, unlike me, she had long legs and striking height that gave her sexy supermodel mojo. She wore a simple white western-style shirt with black jeans, a black leather belt with a big western buckle and boots.

Cody Young was also tall and good-looking with blonde hair and blue eyes. He was dressed in a male version of Michelle's outfit, except his pants were black slacks and he wore a gray-blue tie. Both were wearing white cowboy hats, which they removed simultaneously and set on the coffee table.

"This is Rika Martin," Nick finished.

I barely noticed his mispronunciation of my last name. My eyes flitted from striking Michelle to handsome Cody to hot Nick. I felt like I'd been skydiving and accidentally landed wherever they shoot those shows for that CW channel—the ones where everyone is too good looking to be true.

Cody caught my eye because he was staring at my chest and his lips were twitching.

I glanced down at my t-shirt.

My thighs are moist or your money back, it said on the front. There was a plate of chicken on the back, but they hadn't seen the back, yet.

"It's chicken," I blurted out, not sure who I needed to believe me more, Cody the handsome Ranger, who could surely get whatever woman he wanted on the back of his horse, or gorgeous Michelle, who'd likely be laughing about me later with her equally gorgeous girlfriends.

They just stared at me.

"I'm not selling my thighs," I added.

My statement caused everyone's gaze to jump to my thighs which were completely exposed thanks to yet another pair of LeeAnne's tiny denim shorts.

Cody's lips quirked like he was holding back laughter. "We're not here about your thighs," he said.

"I know," I replied as my face heated. "It's just that the sheriff took my clothes..." I was starting to feel really stupid because I was sure we had more important things to discuss. "These aren't mine."

"Anyway..." Nick said as he threw an *Are you nuts?* look my way. "Everybody have a seat. Can I get you anything to drink?"

Both of them turned down the beverage offer. Cody sat in an armchair. Nick ended up between me and Michelle on the couch. I found myself wondering why the bitch—I mean *Ranger*—hadn't taken the other armchair instead of snuggling up next to Nick.

Well, okay, she wasn't exactly snuggling, but still...

"Rika?" Nick's voice sounded tentative.

I looked up into his face. What had gone wrong now? Were these people here to arrest me for another crime I didn't commit?

"Yeah?" I replied.

"The prosecution has new evidence they're planning to introduce next week at trial."

I frowned up at him. What more could they have? The gum was their ace in the hole and Nick had done a great job of discounting it.

"The lab found DNA evidence in your car."

"What DNA evidence?" I asked. He was taking this really slowly and the centipedes had started crawling around in my stomach again.

"They say it's the victim's DNA...hair in the passenger seat of your car and skin cells on the passenger door handle."

"But..." I began. "But..." I was having trouble putting words in the right order. "That's impossible!"

"I know," he said. "Wade must have planted them. That's why I decided we'd better implement Plan B."

"Plan B?" My head was swimming with the ramifications of Avery Cook's DNA in my passenger seat.

"The plan to get JimBob McGwire to talk," he replied. "I contacted Michelle and—"

"How do you know each other?" I blurted. Why, out of all the questions that could have come out of my mouth, that one was on the tip of my tongue, I did not know.

"Nick defended me." She smiled warmly at Nick.

He defended her? For what? And was it before or after they slept together?

I hated her!

"Why did you need to be defended?" I finally managed to say.

"Bogus police brutality claim," Nick replied. "We got film footage from local security cameras. Got it thrown out of court. No big deal."

"It was a big deal to me," Michelle said. "My job was on the line." She gazed admiringly at Nick again.

Cody broke in, "Between the irregularities in this case and the information we keep getting about an organized crime syndicate that may be operating out of this part of the county, our office decided to get involved. This is not public knowledge right now," he continued. "We don't want Sheriff Strickland to get wind of it before we have a chance to question McGwire."

"He won't hear it from me," I said.

"Rika," Nick said. "You talked about writing a letter to JimBob McGwire offering the bogus trip. How soon can you get that—?"

"I already did it," I replied. "It's on a Word doc on my phone."

"Great," Cody said. "We have letterhead from the dealership to print it on. He'll find it in his mail tomorrow."

"Saturday, we'll be at the dealership," Michelle added, "along with some of the sheriff's officers from that county and Nick, here."

I straightened, "And me."

"No," Nick replied. "Not you. As a licensed attorney, I'm an officer of the court, but having the suspected murderer on the scene wouldn't be a good idea."

Damn it! The best part of the plan—the trip no gamer could resist—was my idea. *I* was the one who wanted to investigate this all along instead of waiting around for a jury verdict, and now I was getting cut out of the good part?

"Can't I at least watch on closed circuit TV from the car or something?" I asked.

"Sorry," Michelle replied, but she didn't look one bit sorry. "Nick's right." She smiled at him again. "Having you there could ruin everything."

Ruin everything. Was she referring to the investigation or her plans to cozy up to Nick? And why was I worrying about Nick's love life when my whole life was on the line?

"Okay," I said as I flashed Michelle a fake smile. "I'll go print out the letter for you to look over."

Nick might know a lot of things about me, but he would never know I gave a crap about Michelle and her stupid long legs. Not after he kissed me in his bathroom and rejected me a minute later.

Asshole.

∾

It was Saturday night and Barr's was dead. LeeAnne had told me why, but I wasn't listening. I was as stressed as a cage animal.

JimBob had taken the bait and made an appointment at the dealership to test drive one of their new models. Nick and Cody and *Michelle* were there, implementing the sting operation created by Nick and me.

Annoying.

Meanwhile, I'd wiped everything in the main room and pool room that could be wiped, I'd swept up, and I'd filled the salt and pepper shakers. LeeAnne was in her office sorting out the bills and Dwight was in the kitchen.

With nothing else to do, I went out to the pickup and pulled out the manila envelope full of evidence copies and brought them inside. There was a chance JimBob wouldn't show up and, even if he did, there was no guarantee Nick and his posse would get any information from him. I might as well have another look at the evidence.

I pulled my phone from my back pocket, checking it yet again for a message from Nick. When there wasn't one, I laid it on the bar, climbed onto a stool and pulled the copies out of the envelope.

For the next twenty minutes I looked through every piece of evidence I had, from the pictures of Avery's body and the crime scene in the emails Nick forwarded to my phone, to the items I'd confiscated from JimBob's truck.

Nothing new caught my eye, so I laid the color copy of the word search in front of me and stared at it for what felt like the thousandth time.

Why couldn't I stop obsessing over this stupid children's puzzle? Just because it was the most interesting scrap of paper I pulled from JimBob's truck didn't mean it was important.

Maybe what was intriguing me was the way the letters were circled. Didn't children like patterns? Like red, blue, orange, green, red, blue, orange, green? The circling of the letters on the word search seemed so random.

Actually, all kids probably didn't like patterns. I liked patterns when I was a kid. My cousin Sofia, on the other hand, loved chaos.

When we were kids, she'd come over and take the clothes off all my dolls. Some, she'd leave that way in a group as if they belonged to the *Toy Story* version of a nudist colony. Others would have their clothes replaced backwards. Some would get their own clothes plus the naked dolls' clothes layered on them or tied in a weird way on their heads.

I hated that. When she left, I'd spend the whole evening straightening everyone out, apologizing to them for my cousin's abuse. I mean, my dolls were always non-judgmental about each other's fashion choices, but what self-respecting Bratz doll wanted to be dressed like a backwards Barbie princess?

So, the lack of color pattern on the word search didn't mean anything. I was grasping for straws. A little kid had simply taken his or her pencils and circled random letters in four colors. That was that.

LeeAnne came in and propped her forearms on the bar. "Whatcha lookin' at?"

"I don't know." I turned the page around for her to see. "Something I got out of JimBob's truck. I kept thinking it could be a clue, but—"

"Oh," she said as she looked down at the page. "It's like the ones they have at church."

Yep. For all the good that did me.

Time to quit obsessing. I'd get LeeAnne to entertain me with gossip until I heard from Nick. "What do you think of Father Heinrich?" I asked.

"I've hardly seen him since he got to town a few months ago," she replied. "When I make it to church, I go to the Bible church, but I'm usually too tired from the night before."

My eye snapped up to meet hers. "They have these at the Bolo Bible Church, too?"

"Yeah, to keep the kids from acting up during the sermon."

I looked down at the page again, intending to flip it around, but my hand stopped in mid-air as my gaze caught and held on a cluster of letters.

Upside-down and from this distance, a few inches farther away than before, the red and orange circles looked about the same and the word I'd thought of as "won" appeared to be circled in the one color. However, from this angle, I realized it could also be the word "now."

I kept scanning the puzzle upside-down, now thinking of the red circles and orange circles as part of the same team. The letters ringed in those two colors formed the words "bod *abajo* move now."

Abajo. A Spanish word meaning "down," "under," "below" or even "bottom," depending on the context.

"LeeAnne, how many of the people around here are bilingual —English-Spanish?"

She tilted her head as she thought about it. "Well, most of the Mexican Americans around here can speak Spanish. Of course, we all learn the cuss words when we're kids." She chuckled. "Plus, it's the only foreign language they offer at the high school and they make everyone take two years of it. I'm not sure how much most people remember, though. I know I didn't retain much."

Great. That narrowed my suspects down to everyone in town. Except maybe the Vietnamese immigrants and Father Heinrich.

Wait. Scratch that. He was European and it seemed like they were often polylingual, plus he couldn't date or have sex, so he'd have to fill his time somehow. Studying foreign languages would be as good a way as any.

But I'd talked to Father Heinrich and didn't think a second meeting would do any good. Plus, I'd tried to cast a spell on him the last time I'd seen him and he might not have appreciated that.

"Do you know who's in charge of the word puzzles?" I asked LeeAnne.

"Well, it could be Ms. Tilly because she practically runs the place. Or Belinda, Tammy Lynn, or ReeAnne. They seem to be the ones who do the most with the kids."

Damn. It would be weird to show up at Sheriff Strickland or Judge Martínez's door. I couldn't imagine Tammy Lynn being of much help, even if I were sure what I was asking.

"Where can I find ReeAnne?" I asked.

"With the rest of them," she replied. "Tonight's the church slumber party for the kids. Remember? I told you that's why it's so dead in here. Most parents have gone off to Meady to the dance hall."

"Hm." I put my palm over my phone and tapped the bar top with my fingernails.

Following up on the word puzzle would be a wild goose chase. Everyone in town could get access to these puzzles simply by walking in the door of either church, or by downloading them off the Internet, apparently.

On the other hand, waiting around to find out if JimBob McGwire spilled his guts for the first time in his life was driving me crazy.

I looked at the clock. I didn't expect to hear from Nick for a couple of hours or more.

"Mind if I take off for the night?" I asked.

"Go ahead." LeeAnne glanced around at the empty bar. "I think I can handle the crowd."

"Great," I said. "Thanks." And I headed for the door.

CHAPTER THIRTY

Rika

When I got to the top of the steps of Bolo Bible Church, the door was unlocked, so I let myself in. The foyer and sanctuary were empty, so I took the hall that ran down the right side of the sanctuary. A series of squeals led me to a room at the back of the building.

The plaque on the double doors said, "Fellowship Hall," and when I entered, kids were fellowshipping the hell out of it.

Nerf balls of various types and sizes were flying through the air, little kids yelling and jumping out of their way.

In one corner, four little girls were stretched out on their stomachs on brightly colored sleeping bags, coloring and chatting. The older girls—probably third and fourth graders—were sitting at a table along the wall, painting each other's nails and holding their hands over their mouths as they talked sideways to each other, their eyes on whatever boy they were discussing.

I approached the nail painters. "Are your, um, teachers around here?" I asked, not sure if "teachers" was the right word.

"Ms. Belinda and them are in the kitchen," said a pudgy strawberry blonde whose Texas accent out-twanged even

LeeAnne's by a country mile. She pointed toward an open door nearby.

I thanked her and said a quick prayer that she'd cut back on the eating or have a massive growth spurt before it was too late. Then I remembered I didn't believe in that religious stuff anymore. Then I hoped I was wrong for her sake. Chocolate milk would be a lot more noticeable in her blonde hair than it was in my brunette.

"Aren't you the Grey Widow?" asked a little Latina with knowing eyes.

Geez, couldn't the adult Bolo-ites, or Bolonians, or whatever they called themselves, be a little more discrete around their children?

And these were the church kids. I could only imagine what the heathens were talking about.

"No," replied the sable-haired future vixen sitting across from her. "She's the one who dresses like a hoochie and works at Barr's."

Up until now, I'd been wholeheartedly against spanking, but these mini-mean girls had me rethinking my position.

"We all dress like hoochies at Barr's," I said defensively. "It's part of the...theme."

Okay, first, I don't know why I felt the need to defend clothes I normally wouldn't be caught dead in, and second, that was the lamest defense I'd ever heard. Where was my lawyer when I needed him?

Oh, yeah. Nick was off trying to catch the real murderer so I could "beat the rap," as my fellow felons put it. Or at least that's how they put it on TV. I hadn't stayed in jail long enough to meet actual criminals.

I walked away from the nail painters before they heaped on any further humiliation.

When I stepped up to the doorway of the commercial-sized kitchen, ReeAnne and Belinda had their hands full, slicing flats of crescent dough in halves and rolling them around tiny sausages.

Tammy Lynn rested her elbows on the counter, directing them on the best way to proceed without getting anywhere near the dough herself.

Typical.

Regardless, ReeAnne and Belinda looked pretty busy. Maybe I'd better wait and talk to them after snack time.

I was about to turn away when another thought occurred to me. Maybe I should go straight to the person who had her finger on the pulse of this congregation.

"Hey, y'all!" I said, hoping I'd put enough drawl on the word "y'all," since it was my first time to use it.

They all looked up at me. "Hey, Rika! What are you doing here?" Belinda asked.

"I'm looking for Ms. Tilly," I replied.

"Oh, she said she had work to do in her office," Tammy Lynn said. "Just take the hall toward the front of the building, go down the stairs, then all the way past the pastor's office to the back of the building again."

When I raised my eyebrows at the directions, Belinda said, "Yes, it would have been a lot more convenient to have a second staircase, but Reverend Jenkins and his cousin, the architect, didn't think of that when they drew up the plans."

All three of them rolled their eyes. Apparently, this omission was a frequent source of annoyance.

"Okay, thanks," I said. "I'll talk to *y'all* later."

The word was kind of addictive once you started using it.

I followed the hall up to the front foyer and found a door appropriately labeled "Stairs."

I'm not sure what I expected, but, since Nick made it sound like people bragged about this church's basement, I didn't expect it to be a bunch of hallways done in cheap wood paneling with cheap laminate squares on the floor like it was.

The hallway that ran along the left side of the church had a sign with an arrow on it that included "Pastor's Office." I took it, passing a series of doors, all shut tight.

At first, I didn't hear a peep from upstairs, but the kid sounds became audible again as I moved toward the back of the building. They were muffled, however, since they were on the right side of the church and I was on the left. When I reached the closed door labeled "Pastor," I paused and tried the handle.

It was locked, though light shown through the slit under the door. I wondered if that meant he was in or if he just didn't remember to turn off the light. I wished I could get a good look at his office, since, after JimBob and Sheriff Strickland, he was the most suspicious person I'd encountered at this church.

I considered trying to pick the lock, but I'd never picked a lock. I'd only watched YouTube videos about it and I didn't have even the most rudimentary tools to get it done. Besides, he could still be in there.

Moving along, I saw an open door at the back of the hall and heard humming coming from inside. I recognized it as one of the hymns the congregation had sung in church the Sunday Nick and I went.

I stepped into a large room with a desk in one back corner, a big metal sink in the other. The area seemed to serve as both office and store room. The walls were lined with aluminum shelving full of boxes, stacks of paper, and plastic bins.

Cardboard moving boxes were scattered all over the floor, some taped up, some empty. Ms. Tilly was in the center of it all, sealing one of the boxes with packing tape.

"Hey, Ms. Tilly," I said as I walked in. I wished I could use the word "y'all" again, but she was the only one in the room and my southern dictionary said it was a contraction for "you all" and shouldn't be used for just one person.

Ms. Tilly straightened and looked surprised to see me, then

tilted her head and looked kind of annoyed to see me. Her expression changed once more to pleasantly surprised.

All this happened in the span of about two seconds, so maybe the one in the middle was her *my back is killing me from all this bending* face. I didn't know her that well.

"Rika! What brings you out here tonight?" She kept working as she spoke, stacking her box on top of another she'd already loaded onto an upright dolly.

"I just had something I wanted to check with you about," I said, "since you seem to be in charge of everything around here."

She chuckled and gestured to her mess. "I guess you can say that again." She leaned in conspiratorially, "If the pastor slacks off any more, I'll be preaching the sermons, too." She laughed. It was a nice laugh, the kind that made you feel warm all over. "We've been looking for a new one for a couple of years now, but nobody wants to come to Bolo. Can't imagine why."

I wasn't sure if she was being serious or sarcastic with that last statement, so I left it alone.

"Anyway...what is it I can do for you?"

I felt a little guilty asking when she seemed to be doing the jobs of several people and one of those jobs included manual labor. Did she use her church work as an excuse not to go home to her jerk of a husband? Couldn't blame her for that.

"I don't want to take up a lot of your time," I said. "I'm just wondering if you've seen this before." I pulled the photocopy of the word search from my back pocket and showed it to her.

She took it from me, pursed her lips, stared at it for several seconds and handed it back. "It looks like the word puzzles we put out for the kids," she said. "But I can't say for sure that was one of ours. ReeAnne usually downloads them and makes the copies."

I glanced around the room again, stalling for time, trying to think of anything else I could ask that might help. I noticed something sitting on her desk and walked toward it. "Is this a replica of

the Washington Monument?" I read the inscription on the base
—*World's Greatest Sunday School Teacher.*

Ms. Tilly laughed again. "I think it was the closest thing my
class could find to a church steeple."

"Well, it's nice," I said as I lifted it from the desk. It *was* nice.
And heavy for its size, a couple of feet tall and made from shiny
white stone. "They must really love you."

"Oh, I feel the same way about them." She peered into
another box, then glanced at her dolly as if making a decision.

I felt like I was interrupting some important work. If there
was anyone I needed to talk to around here, it was probably the
pastor, since he was already mixed up with gambling and loan
sharks, or maybe ReeAnne, who seemed to have her hands full
right now.

I sighed and shrugged. I hated being left out while Nick got to
snag an elusive McGwire boy with my plan.

My eyes landed on a multi-compartment pencil holder on
Ms. Tilly's desk. One compartment contained black and red pens,
another highlighters, and the last...

Four colored pencils. My eyes paused and held on each one.

Blue

Green

Orange

Red

A knot formed somewhere between my heart and my
stomach and rotated there, very, very slowly.

Something thumped at the back of my brain and my eyes
flitted to the award again. The mini-monument was four-sided,
but long. More than two inches thick. Pointy on top.

Very pointy.

I swallowed hard as I realized I was standing *abajo* right now.
Below the main floor, in the basement. In fact, I'd heard people
use the word *abajo* to mean downstairs.

The kid sounds that were farther away at first, were suddenly right overhead, but they barely registered. I couldn't take my eyes off the desk.

"Must be snack time," Ms. Tilly said cheerfully. "The dining room is right above us."

My eyes were still stuck on the monument.

It couldn't be her. Maybe the pastor. His office was two rooms away. Surely, he had access to this place. But did he know Spanish?

Did Ms. Tilly? I'd assumed she was Hispanic when I'd first met her because she'd felt that way to me. She had dark hair and eyes, not so dark skin. I'd never heard her maiden name.

I had to know. "*Está muy ruidoso arriba, sí?*" I said. Meaning, "It's very noisy above, yes?"

"*Pero, está más tranquilo abajo,*" Ms. Tilly replied, adding special emphasis to the word "*abajo.*"

I turned to check her in the face, but my gaze was jerked down to the gun she held in her hand.

She snorted. "You're too smart for your own good."

Clearly, not as smart as I wanted to be or I would have figured this out before staring down the business end of a pistol.

My lips parted, but not one syllable came to mind.

"No matter." Her lips curved up into a sinister smile. Her eyes, once warm and brown, had turned black and empty. "I've been preparing, as you can see. Wade's been getting a little suspicious lately. Asking more questions about where I've been and what I've been doing. Only took him ten years of his wife controlling the heroine trade in three counties. I guess even a moron catches on sooner or later."

I gulped hard, then repeated the action, but the frog wouldn't leave my throat. I cleared it as quietly as I could.

Stall for time, Paprika. "Why'd you kill Avery Cook?" I asked as I wondered if Nick could have found out the truth by now and be on his way over with the state police.

"I had a windfall of smack. Too much for me to move locally.

Avery and I made a deal for him to take it off my hands. He's been running an operation up in the panhandle."

Gun still in her hand, she managed to pick up another box and add it to the dolly without taking her eyes off me.

"I guess the deal went bad?" I figured the longer I kept her talking, the better chance I had at being rescued.

She put her gunless hand on her hip. "He thought he could take advantage of me just because I'm a woman!" she said dramatically.

"Sexist pig!" I said just as dramatically. Maybe if she was crazy enough, we could bond over the patronizing ways of the male gender.

"I know!" Her eyes widened as she nodded at me. "Brought less than half the money we agreed on. Tried to bully me into taking the deal." She snorted. "I still wouldn't have killed him, though, if he hadn't called me an old bat." Her hand tightened on the gun. "An old bat! Do I look old to you?"

I shook my head. "No way!" I cried. As in *no way* was I making the same mistake as that poor asshole Avery. "I thought Sheriff Strickland had taken a child bride."

She smiled and for a moment I saw the warm grandmotherly woman Nick had introduced me to. But a second later, the evil gleam returned to her eyes.

"You're a smart girl," she said. "Too bad you have the worst timing of anyone I've ever met. First, you show up in Bolo when JimBob is dumping Avery's body for me and now..."

Using her foot, she slid one of the empty boxes to the side revealing...

I wasn't sure what.

On the floor, was a duffle bag. I took a step toward it and peered in at the hodgepodge of wires.

Gulp.

"Is..." I had to clear the squeak from my throat. "Is that a bomb?"

"It's my first!" she said proudly. "I mean, it could be better looking, but it won't matter in a little while anyway."

My hand flew to my non-existent pearls, this time rubbing my collarbone, searching frantically for them. "You're going to blow up the church?"

I eyed the bomb again to see if it looked legit. But how many real-life bombs had I seen?

None.

"Where did you learn to make a bomb?" I asked, trying to determine whether Ms. Tilly was a maniacal criminal mastermind or just a crazy old lady. Although, if she'd actually been running a drug ring for a decade under the sheriff's nose...

"I googled it," she said cheerfully.

Wow. Karma really is a bitch.

Where was the nearest bomb squad? Houston? Austin?

Hell, where was her fucking husband? I had to agree with her on this one, I'd thought he was pretty stupid before, but he was definitely a moron if he was just now getting suspicious.

Keep stalling. She likes to brag about herself.

"So, what's the plan?" I asked. "What's the point in blowing up the church?"

"All the evidence against me is in this room," she said. "The bomb will pulverize it. If Wade and the locals conduct the investigation, everyone will assume I died in the blast. It would be better for Wade to let them think so, anyway, rather than inform them his wife's been conducting criminal activities for *fucking ever* without him being the wiser. Wouldn't make for much of a campaign slogan."

The word "fucking" seemed odd coming from her mouth. Like if Mrs. Butterworth suddenly said, "I've been waiting *fucking forever* for you to pour me on your pancakes!"

*Mmm...*pancakes would be really good right now. If ever there was a moment I needed carb therapy, this was it.

Even as I stared at her with a gun in her hand, my mind had

trouble wrapping itself around the fact that sweet, beloved Ms. Tilly was some sort of murderous sociopath.

Keep talking, Paprika.

"What if the feds investigate?"

"I've given them enough to keep them busy for a while." She lifted a spray bottle with remnants of red liquid in the bottom. "If there's enough left of the walls after the blast, they'll find my blood spattered all over them."

I looked where she gestured behind me and noticed the red spray in various places along the wall. "There's a piece of my ear behind the desk, too."

She lifted her hair to show me the spot where the top of her ear would have been. It was sewn up with black thread.

"Did you do that yourself?" I asked, for the moment as intrigued as I was afraid.

She waved her hand dismissively. "It's just a little piece," she said. "Not like I went all Van Gogh or anything."

Okay, she was pretty nuts. For one thing, she thought she was saner than Van Gogh because she was going to blow up a church while only leaving part of her ear behind.

A shriek from above pierced my thought bubble.

Shit! The kids!

"Ms. Tilly? You're not going to set a bomb off while all those kids are in the building, are you?"

She put her hands out and shrugged. "That wasn't the original plan, but it's all fallen together pretty well. I've got enough boom here to blow up this church and the one across the street to boot. Never liked those Catholics, praying to freaking everybody..."

I widened my eyes at her, wondering if she was incapable of seeing the hypocrisy of a murdering bomber judging, well, anyone.

Her eyes wandered off. "My parents were Catholic..." She

looked like she was remembering something and I suddenly wondered what, exactly, happened to her parents.

After only a few seconds she shook it off and smiled. "Anyway, if the authorities find anything at all, they'll be sifting through pieces of a couple dozen kids and, now, four grown women. That will buy me plenty of time to get to my new beach house. Did you know you can buy your own island for just three million dollars?"

"No." I shook my head slowly, using the motion as a way to check my surroundings again. It was looking more and more like I was going to have to get myself out of this situation, but I couldn't identify anything in the room that would thwart a lunatic with a gun. It wasn't like I was a master Ninja pencil thrower or anything.

"No one will have good reason to look for me," she continued. "If the real authorities open an investigation into all the goings-on around here, they'll find Avery Cook's watch and wallet under the seat of JimBob's truck. I put it there yesterday while he was having lunch at the Mary Queen. They'll find messages between Avery and LeeAnne in the trash bin of LeeAnne's email account about how the two of them were going to meet that night. And everyone knows Dwight was fascinated with bombs when he was a kid. Extra materials just like these will be found in his grand-parents' bedroom along with the rifle that shot at you outside Barr's."

Okay, crazy or not, she was definitely a criminal mastermind. She'd actually gone around town, planting evidence on all the most plausible suspects.

"But why would Dwight want to blow up the church?" I cried. I was imagining poor, neat freak Dwight living in a dingy cell with men who had real spider tattoos on their necks.

And LeeAnne! She'd been nothing but good to me and I doubted her.

"Oh, I planted a rambling manifesto on Dwight's computer,"

Ms. Tilly said. "He's the perfect bomber. Loner...antisocial... Sounds angry most of the time."

"But what would that have to do with the murder?"

Ms. Tilly chuckled, a mischievous twinkle in her eye. "Maybe they're not related. Maybe they are. I have complete faith in J.J. Boyle to spin that yarn."

She was right. J.J. would have a blast—no pun intended—concocting a story that made sense out of all the evidence Ms. Tilly had planted.

"Well," she looked at her dolly. "I think I've got everything I want to keep." She looked at the bomb. "I'm sorry I don't have one of those fancy timers like they do on TV." She twisted her mouth to one side as if thinking things over. "I'll tell you what, we'll synchronize so you can watch the countdown to your demise." She checked her wristwatch and the clock on the wall. "Ten minutes should be plenty for me to get this stuff in my car and get far enough away from the building. I'll set my watch timer." She punched around on her digital watch. It was a fancy, high-tech looking thing. I recalled how she'd also had a cutting-edge cell phone that day she used the siren app to startle her husband.

I'd been surprised someone her age was so tech savvy, but I never would have imagined she might be using that ability in her thriving cottage industry.

"There, the timer's set for ten minutes," she said.

Ten minutes? Ten minutes should be enough time to get me and everyone upstairs away from the building after you leave, you nutbag.

I watched her take the left handle of the dolly, then wrap her fingers loosely around the right, while still holding the gun in her hand. She kept her head turned, eyes on me until she'd pushed the dolly into the hall.

"By the way, once the door closes," she said. "I'll be padlocking it shut. I chose this place because it used to be a store room. Easy to lock people in or out."

Okay, I was the dimwit for thinking a criminal mastermind was going to give me a chance to escape.

"Ms. Tilly," I began, trying to think of anything that might stall her a little longer just in case the Texas Rangers were on their way over to arrest her. "You never explained to me...about the word search."

She rolled her eyes. "Well, obviously, I used them to communicate orders to JimBob. He sat in the same place every Sunday and on Wednesday nights. I stuck the word searches in the shelf on the back of the pew in front of him, inside the pages of the hymnal. He knew the message would be in the letters circled in red and orange. This way, no one ever saw us together. No phone calls to trace." She shook her head. "Thought he was smart enough not to just throw the body on the side of the road, though."

I opened my mouth to ask another question, but she wasn't finished.

"But you've figured most of that out already." She narrowed her eyes at me. "I think you're just stalling, hoping someone will happen down here and save you." Her lips curved into a demented smile, "That's not in the cards. The pastor's off gambling across the Louisiana border in Lake Charles, and he's the only one with reason to be down here after hours." She watched the clock on the wall until the second hand was nearly at the twelve. "Your time starts now." She pushed the button on her watch just as the new minute started.

"*Hasta la vista*, baby!" she said sarcastically.

See you later. Very funny.

She closed the door behind her.

I jogged over to it and listened. I heard a clang and a snap that certainly sounded like a padlock. I turned the handle and the door opened slightly, but the padlock held. I hit it hard with my shoulder, which only resulted in a very hurt shoulder. I moved back a few feet, braced on the nearest shelf, and kicked the door.

It wasn't the cheap, hollow interior door I expected, but a hard, solid one.

I tried several more kicks with both feet, but nothing budged.

Okay, forget the door. Think.

Standing in the middle of the room, I turned slowly, focusing on each wall. No secret doors. Just one window up high. Too bad I wouldn't fit through it.

Wait! I looked down at my body. For a moment I'd forgotten about my weight loss. Maybe I could fit through it. I raced to the desk and grabbed Ms. Tilly's Sunday school teacher award taking it over to the metal shelves that stood under the window. They were fairly sturdy and bolted to the wall.

Standing on my tiptoes, I reached as high as I could, managing to set the award on the top shelf. I slipped off LeeAnne's wedges and climbed up. When I got to the top, I wasted no time in grabbing the award, turning my head away and smashing it into the glass.

It worked! The glass broke fairly easily. But there were some sort of burglar bars on the other side. I examined them, then felt all around, looking for the safety release they were supposed to have, cutting my wrist in the process.

But the bloody gash was the least of my worries. The burglar bars weren't the commercially sold kind. They were welded and bolted individually. Even if I had the right tools, it would take me hours to get out of here.

Silverware clattered to the floor right over my head. Kids were laughing.

Oh, my God. The kids. How was I going to get them out of here?

Then, my phone vibrated in my back pocket.

CHAPTER THIRTY-ONE

Nick

I drove toward Bolo, trying to accept what I'd learned at the dealership.

When faced with overwhelming evidence that he was the only one driving his truck and that his truck had been seen at the dump site, JimBob rolled over.

But the crime boss he exposed wasn't Wade. In fact, JimBob seemed pretty sure that Wade wasn't involved at all, despite the fact that the crime boss and murderer was Wade's wife.

A heavy feeling passed through my chest, landing in my stomach. I'd known Ms. Tilly all my life. She'd taught me in Sunday School for Christ's sake. How many times had I run up to her and hugged her when I was a little boy? How many times had she hugged me since I came back from Austin?

This couldn't be true.

But JimBob had provided such detailed information about her operation and how she conducted it—out of her office in the church basement, of all places—that it was hard to doubt his story.

I needed to call Rika and tell her the plan had worked. It

wasn't fair to keep her hanging longer than necessary. However, the idea of saying "Ms. Tilly murdered Avery Cook in a drug deal gone bad" was so unthinkable...

I shook my head and pulled out my phone. After hitting Rika's name at the top of my favorite's list, I took a deep breath, releasing it slowly.

The most important thing was that Rika's innocence was now clear to law enforcement. The charges would be dropped. She'd be free to live her life...

In Los Angeles.

A lump formed in my throat at the idea that I'd probably never see her again once she left.

Shit. Sack up, Owen. You've only known her a few weeks.

I cleared it and swallowed hard just before she answered.

"Nick?"

"Hey, Rika," I said. "It worked. We got everything we need, but you won't believe who—"

"Ms. Tilly," she said.

How the hell would she know? Bolo was fast on the gossip, but we only finished with JimBob a few minutes ago.

"Listen," she said, the urgency clear in her voice. "I came to the church to follow up on the word search and saw the murder weapon. Ms. Tilly realized I knew too much. She's locked me in her office with what she says is a bomb and we have less than eight minutes before she detonates it."

I must have gone numb because I couldn't feel what Rika was saying. Wasn't even sure I heard her right.

"What—?" I began.

"Nick, shut up and listen to me. Ms. Tilly is smart and this thing looks like a bomb to me. No question she believes she's made a bomb, and she's padlocked the door from the outside, so I'm trapped in here. Your mom, Belinda, and ReeAnne are upstairs with a bunch of kids. You have to call and warn them."

My foot pressed harder on the gas pedal. "Okay," I said, not allowing myself to consider the idea that I might lose Rika and my mom in one big blast. The fastest fix would be if Rika could get out of there and warn everyone. I mentally scanned the large store room Ms. Tilly used as an office. "There's a window," I said.

"Yeah, I'm working on it, but it's not looking good."

That's when I remembered there were bars on that window. What were the chances Rev. Jenkins had made sure the church got the kind with the safety release on the inside?

Zero. If the release was there, it was by pure chance.

Half of my brain refused to believe Ms. Tilly was capable of building a viable bomb. But how long had she outsmarted us all? *Decades?*

Maybe she could build a bomb.

"I'm hanging up so you can call," Rika said. "If I don't, um, make it...thanks for everything."

Not *make it*? Fear sliced through me. I couldn't swallow. How could she sound so calm? I had to try to help somehow. "Rika!" I yelled before she could hang up.

"Yeah?"

"Have you tried googling it?" I said, desperately hoping she'd think of something to google.

I could swear I heard her chuckle. "Call your mom, now," she said, and she was gone.

I mashed the accelerator and hit another number on my screen, hoping, for once, my mother answered her damn cell phone.

～

Rika

As I disconnected the call, I was smiling. If I was about to die, I was happy Nick was the last person I spoke to.

A new sound upstairs grabbed my attention. A country song

was suddenly playing. Tammy Lynn's ring tone. I'd heard it before.

But the kids had gotten louder—chattering, squealing, laughing...

No one was answering the phone.

Wrapping my fingers around the bars, I pulled hard, just in case, but my actions had no effect whatsoever.

I thought about the joke Nick made about googling. Or maybe it wasn't a joke. He wouldn't joke at a time like this.

Picking up my phone from where I'd dropped it on the shelf, I climbed down and stood on the floor.

Google it. What could I search for?

I peered into the duffle and looked at the bomb. There were a number of wires, but not a blue one, a red one, and a yellow one, like in the movies. Come to think of it, why would a bomb maker use a standardized, color-coded wire system? That would only make the bomb easier to disarm.

Regardless, I started searching "disarming bomb" on my phone, which was beginning to get slippery with the blood from my wrist. I kept finding images of robots and men in heavy bomb resistant gear and helmets.

I didn't have a robot, gear, or a helmet.

Buzzing began above me. Nick was probably trying another phone, but it sounded like chairs were being folded and put away loudly, and no one was picking up.

I swallowed hard. If I didn't find a way to keep this bomb from going off, half the kids in town were going to blow up with me.

After several more searches, I found a video entitled "robot uses high-powered stream of water to diffuse bomb." After checking the time—I had four minutes left—I watched the video of the robot rolling over to a bomb and spraying. The camera onboard showed wires detaching when assaulted by the spray without the bomb exploding.

I looked over at the elderly metal sink in the corner. It sported one of those separate sprayers we'd had in each of the three places I'd lived in my life, but none of them had ever worked.

My eyes on the clock, I jogged over, turned on the water and sprayed into the sink.

It worked! And the spray was surprisingly strong, but nothing compared to what I'd seen in the video.

Of course, this bomb was smaller than the one in the video too, and more sloppily assembled. But I had no way of knowing if this was the type of bomb that could be thwarted by a strong spray.

I heard another phone ringing upstairs. This one sounded like a house phone, or in this case, the church phone.

It stopped after two rings. I heard something solid hit the floor above me, followed by children's laughter. Had one of them knocked the phone off the hook with their horseplay?

Tammy Lynn's face appeared in front of me like a disembodied ghost. She wasn't my favorite person, but she was Nick's mom! And ReeAnne, bless her heart, and Belinda who'd been so warm towards me. They were moms too, and their kids were a lot younger than Nick.

I had two choices.

One: Wait and see if the bomb went off.

Two: Hit it with a strong blast of water. If it was a dud, it wouldn't matter anyway. If it wasn't, maybe—and that was a big maybe—I would disarm it. However, the pressure of the water might also make it go off early, right?

And what if Ms. Tilly had a change of heart and decided not to detonate? I could blow us all up for nothing.

No. She'd put too much work into her plans, and she clearly had no conscience whatsoever. She would try to detonate.

I was vaguely aware of the blood still streaming from my wrist, but I didn't have time to deal with it now.

The kids had quieted some upstairs, but I couldn't tell if the woman talking over them was instructing them to get out of the building or line up for a game of Simon Says.

I hadn't thought I particularly liked kids, but now, I recalled the image of the littlest girls on their sleeping bags, coloring in *My Little Pony* coloring books.

My heart banged so hard against my ribs, I thought it would burst through my chest.

According to Ms. Tilly's timing, I had twenty seconds left.

I'd waited as long as I could. I crossed myself, just in case it could help, then turned the water on, yanked the sprayer up and pulled it as far out as possible. Surprisingly, it stretched several feet past the sink until it was only a yard away from the bomb.

I pointed the water holes toward the bomb's wires, praying for LeeAnne's amazing aim. I squeezed the trigger on the back of the sprayer.

Water jetted out, hitting the wires hard. I flinched in anticipation of the blast.

Instead, two wires began to wiggle. I adjusted my aim to target those wires specifically.

After wiggling for what seemed like forever, they came loose. I breathed a half sigh of relief, which was interrupted when the two loose wires touched each other, causing a "zuht" sound and a spark.

Shit! Jerking the spray to focus directly on where they touched, I separated them with the stream and they fell limp in neutral corners.

I focused on spraying the remaining wires directly, but they wouldn't detach. I hoped they weren't the important ones.

I heard another shriek of laughter upstairs as I looked at the clock.

Five...four...three...two...

One...

My breath was stuck in my chest, but I kept holding it as I sprayed on, in case Ms. Tilly was just messing with me, waiting until I breathed my sigh of relief to detonate.

I. Will. NOT. Breathe.

A long-forgotten memory floated into my mind. How, when I was young, I used to practice holding my breath. That had been a long time ago, but I held on and kept spraying.

One minute past detonation time. I noticed a puddle of blood was forming on the floor underneath my hand as I held the sprayer.

Two minutes past detonation time.

Three.

Wow. That looks like a lot of blood, I thought, but I didn't relate it to myself. I was starting to feel like I was in a dream, and all I cared about in that dream was keeping the spray on the bomb.

It hadn't gone off so far, but what would happen if I stopped spraying?

I felt like I was about to pass out, but that was okay, I'd spray until I did. Wait, did it make sense to hold my breath until I fainted? I'd been holding it since before detonation time, so I was too oxygen deprived to reason.

"Rika?" That was Nick's voice on the other side of the door. Or was I delirious? "Rika!"

I released the carbon dioxide I was holding and gasped in a big breath. "Nick! Get the kids!" I cried.

"The cops got 'em!"

Still spraying, I listened hard and realized the kid noises were gone.

But Nick was right outside the door. It would be so wrong to deprive womankind of that body by getting it blown to bits.

"Get away from the building!" I screamed. "I don't know if she's tried to detonate yet. Get as far away as you can!"

A power tool cranked up and I realized he was cutting through the padlock.

Seconds later, the door swung open and I was stunned by what I saw.

Nick's hot body—in jeans and a black button-down shirt with the sleeves rolled up—filled the doorway almost completely. In his right hand was some sort of power saw.

Did they set the *Texas Chainsaw Massacre* movies in Texas because everyone in the state drove around with power saws handy?

Nick was yelling at me, telling me to come on, but my feet felt glued to the floor, my hand still squeezing the sprayer trigger. Some wires were still connected and I was afraid if I stopped spraying, the bomb might explode and blow him to bits.

The saw dropped to the floor and Nick strode toward me. He grabbed me below my ribs and flung me over his shoulder like he was rescuing me from a fire. As he jogged us out of there the sprayer ripped from my hand.

He didn't stop running until we were almost to Dill's Dollar Store, where the Texas Highway Patrol had the road blocked off.

Finally, he put me on my feet and panted, "Are you okay?" He noticed the blood and lifted my hand to examine the wrist wound. "It's a big gash. It looks like you've lost a lot of blood."

I glanced down, vaguely taking note of the blood all over my clothes and legs, but replied with, "How did you get a saw so fast?"

Nick's brows drew together, his eyes full of concern and somewhere in the back of my mind I realized that was kind of a crazy sentence to lead with.

Then, my knees buckled. I can't say for sure whether it was from the ordeal I'd just been through, the blood loss, or Nick's now-midnight blue eyes probing mine.

I started to fall, but he caught me and eased me down, then called a medic over. As someone put an oxygen mask on my face, I spotted Tammy Lynn, Belinda, and ReeAnne, surrounded by wide-eyed, chattering kids.

Everyone's safe.

I closed my eyes and sucked in a deep breath.

CHAPTER THIRTY-TWO

Rika

Two days later, I was standing in Nick's driveway next to my car.

It was all over. Matilda Strickland had been captured at the San Antonio airport by the Texas Rangers. She proudly confessed to all she'd done, but also vowed to escape.

Michelle and Cody seemed to think that part was funny when they came by to fill us in. I didn't think it was funny at all. I'd looked into Ms. Tilly's eyes for a good long time. A woman as smart—albeit possibly crazy—and determined as she was would eventually succeed in whatever she decided to do. I had no doubt she could mastermind a breakout.

Sheriff Strickland was so distraught over his wife of thirty-two years, he also confessed what he knew, which wasn't much.

As it turned out, her work at the church had been keeping her out later and later, which made him suspect she was seeing another man. He started investigating and found tens of thousands of dollars hidden under the various seats in his wife's SUV.

By the time the murder occurred, he'd been contacted by the Texas Rangers about a possible crime ring being operated out of his county. He arrested Rika so he wouldn't have to investigate further, afraid his sweet Tilly was somehow involved.

However, he was still shocked to learn she'd impaled Avery Cook personally.

Although I'd had to go to a hospital in a nearby town where they stitched up my wrist and replaced several pints of blood, the biggest shock happened the next morning.

Nick got word from the bomb squad that Ms. Tilly's bomb, despite obviously being made by a beginner, likely would have exploded if I hadn't disabled it. I'd convinced myself it was a dud all along, so the news made me instantly woozy.

Luckily, I was right near the kitchen table when he told me. I grabbed it for support, eased myself down and stayed there until I made myself quit thinking of the bomb and the kids, and the sick feeling passed.

The technician confirmed that the bomb also contained enough explosives to crater the church and anything around it. I knew Matilda Strickland was more than just a crazy old killer, but still...

Holy mother of fucking Zeus! She was a real, live evil genius-maniac and no one had a clue what she was capable of all these years!

A few hours after we got that news, the charges against me were officially dropped by J.J. Boyle, and he didn't seem too happy about it. I felt an apology was in order for making me out to be some sort of homicidal pervert.

J.J. didn't.

So, I'd collected my car, and said my goodbyes to LeeAnne and Dwight. Dwight actually said, "I'm glad you're not dead" before he went back to washing dishes, which I thought was quite a compliment coming from him.

So now, I had no reason to stay on in Bolo. No reason except that every time I'd thought of leaving Nick in the past couple of days, I felt like The Hulk's foot was bearing down on my chest.

I'd been standing in the driveway with Nick for twenty minutes as we recapped our time together and expressed shock over and over again about Ms. Tilly. I'd even asked him about the saw again, which, of course was in his truck because of one of his mom's chores. But, even with that last trivial question answered, I couldn't make myself get into the car.

Running out of things to say, we fell silent and just looked at each other for several long seconds.

"You'll follow the GPS this time?" Nick finally said. "No short cuts."

My lips smiled, but I couldn't force the expression up to my eyes. "I've learned my lesson," I replied. "Never take the short cut."

Nick suddenly reached out with both hands, placed them on top of my head, and smoothed them down the sides, trapping my hair between his palms and my cheeks.

"I'm glad you're okay." His eyes were a beautiful shade of azure out in the sunshine, and he looked at me so intensely, I could feel their glow on my skin. "Really glad."

His touch and the knowledge that I was about to lose it forever was too much. My eyes filled suddenly and Nick turned all fuzzy.

I felt hot liquid running down my face and was so surprised by it, I put both hands to my cheeks, then looked at my palms to make sure it wasn't blood.

No. I, Rika Martín, was *crying*.

Nick cupped my jaw, lifting my eyes back to his. His brows pressed toward each other in a kind of surprised confusion. "*Now*, you cry." His voice was soft and teasing, yet curious at the same time.

I nodded and swallowed, trying and failing to get hold of my emotions.

"You didn't cry when you got arrested," he said. "You didn't cry when you got shot at. You didn't cry when someone tried to blow you up. But now..."

His voice trailed off as he pulled me to him and let me cry wracking, hiccupping sobs into his chest.

When I thought I could talk again, I looked up at him and said, "I don't want to leave you."

His torso tightened like I'd punched him. He breathed in, then exhaled a heavy breath.

"Paprika," he said tenderly. "I'm thirty-four years old and just signed off on my third divorce. I'm not romance material. You're...fresh. And smart. And beautiful. You have a lot of other options out there."

Great. The fancy lawyer version of the *It's not you, it's me* speech.

Bottom line was, he didn't want me. Men went after the women they wanted. Hell, Nick had gone after at least three of them before.

"Sure," I said. "I get it." I turned and stepped toward my car.

I felt his hand on my upper arm as he turned me back to face him. "If you ever need anything. I mean *anything*. You call me. Okay?"

"Sure. Okay." I just wanted to get in the car now so I could cry my way back to L.A. alone. "Thanks," I said. I wiped my eyes and sniffed hard, so a crying snot face wouldn't be the last thing he remembered about me. "Thanks for everything, Nick."

I stepped back and climbed into my Honda, started it, turned it around and headed down the drive toward Zombie Road. When I made the left, I glanced back toward the house.

Nick was still standing where I left him, watching me drive away.

DEAD MEN DON'T EAT QUICHE

SNEAK PEEK

Nick Owen

I flipped over on my left side for the dozenth time since I'd gotten into bed.

Sleeping still didn't come easy, although the reason for my insomnia had changed a few months ago. Johnny Chavez—the innocent defendant in the only murder case I ever lost—had won his appeal and that was a load off my conscience.

Truth be told, though, his face had already been replaced much of the time in my nightly visions with a prettier one. One with big, beautiful eyes the color of chocolate.

My cell phone rang. I turned over and stared at it for a few seconds wondering who could be calling at this hour. Even mom liked to limit her "emergencies" to between breakfast and midnight.

Had to be a wrong number.

I picked up the phone, checked the name on the screen, then blinked a few times to make sure I hadn't conjured it up with wishful thinking.

As soon as I confirmed I wasn't hallucinating, I tapped the screen to answer the call.

"Rika?" My voice came out higher pitched than I was comfortable with, maybe a little desperate. I wished I could have a Mulligan on answering.

"Nick?"

I sat up straight at the distressed sound in her voice. "What's wrong?" I said. "Are you okay?"

"Yes. It's my dad. He's disappeared."

"In Colombia?" I immediately regretted that I didn't know any more than any other dumbass American about Colombia—let's see, coffee...cocaine. Yep, that was it.

"No, he was here...in L.A." I'd never heard her sound so panicked, not even the night she nearly got blown up by the boss of our local crime ring. "He moved here a month ago. Now, his co-worker's been found dead and he's missing!"

Missing? "Missing" in this type of situation usually meant the missing person was the perpetrator...or dead. I suddenly felt like I had a brick wedged in my stomach.

"Are the police looking for him?"

"Yes..." The word came out as a sob. "But they're looking for him as a suspect! He wouldn't kill anyone, but no one's looking for him as a kidnapping victim."

While I tried to process what she was telling me, I heard her clear her throat. She took a deep breath and exhaled it slowly and I knew she was pulling herself together. The Rika I knew last summer was not a woman who cried easily. She made it through her bogus arrest, a shooting attempt with her as the target, and a bomb she had to disarm herself, all without shedding a tear, at least none that I saw.

But she cried when we said goodbye, and the memory of those tears clawed at my heart every single day. I told myself that if it was meant to be between us—if she still felt as strongly as I did once she was back home and wasn't depending on me to get her out of a murder rap—I'd hear from her.

A text. A call.

But I hadn't heard a peep from her since she drove out of my life. I figured she'd come to her senses and moved on with her life.

"I'm sorry." The sob was gone from her voice. "I don't know why I called you. It's just that you were the only person I..."

She seemed to have run out of words, and I didn't want her to hang up before I told her I was coming.

"I'll catch the first flight I can get," I said. "I'll let you know when I'm arriving."

Her sigh of relief whooshed through the phone. "Thanks, Nick... Thanks."

"No problem. See you soon." I hung up and grabbed my laptop to start searching for flights.

Dear Readers,

Don't miss out! Go to NinaCordoba.com and sign up now for my reader group to be notified of my book releases, receive secret intel, and join beta reader or free read for review teams.

You can find book lists, book extras, true stories from my life, and other fun stuff at NinaCordoba.com. (Hint: Check out "Living la Vida Loca" in the blog topics.)

I like to interact with readers, so feel free to friend me on Facebook or contact me anytime through my site.

Thanks for reading!

Nina Cordoba

OTHER BOOKS BY NINA CORDOBA:

86036165R00197

Made in the USA
Middletown, DE
27 August 2018